MW00779460

RED MIST

Praise for RED MIST

"Mitani's second novel wastes no time getting into high action. The reader is encouraged to keep the pages turning in this cleverly crafted roller coaster ride with surprises at each turn. It's a master class in storytelling."

—**Kazunori Yamauchi**, founder of the *Gran Turismo* video game series

"If you ever thought auto shows were boring, step into the fertile mind of Sam Mitani. Mitani was International Editor at *Road & Track* magazine for 22 years, so when he writes a spy novel set in the pampered world of car writers, he knows whereof he speaks. Mitani takes former Navy Commander Max Koga, forced to retire because of psychological trauma, [and has him] pursuing a web of bad guys ranging from terrorists to drug cartels. Mitani has bitten off a big piece of press-program dinner salad here. Does he carry it off? Yes!"

—**Mark Vaughn**, West Coast Editor at *AutoWeek*

"Max Koga moves through a world of danger! Mitani has a keen eye for detail, crisp realism and wound-tight action that will make *Red Mist* a thrill ride."

—**Robert Young Pelton**, New York Times best-selling author of *The Word's Most Dangerous Places* and *Licensed to Kill, Hired Guns in the War on Terror.*

"Talk about a roller-coaster ride! Sam Mitani sends you on one, where the pages fly through your fingers as you search for the next secret surprise. Being a seasoned martial artist, his description of the fight scenes was very real."

—**Hayward Nishioka**, 9th-degree judo black belt, author of *Judo Heart and Soul* and *The Judo Textbook.*

RED MIST

A MAX KOGA THRILLER

SAM MITANI

FORCE POSEIDON
DETROIT

Published in the United States of America by Force Poseidon
forceposeidon.com

Library of Congress Control Number: 2023934577

Force Poseidon hardcover edition – August 2023 ISBN-13 978-1-7375200-6-1

Force Poseidon trade paperback – August 2023 ISBN-13 978-1-7375200-7-8

Force Poseidon eBook edition – August 2023 ISBN-13 978-1-7375200-8-5

This book was produced in Adobe InDesign CC 2023 using
Kuunari for titles and chapter headings and
Crimson Pro Medium for body copy.

Manufactured in the United States of America 

@ForcePoseidon • ForcePoseidon.com

red mist, phrase

— a term used in motorsports when a driver loses all sense of personal safety to win at any cost; a feeling of extreme competitiveness that clouds one's judgment; a monomaniacal desire to win.

Mulholland
Topanga Canyon
Topanga State Park
Santa Monica Mountains National Recreation Area
Tuna Canyon Park
27
Pacific Coast
1
Beverly Glen
San Vicente
Montana
Bundy
Wilshire
Ocean Park
Rose
Marina del Rey
Vista
Santa Monica Bay
Pacific Ocean

Riverside
Forest Lawn
Zoo
Brand
Glendale
Chevy Chase
134
Walnut
Adams
Verdugo
Eagle Rock
La Loma
Arroyo
Fair Oaks
5
York
110
Monterey
Los Feliz
Sunset
Vine
Crescent Heights
Santa Monica
Melrose
Beverly
Burton
La Brea
3Rd
Silver Lake
Cypress
Figueroa
Huntington
Fremont
Academy
Stadium
Daly
Mission
Valley
Temple
Robertson
Fairfax
Olympic
Venice
Hoover
Alvarado
8Th
5Th
Grand
6Th
1St
Cesar E Chavez
60
10
San Pedro
Whittier
Jefferson
Rodeo
Soto
72
Arlington
Martin Luther King Jr
41St
Stocker
Vernon
Bandini
La Cienega
Santa Fe
Slauson
Van Ness
Western
Vermont
Main
Central
Compton
Gage
Centinela
Florence
Eastern
Manchester
Market
Crenshaw
42
Arbor Vitae
Century
103Rd
Tweedy
Abbott
107
120Th
Segundo
Inglewood
105
Prairie
Rosecrans
Aviation
Redondo Beach
110
Alondra
710
Albertoni
Artesia
Paramount
Downey
Grant
Victoria
182Nd
190Th
Normandie
Prospect
Avalon
Amo
Long Beach
Real
Torrance
Madrona
Wilmington
19
Carson
Catalina
405
Cherry
223Rd
Wardlow

RED MIST

Prologue

Seven agents were dead. Their bodies, some of them torn to pieces, littered the stained concrete floor as the stench of burning flesh and gunpowder drifted in thick, moist air.

U.S. Navy Lieutenant Commander Maximilian Koga and his DEA Special Operations Division teammates had just finished setting up intelligence-gathering operations in a remote warehouse in Topolobampo, a port city in Sinaloa, Mexico to monitor the transportation of fentanyl and its precursors from China that were processed and trafficked by the cartels into the U.S.

Their secondary objective was to confirm arms shipments being smuggled into and out of the country. The team had felt secure and hadn't posted any perimeter security, so nothing prevented a compact Mitsubishi pickup packed with C-4 explosives to launch itself into the east side of the large cinder block building. It penetrated the exterior wall and exploded inside, setting fire to nearly everything in the vicinity, including the people.

Then came the solid wall of gunfire. Large-caliber bullets flying at them overwhelmed the DEA agents who had survived the initial blast. Smoke and dust from the explosion and collapsed masonry obscured an unknown number of attackers, who advanced through the opening in the wall.

Both sides fired automatic weapons at each other, but the American agents showed more discipline, dropping attackers flowing through the breach. Still, the DEA defenders were being pushed back, step by step. And there was no place to go.

The battle raged all around them. Fighting off the sting from a bullet graze to his upper thigh, Koga crawled to the side of the newest recruit, Jimmy Slack, who had arrived only the day before. He'd been stacking ammunition when the breeching explosion occurred, and powerful secondary explosions of the ammo had charred the right side of his body black and blood red.

"Sss-sir ..." Slack mumbled. Blood bubbles dribbled from his blackened lips. "I don't ... I don't want to die here ..."

Koga knew the kid wouldn't make it. He just hoped they were concealed in a spot where the invaders wouldn't see them right away.

They were not.

A man dressed in black from head to toe casually walked across the floor to where both Koga and Slack lay. He pointed his AK-47 at Slack and fired a single bullet into the helpless kid's head, the sound of the gunshot echoing off the building's metal walls. The balaclava-clad intruder turned to Koga and paused. He slid his mask up to ensure that the last thing Koga saw before leaving this world was his long, crooked face, half covered by a bushy, jet-black beard. The patch on his shirt showed he was a member of the Eldorado Cartel.

"Hijo de puta!" Koga growled—You son of a bitch! It was all he could think to say as he looked up at the gunman, waiting to receive the hot slug that would end his life. But before the bearded man could squeeze the trigger, another man, with a bald head and wearing an eye patch, entered the building barking loud orders in Arabic.

Koga recognized him right away—Nasim al-Ahmed, the leader of the Aqarib terrorist group, short for *al-Aqarib min Allah*—"The Scorpions of God." He was one of the most wanted men in the world.

What the hell? What is the leader of a radical Islamic terror organization doing with a drug cartel in Mexico?

The gunman responded to al-Ahmed with a curt nod of compliance. He kicked Koga's M4 carbine away from his reach and snapped off its M150 Rifle Combat Optic with a kick. The man went to one knee next to Koga.

"You have lived today, infidel—thanks not to *your* God, but to *mine*," the man said in English. His eyes were wildly red-rimmed, indicating that he obviously was high on something powerful. "But very soon you will die. I promise this. *Allahu Akbar!*"

The man flipped his rifle around with the precision of a drill team and with both hands sent the butt of the weapon hard into Koga's face, knocking him out.

When he awoke, Koga was no longer in the warehouse, but laying half-naked on a metal table in a chilly, empty room that looked and smelled like a medical clinic. His wrists and ankles were zip-tied to a metal chair and a cloth gag kept his jaw from moving. Standing in the room's corner was Ramin Madani, the Aqarib's deputy commander.

Madani was a notorious medical doctor born to affluent parents in Iran, educated in the U.S., and radicalized in Libya. Despite his image as an ascetic, privately, Madani was an enthusiastic consumer of exotic cars and exotic women, always carefully hidden from public eyes.

Also present was a younger man unknown to Koga, arranging miscellaneous tools on a metal tray. He looked up to see Koga watching him, so he showed off the three metal rods, two bone saws, and what looked like a set of wire cutters.

"Ah, you're awake," Madani said in perfect English when he saw Koga's eyes open. "Excellent." He rolled an office chair directly in front of his prisoner and placed his thin body on the seat.

Koga looked back at him with a blank, silent stare.

"I apologize for your accommodations," Madani said. He gestured to the zip ties. "But you don't seem like a man who cooperates willingly."

He removed the gag from Koga's mouth and gestured for his assistant to bring him a separate metal tray from a shelf across the room. On it were two syringes, one of which Madani picked up and, without preamble, stuck into the left side of Koga's neck, depressing the plunger.

Moments after the needle pierced the skin, Koga's vision blurred and everything he saw became tinted in a deep red hue. There followed a sensation of euphoria and relaxation, then an intense pain in his arms and chest that squeezed his lungs empty in a monstrous chemical grip.

"I have injected you with a little cocktail of Anectine, sodium pentothal, and a few other psychotropic goodies of my own design," Madani said with a smile. "The pain will become worse, I'm afraid, and you may die of respiratory failure unless I inject a countering agent. But I won't do that unless you tell me who you have inside the Eldorado Cartel working for you."

Gasping for air, Koga spat out, "I ... I don't know *crap*."

Madani's smile disappeared. He spoke in a more forceful tone.

"We know you're with the DEA and that you're here in Mexico to spy on the Eldorado Cartel. Give us the names of those who have provided you with information."

"I have no clue what you're talking about, and I am not the DEA. Sorry, but you got the wrong guy."

"Regrettably, I do not believe you. You will answer my questions truthfully or I will cut off your fingers, one by one—and then castrate you in the most painful way."

Is there even a less painful way?

"Then I guess you gotta cut away," he said through a forced smile.

Madani laughed. "Your reputation is well founded, Max Koga."

Madani reached for the other syringe and jammed the needle into the right side of Koga's neck. This time, there was instant pain that started in his chest. The pain slowly spread to the rest of his body. He saw his entire arms and legs engulfed in flames, and although he knew it was a hallucination, the searing pain he felt was not.

"Tell me the names of your informants," Madani repeated.

"Ask your momma," Koga grunted before blacking out.

Not aware of how much time had elapsed when he came to, Koga found himself still in the examination room secured to the metal table, but he was alone, for now. His body—still intact—dripped with sweat. Pain hammered in his head, and his eyes struggled to regain their focus. He thought he heard automatic gunfire crackling in the distance, and then he noticed a group of people standing in front of the door to the examination room. They were the members of his team, who he could have sworn perished earlier in the warehouse. Jimmy Slack stood near the front.

"Hey ... what are you guys doing here? You guys okay?" Koga called out. His words slurred from the effects of the drug cocktail that still flowed inside him. The figures stared at him blankly, and then without saying a word, evaporated into thin air.

It was then that he noticed the zip ties around his wrists weren't completely tight. After a few minutes of working his wrists and hands back and forth in the restraints, the buildup of blood and perspiration allowed both of his hands to slip through.

A smoky red haze seemed to fill the room as Koga slowly sat up and marshaled his awareness. He spotted the metal tray holding Madani's tools of torture resting on a nearby countertop. He was just able to reach over and grabbed one of several large scalpels, which he used to sever the zip ties around his ankles. Finding a black jacket someone had left draped over a chair, he slipped it on and gingerly lifted himself off the stainless-steel table. Cautiously, he made his way toward the door with the surgical tool gripped in a slippery hand.

Koga waved an arm in front of him to clear the red fog. It seemed to become thicker by the second, and then he realized the red mist wasn't in the room. It was in his head.

I must have popped blood vessels in my eyes, he thought. *The drugs Madani gave me probably moved that along.*

Despite the intense physical and mental strain of the past several hours, Koga felt remarkably alert and energized. He slowly opened the door and peered down the passageway in both directions. Down the hall to the left, near the front of the building, were three al-Aqarib guards with their backs to him. He looked for another way out and saw that the rear passageway was unguarded. He would have to hurry if he was going to make it all the way to the back door. But first things first.

Koga's bare feet made no sound on the linoleum floor as he made his way toward the guards, plunging the scalpel into the base of the skull of the closest man. These bastards must pay for what they did to my team.

The sound of the guard dropping to the floor made the other two to spin around. Koga jammed the blade into the armpit of one of them, severing his axillary artery, allowing Koga to take hold of the guard's rifle in the process. The third guard hurriedly raised his weapon, but Koga was faster.

Though the weapon was still on the dead guard's shoulder, Koga tilted it up on its sling and fired three rounds into the third man's chest at point-blank range before the guard could get off a shot.

Three threats eliminated in less than twenty seconds. *A personal record,* Koga thought with a lopsided grin. *Kinda noisy, though.*

Expecting a small army to respond to the sound of the gunfire, Koga took shelter behind the cinder block wall with his new rifle at the ready. His mind focused on one thing—to eliminate as many of the opposition as possible.

As expected, the main door of the hospital burst open, and five men wearing body armor and holding Colt M4A1 assault rifles flowed into the lobby. Koga paused when he saw they were sporting familiar combat gear. He blinked his eyes hard to make sure it wasn't another hallucination.

"Friendly here! Friendly!" Koga exclaimed. "American!" He lowered his rifle but stayed mostly concealed. "Are you guys here for me?"

One man lowered his firearm and trotted over to where Koga stood. "Lieutenant Commander Koga?"

"The same," Koga said. He hoped he didn't look as bad as he felt.

"U.S. Navy SEALs—we're here to take you home, bud."

Koga stepped from his hiding spot with his hands raised and looked at the warriors, who faced outward in a protective perimeter. His red mist was lifting and his energy waning. Suddenly overcome with exhaustion and the adrenaline-muted pain making its way back, Koga dropped to his knees and rotated face first to the floor.

The last thing he remembered was being carried out of the building on a combat stretcher and being loaded onto a strange, angular helicopter that made almost no noise at all.

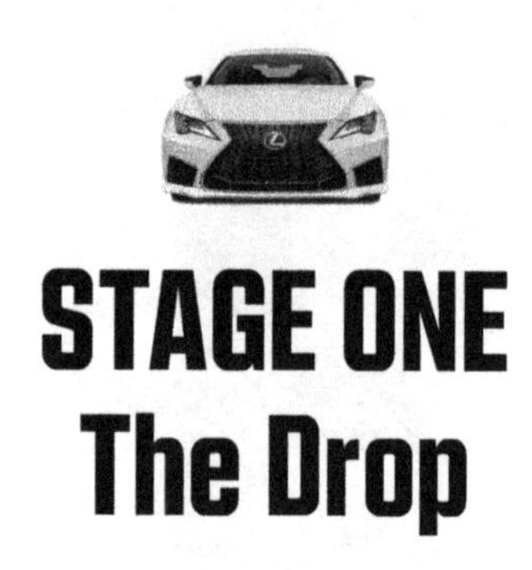

STAGE ONE
The Drop

Chapter 1

Maximilian Koga was quick to mark his territory by placing his laptop on a corner table at the Starbucks on Wilshire and Serrano. The afternoon in Los Angeles' Koreatown district was making its way into early evening and store traffic was low, so it only took a few minutes for the cute Asian barista to whip up his regular brew. She handed it over with her traditional warm, brilliant smile, which Koga thought he might need to investigate further one day.

But not today.

Three months had passed since the DEA had handed him his walking papers after military physicians expressed "concerns" for potential aftereffects from his drug-induced captivity at the hands of terrorists. Thanks for your service, they said. We think you need a long vacation, they said. He was no longer fit to serve, they said, to which Koga countered with legal counsel. But his lawyer informed him that to even have a chance at reinstatement, he would need to pass a psychological test performed by an independent physician of the Navy's choice.

So, against the advice of his lawyer, he submitted to that. He loved the damned job. He didn't know who he was—who he could be—without it.

Since his return to the States, his mind was obsessed with hunting down Nassim al-Ahmed to make him pay for what he had done to his teammates. The time spent under psychiatric observation after the event had been filled with darkness, trapping his soul in an inescapable pit of despair. But the one thing that kept him focused was the thought of seeing al-Ahmed and Ramin Madani bleeding at his feet, their pitiful and unanswered cries for mercy filling his ears.

It was the first time in his life that he felt so much hate that he wanted nothing more than to kill the perpetrators himself, slowly and creatively, such that his hands trembled at the prospect.

Bringing the two in alive was not going to be good enough.

The whereabouts of al-Ahmed and his men were currently unknown. They had dropped off the grid after the Mexico episode, with no chatter as to their whereabouts on the streets or even the dark web. And Koga knew full well that finding them would be impossible outside the resources of a government agency. Being restored to duty meant everything to him, not only because he still felt a duty to serve his country. No, it was more than that now. It was personal.

With the results of his evaluation due later that day, Koga passed the afternoon scanning job postings on websites that might suit a former Naval Intelligence officer with a three-year stint in the DEA, just for the hell of it. He had no actual interest in pure civilian life yet, and might never have any.

The automotive section on LinkedIn came first. Koga was a car guy, born and bred. When he was ten, his father, a successful race car driver, died in an event in Argentina when a suspension arm on his rally car snapped and whipped his car headfirst into a tree. Despite this tragedy, young Max still wanted to follow in his father's footsteps. But his mother would have none of that and took him as far away from racing as possible, moving in with her father, a World War II veteran, in Kaneohe, Hawaii—a state where no racetracks existed.

Nevertheless, Koga had still developed a natural liking for cars and spent his teenage years fiddling mostly with Japanese cars. He had rotated through a handful of different makes and models in those years, but his favorite ride was a hot Toyota 86 that he occasionally ran up and down curvy Tantalus Road between Telephone Road and Round Top Drive. If he'd worked his brakes too hard, he'd pull into the parking area at the Pu'u Ohia

Trailhead and talk cars with the other motorheads until the binders cooled back down.

In the end, although his mother had successfully kept him away from competitive driving, to her dismay, Koga ended up choosing an even more dangerous career: serving in the U.S. armed forces as his grandfather had. He became an officer in the U.S. Navy upon graduating college.

As Koga scrolled through the LinkedIn listings on his laptop, his peripheral vision spotted a large man in a black leather jacket and baggy khakis enter the coffee shop. His large oval head was topped with jet-black hair cut right above the ears, and his piercing brown eyes conveyed that he wasn't someone to be messed with.

Out of instinct, Koga watched him while keeping his head tilted toward his laptop. Without stopping at the order counter, the man grabbed an empty chair and slid it toward Koga's table, plopping his linebacker's body down in front of him.

"I'm Paul Verdy," he said, placing a business card on the table.

"Okay. Why do I care?" Koga asked.

"I run a company called Argon Securities. We provide intel services for various organizations around the world. I was told you were available for new opportunities, so I'm here to assess your interest in one." He pushed his business card a few inches closer to Koga with a stubby index finger. "Sorry to hear how the DEA jammed you up, by the way."

Intrigued but wary, Koga closed his laptop and gave the stranger his undivided attention.

"Thanks. I guess. So, how, and especially why, do you know me?"

"Like I said, Argon is a private intelligence company. We're in the information business."

Koga studied the imposing figure, trying to read his facial expressions and body language, but the man gave up nothing, sitting perfectly still with a poker face that might have been whittled from stone.

"Sounds like you're offering me a job with a PMC," Koga said.

"Technically, I suppose I am," Verdy answered.

Koga was well-versed with Private Military Companies. They were all the rage when the wars and semi-wars bloomed in the Middle East. Now that many hostilities there had subsided, the PMCs were often looking for work and frequently for trouble. Some weren't above starting it themselves.

Koga had worked alongside outfits like Executive Outcomes, Academi, and DynCorp when he was with Naval Intelligence. He could never fully trust someone who was in the business of war for profit. But *Lord*, there was a lot of money to be made. And war was a growth industry.

In Koga's mind, PMCs often were comprised of lawless bands of greedy mercenaries who usually did more harm than good. For them, it was all about being paid and a sense of duty coming in a distant second. Sure, their best recruits were former active-duty military, especially the prized special operators—SEALs, Rangers, Green Berets—with their exotic training and extensive combat pedigrees. But PMCs needing to fill slots also employed folks whose principal skill was pulling a trigger, not thinking.

"Sorry, Mr. Verdy, I appreciate your offer, but I have no interest in working for a PMC. The last thing I want right now is to be in some hot, dusty country with poor sanitation and foul drinking water escorting snotty politicians and corporate jerks to their hotels. I've *had* dysentery and I'll pass on a rematch. The Pepto diet for a week wasn't fun."

Verdy leaned back in his chair and looked directly into Koga's eyes.

"I understand your concerns, but let me tell you that Argon Securities is different. I know your clearance doesn't expire for a few more weeks, so I will tell you now that we operate within the articles established by the United Nations Regulations on Private Military Contractors—and our main client is Uncle Sam, who currently has us working undercover globally as an online automotive magazine."

Koga couldn't hide his disbelief at that last part. Verdy's candor was as surprising as what he'd just said. "Should you be telling me this?" he asked.

"I know you're a car guy, and I needed to grab your attention. Besides, you have a current Top Secret-SCI clearance. I also saw that your service to this country has been exemplary. You have a Meritorious Service Medal, a Bronze Star, and a Navy and Marine Corps Medal, a Purple Heart, and you're the grandson of a 'Go For Broke' World War II veteran of the 442nd Regimental Combat Team. There's more, but I suppose you know your own pedigree."

"You left out my Good Conduct Medal ... *general.*"

Verdy chuckled. "So, you do know me."

"To tell you the truth, sir, it just came to me. You retired before I joined the Navy, so I wasn't exactly sure at first." Koga reached across the table and shook Verdy's hand. "It's an honor, sir. Forgive my earlier attitude."

"Not a problem, mister. I've been there a few times. So, Max, why did you choose to go with the DEA? Navy Intel is a growing field. If you stayed, you would have made commander by now. Or you could have worked with other three-letter agencies, like NSA." The general squinted and cocked his head. "The CIA would also have been a good fit for you because of your ethnicity."

"If you're referring to my Asian heritage, I don't speak any Chinese or Korean, much less Japanese, except to order two beers in a sushi bar and say, 'My friend will pay.' But the DEA's international work intrigued me for a time, especially in its attention to arms traffickers and its role in dismembering Colombian drug cartels. It felt like a place where I could really make a difference," Koga said. "The flirtation was brief but memorable, and then it didn't work out. Now, may I ask you a couple of questions, sir?"

"Shoot," Verdy responded.

"Why would a retired four-star Marine Corps general be running a PMC? Shouldn't you have a posh consulting job or, like, a contributing national security gig on CNN?"

Verdy smiled, as if he had expected the question. "That would've been nice in a parallel universe, I guess, but the previous president asked me to help protect this country from outside of the Washington system. Former President Williams doesn't trust his incoming replacement. He thinks the man could be a threat to national security instead of its caretaker. Turns out, he was right to be concerned. President Raymond Pugh has made our national security agencies ineffective, placing political cronies at the top of the CIA and FBI, and ignored every recommendation made by the people who really know the score. And we know Pugh has ties to, let's just say, some sketchy characters."

Verdy sat back then and slipped his large hands into the side pockets of his jacket. He drew a deep breath and exhaled.

"He's not that bad, is he?" Koga asked. "I mean, he's a politician, but..."

Verdy shrugged his shoulders. "I just calls 'em like I sees 'em. Anyway, we finalized a long-term IDIQ contract with CIA just before President Williams left office, so as much as President Pugh hates us, he can't get rid of us so easily. Or inexpensively."

An Indefinite Delivery-Indefinite Quantity contract is the gold standard of government contracts. With it, companies received a large retainer to be on standby to deliver what is required by the contract. With Argon Securities, the services delivered had a broad and creative spectrum, and also covered payments for training and equipment development between assignments. And it would cost, as the saying goes, a shit-ton of money to cancel.

"So, why are you posing as a real car magazine?" asked Max.

"I can't share the details of that one just yet, but let's just say that it can be a convenient way to investigate international criminals who may use oblivious car companies as fronts to move money and weapons around the planet."

Verdy reached into an inside jacket pocket and produced a remote key fob. On its face was the distinctive "L" of the Lexus automotive brand. He placed the ornate piece of carbon fiber and metal on the table next to the general's business card that Koga had yet to touch.

"Are you trying to bribe me, sir?"

"No. That would be unethical. Let's call it an incentive. It belongs to a Lexus RC F that's parked in a 24-hour lot around the corner. You come work for me, the car and the pink slip are yours. Call it a signing bonus. Whatever you think of PMCs, at Argon we're in the business for the right reasons—and yes, it can be lucrative. I won't apologize for that. We work hard, and sometimes in dangerous places, for those tax dollars. And our ROI is pretty good."

Koga looked down at the Lexus key fob and wondered what color the high-performance sports car might be. If he's thinking of giving this to me as a signing bonus, the pay must be pretty friggin' good, Koga thought.

Verdy saw his look and read Koga's mind. "You'll make double-plus what you were making with the government."

Koga hesitated and then said, "It's very generous of you, but ... I'm not really interested."

Verdy rose from his chair.

"You are a stubborn son of a bitch, but let me say this. We can use a guy like you today, especially with your intel background and automotive knowledge. Oh, and we know you have some unfinished business with a certain terrorist named Nasim al-Ahmed and his little buddy, Doc Madani." Verdy half-smiled. "We may help with that, too."

At that moment Koga's cellphone, muted on the glass tabletop, vibrated across the surface with an incoming call. Koga glanced down and saw the Caller ID. It was his lawyer on the line with his test results.

Verdy said, "If you want to keep protecting this country, joining Argon is the only option left to you." He pointed at the buzzing phone. "You should let that go to voicemail." The general frowned paternally and shook his head slightly. "It isn't good news."

Without waiting for a response, Verdy turned and walked out of the store, leaving the electronic car key and his business card on the table.

Chapter 2

Max Koga took a few minutes after General Paul Verdy left the coffee shop to consider all he'd said. The Argon deal sounded great on its face, and that alone was enough to suspect it. Koga had never felt at home anywhere but in the Navy, and later the DEA.

He believed, like many veterans do, that pure civilians, with no military experience, were different from vets. Not all of them, but certainly enough that he didn't want to work next to them. They often had different sensibilities and different priorities, all mostly self-serving. Vets understood sacrifice was more than running out of money on dollar-beer night.

He let the lawyer's call go to voicemail while he looked up Argon on his laptop, but the pressure to know his fate was too much to ignore. He opened the phone app. His lawyer's voicemail had been transcribed, so Koga didn't need to hear the words, though they played as he read them.

"Max, hey, it's Tom Steinway," the message read. "I received an email from Dr. Richard Phillip Harris, the independent psychiatrist the government tasked with your psych eval and medical file review. In short, the email says, 'After carefully evaluating Maximilian Koga's test results, I cannot recommend reinstatement at this time.' Sorry, man. Call me and let's figure out next steps. Bye for now."

At this time. That's what people always say after they've kicked you in the guts and never plan to call you again. They think the false hope fools people because it implies, *So you're saying there's a chance*. But people are never fooled. It's the final kiss-off, that's all.

It took a few seconds for the message to sink in. When it did, Koga felt completely bewildered for the first time ever. The main purpose in his life—protecting his country from all enemies, foreign and domestic—had been ripped away from him for good, ending in the form of a voicemail, no less. How frickin' modern and efficient.

Equally painful was no longer having an official way to avenge his dead colleagues, which he swore to their memory and to himself that he would do. Koga looked down at Verdy's business card and then at the Argon profile in the Military Times on his laptop screen. His eyes defocused, and he pondered where his path would take him next. The General's offer suddenly became more enticing, but there had to be another path.

Another buzz of his cellphone. The screen showed a text from Donald Rawlings, one of his closest friends from their Navy days. They had shared an apartment and many good times together in Coronado, California, back when Koga was with Intel and Rawlings was with SEAL Team Five. Nowadays, they only connected once or twice a year.

Yo, my man! How are u doing? the message read.

Koga picked up his phone and typed: *Hey Donnie. Long time, bruddah. How's it?*

Rawlings replied, *Just wanted to check in with u. Been hearing things. U G2G?*

"Haha, no," Koga said aloud. "I definitely ain't good to go."

Koga wasn't ready to talk about his recent misfortunes yet, so he steered the conversation in another direction.

I remember you saying that you were thinking of leaving the Navy. Whatever happened to that? Koga typed.

That's what I wanted to talk to u about. Gotta sec?

Koga paused, for the last thing he wanted to do now was talk. But considering it was one of his best friends, he wrote *Gimme 5. Let me step outside.*

After gathering his belongings he gave the Lexus key to the barista. "I found this on the floor." She smiled and tossed the fob under the counter.

I need more time to think about it, General.

Koga stepped out of the Starbucks to look for a quiet spot along the sidewalk, when he noticed a black mid-nineties Chevy Tahoe driving slowly by on the main road. It wasn't the front-end damage, blacked-out windows, or blue smoke from the tailpipe that got his attention.

It was the missing license plates.

Koga's eyes followed the boxy sport-utility as it passed several open parking spots and then stopped in the middle of the street immediately next to his third-gen Mazda RX-7 parked a block away.

In case things got weird, Max thumbed a *gotta go more soon* into a text to Rawlings, shoved the phone in his back pocket and hid behind a column.

Then things got really weird. Suddenly and unexpectedly, the driver's door of the Tahoe flew open and a short man jumped out with what appeared to be a tire iron gripped tightly in his hand. He looked around nervously and, seeing no one nearby, he closed in on the Mazda. The man's face was mostly concealed by a pair of military-style aviator sunglasses and a Yankees baseball cap, and the color of his hair and skin suggested he was of Latino or Middle Eastern descent, making him virtually anonymous in L.A.

He peered into the RX-7 through the driver's window, one hand shading his eyes.

Before Koga could approach or yell a warning, the man stepped to the back of the Mazda and swung the metal bar against the rear window, shattering the tempered glass into a million pieces.

"Hey, that's my car!" Koga called out.

The man didn't respond. Instead, he took a plastic-wrapped package from under his shirt and tossed it into the Mazda's rear luggage compartment. Then, keeping his head low and turning away from Koga, he jumped back into the Tahoe and sped off.

Koga chased the SUV on foot, but it was long gone. The location of the area hardly made his car a worthwhile target for theft or carjacking, and it didn't seem like the perpetrator was looking to steal anything, anyway.

All the same, Koga walked to his RX-7 with care, ready to drop to the ground in case the man had left behind an Improvised Explosive Device, as

Koga had seen planted in more than a few cars in Afghanistan and Mexico. As he peered into the car's rear compartment, he saw the white plastic bag, taped shut, with the words "To Agent Maximilian Koga DEA CIA FBI" sloppily written on it with a black marker.

The package itself was flat and small, and the absence of obvious wires convinced him it wasn't packed with explosives, so he fetched a pair of disposable surgical gloves from a thin box he kept in the door pocket of his car and pulled them on.

Max carefully reached through the jagged hole to lift the object out of the car and, holding it away from his body, moved to the hood and set the thing down. He drew a Ronin Tactics "Sakura" combat blade from a horizontal scabbard attached to his belt and carefully sliced open the top of the plastic bag.

No clear liquid or white powder, which meant it wasn't obviously booby-trapped with poison. Instead, there was a single dirty manila folder with a letter written in ballpoint pen and several photographs, all blurry and faded. But the key person in every image was unmistakable: Nasim al-Ahmed.

The photo that caught Koga's attention showed the bald and bearded one-eyed terrorist in the driver's seat of what appeared to be an exotic sports car captured head-on stopped at a traffic light. Judging from the small cross-section of the car that was visible, it was a model that Koga had never seen before.

Then he read the letter

My name is Abdul Hassan, and I am the cousin of Nasim al-Ahmed. I was there when Dr. Madani tortured you. I am sorry I could not help you then. I can supply you with the location of my cousin in exchange for protection and the posted reward money of fifteen million U.S. dollars. In good faith, I am giving you the location of an active Al-Aqarib cell in the United States. If you agree to my terms, please write four Xs on the electrical box at the corner of 166th and Denker in the city of Gardena. I will then contact you. Bring fifty dollars U.S. in cash. This is not a trick or trap. I implore you to trust me, for I risk my life doing this.

Koga reread the note, then read it a third time. He looked up at the darkening purple sky. It would storm soon. He visualized the faces of his dead comrades among the roiling clouds and wondered if they were sending him a message.

❖

Dusk had already descended on greater Los Angeles when Paul Verdy stepped out of the Argon Securities office in Marina Del Rey. It was a convenient location for a center of operations, with Los Angeles International Airport nearby, and the added perk of being only a few miles away from the ocean. Among Argon's neighbors were satellite offices of several big tech companies, including Sony and Google, prompting some to refer to the area as Silicon Beach.

Verdy pressed the unlock button of his remote key fob, returning a honk and a flash of headlights from his Infiniti QX60. Then, the distinctive growl of a naturally aspirated V-8 engine roaring in the distance made him pause in mid-step, a brief smile creasing his leathery face. He stole a look at his MIL-W-46374-spec Marathon GSAR watch, issued only to Marine Corps general officers, and awarded to him when he'd retired. A moment later, an electric-blue Lexus RC F appeared and made a smooth halt in front of the retired four-star general.

The driver's-side window of the sports coupe lowered, revealing the face of Maximilian Koga.

"General," he said, "upon further reflection, I believe I'll examine your offer of employment in greater detail."

Chapter 3

The response from Paul Verdy was unexpected. There was no smile or welcome-to-the-team handshake, just a curt, direct order.

"You're late. Park the car and get in with me. Review this on the way," he said, handing Koga a thin file through the open window.

"Yes, sir," Koga said, parking the Lexus and jumping into the passenger seat of the Infiniti QX60.

Verdy steered his SUV north on Highway One as Koga opened the manila folder. He saw his medical evaluation inside, the one prepared by Dr. Richard Harris.

"So, you knew that I was rejected. Does this mean the job offer is no longer on the table?" Koga asked.

"If that were the case, you wouldn't be in this vehicle with me, would you?" Verdy responded.

Max hadn't bothered to ask Dr. Harris for the details of his evaluation, and he hesitated to even look at the report. But it was a reality he needed to face eventually, so he began to read.

Maximilian Koga suffers from Complex Trauma, resulting from the shock of his father's death at an early age and losing his team in the Mexico incident [Tab D]. The latter seemed to have triggered synesthesia that accounts for his peculiar red vision tinting. With most synesthesists, colors are associated with taste or smell or letters of the alphabet, but in his case, it seems to be set off by emotions. As this is highly unusual, I recommend continued monitoring.

"The thing is, I've never felt better in my life. Apart from being a bit out of shape these days," Koga commented.

"Keep reading," Verdy instructed.

He took up where he left off.

What is primarily concerning is that Mr. Koga's original report claimed terrorists held him for a few hours, while in reality, it was three days. This suggests he may have undergone some form of mental conditioning, or brainwashing, and thus I cannot sign off on his reinstatement at this time. I recommend Xanax to help control his ocular tinting symptoms. A follow-up exam should be performed in two to four weeks.

Koga scoffed. "Does this doctor know what it's like to be held inside a windowless room while being tortured? It's easy to lose track of hours, even days."

Verdy kept his eyes forward as he spoke. "Max, I don't believe in brainwashing. But if there was such a thing, it would have required your captors to break you and make you question your identity, which obviously didn't happen. And, as far as the complex trauma is concerned, I've seen my fair share of it, and it affects different people in different ways."

Koga breathed a sigh of relief. "About this vision-tinting thing, it's happened only once, but when it occurred, it infused me with some kind of special energy that I've never experienced before. It gave me a feeling of invincibility and sharpened my senses. I'm wondering if it's kind of like the 'red mist' race drivers supposedly get."

"What's that?" Verdy asked.

"There's an old myth that when race drivers see an imaginary red mist, they become hyper-alert, but lose all sense of self-preservation. Without a second thought, they perform risky driving maneuvers with no regard for their own safety. They become reckless and put everything on the line to win at all costs."

"Well, let's hope it's not that." Verdy pointed to the bag. "There's Xanax in there. Our doctors said to take it when you feel your vision starts to tint. It's supposed to keep you level, but you decide for yourself if you need it, if or when. But be careful. They can be addictive."

Koga gazed down at the bottle of pills, wondering if his tinted vision had any relation to the recurring visits from his dead colleagues, which, for obvious reasons, he wanted to keep to himself.

The QX60 turned into the parking lot of a weathered building with large garage doors. A subtle stainless-steel sign affixed to the structure was backlit in soft blue and read *Automobile Digest.*

"We're here," Verdy said.

"*Automobile Digest? That's* your undercover car magazine front? You are kidding me right now," Koga said. Incredulous, he could only shake his head and laugh. "This is your cover?"

Verdy offered nothing but a sly grin as he parked the vehicle. They exited, and he led Koga through the frosted glass doors of the two-story structure.

In stark contrast to the exterior of the building, the lobby was a car lover's dream. The walls were decorated with posters of race cars from various eras, including legendary Alfa Romeos, classic Auto Unions, and modern-day McLarens. A row of framed photos of Jim Clark, Ayrton Senna, and Mario Andretti hung on the far wall. On a stand to the side of the lobby was a Kamita GT1, a supercar of which only ten examples were produced. It was the last model introduced under the legendary industrialist Testuro Kanda.

"When you're done ogling, Max ..." Verdy said, holding the elevator door open.

"Sorry, sir," Koga said, stepping inside.

"This building was the photo studio for the *Digest* until about three months ago," Verdy explained. "But ever since it moved to a new location, it's been our base of operations. For now, we're the only ones allowed to set foot here. Press the second-floor button and 'G' at the same time to access the basement. That's where your new office is, at least for now."

"If we're here, who's at the main office in Marina Del Rey?" Koga asked.

"Most of our staffers manage lower-profile clients there, such as private firms and individuals. We have forty-three employees at Argon, and another twenty or so freelancers, most of whose identities are kept secret.

Only four, including you, are tasked to this secret special operations unit."

"When you said you were fronting as an automotive magazine, I never expected it to be *Automobile Digest*," Koga said.

"The owner, who you'll meet later, worked with the CIA a while back, and he's agreed to help us. It's worked out well beyond our expectations."

The owner of the Digest was a CIA officer? Koga thought.

Before Koga could recover, the elevator doors slid open, revealing a hallway that ended with a polished metal door. Verdy placed a right thumb on the fingerprint scanner on the wall, and with a soft click, the door hissed open. Inside was a long state-of-the-art conference room with flat-screen monitors on the walls and workstations in the back.

Then, sitting in a chair at the rectangular center table, was Koga's best friend, Donald Rawlings.

"Donnie? What ... what are you doing here?" But Koga felt he knew that answer.

"You never called me back, bro," Rawlings said with a wink. He stood and shook Koga's hand.

Lean and muscular, Rawlings had the chiseled look of an NFL defensive end, standing two inches north of six feet—four inches taller than Max. Rawlings often compared himself to Denzel Washington, but Koga had always told him he exuded more of a Kanye West vibe, which Rawlings didn't much appreciate.

"Is this what you wanted to talk to me about earlier?" Koga asked.

"Yup. I joined Argon three months ago as tactical director. I wasn't allowed to mention this to anyone, not even my mom, but Paul gave me the okay to talk you into getting your butt in here."

Koga looked at Verdy, who shrugged his shoulders.

"What can I say? I don't like taking no for an answer," Verdy said. He turned to the other desks. "Let me introduce you to the rest of your team. That lady over there is Denise Johnson, our lead analyst. The guy behind the three computer monitors in the far cubicle is Raja Singh, our principal hacker—uhm, that is 'information specialist.'"

"Pleased to meet you," Johnson said. "I've heard a lot about you." She spoke with a minor southern twang and a megawatt smile that could melt ice at fifty meters. Everything about her seemed fiery, from her firm grip to her bright red hair that dropped over her shoulders.

Singh stood from behind his cube and walked over to Max. "Hey. Call me Raj," he said in a light Indian accent.

"Pleasure," Koga said, taking Singh's outstretched hand.

"We have a good core crew here," Verdy said. "Denise was a ten-year veteran intel analyst with CIA, and Raj worked as a computer scientist for the Pentagon. And he slings a mean curry, too."

Singh just grinned and raised a thumb.

Then Koga noticed a man sitting in the corner in a buttoned-down shirt over a stocky build and no tie, his round, freckled face topped with wavy red hair. He looked to be in his early fifties.

"And last, but certainly not least, is our primary client, the chief operating officer of the CIA, Andrew Roberts," Verdy announced. "He was in the neighborhood and wanted to stop by to see what we're up to."

Roberts stood up and shook Koga's hand. "I've heard a lot about you, Max. Glad to have you on the team."

"Glad to be here," Koga answered, still slightly bewildered.

Verdy cleared his throat and took a seat at the head of the table. "Now that we have our director of counterintelligence on board, let's get him up to speed. Can someone call Stockton Clay and have him join our meeting now?"

Chapter 4

Stockton Clay was the owner and editor-in-chief of *Automobile Digest*, and already a modest legend in magazine publishing. He strolled casually into the Argon conference room, looking no more than thirty years old. He wore a boyish grin on his lightly tanned face, and his slicked-back dark brown hair glistened under the fluorescent lights. His blue suit seemed one size too large, but what particularly caught Max Koga's eye was Stockton's faded green Gran Turismo 3 T-shirt.

Before taking a seat at the table, Stockton Clay did a double take at the sight of Andrew Roberts in the far chair.

Verdy said, "I'm sure you know Andy Roberts, Stockton?"

Roberts leaned back in his chair. "General, Clay and I go way back, ever since our little adventure in Japan, years ago. Isn't that right, buddy?"

"Yes. And calling it a 'little adventure' is a gross understatement, chief. It's good to see you again," Stockton said with a smile. He turned to Koga. "And it's very nice to meet you."

"Likewise," Koga answered. "I'm a big fan of your work."

Koga knew Clay's bio by heart. Seven years ago, the wealthy boy wonder had taken the reins of a moribund *Automobile Digest* and transformed it into the most visited and widely read automotive website in the world, with over seven million YouTube subscribers and a popular weekly television show to boot. While they still produced a printed version of the Digest, the bulk of its revenue came from the internet, which included several online magazines, a dozen social media sites, as well as plenty of streaming content.

Verdy motioned Stockton to take a seat at the table.

"Max, I take it you knew Stockton Clay before we brought you in. What you probably don't know is that he's a large stakeholder in Argon Securities, and he's helping us by letting us use his magazine as a non-official cover for our operations. He has a full Top Secret/SCI security clearance, so consider him one of us. Also, in case I have to say it, everything you see and do, or that anyone else does, is classified. Are we clear on that?"

Nowhere else, not even in the Navy, Koga mused, would he be able to go undercover as an automotive journalist and hunt bad guys. It was better than hitting the Lotto jackpot.

"Are we clear on that, Max?" Verdy repeated.

"Yes, sir. Crystal," Koga responded.

"Good," Verdy said. "Last week, Stockton contacted me about a car company called Song Motors, saying something wasn't right with them. Stockton, can you fill Max in from the beginning?"

Stockton Clay swiveled his chair so it faced Max. "At the Beijing Motor Show a few months back, Song Motors, a Chinese company we had never heard of, displayed an electric SUV concept vehicle called the CruiseStar. The reported price tag for the production version of this vehicle was two million dollars. Our reporter covering the show asked for more information, but the company didn't seem to have a public affairs office, so no information was forthcoming. I had our best investigative reporter, who also speaks fluent Mandarin, travel to China to see if we could get an exclusive on it. Three days after he left, he called in to say he was quitting his job."

"Why?" Koga asked.

"He said gangsters threatened him. They roughed him up a bit, took him to the airport, and told him never to come back," Stockton said. "They told him if he continued to look into Song Motors, they would come after him and his family—and then sweetened it with $50,000. It was such a strange exchange that I mentioned the incident to Paul, and here we are."

The CIA man, Roberts, broke in. "Looks like I picked the wrong day to visit. They seem to be a pretty small-time operation. I hope you're not wasting your time with this one."

"Not so fast, Andy. The more we looked into them, the more intriguing this 'small-time' operation became," Verdy said. "The company has a subsidiary in Sudan under another name that's quite cozy with a few bad guys in that part of the world. Our people on the ground discovered that this satellite company recently shipped 'prototype' vehicles to Iran, Yemen, and Pakistan that we suspect were simply containers that smuggled cash, drugs, and arms. In any case, I was notified a few hours ago that a cargo ship rented by Song Motors arrived at Port Hueneme earlier today."

Stockton turned his attention to the general. "They're probably bringing in a high-end concept vehicle to the Los Angeles Auto Show, which takes place next week. Some companies use the smaller ports, like Port Hueneme, to bring in their top-secret products for more secrecy."

"Or it could be another 'prototype' they're using to smuggle something in," Verdy added.

"Whatever it is, it will have to pass customs," Roberts said.

"I know the Port Hueneme area fairly well," Koga said, making sure what he implied was clear. "I've been to the naval base there a few times ... "

Verdy looked over at his new employee. "Are you saying you want to check it out?"

"Yes, sir."

"Okay, but recon only. Andy, can you make sure whatever is inside the cargo hold will remain on that boat until at least tomorrow morning?" Verdy asked.

Roberts nodded. "Consider it done."

Verdy smiled. "Perfect. Ask around to see what's up with that ship and crew, but do it discreetly. I don't want to have an international incident that can risk our cover. No engagement whatsoever. The name of the ship is the *Mucho Gusto*, registered in Panama."

Rawlings chuckled. "Registered in Panama, huh? Which means pretty much nothing. Most private cargo companies register their vessels with a different country, usually for favorable tax advantages. I'd love to go with you, Max, but I need to be somewhere else in an hour."

"I'm a big boy," Koga said, flashing a thumbs-up sign. "I can handle it."

Verdy said, "Good. We meet tomorrow at zero-six. Everyone knows what they need to do. Any other items to address?"

Koga cleared his throat and unzipped his Oakley duffel bag.

"Yes, sir," he said in a clear voice. "As a matter of fact, I do have something."

Chapter 5

Before getting into the meat of his story, it took Koga all of ten minutes to fully describe the events of the Aqarib ambush in Topolobampo, Mexico.

"I'm sorry to hear what you went through. I had no idea," Stockton Clay remarked after Koga had finished.

Donald Rawlings gripped Koga's shoulder. "Nothing worse than losing a colleague, much less your entire team."

Andrew Roberts explained that Nasim al-Ahmed and his number two, Ramin Madani, had escaped from their hideout, an abandoned hospital in Navolato, Mexico, minutes before the SEALs came knocking.

"DOD evidently discovered the hideout after a courageous local resident recognized Nasim al-Ahmed and notified the local police."

Koga said, "Whoever that person was should get some bounty money or something."

"Agreed," Roberts said. "When we looked him up to do that, we learned this man had been killed. 'Stepped in front of a bus' was the cause of death."

"Good lord," Denise said.

"Yeah, that's Mexico," Paul Verdy said, shrugging. "So, what did you want to share with us?"

Koga recounted the incident outside of Starbucks earlier that day, with the man claiming to be al-Ahmed's cousin. Reaching into his duffel bag, Koga produced the folder Abdul Hassan had left in his car, spreading out its contents on the conference room table.

Raja Singh took particular interest in the photos, donning a pair of cotton gloves and inspecting each one up close.

"I'll try to see if I can find out where these were made. Maybe I can find some hidden faces in the reflections. By the way, what type of car is this?" Singh asked, holding up the photo of al-Ahmed seated in an automobile of which only a small section was visible.

Taking a long, hard look at the image, Stockton Clay shook his head.

"I wish I could make out more of it, but it's nothing I'm familiar with." He turned to Koga. "Max?"

Koga took a long look at the low-resolution image.

"Yeah, nothing from me."

"I'll run a recognition program to see if the A-pillar shape and door opening matches anything," Singh said. He collected the photos and carried them to his cubicle.

Denise took Hassan's letter and read it as Rawlings peered over her shoulder.

"I would like to search this for matrix points," she said. "We need to see if this guy is on the level or not. It's already obvious that he's versed in intelligence. He found you pretty quickly, Max, and asking you to mark the electrical box is classic tradecraft."

"Or he picked it up from watching *The Americans,*" Koga said with a wink.

"Yeah, or *Homeland*, maybe. I wonder why he wants you to bring fifty dollars?" Denise asked.

"Saves him a trip to the ATM?" Rawlings joked.

Roberts looked at the letter. "I'd appreciate it, Paul, if you'd keep me updated on this as well. We've been after Nasim al-Ahmed and the Aqarib for years. If these are genuine, it could be the opening we've been looking for."

"Of course," Verdy answered before addressing his team. "While our priority is still on Song Motors because that's what this task force was created to investigate, it can't hurt to vet this Hassan character at some point. If he checks out, we'll discuss how to move forward with him. He has the potential to be a valuable asset, if not for us, certainly for Langley. In the meantime, Max, tell me what you find at Port Hueneme, but be discreet."

"Roger that. By the way, do we actually do any work for the magazine?" Koga asked.

"Dude, you know I hate to write," Rawlings said.

"And Raj is a terrible driver," Denise smirked.

"We have freelancers who do all that for you, so you guys can focus on your actual jobs," Stockton said. "Your articles will have your cover names attached to them. That way, if anyone looked you up, you would be legit."

"If you see anything written by Darius Hightower, that's me," Rawlings noted. "And check out my column, 'Auto Rhythms.'"

"And," Stockton announced, returning the attention back to him, "I've told everyone at the *Digest* that you're all part of a new team working on a special future issue. We have many outlets in our organization, so no one will take the slightest notice of your presence here. Oh, and I have something for you, Max."

Stockton reached down and opened a stainless-steel Rimowa briefcase that rested next to his feet. He took out a large envelope and slid it across the table to Max, who spilled its contents onto the tabletop. The items included a California driver's license, a Motor Press Guild membership card, a company ID, and a hundred business cards, all with the cover name "Mack Katana" printed on them.

"Mack Katana?" Koga asked.

Verdy grinned. "I came up with that myself. You like it?"

"Yeah, sure. I mean, I guess so, sir," Koga said, putting on his worst poker face. "I mean, I should be able to remember the initials, right?"

"Well, you'll get used to it," Verdy growled.

With a nod to his new boss, Koga rose from his seat, eager to get on with his first assignment, when Rawlings stopped him.

"Hey, bro, before you go, I need to provide you with our standard field gear. Follow me," he said.

"When you're done there, you need to fill out some onboarding paperwork," Denise added. "I imagine you will want to get your pay, right? There are employment forms and insurance papers on your desk, stuff like that. Please don't leave the building until you get those back to me. I'll forward them to HR."

An hour later, Koga was equipped with a secure cellphone, a micro compact 9mm Sig Sauer P365 SAS handgun, and several pen-size canisters filled with a propofol-derived anesthetic they called Hypnos, after the Roman god of sleep. It was a prototype knockout drug Rawlings said rendered an enemy unconscious for up to six hours by inhibiting nerve transmissions in the central nervous system. In short, it was like a powerful general anesthetic. Just pop the needle out like a ballpoint pen and stab, Rawlings instructed.

Tossing his electronic key fob into the air, Koga jumped into his Lexus RC F and pointed the car north toward Port Hueneme.

Chapter 6

Max Koga peeled the Lexus RC F off Pacific Coast Highway at Exit 109, and after entering the Port Hueneme parking lot off Dock Drive, he parked the electric blue sports car in a secluded spot, away from the overhead lights in the corner of the lot.

The sun had long since set, and the harbor was well-lit from the wharf lights that were mounted to a dozen square metal buildings lined against the water. The Navy grounds were on an adjacent piece of property, separated from the main dock.

After stepping out of the car and checking the vicinity of video cameras, seeing two, Koga made his way to a small gate that marked the entry to the marina. The security guard—a large, blond Caucasian man in a black and gray rent-a-cop uniform—emerged from a wooden booth and walked along a chain-link fence, stretching his arms over his head and yawning.

Taking a pack of Marlboro Reds from his pocket, he placed a cigarette into his mouth, lit it with a disposable lighter, and took a satisfying drag.

"Hey there," Koga called out, approaching the guard shack in the dark.

Startled, the guard walked back into his shack and slid open a plastic window disfigured by scratches.

"Can I help you?" he asked.

"How are things tonight?" Koga asked.

The heavy-set guard had a pink, sunburned face, and the skin around his eyes was two shades whiter than the rest. "Oh, you know. It's pretty quiet, like always," he said. "Whadda you need, sport?"

Koga displayed his business card. "I'm with *Automobile Digest*, and I have an interview with a guy who came in on that boat over there," he said, pointing to the *Mucho Gusto*. "Okay to go inside?"

"Mack Katana," the guard said, reading the business card. "Cool name. Sounds like you should be an actor in karate movies." The guard slid his window closed and stepped back out of the shack. He made a few squiggles on his clipboard and handed the card back to Koga. "Sure, be my guest. But be careful, because those crew members are a little off, if you know what I mean."

"Actually, I don't," Koga said.

"Well, for starters, the captain was getting chewed out by his own crew right after they moored. I mean, it's usually the captain doing the yelling, right? But this crew was slapping him around. I mean, it looked like a full-on mutiny."

"Could you hear what they were saying?"

"Yeah, but they were yakkin' in Spanish or some damn thing."

"Thanks for the tip. I'll try to keep clear of them," Koga said, walking through the gateway onto the dock.

The *Mucho Gusto* was a private single hull, break bulk container ship of the Feedermax class, painted white with a blue hull. As far as cargo ships that crossed the Pacific went, it was on the small side, with a length of about six hundred feet and a breadth of about sixty. On board was a central superstructure with dim lights hanging near the bridge that illuminated the fore-and-aft decks.

As Koga approached the ship's gangway, he noticed they had chained it off with a large DO NOT ENTER sign hanging from its links. He called out in a loud voice.

"Hey, hello? Is there anyone there? Permission to come aboard?"

The only response was the sound of seawater slapping the ship's hull, so he tried again with a louder but more timid voice.

"I'm with *Automobile Digest* magazine, doing a story on sports cars? I'm here to speak with the captain?" He waited a few seconds, but still nothing.

Koga weighed his options. The smart thing to do was to wait until someone showed up, ask a few questions, and get out of there.

But an overwhelming desire to board the vessel took hold of him and would not let go.

"I hope I don't regret this," Koga said aloud to himself. He ducked under the chain and made his way up the gangway.

Chapter 7

Mucho Gusto was how Max Koga expected a ghost ship to appear in movies, but at least there were no lurid blood trails on the walls. The deck was devoid of people, no watchstanders at the top of the brow, no crew moving about, just a trio of overhead lights casting long shadows on an empty, bare-metal floor.

Amid the odor of diesel fuel and seawater, he stuck to the shadows and made his way to the superstructure located amidships. There, he found a thick metal hatch, which he undogged. It swung open easily, allowing a peek inside. There was a short passageway, and for the first time, he felt—or, rather, heard—the presence of people aboard, as voices emanated from one of the far rooms.

Koga spotted a ladder leading below, just inside the main hatch. It likely led to cargo holds and crew quarters. And from the darkened state of the deck below, there didn't seem to be anyone standing guard. Making sure that his Nike cross-trainers made no sound as he walked, he stepped into the superstructure and descended the ladder as quickly as possible.

Once he reached the deck, he came upon a narrow passageway that led forward. The first hatch was dogged tight and secured, but it had a small viewport at eye level. He peered through the thick tempered glass and made out the dark silhouette of something the size of a car sitting under a silky fabric tarp in the middle of an empty space.

Giving up on going any deeper into the ship, Koga turned to head back up to the bridge level when he heard heavy footsteps on the deck above him.

Koga tried the hatch again, this time with more force, but still no luck. He didn't dare venture deeper into the ship and risk running into other crew members. A confrontation seemed unavoidable. Without other options, he checked his handgun and returned it to its holster.

He hoped he wouldn't need it.

With his heart racing faster, his vision tinted a slight shade of pink. He pulled a Xanax pill from his pocket and popped it into his mouth, grimacing at the bitter taste as he chewed it up and swallowed it dry. He leaned against the bulkhead and centered, slowing his breathing while listening intently. The pink mist never reached the red stage, and it dwindled slowly. A wave of tranquility settled onto his nerves.

Well, whaddaya know—the damned things work.

He backed up against the far wall and ducked under the stairwell. He bent his body into a compact ball and backed himself into the cramped space.

The steel deck plates shook when a large man touched down.

From his crouched hiding position, Koga could only make out a pair of boots: large green, rubber-soled, military types caked with brown dust. Not your typical deckhand footwear. Another pair of boots followed, but these were smaller and cleaner. Both pairs of boots made their way to the cargo hold hatch, where one man undogged it, preparing to step through.

Time to move. Koga pulled out one of the Hypnos injectors he'd received from Rawlings. He popped off the cap, leaving the plastic cover on the floor, and then crawled out of his cubby, assuming a sprinter's starting stance.

He rocked back once and launched his body forward, springing from his hiding spot with the metal injector gripped tightly in his right hand.

It took exactly three full strides to reach the first man. Koga threw a high left hook into the head of the smaller deckhand, striking him between the lower right ear and spine, rendering him unconscious before he hit the deck. Koga followed up the strike with a choke hold on the larger man, wrapping his left arm around his throat and stabbing his neck with the knockout drug.

The big man had no time to react and the drug went to work instantly, causing his body to fall limp onto the cold metal deck next to his comrade.

"*Buenas noches,*" Koga said.

After dosing the smaller man with another injector, Koga searched the pockets of both deckhands. Under the lone ceiling light, he could see that they had dark complexions, long hair, and thick beards.

The larger one had a tattoo of a scorpion on the side of his neck where the drug injector had penetrated. The smaller man had the same symbol emblazoned on his wrist. They both had handguns wedged inside the pockets of their camouflage pants—Russian-made MP-433 Grachs—that Koga confiscated and shoved under his own belt.

The cargo hatch swung open wide, and Koga dragged each man inside, stashing them next to the bulkhead where they wouldn't be seen by anyone making a casual glance through the viewport. He turned to the object in the middle of the open space, lifting the tarp to see what lay underneath.

It was indeed an automobile—a low and wide sports car in fire-engine red. Round exposed headlights highlighted the front fascia, while flared front and rear fenders made the thing appear race-car wide. The badge on the hood read MachStar, and the absence of a grille and tailpipe suggested it was an electric vehicle, or perhaps hydrogen powered. He noticed a fresh scratch on the lower part of the passenger-side door, which might have explained why the captain was being chewed out earlier in the day.

Koga opened the driver's door and dropped his body into the cockpit, checking the cabin for hidden compartments. But other than the glove box and a storage slot in the center console, there was nowhere to stow anything larger than an iPad. After lifting himself out of the car, he popped open the hood behind the passenger cell, where he found a large battery pack that had plenty of extra room to hide drugs, money, or even weapons.

He checked the luggage compartment at the front of the car—the "frunk"—but it was empty. Then he noticed the car's A-pillar. It looked the same as the one in Abdul Hassan's photo, but it couldn't be—could it? Koga took out his cellphone and snapped a shot of the car's profile, texting the JPEG file to Raja Singh with the message: *Is this the same car as the one in the picture?*

He covered the car with the tarp and hurried back up the ladder, trying to imagine if a Chinese car company, a radical Islamic terror group, and the Eldorado Cartel could be associated with one another. Logic dictated that there was no way in hell, but the world has seen stranger things happen throughout history. When he reached the bridge level, he could still hear voices emanating from the compartment furthest down the passageway, likely the mess where the crew took their meals.

Was it worth the risk to have a quick look?

Taking a moment to listen to their voices carefully, Koga made out a few Arabic words, such as *ghidha*, meaning food, and *albanadiq*, the word for gun. Feeling as if he had overstayed his welcome, and not wanting to press his luck any further, he made his careful way out of the superstructure. He dashed across the open deck, hurried down the gangway, and onto the pier. After waving to the security guard on his way to the parking lot, he jumped into the Lexus, when his new cellphone vibrated.

It was a message from Singh: *Veh ID positive. It's the same car.*

Koga pushed the speed dial button for Paul Verdy, whose voice instantly sounded through the car's audio system.

"Find anything interesting?" Verdy asked without a greeting.

"Sir, I just had a quick look inside the *Mucho Gusto*, and I think I found something."

"You went inside?" Verdy asked in a tone. "Didn't I specifically say ..."

"I'm on my way back to the office now," Koga said, interrupting him.

"Okay, but what did you find?" Verdy asked.

"There was a car onboard all right, and Raj just confirmed that it's the same as one in the photo with Nasim al-Ahmed."

After a long pause, Verdy asked, "Are you saying that the Aqarib are customers of Song Motors, or are you saying that they may be connected in some other way?"

"I can't say for sure, sir," Koga said, "but the ship's crew were speaking Arabic and a couple of them had tattoos of scorpions on them, which is the Aqarib insignia."

"I think it's time we have a chat with your new friend, Abdul Hassan," Verdy said. "Let's bring him in."

Chapter 8

Night had descended on the Southern California coast as Max Koga drove back to the *Digest* offices in Malibu. A ding notified him he'd received a text on his new company satellite phone. He raised the device to look at the monitor and saw that it had come from Donald Rawlings.

Heard u hit jackpot at the boat. Let's get a drink. See u at Gin's Joint, one hour?

Koga checked his watch. Only ten p.m. It would be helpful to brief Rawlings personally on what he had just found, he thought, and also get his advice on what to do next.

See you there, he typed.

After an hour on the road, he peeled off Pacific Coast Highway and made his way to Lincoln Boulevard in Venice. In his rearview mirror, he noticed a motorcycle taking the same turns he'd made since exiting the Interstate. Its double headlights shone bright, making it difficult to tell the make and model of the bike. It maintained a discrete distance of about six or seven car lengths. It was probably just coincidence, he thought, but he did a surveillance detection route to see if the bike followed.

Koga made a quick turn into a narrow alleyway that took him across the back parking lot of a strip mall.

The bike continued straight ahead. False alarm.

Back on his way, Koga soon noticed what looked to be the same headlights in his side mirror about four car lengths back in the adjacent lane. This time he could see the make and model of the bike when he passed under bright streetlights—a Yamaha R1. Now, he was convinced it was a tail.

It might be the Aqarib. Had Abdul's defection been discovered, or did he just play me?

While steering with his left hand, Koga reached under his seat with his right arm and pulled out his handgun, placing the firearm on the seat between his legs. He sped up slowly, not wanting to let his pursuer know he was on to him, but enough to create more distance between his car and the bike. Then, without touching the brakes, he yanked hard on the wheel, turning onto a side street and immediately pulling into a parking garage, the entrance of which was blocked by a lowered gate arm. He switched off his headlights.

A man wearing a worn, light blue windbreaker, stepped out of a small wooden booth near the barrier gate.

"Twenty bucks," he said.

Koga lowered his window. "I made a wrong turn," he said. "I'm going to back out. Can you keep the space behind me clear?"

"Yeah, sure," the parking attendant said.

Koga glanced at his rearview mirror, waiting for the motorcycle to pass, but a dark red BMW sedan pulled up behind him, blocking his rearward path. A moment later, the Yamaha motorcycle passed by, unaware that the Lexus was sitting at the entrance of the parking garage. The Bimmer provided cover, which was a good thing, but now Koga's car was stuck.

Seeing this, the parking attendant called out to him. "I'll open the gate for you, just make a U-turn and leave out through the exit." He pointed to the empty exit lane.

Koga gave him a thumbs-up sign. "Perfect."

Returning to the booth, the man raised the plastic gate arm by pressing a button inside, allowing Koga to enter the parking structure and turn around. With the headlights of his Lexus still turned off, he headed in the motorcycle's direction.

The motorcycle's red taillight shone about a block ahead. The bike had slowed down considerably, the rider probably scanning the area for the RC

F's distinctive L-shaped taillights. Koga moved to within about five car lengths, staying behind a Metro bus and a couple of yellow taxi cabs.

Then the Yamaha R1 stopped and performed a fishtail turn, spinning around one-hundred-eighty degrees and stopping, causing motorists to lean on their car horns and shout obscenities. But the motorcycle just sat motionless in the middle of the road.

Realizing they had probably made him, Koga pulled to a stop at the side of the road, his eyes fixed on the rider. The pursuer was dressed in a black leather jumpsuit and wore a black helmet with a darkly tinted visor. Koga lowered both windows and placed his right hand around the cold grip of his gun.

As if on cue, the Yamaha's rear tire spun wildly, spitting out white smoke into the night air as the front tire lifted off the ground. The bike sped down the street, doing a high wheelie toward the parked Lexus.

Undoing the safety of the pistol with his thumb, Koga watched the rider's hands for any sudden or suspicious movements, but the bike passed by without incident. He watched it go by, trying to make out the rider's identity, but the face remained hidden under the full-face helmet.

The front tire of the Yamaha touched down as the bike kept going, speeding down Abbot Kinney and disappearing around the first corner. Koga considered giving chase, but he knew the bike would be out of reach before he could even get his car spun around. He stowed his handgun back into the cubby, switched on the headlights and drove off toward his rendezvous with Rawlings, checking his rearview mirror for any other suspicious vehicles on the road.

To his slight disappointment, there were none.

Chapter 9

J.M. Gin's Tavern, which everyone referred to as Gin's Joint, specialized in Asian fusion cuisine. It was one of several places to be in Venice on a Friday night, with almost every seat in the house occupied despite the late hour. The smell of grilled *bulgogi* tacos and the sound of live pop music filled the air of the jam-packed restaurant.

Max Koga squeezed past a trio of men sipping drinks near the front door and spotted his friend at a table tucked away in the far corner of the dining room. Donnie Rawlings waved his arm.

Using his right hand as a wedge to slice his way through the crowd, Koga worked his way to the table where Rawlings and Denise Johnson were working on their second drinks of the evening. A couple of light hugs later, Koga sat down between them.

"Sorry I'm late," he said. "No Raj?"

"He doesn't drink. Plus, I think he's busy studying those photos from the boat you sent him," Denise said.

A brunette waitress dressed in a tight black T-shirt and a matching waist apron approached the table. "What can I getcha?" she asked Max.

"He wants a Bulleit Bourbon, straight," Rawlings answered.

Koga raised both hands in protest, handing her a credit card. "Oh, no, not tonight. I'm tired, and I'm driving. Make that a tall Sapporo in a glass. And put everything on my tab."

Rawlings clapped in approval. "Now, that's being a team player."

"We can't let him pay, Donald. It's still his first day on the job," Denise retorted, but her words fell on deaf ears because both Rawlings and Koga had turned their attention to a woman who had just entered the restaurant.

The newcomer looked to be in her late twenties, wearing a black felt hat over medium-length platinum blonde hair. A pair of tinted glasses with large turquoise frames partially covered her face and a light green designer scarf hung loosely over a form-fitting black blouse with a plunging V-neck.

With a slight smile that highlighted her high cheekbones and full, ruby-red lips, she strutted her shapely figure to the bar, aware that almost every man in the room was watching her as she sat down on the only empty bar stool.

The bartender went straight over to take her order.

Rawlings got up from his seat. "Hey, yo, I'm going to see if I can get her number before someone else beats me to it," he said.

"I thought I was your date tonight," chided Denise, but he was gone before she finished her sentence.

Not more than a minute later, Rawlings returned.

Koga couldn't help but snicker. "Swing and a miss," he said in his best Vin Scully impression, mimicking a batter swinging a baseball bat.

"What happened?" Denise asked.

"Not a thing. Our conversation comprised exactly three words. 'Hi,' and 'Not interested.'"

The waitress returned with an Amstel Light for Rawlings. Koga's Sapporo came in a chilled glass. And she also placed a dirty martini on the table.

"Miss, we didn't order the martini," Rawlings said.

"That is compliments of the lady over there," she said, pointing to the bar and placing the drink in front of Koga.

The woman looked Koga's way and flashed a smile that could put a politician behind bars.

"Whoa, did you see that?" Rawlings exclaimed. "Dude, you need to go over there right now. Get me some revenge."

"I wouldn't put it as poetically as that, but he's right, Max," Denise said. "You should definitely go see what her deal is."

"I guess it couldn't hurt," Koga said, rising from his chair with the martini in his hand.

When he reached the bar, he cleared his throat, prompting the woman to spin in her seat. Her perfume had the scent of sweet jasmine.

"How did you know I liked dirty martinis?" he asked coolly.

"You look like the type," she answered in a low voice.

"I'm grateful for the drink. Thank you." He raised his glass.

Without touching her beer, she replied, "I'm not usually into Asian guys, but you caught my eye."

"I think there's a compliment buried in there. My name is Max," he said, raising his drink again, but closer toward her.

The woman picked up her purse and slid off the bar stool, leaving her untouched glass of beer on the counter. She was taller than him, which he didn't mind at all, but what bothered him was that she ignored his raised glass.

"Maybe I'll see you around again. Enjoy the drink," she said and walked past him toward the exit.

Koga watched her squeeze through the crowd without looking back once. After standing in place for a good fifteen seconds, he returned to his table.

"No-no, don't tell me," Rawlings said when he saw Koga approach alone. "Not you, too."

Koga shrugged his shoulders. "'Fraid so."

"Well, at least you got a drink out of it. I didn't get jack."

Denise, who was now smiling from ear to ear, said, "I kinda like her style. Did she say why she bought you the drink?"

"Nope. Only that I caught her eye," Koga answered.

"Maybe she didn't like what she saw when it was up close," Rawlings said with a laugh. "You always did look best from fifty meters in dim light."

Ignoring the remark, Koga gazed at the entrance of the bar and watched several patrons slowly make their way out.

"Well, here's to us and those like us," Denise said. "Til Valhalla."

"That's right," Rawlings said. He placed a consoling hand on Koga's forearm. "And there's plenty more fish in the sea, bro."

"Not many like that one," Koga responded. "Don't ask me why, but there's something oddly familiar about her, like I've seen her somewhere before."

Chapter 10

Last call had come and gone when Max Koga waved the waitress over to settle the bill. He insisted that Donald Rawlings and Denise Johnson not wait for him, so they had thanked him for the drinks and taken their leave.

Once the check was paid, Koga stepped outside into the cool night air and took in a deep, satisfying breath. The roads were empty, and there was a calm peacefulness about the town. As he walked toward his car, he heard footsteps behind him. It was more than one person.

His gut told him to be on guard. Without turning around, he stepped into the narrow alleyway to let whoever was behind him pass.

They followed him in. There were three of them, each one built like a fire hydrant, and all of them with shaved heads. They stood three wide, occupying the entire width of the alleyway. The biggest one, dressed in a tight camo T-shirt that showed off a massive chest and thick, tattooed arms, took up the middle position. The other two, in flannel shirts and faded black jeans, wore crooked grins as they pretended to crack their knuckles.

He hoped that none of them were armed. That was always messier.

Now standing face to face with them, Koga asked, "So, you boys lost, or are you just trying to get my number?"

Alpha Male took a step toward Koga. "What, you a tough guy?"

The two others positioned themselves on either side of Koga as Alpha Male grabbed Koga's shirt. He was at least three inches taller and twenty pounds heavier.

"Just so you boys know, I don't have any cash on me, and I bite back when provoked," Koga cautioned with a sly smile.

Alpha Male pulled him in closer. "How about we throw you onto a boat and send you back to China where you belong?"

Koga smiled. "I'm from Hawaii, actually."

"Hawaii? You should go back to your shitty little island and take your shitty yellow friends here with you," Alpha Male said as his mates joined in with laughter.

"Ah, I should have known by the smell—white supremacists," said Max. "So, what's it going to be? Are you going to walk away from this and spend tonight in your own beds, or would you rather I send you guys over to Cedars-Sinai?"

With a laugh that was more a bark, Alpha Male pulled back his right fist. The man seemed to move in slow motion as Koga easily blocked the oncoming attack with an open hand, slapping it downward while pulling his body away from Alpha Male's grip. Then, in one fluid motion, Koga turned and delivered a rotating side kick into his adversary's gut, sending him stumbling backward off the sidewalk. Ten years of *jiu-jitsu* lessons growing up, and five years of *Muay Thai* while in the Navy can make a person a fairly effective weapon.

The other two men stood motionless, seemingly in shock at the sudden counterattack, giving Koga more than enough time to follow up his attack with an uppercut into Alpha Male's face. The impact crushed the bone in his nose, causing him to yelp in pain and fall on his back as blood gushed out of his nostrils.

One threat eliminated.

Koga kept low, almost in a squat position, as he turned toward the remaining two men, pausing to give them an opportunity to run away. They didn't take it. The youngest-looking kid dove for Koga's legs. He countered by sprawling, distancing his legs from the attacker's grasp. Pressing the kid's face into the ground, Koga grabbed his wrist and locked his shoulder into a standing submission hold.

Eying the last kid as he held the younger one down, Koga said, "If you're thinking of joining in, I'll break his arm, and then I'll smash your ugly freckled face."

The third man didn't listen, or perhaps didn't hear him, because he screamed from the top of his lungs and charged with his fists flying. Koga put extra pressure on the young kid's arm, popping the shoulder out of its socket. The cry of pain temporarily slowed the final attacker's momentum, which allowed Koga to jump forward and headbutt him in the face. The blow landed on the bridge of the attacker's nose and he staggered back with his face in his hands.

Koga returned to the kid, who was now writhing on the ground, holding his limp arm.

"*You broke my arm,*" the injured man whimpered, his eyes tearing.

"No, I popped your shoulder out. I'll do worse if you don't tell me why you guys targeted me. There were plenty of non-whites that came out before me tonight. Why me?"

"It was your wife."

Koga paused. "My what?"

"Your wife, man. She gave us three hundred dollars each to rough you up. She said that you were beating her."

Koga laughed. "I don't know how to break this to you, but I'm not married. Hell, I don't even have a girlfriend."

"What?" The kid started sobbing loudly. "*What?*"

Maybe I should have gone easier on them.

"When and where did this woman approach you?" Koga asked.

"Outside the bar a few hours ago. We waited until you were alone. That's all."

Koga grabbed the kid's arm, pulled on it and twisted it clockwise. With a loud pop, the shoulder snapped back into place.

Winded from the skirmish, Koga leaned against the wall for a quick breath when a pair of headlights shone on him from down the street. The howl of a motorcycle's inline four-cylinder engine whined up as the lights became brighter. Koga watched it approach and pass him slowly. It was the same Yamaha that trailed him earlier, but this time Koga got a good look at the size and build of the rider.

It was a woman, and judging from the few strands of platinum-colored hair that dropped under the black helmet and a light green scarf loosely tied around her neck. By her distinctive contours, it was likely the same woman who had bought him the martini earlier.

But who she was, and whether she was somehow connected to al-Aqarib, he had no idea.

Chapter 11

As the sun peeked above the eastern horizon, Max Koga walked along the cracked sidewalk of 166th Street in the city of Gardena, about a half-hour's drive south of downtown Los Angeles. Brian Panackia, who managed Argon's safehouses, surveilled the surrounding area from inside a beige GMC Denali parked a block away.

"I appreciate you coming along on such short notice, Brian, and sorry to get you up this early in the morning," Koga said through the microphone attached to his earpiece.

Panackia, an Army veteran in his mid-forties and a seasoned mixed martial artist, laughed at the comment. "You call this 'early'? Y'all Navy boys are too damned soft."

"That's all right, but you're thinking of the Air Force." Koga chuckled at the remark as he came upon the green electric box described in Abdul Hassan's letter.

The previous evening, Raja Singh had established the authenticity of the photographs, confirming that they were the real deal, and Denise Johnson had run a deep background on Hassan that verified he was indeed the cousin of Nasim al-Ahmed.

Born in Saudi Arabia and educated in the U.S., Abdul Hassan had graduated from the University of Colorado with a bachelor's degree in philosophy but was forced to return to his home country when his student visa expired. Not long afterward, he joined al-Aqarib after the fall of ISIS. He quickly worked his way up the ranks to become one of the organization's five top lieutenants. He ranked fifteenth on America's most-wanted list.

Denise had concluded that nothing in Hassan's letter suggested he was lying. The location of the Aqarib cell checked out, with the FBI having since raided the house in Matthews, North Carolina, apprehending five suspected jihadis. She also noted that he was trained in Somalia by Harkat al-Shabaab al-Mujahideen, or more commonly known simply as al-Shabaab. His ability to suggest a technique often used to mark dead drops revealed that espionage was part of that training.

While leaving markings on public property was hardly sophisticated tradecraft for handlers to communicate with their assets, it was still an effective technique. No one would notice a random mark in a neighborhood already rife with graffiti except the person looking for it. What piqued Koga's curiosity was how Hassan planned to make contact.

The residential neighborhood was relatively quiet because of the early morning hour. Koga stopped and surveyed the area around the electrical box. Aside from a feral cat sniffing for scraps in an open trash bin, nothing seemed out of the ordinary. He took out a thick, yellow piece of chalk from his pocket and drew four large Xs on the side of the box.

"Any movement?" Koga asked into the mic at his wrist.

"Negative," Panackia said.

"Okay, I'll walk around the block a couple of times and give him some time to think about it. If he doesn't show by then, come and get me at the designated spot."

"Roger that," Panackia responded.

As Koga made his way down the street, a boy of about ten years old ran out of a nearby apartment complex.

"Hey—hey, mister," he called out. Koga stopped and turned around.

The boy was Hispanic with straight, dark hair, and he wore a Lakers jersey over a white long-sleeve T-shirt.

"Yes?"

"Man said I'm s'posed to give you this." The kid held out a folded piece of paper.

Koga took the paper and opened it up. On it were the words: "De Portola Park. Bench, NW corner. Midnight. Bring signed hard copy of agreement or no deal."

"Who gave this to you?" Koga demanded.

"Some guy with curly hair and a beard," the boy answered. "He paid me fifty bucks to hand this to whoever drew a yellow mark on that box."

"When did you see this man?"

"Yesterday, while I was playing with my friends. He gave four of us each fifty bucks to take turns waiting for you to show up. And he said you would pay the person who gave this note to you another fifty," the kid said with an open hand.

"Have you ever seen him before?" Koga asked, handing the kid two twenties and a ten.

The boy shook his head.

Hassan had evidently hired the children to watch the electric box during the day, and probably recruited an adult—a homeless person, perhaps—to monitor it at night, while he himself kept a safe distance away. Clever, Koga thought.

"The asset just made contact," Koga reported to Panackia. "A note delivered by a kid in the neighborhood. Meeting at midnight tonight at De Portola Park. Ever heard of it?"

"I have," said Panackia. "It's about a twenty-minute drive from here, in Country Hills."

After one last look down both sides of the street, Koga started back to the parked Denali. "I say we go check out the park before our meeting. I'd like to make sure we're not walking into some sort of trap."

Chapter 12

De Portola Park was an ideal meeting place for those who didn't want to be noticed. Located in the middle of an upper-middle-class residential area, the park itself was small—a grassy plot of square real estate just off Rolling Hills Road. At its center was a playground for children, complete with a slide, a miniature merry-go-round, and a quartet of swings. A solitary wooden bench was along a walkway, hidden from the homes to the east under dim overhead lights.

Earlier that day, Brian Panackia, disguised as a retiree walking his dog, did a recon of the entire area, looking for any potential danger points. All clear was his report. As the hour approached midnight, Koga strolled into the darkened park that was eerie when empty. Taking in the surrounding area, he took a seat on the lonely bench as a heavy fog descended from the night sky, obscuring everything over twenty yards away. He patted the Sig in the pocket of his fleece jacket to reassure his nerves when the chime of a cellphone broke the silence. It didn't originate from any of his devices.

The sound came from below, prompting Koga to look under the bench. Duct-taped to the bottom corner of the seat was an old-style flip phone.

Brian must have missed it when he swept the place earlier, or perhaps it was placed there after he left?

He peeled the device off the tape and answered it. "This is Max Koga."

"Mr. Koga. I am glad you came," a voice said in a slight Arabic accent. "I see that you have rounded up my colleagues in North Carolina. Does that mean you have agreed to my terms?"

"Yes, definitely," Koga answered. "Do you have the location of Nasim al-Ahmed?"

"I do."

"Great. Then why don't you come out, and let's talk."

Hassan laughed. "And let your fellow agents subdue me like a criminal? I think not. I know what happens to people like me. We're taken to Guantanamo Bay, correct? I need to make sure that I am paid those fifteen million dollars with guaranteed immunity and protection. Then, I will show myself to you. As well as others."

"It's your call, but that money can't be released unless we have Nasim al-Ahmed. And you're probably already in hot water with your cousin for giving up your fellow jihadists in North Carolina. Al-Ahmed is going to want to know who ratted them out."

"You would double-cross me like this?" Hassan asked with concern.

"No," Koga replied. "But it was the FBI that raided the hideout, not my organization. And your cousin may have informants inside the FBI who can trace the tip back to you."

"I am not an idiot, Mr. Koga. I have made precautionary arrangements in case things like that happen," Hassan retorted.

"Look, Abdul, if I may call you that, I'll be honest with you. There is a car parked down the road with my colleague inside. He's supposed to be keeping an eye on me, but because of this fog, he probably can't see what's happening here, and I chose not to wear a wire. So, it's just you and me. I have the agreement with me that promises you the reward money if you deliver. I believe you want out of your organization, so why not trust me, and let me take you somewhere safe? Like Jerry Maguire said in that movie ..."

"... help me help you," Hassan completed the sentence for him.

"Yeah," Koga responded with pleasant surprise. "You've seen it."

After a long pause, Hassan said, "Please wait there for five minutes." The call ended abruptly.

In less than half that time, a man approached from the north side of the park on an electric kickboard. Koga stood and raised his arms in a show of good faith, but the reassuring weight of the Sig in his jacket pocket was comforting. Obscured by the darkness and fog, the man stopped about fifteen yards away, just out of the overhead lights. Koga could make out the silhouette of a short man with curly hair. Although his face wasn't completely visible, Koga was certain that it was the same person who broke the window of his RX-7.

"Abdul?" Koga asked.

"If I am to go with you, I must first see the agreement," Hassan said.

"All right. I'm going to reach into my back pocket to get it. The contract says that if you provide us with information leading to Nasim al-Ahmed's capture or death, you are entitled to the reward money, as well as placement for you and your immediate family members in our witness protection program. It's signed by the U.S. Secretary of State himself."

"Please do it slowly," Hassan instructed.

Despite the lack of visibility, Koga was sure Hassan had taken out a pistol and was now pointing it at him, because that's what he would have done. After turning around to show the white envelope stuffed into his pocket, Koga pulled it out and tossed it onto the moist grass in Hassan's direction.

The man in the shadows took a moment before dismounting his kickboard. Then, taking one step toward the envelope, he bent to retrieve it. The overhead light caught part of his face, revealing a gentle-looking man with soft features and a thin beard; he looked years younger than his purported age of thirty-eight. He smiled when he saw the paper inside the envelope.

"You understand, I must take precautions," Hassan said as he took out a cellphone and snapped a photo of the piece of paper.

"Of course," Koga answered. "If you're done, shall we go?"

Hassan's smile faded when the reality of what he was about to do set in.

"We need to leave now," Koga pressed.

Hassan took a deep breath and stepped fully into the light, offering Koga his pistol, grip first.

"I am ready," he said.

Chapter 13

The drive from De Portola Park in Country Hills to Argon's safehouse, dubbed "the warehouse" by staffers, took about a half hour at night. In Downey—a city whose claim to fame was producing the Seventies soft-rock band The Carpenters—a nondescript two-story building served as an ideal spot to conceal high-value informers because of its location behind an empty industrial park. Being only fifteen miles from Long Beach Airport and twenty miles from LAX, the location was convenient for sneaking in or whisking away informants.

For the duration of the trip, the three sat in silence. Brian Panackia, the safehouse's manager, drove while Max Koga sat next to Abdul Hassan in the rear seats, who wore a blindfold and headphones to keep from discovering the location of The Warehouse. His wrists were in handcuffs, but in front.

After waving to an armed Argon guard at the front gate, Panackia parked the Denali in front of an abandoned warehouse building next to Koga's Lexus RC F. He then lifted his solid 230-pound body from the driver's seat and led his guests down a narrow stairwell to an orange metal door, where he placed his thumb on a round print scanner on the wall, activating a state-of-the-art security system. The door opened, and all three men stepped inside.

"Welcome to The Warehouse," Panackia said. "It's vacant right now, so you have the entire place to yourself."

"Is there a quiet place where we can chat?" Koga asked, removing Hassan's blindfold.

“Right this way,” Panackia said, walking them through a hallway lined with small offices. The first was a surveillance center, where a security officer spent his seven-hour shift monitoring live video feeds from cameras posted all over the neighborhood block. Next to the surveillance room was a small kitchen area, and next to that was another office with a large desk and a computer.

The last room was the interrogation room, which Panackia laughingly referred to as the Karaoke Box because guests were invited to sing there.

“Look up at that camera and wave to let us know if you need anything. One of our staffers will come right away,” Panackia said, leaving the room.

The Karaoke Box was a square chamber that mimicked the interrogation rooms of federal detention facilities. Lit by overhead fluorescent lights, the room had a simple metal table with a ring for restraints, and two metal chairs, all bolted to the bare concrete floor. The walls were gray and blank, save for the one with a large two-way mirror that reflected the entire room. Video cameras occupied all four corners of the ceiling.

After offering Hassan one of the two chairs at the table, Koga grabbed the other seat and took out a notebook and voice recorder.

Koga asked, “Do you need a coffee or something? Water? Anything but booze, I think we have it.”

Hassan shook his head. “No, thank you. I’m all right.”

“Okay then, let’s get started. What was the Aqarib doing in Mexico where seven of my agents were killed?”

Hassan closed his eyes and took a deep breath before answering. “It is very complicated, but the simple answer is that Al-Aqarib was running low on money, so Nasim moved in on the drug business in Sinaloa. He took over the Eldorado Cartel and started eliminating all the smaller gangs in the area. As a result, we reaped the financial rewards of the drug trade and set up a base within striking distance of his hated enemy, America.”

“How did al-Ahmed take over the Eldorado Cartel?” asked Max. “The Mexican cartels don’t let outsiders come in and simply hand them the keys to the kingdom. He couldn’t have done this on his own, especially without the U.S. knowing about it. Did he have help from the inside?"

"I do not know for sure, but Nasim has a new benefactor who he has kept very secret, even from me. Apparently, this new friend is very influential and has powerful friends in high places. This mystery man also supplies our organization with weapons and money."

"And you don't know who this benefactor is?"

Hassan nodded. "Only that he's an Asian man. Probably Chinese, but I can't say for sure."

"Asian? Is it the person in the photo that you gave me? The one with al-Ahmed inside the car?"

"I think so, but I can't be sure."

"Have you ever heard of Song Motors?" Koga asked.

Hassan shook his head.

"They're the ones who made the car that your cousin was sitting in. Did your cousin ever mention anything about a car company?"

"No," Hassan answered. "Not to me."

"How did al-Ahmed get into Mexico in the first place? The bastard's name and face are plastered on the wall of every airport in the world. And that face isn't one you can easily disguise."

"His new benefactor provides him with access to a jet that transports him wherever he wants. He uses only private airfields, so there is no concern about immigration or customs."

Koga leaned back in his chair and let out a long breath. If Hassan was telling the truth, America's national security faced a grave additional risk: A Middle Eastern terror organization had set up shop within spitting distance of America, with money and weapons supplied by what was most likely a hostile Asian government.

"Why was I the only one spared in Mexico?" asked Max.

"It was completely accidental. Call it natural selection, like Darwin—you were the toughest of the bunch, so that allowed you to survive. The plan was to leave one of you alive to bring in for our questioning, to find out if the DEA had informants inside the Eldorado Cartel."

"You mean for torturing," Koga corrected him.

Hassan just shrugged.

"And how did you track me down in L.A. afterward?"

"It was you who told me. When I secretly visited you in your holding cell, in your delirium, you told me you were based in the Los Angeles DEA office. I then asked Nasim if I could go to America to help organize our cell in Southern California. When he finally agreed, I waited near the DEA office every day looking for your car, which you had also described to me. I'm glad that there are very few of those RX-7s on the road," Hassan said.

A chill ran down Koga's spine. He had no recollection of the conversation. "What else did I say to you?"

"Nothing of consequence, only babbling. Dr. Madani mentioned that he never saw anyone resist his truth serum as well as you did. He was going to resort to physical torture, but your military force came in before he had a chance. I was the one who loosened the binders around your wrists so you could escape. But in the end, I suppose, there was no need."

So that's why they were loose.

Koga gave Hassan a nod of appreciation. "I appreciate that, and it helped," he said. "Now, I'm ready for you to tell me where to find al-Ahmed."

"I'll write down his exact coordinates and address. I expect to be paid in full when you capture him," Hassan responded.

It was clear Hassan still believed Koga was with the DEA, which was fine by him. Koga took out a piece of paper and a fine-point Sharpie from his carrier bag and placed them on the table. Hassan took the items and scribbled down longitude and latitude coordinates, as well as a street address, and then slid the paper back to Max.

Koga scanned it and looked at Hassan. "You're kidding, right?"

Hassan shook his head. "I'm not. Nasim al-Ahmed is in San Diego, California. Right now."

Chapter 14

No other entity in the world can rival the Mexican cartels for tunneling. More than a hundred secret passageways of all sizes and lengths—some stretching a full mile—crisscross beneath the U.S.-Mexico border at any one time for smuggling drugs and, even more tragically, humans.

Abdul Hassan explained how Nasim al-Ahmed had used one of these tunnels to cross the border into the States. "From Mexico, he secured cartel cooperation to set up a secret al-Aqarib cell in Chula Vista, ten miles south of San Diego. He is planning a large-scale attack here. It must be very important, or he would not have risked coming into America."

"How do you know he's there now?" Koga asked.

"I'm scheduled to meet with him at a house there at dawn tomorrow. He plans to unveil the details of the operation to our team, which is his usual eleventh-hour practice. He never reveals a plan until the very last minute, even to participants."

"Why didn't you wait to come to me until after he told you about this attack?" Koga snapped. "Then we could've been prepared to stop it."

"If I did that, I wouldn't have been able to provide you with his location. He will disappear again right after our meeting. This was the only way to know where he was going to be beforehand."

"I'll be right back," Koga said to Hassan, then stepped from the room. He took out his cellphone and briefed Paul Verdy on the conversation he'd just had with his new asset and what he expected for the raid. "I'd like to be there when everything goes down. It's only a two-hour drive from here."

"Negative," Verdy responded. "We need to leave this to the government agencies now. Our job is done. I know how bad you want this guy ..."

"I don't think you do, sir."

"Take it easy. Donald and I will head there now to keep an eye out. You need to take your personal feelings out of this. Bad stuff happens when you make things personal. When I hear something, I'll call you."

Click. End of conversation.

Disappointed, Koga headed straight home without even stepping back into the interrogation room. Once there, he jumped into the shower and went straight to bed. It took a while for him to fall asleep, but when he did, a sound of distant gunshots galvanized him awake.

The nightstand clock that showed four a.m. He had been asleep for only an hour—and he wasn't alone. At the foot of his bed were his seven dead colleagues, all looking at him with blank expressions.

"I really wish you guys would stop visiting, or at least tell me what you want," Koga said as he sat up against the headboard.

They laughed silently, as if he had made a joke. Then their faces turned grave. They opened their mouths as if they wanted to tell him something important.

"So, this is what PTSD on steroids looks like," Koga said to himself. Then the ring of his work phone interrupted the moment, causing the visions to evaporate into the darkness.

He looked at the Caller ID. It was Verdy.

"Did you get him?" Koga asked.

"No, we did not," his boss said.

Koga cursed quietly under his breath. "What happened?"

"The Feds showed up at the house, but it was empty. The neighbors confirmed that Middle Eastern-looking men rushed out of there earlier in the evening with a couple of moving trucks, but the arrest team got there too late. The FBI director thinks we were set up. He wants to meet with us at their San Diego field office at zero-seven. I need you to take point on this because it was your asset who provided the information."

"I'd be happy to, sir. Sorry it didn't work out. Sounds like the info was good, but the timing wasn't."

"It was a solid lead, Max. We just need to convince our clients of that. You can take the helicopter. It's parked at the Long Beach Airport. I'll have my secretary send you the details."

"We have a chopper?"

"Like I said before, PMCs are a lucrative business," Verdy reminded him and ended the call.

Koga jumped out of bed, dressed quickly, and headed out the door of his townhouse. Before going to the airport, he needed to have a follow-up conversation with Abdul Hassan. The supposedly turned terrorist had some explaining to do.

Chapter 15

If the NO TRESPASSING signs didn't keep visitors clear of The Warehouse grounds, the armed guards posted around its perimeter certainly did. After driving through the main entrance, Max Koga parked his Lexus in the lot and walked to the hidden entrance. His watch showed five a.m., giving him about twenty minutes if he was going to make his seven o'clock. He put his thumb on the scanner that unlocked the door. He heard the electronic lock click and pulled the door open.

On the other side of the doorway at a desk sat a muscular bald man, mid-forties, in a tight black T-shirt and black jeans. He looked Koga over from head to toe.

"How can I help you, sir?" the man asked, standing.

"Where's Brian Panackia?" Koga asked.

"He's probably home sleeping. I'm Jayson Spence, night manager. Call me Jay."

"I'm Max Koga, new guy. I need to speak with my guest. Urgently."

"This way," Spence said, getting up and leading him to the interrogation room. "I'll bring him right away." He towered over Koga, standing a full six feet, four inches.

"Thanks, and don't bother restraining him," Koga instructed.

Several minutes later, Spence returned with Abdul Hassan, who wore a Yankees baseball cap, faded Levi jeans, and a Boston Celtics T-shirt.

"Oh, it's you Mister Koga. What can I do for you at this unholy hour?" Hassan asked, rubbing the sleep from his eyes.

Koga ignored him, instead turning his attention to Spence.

"Can you leave us alone for a few minutes?"

"Would you like for me to turn the cameras off?" he asked.

Koga paused. "That's against company policy. That won't be necessary."

"Understood," Spence said as he stepped out of the room.

Judging by the way Spence looked and moved—alert with no wasted motion—Koga guessed he might have been a special forces soldier in his previous profession.

"Sit down," Koga said, turning to his guest.

Hassan plopped onto the metal chair. "Well, what is it?"

Koga positioned himself behind Hassan and knocked the baseball cap off his head. He then took a handful of his curly hair and pulled Hassan's head back.

"What are you doing?" Hassan cried.

Lowering his own head so his mouth was an inch from Hassan's right ear, Koga said, "We just visited your so-called secret cell in San Diego, and guess what? No one was home. Now, have you been playing me?"

Hassan raised his hands in a show of surrender.

"Please. Everything I told you was true. I've been there a few times myself. I swear to Allah."

Koga eased his grip on Hassan's hair. "Then why wasn't he there? Why wasn't anyone there?"

"I don't know. Maybe one of you tipped him off?"

"Impossible," Koga answered. "This mission was close-hold."

"Then I don't know. You must believe me."

"I'm very dissatisfied with our little arrangement, and I'm considering other options. For us, but most especially for you."

Hassan froze. "Please, I promise you. I told you nothing but truth."

While some military contractor companies and rogue governments around the world still resorted to what the CIA called Enhanced Interrogation Techniques—the classic method being waterboarding—Koga didn't believe in torture. Not only did it violate the rules of human decency, to him, befriending a captive and winning his confidence often provided better results. The operating manual at Argon, which Koga had read the day before, prohibited EITs such as waterboarding and sleep deprivation, but it didn't oppose slapping around an uncooperative guest from time to time. Fear is a powerful motivator.

"Who said anything about hurting you? I'm thinking of letting you go," Koga said. "If someone else wants to hurt you, that's none of my business."

Hassan showed panic. "Nasim knows by now that I have betrayed him. I'll not last a day in the open."

"Especially not if you wear a Celtics jersey in this town."

Hassan didn't get the joke. "I have done everything you asked. I have told you everything I know. I'm still entitled to the reward money, yes?"

"Not a chance. You're worthless to me now," Koga said, facing a camera and pointing at the door.

"What have I done to deserve this?"

"It's what you haven't done that's the problem, brah."

A moment later, Spence stepped into the room. "All done, sir?"

"Yes. Take him back to his quarters, and thanks."

Spence nodded and held the door open.

Hassan slowly made his way to the exit, then stopped when he reached the doorway. "I detest what my cousin is doing. America is a place I love and respect. I love and respect all good people. I hope you believe that."

"We'll see," Koga said, as Hassan was escorted away .

Koga walked to the mirror and frowned in displeasure at a five-foot-ten-inch frame and pinched a small gut that had formed on his formerly lean one-hundred-and-eighty-pound body. The meeting with the FBI awaited, and he wondered if the only reason he was being asked to attend was because they needed a warm body to throw under the bus.

Chapter 16

The trip from Long Beach to San Diego in Argon's Bell 206B Jet Ranger took less than an hour, about a third of the time it would have taken by car. And it offered a scenic bird's-eye view of the coastline from Los Angeles to Camp Pendleton under the early morning sun.

Once the chopper touched down on the heliport at San Diego International, Koga met a Lyft ride summoned by an app and went straight to the FBI's San Diego field office near the ritzy Torrey Pines community, home to a famous golf course of the same name. Koga had visited the office during his DEA days, when he was part of a joint task force weeding out drug runners in the Chula Vista area.

He entered the building and passed through a metal detector. Once he and his effects were cleared and he'd surrendered his cellphone for a receipt, a visitor's badge with a thick red border was clipped to his collar, and he was escorted to the highly restricted eighth floor. Two women in dark business suits, one of whom he recognized from his last visit, staffed the reception counter.

"Hey, Mocha. Good to see you." He stole a fast look at his watch. On time. "The director is expecting me," Koga said.

Mocha Imada looked down at her appointment calendar and typed quickly on her keyboard. When she looked back up, she flashed a smile.

"Well, if it isn't Maximilian Koga. They're waiting for you in the conference room, sir," Mocha said. She rose and shook his hand. "Good to see you again. This way, please." Her colleague buzzed them through the door.

Pleasantly surprised that she remembered his name, Koga flashed her an awkward smile before being led down a short hallway that ended at a pair of double doors. After a light knock, Mocha opened the door and Koga entered the conference room. FBI Director Edward Womack sat at the head of a long, rectangular table, his head propped up on one arm and a pair of reading glasses hanging off his nose. A businessman by trade with no national security experience whatsoever, he'd been appointed as acting director to the FBI's top spot by the new President. The press had discovered afterward that he'd received his posting after donating three million dollars to the President's inauguration.

"Hello, Max. Come in, and please sit down," Womack said, extending his arm to an empty chair.

Already seated in one chair was Paul Verdy, dressed in his signature black leather jacket, zipped halfway up over a white dress shirt unbuttoned at the neck. CIA's Chief Operating Officer Andrew Roberts occupied the seat next to the general, his disheveled red hair and wrinkled clothes making it seem like he had spent the previous night in his car.

Verdy merely nodded with a grunt.

"Nice to see you again, Max," Roberts said.

Koga gave Roberts a slight nod. "Likewise, sir."

Ed Womack cleared his throat. "We'll skip with the pleasantries. What's your take on what happened last night? Or should I say, didn't happen?"

"Our source was good, sir. I feel someone must have tipped them off," Koga answered.

Womack sifted through a stack of paper on the table and shook his head. "We can't confirm if the target was there at all. By every account, it looks like your Arab friend played you like a Stradivarius. I wasted a lot of time and men on this wild goose chase you put us on."

Koga's eyes swiveled to Verdy and then back at Womack. "Is this some sort of hearing or official inquiry?"

"Not official, at least not yet," Womack said, removing his reading glasses and holding them lightly. "But we have our concerns with Argon."

"Come on, Ed," Roberts interjected. "They've been an extraordinary benefit to the CIA. Honest and effective companies like Argon aren't common. Give them more time. I don't know if you're aware, but General Verdy is a national hero."

"I know all about the good general," Womack snapped. "And I have the greatest personal and professional respect for him, but so far I'm unimpressed with his organization. At the South Carolina location, we captured five cell members. We were told to expect a dozen."

"We never said there would be a dozen," Koga pointed out.

"That really doesn't matter now, does it? Who says Nasim al-Ahmed wasn't setting you up from the start? Didn't it occur to you that maybe your source is a dangle, someone sent to provide you with misinformation?" Womack asked.

Koga said: "Of course I considered the possibility, but I deemed it highly improbable that he was sent solely to deceive because it seems clear he wants out of the organization. And he's after that reward money. My opinion is that al-Ahmed got a tip that the San Diego cell was about to be compromised, so he hightailed it out of there before you guys showed up. Check the electrical records, and I'll bet someone was using the power at the house until the very last minute."

"You're suggesting that there's a leak somewhere?" Womack asked.

"Yes, sir—but only suggesting. I have no proof, but it bears discussion."

Womack leaned forward and rested his elbows on the dark mahogany table. "Do you have a name, a suspect? Anything actionable at all?"

Verdy jumped in before Koga could answer. "We're working on that now, and we have a new lead. We strongly believe that Nasim al-Ahmed is working with a Chinese car company called Song Motors, but for what reason, we have yet to find out."

Roberts twisted in his seat and looked at Verdy. "When did this come about, general?"

"Max here found al-Aqarib operatives aboard a ship that transported a

Song Motors concept car to California."

Womack scoffed. "That means nothing. Cargo ships transport many cargoes at one time."

"True, but we also have a photograph of al-Ahmed in that same show car," Verdy said. "And just before our meeting here, our computer guy discovered that the other person in the photograph is a man named Xavier Qiu, the president of Song Motors."

This was news to Max. How Raja Singh managed to identify Qiu from a blurry image of the side of his face was nothing short of sorcery.

"And who exactly is Xavier Qiu?" Womack asked.

Roberts leaned forward in his chair. "Who indeed?"

"He keeps under the radar, and he's not exactly a law-abiding citizen," Verdy said. "What we know for sure is that he rose in the Hong Kong financial sector through ties with mainland Chinese politicians and mobsters. He's brokered arms deals and drug deals, mostly heroin from poppies grown and processed in Vietnam and Thailand."

"Now, why would a Chinese drug dealer and car mogul be sympathetic to the causes of an Islamic terror group?" Womack asked. "What does he get out of sleeping with the Aqarib?"

"That would be the billion-dollar question," Koga answered.

Roberts began rising out of his seat. "I need to run this up to my boss immediately."

Womack turned to Verdy. "I'll give you guys another chance, but keep me updated. Make sure I'm in the loop on everything. Any funny stuff from either of you..."—he wagged an index finger at Verdy and Roberts—"and I'll recommend to the President that your services be terminated immediately."

"Wait a minute, Ed," Roberts protested. "Their contract is with us, with CIA. You have no right or authority to do such a thing."

Womack's eyes narrowed. "Beside the President, I also have CIA Director Nigel McKeen's ear, who I believe is your boss. Don't forget that, Andy."

Roberts responded to the comment with a cold, hard stare of his own.

"I'll try not to," he said through gritted teeth.

"Good day to you, general," Womack said. "And you, Chief Roberts." Without addressing Max, he placed his reading glasses onto his nose. "That's all."

When the three men stepped into the hallway, Koga turned to his boss, "That was certainly enlightening. Since when have we been on the chopping block?"

"Ever since Womack got the director's job," Verdy answered.

Roberts stepped forward.

"You guys see that this son of a bitch eats his words. The whole U.S. intelligence community has become a spectacle, starting with that clown. In the meantime, I'll do what I can to back-channel and keep him off our backs."

"That will be helpful, Andy. Thanks," said Verdy.

"Perhaps this Qiu fellow can lead us to al-Ahmed," Koga pointed out.

Verdy nodded. "I'm betting on it. Which reminds me, Stockton said he received an invitation from Song Motors to some fancy dinner party in L.A. He asked if one of us wanted to attend it with him."

"I'd be very interested in going," Koga said.

"I thought as much, so I already told him you're in. He's emailing us the details. They're putting you guys up in some swanky hotel nearby."

"Make sure you keep me posted on everything," Roberts said. "I can't protect you if I don't know what you're up to. There's a lot going on here that we still don't know about, and one wrong move might cost lives."

Verdy put a hand on Roberts' shoulder. "We're aware of that, Andy. Well aware."

Chapter 17

The slight morning chill produced clouds of white vapor from Max Koga's mouth as a big Audi Q8 in gleaming white approached the curb in front of the FBI building. It dwarfed the Toyota Corollas and Honda Civics parked in metered spaces nearby. A tinted passenger-side window of the vehicle slid down, and the familiar face of Donald Rawlings smiled from the driver's seat.

"Going my way, stranger?" he asked.

Koga took a step back to examine the full-size SUV, this one tuned by Germany's aftermarket high-performance specialist ABT, the Mercedes-AMG of Audi products.

Paul Verdy had left with CIA chief Andrew Roberts, taking the company helicopter to Las Vegas where they had a meeting with the energy secretary of Bosnia. So Rawlings, who'd driven into San Diego the previous evening, offered to take Koga back to Los Angeles.

"What happened to your Camaro SS?" Koga asked, jumping into the passenger seat.

"Sold it. This was part of my Argon employment package. What do you think?"

"I like it, except for the chrome wheels. You should've left the stock ones on."

Rawlings shot him a crooked glance. "It's what makes this ride so special. People think I'm a baller or a rap star when I pull up in this thing."

Koga laughed. "Okay, sure—like who, MC Hammer? Tone Loc? When did they peak, like, the Eighties?"

Rawlings shook his head. "I'm gonna let that slide because you bought drinks last time."

Traffic on northbound Interstate 5 was reasonably light, and they reached the Orange County border in just over an hour. They discussed details of the Aqarib cell house, which Rawlings inspected after the raid and the FBI had moved out. He'd found nothing of note but dirty dishes and a refrigerator full of food.

When the Q8 entered Los Angeles County, he slowed the vehicle and exited the fast lane. "I think we got a tail," he said, his eyes darting to and from the rearview mirror.

Koga turned in his seat. "Well, that didn't take long. Motorcycle?"

"Negative. Why do you ask?"

"Never mind. How close are they?"

"Not too far. Maybe a few car lengths. It's a beige Ford Explorer. Ring a bell?"

Koga shook his head, spotting the SUV for the first time in the side mirror. "Whoever it is needs a bit more practice."

"Who all knew you were going to be at the FBI building?" Rawlings asked.

"Only a couple of people besides you."

Rawlings looked closer into his side mirror. "Whoa, there's a sweet Asian lady behind the wheel, and she's alone."

Koga squinted to get a better look. "Now I definitely want to know who it is."

"That makes two of us. Damn, I hope she's after me and not you. What do you want to do?"

"Let's find out who it is. Can you give me a small gap?" Koga asked, referring to a technique that would break visual contact from their pursuer for several seconds.

Rawlings smiled. "You got it, bro. Just like old times."

He pressed down hard on the accelerator, then steered the Audi off the freeway and into a rural neighborhood in Long Beach. The Ford also sped up, keeping pace with the Q8, following it off the exit ramp. Rawlings made two successive right-hand turns and slammed the brakes.

During the few seconds the Q8 was out of view, Koga flung his door open and jumped onto the street, hiding behind a large oak tree on the sidewalk. The Audi continued forward before pulling to the curb three blocks away, its hazard lights flashing. A moment later, the Ford Explorer drove past and parked a block behind the Q8.

The neighborhood was quiet, as most neighborhoods were on an early Sunday morning. The Explorer sat motionless on the side of the road with its engine still running. The hot red brake lights showed that the transmission was still in Drive, meaning that the driver was making sure she could flee the scene quickly at the first sign of trouble, further confirming that she was most likely alone in the vehicle.

Making sure no eyes were on him, Koga crouched low and scurried to the back of the Ford, where he squatted and leaned against the rear bumper. He lifted his head and peeked into the cabin through the rear glass. The woman sat motionless in the driver's seat with her hands on the steering wheel, her gaze forward.

Convinced it wasn't the same person as the motorcycle rider from two nights before, Koga rose to his feet and causally walked to the Explorer's driver-side door and tapped his fist on the window, causing the Asian woman to jump and clutch her chest. She looked to be in her early thirties, with long black hair parted to the side. She had a small, attractive face with large brown eyes that looked up at Max.

"Roll your window down," Koga instructed, making a circular motion with his right hand as if he were cranking on a lever.

She pressed a button on the armrest, lowering the window. "What do you want?" she asked.

"Oh, I don't know. How about we start with why you're following us?"

"I don't understand what you mean. I just pulled over to respond to a text," she said, holding up her smartphone. She was confident, unafraid.

Koga laughed. "Nice try. You're as bad at lying as you are at tailing. I have your license plate, and my buddy has the cops on speed dial, so if you don't tell me who you are and why you were following us, we're calling the police to get you sorted out." Koga offered a half grin. "But I'm guessing you don't want that."

She stared at Max, studying every detail of his face.

"You don't look much like your profile photo, do you?" she said. She shifted the Explorer into Park and reached for her purse in the passenger seat, prompting Koga to take a step back.

"Okay, what are you doing?" Koga asked, unzipping his jacket.

"Take it easy, cowboy." She slowly slid her hand into her bag and pulled out a credential wallet with a gold badge and ID card that read Special Agent Beth Hu, FBI.

Koga placed his hands on the driver's side window opening and leaned in. "For what plausible reason would the FBI be following me?"

She kept her eyes fixed on him. "Are we going to have this conversation here or do you want to get in?"

"Will you give me a lift back to my place?"

She paused, then nodded. "Sure."

"Don't go anywhere." He jogged to the parked Audi. Rawlings sat with the driver-side door partly open and his Sig Sauer pistol resting on his lap.

"Restoring an old one-night stand?" Rawlings asked with a leer.

"It's more complicated than that. I'm going to catch a ride with her."

"Thataboy, getting back in the saddle again. I knew you had some magic left in you. And from what I can see from here, she's pushing a solid eight."

"You're a sexist pig. I look forward to reporting you to HR for creating a hostile workplace."

"Okay, whatever," Rawlings said, grinning. "But watch your six, yeah? I'd like you to get paid at least once before someone takes you off the field."

Koga returned to the Explorer and threw his jacket into the rear, climbed into the passenger seat, and buckled up. He turned toward his female driver. "This is my first experience with a stalker. Be gentle."

"You're Maximilian Koga, formerly Naval Intelligence, then DEA, and now working at Argon Securities for Paul Verdy," Hu said as she punched Koga's address into the navigation system.

"And I see you won't be needing directions."

Agent Hu just smiled and pulled the vehicle away from the curb.

"Your boss, FBI Director Ed Womack, wants to keep an eye on me, is that it?" Koga asked.

"It could've been worse. We could have assigned someone else to follow you."

Koga shot her a quizzical look. "And why should I be happy it's you?"

"Because I'm on your side on this, and I happen to be good friends with General Verdy. I'm also very curious about what Song Motors is up to. We've been monitoring them for the past several weeks."

"What do you have on them?" Koga asked.

"Nothing much, really, only that a Chinese gang called the Tangs does most of the company's dirty work at home and overseas."

"Dirty work?"

"The big three—drugs, human trafficking, extortion. They're some of the main players sending fentanyl to Mexico, which then gets trafficked up here."

"Never heard of them."

"Neither did we until recently," Hu said, "but the CIA has shared a thick file on them."

Koga was silent until the Explorer pulled to a stop in front of his townhouse. His bright red RX-7 was parked in the driveway, complete with new rear glass.

"Thanks for the lift. It's been educational," Koga said, stepping out of the vehicle.

With a grin and a nod, she drove away. When the Explorer was out of sight, Koga took out his cellphone and dialed Paul Verdy, who picked up on the first ring.

"What've you got, Max?" he asked.

"Hi, boss. I just wanted to tell you I made a new friend today. It was someone from the Bureau."

Verdy grunted. "Don't tell me, Womack had someone follow you."

"He did, but this agent said she was a friend of yours. She actually mentioned you by name."

"You must be talking about Beth Hu. I can vouch for her. She helped me interrogate a Chinese informant a while back, and she was very effective. Speaks fluent Mandarin and Cantonese. Still, let me make a few calls and see if I can't get her to back off."

"Can you hold off on that, sir?"

"Why? What are you thinking?" asked Verdy.

"She mentioned a crime organization called the Tangs. Have you heard of them?"

"Can't say that I have."

"Me neither. But according to Agent Hu, the CIA seems to know about them, and they seem to be connected with Song Motors, which leads me to believe that Andrew Roberts and the CIA haven't been very upfront with us."

"I'll squeeze Langley. You work the FBI angle through Beth," Verdy said.

"You read my mind, sir."

"But let me be the first to warn you, Beth is as razor sharp as they come. Be careful you don't end up getting sliced into pieces by her."

Chapter 18

"Are you prepared to give up your life for Allah, Hector?" Nasim al-Ahmed said in Arabic to his translator.

The translator repeated the words in Spanish to the teenager kneeling with his hands clasped tightly in front of him. Dressed in a worn T-shirt and cargo shorts, Hector Espinoza was a month shy of his twentieth birthday, but his scruffy beard made him look at least five years older.

"I am prepared," Hector said without hesitation.

Forty-eight hours before, roughly four hours before the raid on the Aqarib's San Diego cell location, al-Ahmed had received word via an encrypted communications app that the American authorities had discovered his location. He immediately dispersed his men and headed to a shoe store at the U.S.-Mexico border, taking a tunnel into Tijuana. Once in Mexico, a private helicopter transported him to the summer home of Mauricio Duarte, the governor of Sinaloa, where he was instructed to stay until his new facilities in San Ignacio were ready. His second-in-command, Ramin Madani, joined him in Mazatlán earlier that day.

Al-Ahmed placed his palm on Hector's head. "When your time comes, you will be cast into the highest levels of heaven, and your family will never go hungry."

"I am honored," Hector said, after hearing the translation.

"Now, go to your room. We will call upon you when you are needed."

Hector bowed, kissed his leader's hand, and left the room.

Madani watched the proceedings quietly from a sofa against the wall.

"It's much easier to find converts in the poorer areas, isn't it?" He spoke with a soft lilt just short of a chuckle, like he was in on an inside joke.

Al-Ahmed chuckled. "Allah provides, brother."

A Sunni from Saudi Arabia, al-Ahmed treated Madani, who was an Iranian Shia, like a brother. While a Sunni and a Shia hardly made for common bedfellows, al-Ahmed believed all Islamists needed to unite and fight the evil influence of the West. At first, his revolutionary ideals were met with resistance. But as more converts joined his movement, he became a folk hero, strengthening his organization.

"Are you sure you don't want to use the people we brought in from Qatar?" Madani asked in Arabic, one of several languages that he spoke fluently. "We have four candidates trained and ready to go now."

Al-Ahmed, dressed in the same fatigues as Madani, ran his fingers through his bushy beard and adjusted the eye patch that covered his left eye. "It makes much more sense to use someone here. Locals arouse less suspicion, and they will encourage others to join our cause. We must be a unique brand of jihadi, different from our Islamic State and Taliban brothers, Ramin. We need to be more international."

"And more careful. Must I remind you they nearly captured you in San Diego?" Madani said.

"You're right, of course. That we were informed before their arrival was a blessing. Allahu Akbar."

The temporary base in Mazatlán was a stark improvement and much safer than the Aqarib's previous operation center in Waziristan, a place the Arabic news channel Al Jazeera has dubbed the most dangerous place in the world. Situated on a cliff overlooking the Pacific Ocean, the mansion in Mexico came with several perks, including servants and a swimming pool. But as luxurious as it was, al-Ahmed felt trapped.

He had no way of contacting his soldiers throughout the world, and although the hideout was tucked away in a secluded part of the city, the town center and surrounding areas were major tourist destinations, so he had little choice but to remain indoors. For the time being, he ran his operation from the mansion's four-car garage.

One of the male servants knocked on the door. "The governor has arrived. He wishes to speak to you," he said in English.

Al-Ahmed nodded. "Let's go," he said to Madani. "This should be a very interesting conversation indeed."

The two jihadists followed the servant to the living room. A large couch and a loveseat faced each other in the middle of a marble floor. Sitting on the smaller sofa was a man with a dark complexion, short brown hair, and broad shoulders. His shiny Armani suit gleamed in the sunlight coming in from the window.

"Please, my dear guests, sit down," Mauricio Duarte, the governor of Sinaloa, said in perfect English. "I hope my humble home is to your liking."

Taking a seat across from Duarte, al-Ahmed said, "We appreciate your generosity, Señor Gobernador. Thank you for flying us out of Tijuana."

"It's my pleasure, and please call me Moe. And don't thank me, it was Señor Qiu who made all the arrangements, as we all have a shared interest in your new business venture here. Thanks to your men, you've empowered the Eldorado Cartel and taken out the small timers. Because of that, the murder rate in my state has dropped by half, and my poll numbers have risen astronomically."

"I'm glad that we've been of service," al-Ahmed said with a bow. "It helps when the law enforcement agencies are on our side for a change."

"It's the least I can do, and as a result, local police deaths have dropped drastically, too, thanks to the protection you have provided them. If there's anything you need, just tell one of my people, and I shall see that you get it."

Al-Ahmed rubbed his shaved head. "There is one thing. Is there nowhere else we can stay? As beautiful as your retreat is, being in the middle of a resort town is not what I call ideal for an organization such as ours."

"I understand your concerns, but it's the hurricane season, so there are very few tourists now, and the Americans would never imagine looking for you here. As long as you stay inside, you are safe," Duarte assured him.

"We dislike being trapped like dogs, Señor Gobernador."

Duarte leaned back on the sofa. "You can't underestimate the Americans. They've been a thorn in my side for years. They were just about to label the cartels here as 'terrorists,' which would have given them a free pass to violate Mexican sovereignty with their guns blazing, so to speak. But, thanks to you, peace is restored and they have no reason now to invade. Little do they know real terrorists have taken their place."

"That is an offensive term. And if the Americans did come, they would have exposed you for the hypocrite that you are and hauled you away in chains," Madani said with a laugh.

"I take offense at his tone," Duarte said to al-Ahmed.

"What he speaks is true, is it not?" al-Ahmed responded. "You're only in it for the power and money. Everyone knows that you've been on both El Chapo's and the Eldorado Cartel's payroll for years. How else can you afford to live in such luxury? I also know that Mr. Qiu paid you handsomely to help arrange our takeover of the Eldorado Cartel. So, my dear Señor Gobernador—er, Moe—I suggest you continue to play the role of the obedient dog and allow us to keep doing God's work, or you may not have the opportunity to spend all your newfound money."

Chapter 19

Two hundred kilograms of a custom-blended military-grade explosive, covered in a blue vinyl tarp and delicately placed into the bed of a late-model Toyota HiLux pickup, was enough to take out a small neighborhood block. Nasim al-Ahmed had originally asked his benefactor for a nuclear weapon—a request denied—but he was provided with one of the next best things: Heptanitrocubane, or HNC, a chemical that possessed approximately thirty times the power of HMX, an explosive used almost exclusively by the military.

Compared to C-4 and Semtex, the longtime favorites of terrorists, HNC was much more powerful, and its expensive nature made it the current Bentley of explosives.

Nasim al-Ahmed and Ramin Madani watched quietly as their chief bomb maker, Ifran, installed a cellphone detonator under the vinyl cover to the metallic casing of the bomb.

"Although I don't fully trust our friend Mr. Qiu yet, his support has been quite generous," al-Ahmed commented.

The truck sat in the middle of Mauricio Duarte's three-car garage. On usual days, the garage housed a couple of Porsche 911s and a Lexus LFA, but when the Aqarib leader told the governor that he would use the space to build and store weapons, Duarte immediately instructed his servants to move the cars to a nearby auto shop.

With polished cement floors and pristine white walls, Duarte's garage was larger than many of the surrounding homes in the city. But the place disgusted al-Ahmed, for it served as a constant reminder of why he hated the West and corrupt politicians. He made a vow to kill Duarte or, at the very least, take away all that he held dear.

Ifran wiped his forehead with a towel and approached al-Ahmed. "It's ready to go. I can detonate the device by calling the cellphone we attached to it or by flipping a timing switch installed under the dashboard."

Al-Ahmed put his hands on the older man's shoulder. "Ancient school. I love it, Ifran. I'm looking forward to seeing firsthand this gift from Mr. Qiu in action."

"But I must again caution that we don't know if it'll work as desired," Ifran warned. "This is a highly complicated weapon, and unless we synthesized the HCN just right ..."

"Yes, yes—that's why we're treating today's mission as a trial run," al-Ahmed soothed. It wouldn't do to have a nervous bomb maker.

"I still think we would have been better off with something biological, or aggressively viral."

Al-Ahmed shook his head. "You remember the last time the Chinese and Americans tried to weaponize a virus, don't you? It caused a worldwide pandemic. They're too unpredictable, my friend."

"Yes, Covid took a great number of our brothers. Still, Duarte will not be pleased with our strike tonight," Madani noted.

"I know you have no concern for the governor's wishes, and nor do I." He nodded toward the door. "Bring our martyr-to-be."

Madani left the room and soon returned with Hector Espinoza.

Al-Ahmed laid both hands on the boy's shoulders. "The time has come, Hector. It's time for you to go to Allah and collect His rewards, and we on this earth shall glorify you until the end of days," he said to the young Mexican.

Hector bowed.

"And you'll take care of my family? My mother and my sisters?"

"Rest assured, brother. I give you my word that they'll never go wanting. And angels and beautiful virgins who will do whatever you desire will surround you."

"Then I am ready. Allahu Akbar! What do you want me to do?" he asked.

Al-Ahmed opened the driver's door of the Toyota HiLux. "Simple. Drive this vehicle to a toy manufacturing factory in Durango. We'll give you direction and will follow you. Once you crash through the gates and enter the facility, flip this switch."

The color drained from Hector's face.

Al-Ahmed's eyes narrowed. "Paradise awaits."

"I ... I understand," he stammered, looking at the faces of the strangers around him.

Madani asked quietly in Arabic, "It's a long drive from here to Durango. Maybe three hours. What if he reconsiders?"

"That's why you and our trusty translator are going to ride with him. Continue to provide encouragement. I'm putting my trust in you, Ramin," al-Ahmed replied.

"As you wish, *sayyid*," Madani responded, using the Arab honorific for master. He then turned to the boy. "Shall we depart, Hector?"

Hector nodded and climbed into the truck, followed by Ramin and the translator.

The garage door opened, revealing two old Mitsubishi Monteros in the driveway outside. Al-Ahmed and Ifran walked to one of the SUVs and jumped in. The other was a security trail vehicle. Then, all three four-by-fours drove off the property, with the HiLux sandwiched in the middle.

Precisely three hours into their journey, the Toyota pickup pulled over to the side of the road, where Madani and the translator stepped out and jumped into one of the Monteros, leaving Hector alone in the pickup.

"How is our friend?" al-Ahmed asked when Madani joined him in the rear seat.

"He's scared, but he won't fail us. *Inshallah*."

If Allah wills it.

"Good."

The HiLux continued straight on the road to the outskirts of Jalisco, a historical city known as the birthplace of tequila. Two rings of twelve-foot-tall chain-link fences enclosed the toy factory—which doubled as the Navarro Cartel's drug-processing facility. A dozen armed guards with pit bulls patrolled its perimeter.

About a quarter mile away, the two Mitsubishis parked behind trees atop a dirt hill that looked down upon the factory. Al-Ahmed, Madani, and Ifran stepped out of the vehicle and walked to the edge of the hill, where Ifran surveyed the factory grounds with binoculars.

"The Toyota should arrive at the front gates in about three minutes," he noted, holding a cellphone with his thumb on the call button.

Two and a half minutes later, a lone truck barreled down the two-lane road that led to the front gates of the factory. Al-Ahmed watched in silence as the HiLux burst through the outer entrance fence in a hail of defensive security gunfire, blasting the gates off at their hinges and dragging one barricade under the front bumper.

A streak of orange sparks followed in its wake. Four guards fired with their automatic rifles from the inner entrance gate, but most of the bullets seemed to catch the grille, with a few taking out the headlights. Several more guards came running out of the main building, unleashing their rounds into the side of the HiLux. The bullets ripped through the side of the truck, blowing out its left rear tire. The damaged truck skewed left into the concrete wall of the factory building, grinding off the mirror and door handle on the driver's side before screeching to a halt.

"Now," al-Ahmed said.

Ifran pushed the call button on his cellphone just as Hector reached to his head with both hands.

A moment later, a mammoth orange fireball engulfed and consumed the main warehouse, blowing security men and their vehicles high into the air. The bright flash of orange temporarily blinded al-Ahmed, who closed his eyes and turned his face away.

An intensely fierce shockwave of the explosion nearly knocked him over a few seconds later, followed by the enormous concussive blast. The sound of the explosion would cause his ears to ring for the next two days.

A plume of gray-white smoke rose into the black of the night, lit from below by raging fires fueled in part by the components of drug production. This test was a wildly successful one, causing al-Ahmed to smile.

"You're next, America," he whispered to himself. "You are next."

STAGE TWO
Song Motors

Chapter 20

With its shiny marble floor, wood-paneled walls, and ornate furnishings, the spacious lobby of the Sheraton Grand Los Angeles exuded a tasteful blend of art déco with a splash of old-world charm. Koga studied every person near the entrance as he checked in with the receptionist, a Latino man with Hollywood good looks, who handed him a card key to a room on the tenth floor.

"I have a fear of heights. Can you give me something on a lower level?" Koga asked. Never take the first room assigned.

"Let me check," the receptionist said, punching his keyboard. "Ah, yes. I have a double room on the sixth floor. Will that do?"

Koga nodded. A few more keystrokes later, he took his new card key and headed toward the elevator. Once in his room, he promptly swept it for listening devices, looking inside the lamps and inspecting vents and smoke detectors. The room was clean. He laid his suitcase on his bed and, with most of the day to kill before the Song Motors dinner, headed back outside for a brief walk and some fresh air.

Koga ducked into Bottega Louie, a restaurant down the block from the hotel, and he treated himself to a long lunch followed by a shot of espresso. While waiting for his food to arrive, he perused a brief profile on FBI Special Agent Beth Hu that Denise Johnson had prepared for him at his request.

Elizabeth Hu, second-generation Chinese, was the only child of Dr. Qiang Hu and Natalie Hu. Dr. Qiang Hu was a prominent radar scientist who taught at MIT while working part-time for Raytheon. Elizabeth had a typical Chinese-American upbringing, taking piano lessons as a child and studying tirelessly under the watchful eye of her tiger mom. She graduated salutatorian in East Asia Studies from Princeton. Her life took a turn in her final year at Yale Law School when her father inexplicably disappeared.

The impending police investigation turned up nothing, prompting Elizabeth to leave school and join the FBI, vowing to locate her father. That was seven years ago. She has come no closer to finding him.

As Koga casually sipped the thick coffee, he looked up from his phone, when his eyes stopped on a man wearing a black golf cap, a light blue shirt, and dark brown slacks seated on the patio of a café across the street. He'd seen this getup an hour earlier in the hotel lobby. It belonged to a husky Asian man with a scar on his lip, who sat on the sofa while fiddling with his cellphone. That same man was now dining alone across the street.

Coincidence?

After paying his bill, Koga left the restaurant and strolled past the café to get a better look at the man in the black golf hat. Nothing about him seemed suspicious. He appeared to be a tourist enjoying a slice of apple pie and a cup of hot tea, but something seemed off.

Koga moved past him, continuing straight on Grand Avenue. To be safe, he scanned the reflections in the windows of the surrounding buildings as he walked to see if he had a tail. After three blocks, his eyes caught sight of the man in the black golf hat walking alone on the other side of the street.

Well, that pretty much settles it.

Without looking the man's way, Koga quickened his pace and took a right turn at the next intersection, placing himself out of the view of his pursuer. He then ran in a full sprint toward a narrow brick office complex at the far end of the block. Without slowing his pace, Koga entered through the building's open double doors and climbed the stairs to the third floor.

He headed to the nearest room, marked "Malena's Art Gallery," where he stepped into a compact showroom and positioned himself next to a large window that overlooked Olympic Boulevard. Not a minute later, a tall forty-something Latina woman with brown hair approached.

"Hello—may I help you?" she asked with a warm smile. Her mild Hispanic accent sounded South American and floated on the air like music. "I am Malena Casal. I own this gallery."

Koga shook his head. "Nice to meet you. I'm just looking."

She turned less hospitable. "We only take appointments. Do you have an appointment today?"

"Uhm, no, but my uncle has asked me to pick out some paintings for his new penthouse apartment in Beverly Hills. Would it be all right if I look around a little?"

When hearing the words "Beverly Hills," the woman's demeanor instantly changed. *Money.*

"Of course, dear, take your time. This month we're featuring the latest collection from an exciting new Venezuelan artist named Sasha," she said as she strode forward and shook Koga's hand firmly. "Let me know if something catches your eye."

"My name's Mack," he replied. "I'll come get you when I see something I like," Koga said.

Casal walked back into her office, six-inch heels clicking on the polished floor, and Koga returned his gaze to the window. As if on cue, the bulky Asian man in the black hat appeared, meandering down the sidewalk. Two other men joined him, both Asians, but younger. Koga took out his cellphone, opened the camera app and zoomed in on their faces, snapping away as the three men exchanged words before going off in different directions.

Koga sent the photos to Raja Singh and waited to see whether the Asian men had returned. Ten minutes elapsed with no sight of them. He gave them another five minutes, then called for an Uber. Sneaking past Casal's office and out the back of the gallery without getting trapped by her unctuous smile and broken expectations, Koga met the ride on the next block and jumped into the rear seat of a late-model Honda Accord.

The driver greeted him but got the hint when Koga didn't reply. Instead, Koga studied the photos of the three Asian men on his phone. The car pulled away from the curb and pointed toward the Sheraton Grand.

It wasn't a shock that none of the Asian males in his photos looked familiar. But someone inside Argon or the U.S. government was leaking information. No one outside of his small circle of associates knew he would be at the Sheraton Grand that day.

It was vital that he expose the spy among spies soon, or he was as good as dead.

Chapter 21

Hey, Max—I mean, Mack—over here," Stockton Clay called out from the center of the Sheraton Grand Los Angeles lobby.

Koga stepped out of the elevator dressed in a charcoal-gray suit with a nearly invisible chalk stripe, white shirt, and no tie. "Did I keep you waiting?" he asked.

"Nope. Right on time. You ready for this?"

Koga gave him a thumbs-up sign. "I've been looking forward to this all day."

They exited the hotel through the main revolving doors and headed to the U.S. Bank Tower, the venue for the Song Motors dinner.

On Fifth Street, the U.S. Bank Tower was among the tallest buildings in downtown Los Angeles. Taking up the seventieth floor of the cylindrical edifice was Skyspace L.A., the location of the state's tallest observation deck. A popular tourist spot, complete with a glass slide and a virtual-reality center, the entire facility was rented out to big corporations a few times a year for their special events. During the ten-minute walk from the Sheraton to the VIP dinner venue, Stockton gave Koga a rundown on the automotive journalists expected to attend, noting those who were friendly and those who were to be avoided.

"Usually, the older they are, the snobbier, and thus horrible dinner companions to boot, so try not to get trapped by anyone who looks north of sixty," he suggested. "And those in their thirties think they know it all when they don't know jack, so avoid them too."

"Aren't you in your thirties?" Koga asked.

He grinned the boyish grin that was his trademark.

"When I make rules, I never mean they apply to me."

They were met at the entrance of the building by a young Caucasian man in a tuxedo, who ushered them through an adjacent entrance to a waiting elevator. He leaned in and, without stepping inside, pushed the button to the seventieth floor.

"Enjoy your evening," he said as the elevator doors closed.

The elevator shot up so fast that Koga felt like he was briefly twice his weight. When it slowed to a stop and the doors opened, he and Stockton stepped into an expansive circular room with windows providing a panoramic view of the city. An older woman with perfect silver hair in a casual but expensive Nic+Zoe sweater sat behind a mahogany desk at the entrance. She was reading her laptop and absently playing with an impressive string of pearls when she looked up.

"Welcome to the Song Motors dinner. May I see your invitations?"

Stockton handed her two envelopes. After looking them over through her reading glasses, she picked out a couple of name tags.

"Mister Clay and ... Mister Katana. Welcome. Enjoy your evenings."

Stockton collected the tags, handed Max's to him, and they walked onto the observation deck, where a young Asian woman in a cocktail dress handed each one a glass of champagne.

The view of metro Los Angeles was breathtaking. Not only could one look directly down at what was formerly known as the Staples Center, the home of the Lakers and Kings sports teams, but the Santa Monica Pier was visible more than fifteen miles away. Even Catalina Island, about fifty miles due west, was easily seen on this cloudless day.

The entire floor was bustling with people. The journalists and influencers were clumped together in groups of three to five, mostly men but a fair sprinkling of women, huddled in light conversation about cars, who was dating whom, and who was jumping from one magazine job for another. Koga's eyes locked onto a gang of six gathered near the glass slide, where a distinguished, salt-and-peppered-haired Asian man dressed in a white tuxedo held court.

Koga recognized Xavier Qiu from magazines and the photos Raja Singh had provided. The Chinese businessman stood just shy of six feet and looked to be in his early forties, with a chiseled, handsome face that wouldn't have been out of place in a Hong Kong action flick. Next to him was a tall, striking Caucasian woman, dressed in a form-fitting one-piece that showed off her lithe, athletic build. Her auburn hair fell to the small of her back, and she graced her admirers with a dazzling smile that might actually have twinkled.

"Stockton, go on ahead. I'll catch up to you later," Koga said, heading toward Qiu.

He took up a position at the back of the pack where Qiu waxed on in flawless English about the company's future product, called the MachStar, saying how it was going to revolutionize the supercar genre.

Time for some fireworks.

Koga edged his way between two gray-haired gentlemen from *Businessweek*. "Mack Katana, *Automobile Digest*," he said, holding a business card out with two hands. "We're big admirers of your company and your new car."

"Please, call me Xavier," Qiu said, taking Koga's business card and briefly glancing at it before handing it to the tall woman, who tucked it into a small black clutch hanging from her shoulder on a gold chain.

Koga reached out to shake Qiu's hand, but he raised his hand flat and leaned slightly back. "Thank you for your courtesy, Mr. Katana, but forgive me. I do not shake hands."

"Oh, that's fine. I understand. I apologize." He turned to the tall redhead, offering another business card. "It's nice to meet you, too, um ... Mrs. Qiu?"

The woman laughed. "Thank you, Max—" He frankly liked that she used an informal greeting. "—but no. I'm Cynthia Blackwood, executive assistant to the president."

The surrounding journalists flashed disapproving looks at each other. None of them had gotten Cynthia Blackwood to smile, let alone laugh like that. One stepped forward. "I don't know who you are, but we were in the middle of a conversation," he said.

Ignoring him, Koga spoke to Qiu. "So, Xavier, I wanted to ask where you got the money to start such a big company from scratch. Can you shed some light on this?"

"We have a diverse group of generous investors," Qiu answered, nodding and smiling.

"And they are?" Koga pressed.

Qiu's smile slipped a little as he tried to steer the conversation. "They prefer to support us behind the scenes, to let our company and our innovative motor vehicle have the spotlight." Qiu turned his head slightly and squinted. "Who are you with again?"

"*Automobile Digest*, the largest automotive media group on the planet."

"Well, Mr. Mack Katana of *Automobile Digest* ... an interesting name, by the way ... our laws in China do not require us to reveal our financial sources, so I'm afraid I have no additional comment regarding that matter."

"I see, but there have been rumors—and please forgive me for being so candid—that Song Motors has financial ties with the Chinese mafia." He paused for dramatic effect. "Possibly others. Would you care to comment?"

The journalist group around Koga and Qiu backed away in slow motion.

"I suggest you re-check your sources because what you are saying is ridiculous and untrue, certainly salacious, and likely libelous if printed. However, this is a celebration and not an inquisition, is it not?" He smiled and raised a hand to acknowledge the silent senior writers, who had stopped breathing. "Dinner is about to begin," he said, gently pulling Blackwood away by the arm. "Shall we go in?"

Koga watched the couple walk toward the dining area trailed by the gray-suited, gray-haired business journalists. He felt a tap on his shoulder.

"You have to work on this shyness problem," Stockton said. He made a disapproving face. "Now Xavier Qiu hates our guts, and we've lost any chance at an exclusive on the stupid car."

"I thought he already hated your guts. Hasn't he threatened one of your journalists once already?"

"Okay, good point. I guess no harm done then."

"Well, I need a drink. Can I get you something from the bar?"

Stockton shook his head. "I'm fine. I'll save you a seat next to me inside. Table One." In classic fashion, Qiu and his executives and most-favored guests would sit at Table One. That meant Koga and Stockton were going to be close enough to mend bridges with Qiu.

Or burn them down.

The Garden Bar specialized in beer and wine, but for the Song Motors event, it had been converted into a full premium bar with a broad selection of exclusive whisky and Scotch brands, including seventeen-year-old bottles of Hibiki Japanese whisky and twenty-year-old Balvenie single malt Scotch. Behind the counter was a young bartender, no doubt another aspiring actor, wearing a black bowtie.

"Yes, sir, what can I get you?" he asked when Koga approached

"Warbringer, neat," Koga said.

The bartender filled a large glass with three fingers of the American whiskey and placed it in front of Max, just as a man walked up next to him and leaned an elbow on the bar counter. The man looked straight ahead, not even trying to acknowledge Koga's presence.

Not the friendly type, Koga thought, giving the man a once-over. Then he saw it. On the back of the young man's wrist was a tattoo. It was mostly hidden under the cuff of his sleeve, but there was no mistaking the small pincers and stinger of a scorpion, the insignia of *Al-Aqarib min Allah*.

Chapter 22

The scorpion was small and integrated into a larger design, making it hardly noticeable by a passing observer, but to Max Koga, it might as well have been highlighted in fluorescent colors.

"Perrier," the tattooed man said to the bartender. He was about Max's age and height but looked at least twenty pounds heavier, all of it muscle. His complexion was dark, and he wore a thin beard in the Islamic style.

The bartender opened a small refrigerator on the floor and found it empty. "Sorry, I need to get some from the stockroom. I'll be right back," he said, ducking into a back room.

"Do you know why sometimes whisky is spelled with no 'e'?" Koga asked out of the blue.

The man responded with a roll of the eyes and an apathetic shoulder shrug, conveying that he didn't care in the slightest.

Koga continued. "Both are technically correct, but whiskey-with-an-e refers to grain spirits distilled in Ireland and the United States. Whisky-without-an-e refers to Scottish, Canadian, or Japanese spirits."

The man with the scorpion tattoo kept his gaze the other way until Koga pointed to his exposed wrist.

"Where'd you get that tattoo there, bro? I'd like to get one like that," Koga said with fake enthusiasm.

"Nowhere," the man said, pulling his sleeve down.

"I'm Mack," Koga said, offering a fist bump.

The man hesitated, frowned, and tapped it lightly. "Nice to meet you."

"And you are?"

The man frowned and looked for the missing bartender.

"Ali," he said without looking Koga's way.

"Who do you write for? I'm with *Automobile Digest*."

Ali let out an exasperated sigh. "You Americans are so incredibly talkative. What does it matter?"

"Hey, it was just a question. No offense, brah."

"I'm a blogger from Jordan."

"I didn't know Jordan had much of a car culture," Koga noted.

Ali glanced impatiently at his watch and breathed a sigh of relief when the bartender returned. Without saying a word, Ali tossed him a ten-dollar bill, took his drink, and headed to his table.

"See you around campus," Koga called out, but Ali didn't respond.

As most of the guests were already seated, Koga searched for his table, which he found in the center near the front. Before taking his seat, Stockton Clay introduced him to a sixty-something man with a tanned face and a head full of wavy, dirty-blond hair.

"Mack, this is Mark Tyler, editor-in-chief at *Car News Weekly*. He's a good friend of mine. If you need an introduction to anyone here, he can provide it," Stockton said. "He's sitting next to you."

Koga shook Tyler's hand and stole a glance at the far side of the room where Ali sat. Then, Stockton, Mark, and Koga took their seats in front of place cards with their names on them, directly across from Xavier Qiu, who had yet to appear.

Several minutes later, Qiu stepped onto a small stage at the front of the room and recited a lengthy welcoming toast, while waiters circulated with a first course of truffle salad with walnuts and olive oil. Stockton and the others picked up their forks and dug in. Two Japanese journalists from a digital magazine called *Gran Torino*, who were also at the table, commented on how wonderfully balanced the ingredients were. But Koga just sipped his Warbringer and kept his gaze on Ali, who suddenly stood from his chair and walked out of the dining room.

"Any fun cars you've driven lately?" Tyler asked Max.

"I'm sorry. Will you excuse me for a second?" Koga said, getting up from his seat.

Tyler laughed. "Was it something I said?"

Ali was headed toward the restrooms, which were located outside the dining area in a semi-secluded part of the floor.

Koga followed Ali into the men's room. Ali had walked up to one of the urinals and Koga strolled past him, pushing lightly on each of the three stall doors to check if any were occupied. All clear. He took up the urinal immediately next to Ali and pretended to unzip his fly.

"Hey, man. Nice to see you again," Koga greeted.

Ali ignored him.

Undeterred, Koga said, "By the way, do you know of any decent topless bars in the area?"

Ali shook his head in disgust and mumbled something rude in Arabic.

Koga stepped back and reached into his jacket pocket and palmed an injector containing the knockout drug. "Oh, that's right. You Aqarib scumbags prefer sex with goats and children."

Ali's eyes opened wide. The shock on his face told Koga all he needed to know. In one fluid motion, Koga pulled out the injector and popped the cover off with his thumb. He went straight for the back of Ali's neck, but the big Arab's reflexes were quicker than Koga expected. Ali ducked the attack and threw a short right hook that landed squarely on Koga's chest, knocking him backward on the slick ceramic tile.

Chapter 23

Ali was the bigger of the two, but that didn't deter Koga. Keeping a tight grip on the injector, Koga led with a low kick that Ali blocked with his leg. The so-called Jordanian countered with a straight left to the face that Koga dodged by leaning back. Unfortunately, Max failed to notice a small puddle of water on the floor behind him, causing his heel to slip and sending him stumbling backward.

Ali didn't let the opportunity pass as he wrapped his arms around Koga's thighs and drove forward with his shoulders, sending both men onto the cold tile floor with Ali on top. Ali quickly unleashed a barrage of punches to Koga's head.

Koga raised his arms to block the blows, which kept the heaviest punches from doing much damage, but Ali's fists were eventually going to break through his guard. The man was as powerful as a bull. Koga rotated his torso, keeping his head covered the entire time.

Ali wrapped his legs around Koga's hips and immediately went for the neck with his arms, looking to put Koga in a sleeper hold. Before Ali could lock it into place, Koga slipped his left hand between his throat and Ali's forearm, which eased some of the pressure. But Ali simply squeezed tighter.

With the syringe still in his other hand, Koga desperately tried to stab the point of it into Ali's leg, but he couldn't generate enough thrust to prick the skin with the needle.

Koga was completely helpless, and in a few seconds, he would pass out. As the black veil of unconsciousness crept in, Ali's grip loosened. Koga thought he was imagining it at first, but a moment later, Ali's weight had completely lifted off his back.

Struggling to turn over to see what was happening, Koga saw Ali on his back, holding his hands near his neck with his legs flailing in the air. Someone was under him and had put Ali in the same hold that he'd had Koga in. As he rose to his feet, Koga saw Stockton Clay holding Ali's torso between his legs from behind, with his arms wrapped around the Arab's neck.

"Holy cow, this guy is strong," Stockton mumbled. "Little help, please."

Koga picked up the syringe. "Hold him tight," he said as he buried the needle into Ali's chest.

A moment later, Ali's eyes rolled back and his arms dropped lifelessly to the floor.

Stockton let out a long sigh, pushing Ali's limp body off of him. "That's some potent stuff you got there. What is it?"

"It's a prototype knockout drug. Thanks for tapping in. I thought I was a goner," Koga said, shoving the empty injector into his pocket.

"I suspected something was up, the way you abruptly left our table, so I checked up on you. Glad I did. So, now what?"

Koga knelt next to the unconscious Ali. "Can you make sure that no one comes this way for the next few minutes? I need to get him out of the building."

Stockton nodded. "Consider it done."

"By the way, where'd you learn that choke hold, brah?" Koga asked.

"I have a black belt in judo," Stockton said.

"Good to know," Koga said.

Stockton left for the dinner. Koga tossed one of Ali's arms over his shoulder and wrapped an arm around the big man's waist. With nearly all of Ali's weight on his right hip, Koga slowly dragged him out of the bathroom. The coast was clear. There was no one between him and the elevator. But Ali's heavy build made the short journey harder than expected. Just as he reached the elevator door, a voice stopped him in his tracks.

"Are you guys okay?"

It was one of the Japanese journalists at his table. His nametag read Taku.

Max put on a fake smile and laughed. "My friend here had a few too many, so I'm taking him back to his room."

"You need any help?" he asked in good English.

Koga shook his head. "Ah, no thanks, I can manage. He does this all the time. Could you push the down button for me, though?"

Taku hurried to the elevator and pushed the button. The elevator bell rang immediately. "I won't tell anyone I saw you leaving," he said with a wink.

"*Domo arigato*," Koga said with a curt bow, wondering what exactly Taku thought was happening. He stepped into the open elevator and gave his new Japanese friend a nod as the doors shut between them.

Chapter 24

Abdul Hassan thought that if he was indeed being held captive at a CIA black site, it wasn't nearly as bad as what he had expected. He'd spent many nights in far worse places that weren't even considered confinement.

There were no windows in his small room, nor was there any privacy. A trio of cameras mounted near the ceiling surveilled the main space with a fourth in the bathroom, and he was sure they were monitoring his every move. Hassan didn't mind. He had nothing to hide and relished his temporary quarters, comprised of a steel-framed bed, shower, sink, a functioning toilet, and regular, fairly well-prepared meals.

A large speaker mounted on the far wall was a cause for concern though—no doubt, it was there to keep captives awake. But he gave his hosts no reason for it to be used. He did everything he was told, without lodging a single complaint.

Despite his religious convictions, he had always admired America—the pretty girls, the lifestyle, and especially the sporting culture. He'd become a devout fan of the New York Yankees and Boston Celtics. For several years, he had waited patiently for his cousin, Nasim al-Ahmed, to send him to the land of infidels so he could disappear and leave the accursed world of radical Islam forever.

During Koga's captivity in Mexico, Hassan snuck into the American agent's makeshift cell several times to ask him the best way to defect. Although their conversations were short and occurred while Koga was partially sedated, Hassan had gathered enough information to formulate a plan.

A month later, al-Ahmed finally asked him to travel to America to prepare the Los Angeles and San Diego cells for his visit. Soon after moving into a rented house overlooking De Portola Park in Country Hills, Hassan put his plan into action. It took patience, but after nearly two weeks of staking out the DEA building in downtown Los Angeles, he finally spotted Koga's red Mazda RX-7 traveling on First Street near Little Tokyo. He followed the car and patiently waited for the opportunity to deliver his special packet with his offer.

All went exactly as he had planned ... until the incompetent Americans botched the attempt on his cousin's life, instantly transforming his American dream into a tragic nightmare.

Hassan sat on his bunk, wondering if he was being punished by Allah, when the door swung open. The man in charge of the safehouse walked in.

"We're going to another room," Brian Panackia said.

"Where are you taking me?" Hassan asked.

"They asked me to transfer you to another room. No more questions," the husky man snapped, handcuffing Hassan's hands behind his back.

Hassan didn't resist his captor pulling him by the elbow and leading him down a hallway. "You're not going to give me up to Nasim, are you?"

"My orders were to take you to another room. That's it. Now shut your trap."

They crossed the outdoor atrium and entered another building, where Panackia led him to a small door, opening it with a card key and pushing his prisoner inside. Max Koga sat inside with his legs crossed.

"Thank you, Brian. I'll call you again when we're done here," Koga said.

"You know where to find me," Panackia said. He turned and walked away.

Koga looked at Hassan without expression. "Congratulations, Abdul. You get another shot at helping me out."

The room had the look and smell of a cheap motel room. The walls were brown, and the torn carpet appeared stained from cigarette burns. It was not a room for VIP guests, that much was obvious. A video camera sat on a tripod facing a double bed, where a man laid on his back with his eyes closed. Hassan recognized Yousef Badawi immediately, a trusted Al-Aqarib lieutenant and one of Nasim's trusted bodyguards. Originally from Saudi Arabia, Badawi joined the organization as a disgruntled teenager after his parents disowned him. He then found new meaning to life, or at least he thought he did, in the gospels of Nasim al-Ahmed.

"Do you know him?" asked Max.

"He is Yousef Badawi," Hassan answered. "He is one of Al-Aqarib's advisers and a bodyguard."

Koga chuckled. "And he told me his name was Ali. Anyway, we shot him up with a strong sedative, so he's going to be groggy. I want him convinced that you saved him. Make him tell you why he was at the Song Motors dinner tonight."

Hassan nodded, and for the first time, noticed that there was another person in the room: a dark-skinned man with close-cropped hair and an athletic physique who stood with arms crossed. Hassan shifted his gaze from Badawi to Koga and then to the dark-skinned person.

"That is my associate," Koga said. "He speaks and understands Arabic and Farsi, so don't try any funny stuff. Am I clear?" Hassan nodded.

Koga slid his plastic chair beside the bed, pulled out a syringe from a small bag, and stuck the needle into Badawi's forearm. Once the clear liquid contents were emptied, Koga stood and gestured for Hassan to take his seat.

"He'll be coming around in a few seconds," Koga said. "My associate and I will be in the next room watching every move you make and listening to every word. Make him divulge as much information as possible, and if you prove successful, we'll put some of that reward money back on the table."

Praise Allah. You have not forsaken me after all.

Koga held out a wireless device, which Hassan took and wedged into his left ear.

"I will do my best," Hassan said with a smile.

Chapter 25

Yousef Badawi's eyes cracked open, but his eyelids only made it halfway up. The black pupils within brown irises were dilated, struggling to focus on the familiar face in front of him.

"Yousef, it's me," Hassan said in Arabic, his face inches from Badawi's.

Badawi blinked hard a couple of times and, on the third try, gave up, keeping his eyes shut. "Where am I?" he mumbled. "Is it really you, Abdul? Our leader told us you had been captured."

Hassan paused. "No, I've been in hiding because the Americans started following me. Be assured that I'm still part of our holy cause. I spotted you being carried away, so I had my men jump the American agents and shoot them. We brought you here, to a safe location. There's no worry now, brother."

Badawi smiled and raised his hand. "Praise Allah that you found me. The Americans will pay soon enough."

Hassan took Badawi's hand and held it to his chest.

"What are you doing here, Yousef? Why are you in America?"

Badawi grimaced but didn't answer.

"What are you doing here?" Hassan pressed. "I wasn't informed you were in Los Angeles."

Badawi spit out short breaths as droplets of sweat formed on his forehead. Hassan could see his former colleague trying to fight off the effects of the drug Max Koga had injected.

Badawi mumbled, "They sent here me to keep an eye on the Chinese car people. Our leader doesn't fully trust them, so he arranged for Arash, Karim, and me to be with them until the moment of truth."

Hassan heard Koga's voice through the earpiece.

"Find out more about this."

Hassan nodded to the video camera and then looked down at his former colleague. "What is the moment of truth? What's happening, Yousef?"

Badawi's body twisted in the bed. "I need some water. Please, water."

"I'll get you water, but first, tell me. What is this moment of truth?"

"A colossal explosion. There will be many casualties."

Through his earpiece, Hassan heard Koga say, "*Damn* ..."

"I had assumed that it was aborted," Hassan said.

"No, it's still on. He brought in the Waziristan men to carry it out."

"I see. This attack will be in Los Angeles?"

"Yes. It'll cripple the world economy and strike fear in the West, and it will come very soon. I cannot say anymore," Badawi said.

"Thank you, Yousef. I'm sure it will be spectacular, *inshallah*. Let me get you that water now." Hassan rose from his chair, walked to the door, and knocked softly twice. Koga answered and led him into an adjacent room, one that was encased in soundproofing material. The black man sat at a table wearing headphones.

Hassan noticed the entire conversation with Badawi was already translated into English on a laptop computer. The words "LA" and "bomb" appeared many times on a yellow notepad.

Koga handed a plastic water bottle to Hassan.

"See if he knows anything about Song Motors and a man named Xavier Qiu. I want to know the real motive behind the creation of this car company. And then, we'll circle back to the attack."

"Promise you'll hold up your end of the bargain. I'm as good as dead if I don't have protection," Hassan said.

"You'll be safe. Don't worry."

"I'll get my money too, yes?"

Koga rested his arm on Hassan's shoulder. "If we end up saving American lives, I'll cut you a check myself. Now go."

Hassan returned to the holding room and cradled his former colleague's head with one arm, carefully pouring the mineral water into his open mouth. Badawi coughed, creating a small puddle on the bedsheets.

"How is this car company connected with us? I was told by Nasim that I should get to know them better, too," Hassan said.

Badawi tried to open his eyes again, but couldn't. "Our main ... benefactor ... is the owner of the car company, the man who helps us financially."

"Mr. Xavier Qiu, yes," Hassan said. "I was told this recently."

"No, Qiu is only a puppet. Only our leader has ever met the true owner of the company, but I ... I think he is a high-ranking Chinese military officer."

"Do you know where Nasim is now? I must warn him about the Americans, that they are investigating this Chinese car company."

"I don't know. We were told to stay in Los Angeles and monitor Qiu until our attack."

After a few light coughs, Badawi's head fell to the side and he slipped back into dreamland. Hassan slapped Badawi's face twice, but the man was out.

"He's sleeping again," Hassan said in English to the video camera.

A moment later, Koga and his colleague stepped back into the room.

"You did good, Abdul. Your friend probably won't come to again for another hour, so Brian will take you back to your room, and we'll try this again then," Koga said.

Hassan could have cared less about how they treated Yousef Badawi. The only thing that occupied his mind was the money.

"And what of our agreement?" he asked.

"If this leads to something, you'll be set for life," Koga said.

Hassan bowed.

"If it doesn't lead to something, you'll be set for life in a different way."

As he watched Koga and his colleague turn to leave the room, the feeling overcame Hassan that he would never see a penny of that reward money.

Chapter 26

Koga stepped into the open-air atrium of The Warehouse with Donald Rawlings right behind him, taking in a deep breath of the chilled night air. After being crammed inside the observation room for more than an hour, that air felt good in his lungs.

"What's our next move?" Rawlings asked.

"Can I hitch a ride with you?"

"Absolutely. Where to?"

They walked together in silence to the parking lot and the Audi Q8.

"Downtown."

As they climbed into the SUV, Koga pulled out his cellphone and dialed the boss. Paul Verdy picked up on the first ring.

"Talk to me, Max," he said.

"Our new friend told us that there's a major attack happening somewhere in Los Angeles soon. It's the reason for al-Ahmed's visit to San Diego."

"When and where?" Verdy asked.

"We didn't squeeze that out of him yet, but he did mention that it would be a symbolic blow to the world economy. He'll regain consciousness in an hour or so. In the meantime, I'm going to check something out. It's only a theory, but I think it has merit."

"Listening," Verdy said.

"The subject mentioned there would be a lot of casualties, so I'm thinking the connection with Song Motors makes it highly probable that something is going to happen at the Los Angeles Auto Show. Media day is tomorrow, and then it opens to the public in two days."

"You're saying they want to blow up the auto show? Sure, it would make for big news, but will it be enough to disrupt the world economy?" asked Verdy.

"The heads of Kamita Motors, GM, Hyundai, and Volkswagen are scheduled to have a kind of summit meeting on the first public day—just something ceremonial to open the show, followed by a big press conference. Stockton said that they're announcing a global coalition to build clean public transportation systems for third-world countries. If four of the biggest carmakers in the world all lost their leaders in a major terrorist attack on live TV, it might well send the world economy into a tailspin."

"Don't forget to mention the high-ranking Chinese military official being the real owner of Song Motors," Rawlings reminded Max.

Koga nodded. "And right now, that's all we have on that. But if that's true, chances are that the man behind all of this could be someone from the Chinese government. The fact that they would do something to potentially start World War III sounds more than a bit off. I, for one, think there's something else brewing. Maybe a rogue agent."

A long pause followed before Verdy spoke again. "I agree. I doubt that the Chinese government would sponsor such a serious attack. The rogue-agent theory sounds more likely. And it says here on the website that before the pandemic, the L.A. Auto Show attracted about a million people every year. And every year after, attendance has been steady, so they're expecting tens of thousands of show-goers per day. And, yup, there's a big announcement scheduled from the four major car manufacturers the day after tomorrow. Is Rawlings with you?"

"Aye-firmative," Koga answered.

"Good. I want both of you to go to the Convention Center. I'll ask Beth Hu to join you. She can provide access to the building and keep things cool with the police if they end up crashing your party."

The line went dead.

"So, what did he say?" Rawlings asked after Koga put his phone away.

"We're to check out the Convention Center."

The Q8 weaved through slower traffic on the 110 Freeway and made its way to Figueroa Street before pulling up along the curb directly in front of the West Hall of the Los Angeles Convention Center, right behind a beige Ford Explorer.

"I remember that ride. That's your new girlfriend's, isn't it?" Rawlings asked.

"She's not my girlfriend."

"But you want her to be," Rawlings said with a wide grin.

"Over here," Beth called out from the shadows. She emerged from the darkness, dressed in black stretch pants and a Patagonia jacket. She wore little makeup even though her naturally attractive face required none, and her full, black hair bounced with each step.

"Beth, this is Donnie. He works with me at Argon," Koga said.

"Are you guys auditioning for a new *Rush Hour* movie?" she said with a chuckle.

"She's also a crappy comedian," Koga added.

Rawlings gently took Beth's hand, lifted it to his face, and kissed it softly. "Your wit is as sharp as your appearance, m'lady."

"Wow, a real Romeo," she responded with a blush. "I just called security. They're sending someone down to let us in. General Verdy said that you'd explain everything to me when you got here." She handed him a rectangular placard printed with the auto show logo, a serial number, and a big blue PRESS. "Take this and put it on your right front dashboard. It will let you park right here."

"It could be nothing," Koga said as the security guard, an elderly man with tangled gray hair and a pot belly, approached from the other side of the glass door. "But I think there's a bomb in there somewhere. And if so, we need to find it, or a lot of people are gonna die."

Chapter 27

After taking a long look at Beth Hu's FBI creds, the rental security guard unlocked the door and let her, Max Koga, and Donald Rawlings into the building.

Beth looked at the guard's nametag and said, "Thank you, Mr. Langdon. We appreciate your help today."

He touched the bill of his ball cap. "Yes, ma'am, happy to help."

She pinned him with a big, appreciative grin. "We may need to call upon you again."

Langdon's smile glowed. "Yes, ma'am, and I'll be here if you need me."

As the three walked away, Beth said, "It never hurts to make sure potentially obstructive elements are on our side."

"Where's the Song Motors booth?" Koga asked, taking in the details of the lobby that had several supercars on display, including a new Lotus Eterna and a scattering of brightly colored Lamborghinis.

"Well, it's either here or in the South Hall. But shouldn't we be calling in the bomb squad or something?" Beth asked, grabbing a floor map of the auto show from a nearby table.

"Not yet. We have nothing to say to a bomb squad. As of now, I'm just acting on a hunch," Koga said. "Let's start here in the West Hall."

The three of them jogged up a flight of stairs and entered the West Exhibit Hall. It was the size of a large aircraft hangar, with high ceilings and carpeted floors, and yet, most every square foot was occupied by elaborate vehicle display booths. The stands for Toyota, Nissan, and Kamita Motors were front and center, while Mercedes-Benz, BMW, and Audi lined the back wall. Ford and Chevrolet were situated in the far corners, and the niche companies, such as Mazda, Jaguar, and Tesla were scattered in between. Except for a couple of uniformed security guards roaming various sections of the complex, the hall was devoid of people at this hour.

"There it is," Rawlings said, pointing to a large Song Motors sign on a white partition.

The Song Motors booth was smaller than most of the others. It was next to the Jeep stand, where a new Wrangler sat on a mound of real rocks and dirt. In the middle of the Song Motors booth was a circular stage in an unlighted section of the display floor. The car was car covered by a thin fire-engine-red tarp. The covering was securely locked to grommets in the floor in eight places to foil the curious, or journalists looking for a scoop.

"This is the Song MachStar," Koga said, recognizing the low-slung silhouette. "If there's a bomb here, it's probably in there. The press intro is supposed to be the big product hit of the L.A. show, so this entire area will be elbow-to-elbow at press conference time." He looked at Beth and Rawlings. "All the TV and phone cameras will be recording. What better time to blow up something really big?"

They approached the booth from three different angles. Rawlings leaned forward and ran his hands over the silky cloth, using the Braille method to determine what was underneath.

"Sweet Jesus," he said. His eyes closed as his hands flowed across the sleek lines of the electric sports car. "This is like running my hands over a fine woman in lingerie. I don't care what this costs—I want this beauty in my garage yesterday." He did a happy little jig next to the car.

"Where did you find him again?" Beth asked.

"The animal shelter on Tenth," Koga said. He turned to Rawlings. "We aren't going to get very far with interpretive dance, brah. Stand back and let the master work his magic."

Koga pulled a folded leather trifold from his right rear pants pocket and removed a few thin pieces of steel. A few moments later, he'd lock-picked open the two front locks and two on each side of the car.

"I had tougher locks than these on my high school gym locker." He tossed back the silky tarp and reached into the driver's side door to unlatch the hood.

Koga opened the front-hinged hood to expose the "frunk," the front luggage/trunk area with access to vehicle electronics. He then used a Swiss pocket tool and unfastened the screws that secured the CPU box, which he removed and placed on the carpeted floor. After activating the flashlight app on his cellphone, he peeled away an additional plastic cover that was painted to look like the top of a battery case. When he glanced underneath it, he found a hollow metallic box with nothing inside.

"Nothing here," he said. "This CPU box is just for show."

"Should we check the trunk?" Rawlings suggested.

"It can't hurt to look," said Beth.

Koga opened the car door and searched for the trunk actuator under the dash. His fingers found a small button and, with a click, the lid to the rear luggage compartment popped loose and slowly rose into the air.

Beth reached into the tight compartment and pulled out a small Gucci suitcase.

"This is the only thing in here, and it's empty," she said, shaking the designer luggage piece with both hands.

"That probably comes with the car," Koga said. "And besides, if they were going for maximum casualties, they'd need an explosive device a lot bigger than that."

"You think your Arab friend was lying?" Rawlings asked.

"Mmm, doubtful. I must have interpreted the clues wrong, but it made so much sense."

"How large would a bomb have to be to cause serious damage?" Beth asked.

Koga pointed to a miniature two-seat car in a nearby Mercedes-Benz booth. "If they had military-grade stuff, probably about the volume of that minicar there. Something that size could take out this entire hall."

“I’ll say one thing. There’s a whole lot of places to hide a bomb here,” Rawlings said, looking at the sea of vehicles scattered throughout the floor.

Beth nodded. “Yeah. It could be in any one or more of these cars.”

Koga also surveyed the showroom floor. “It’s possible, I suppose, but unlikely. The manufacturers check their display cars all the time. The chances would be too great that it would be found before the show started.”

They stood quietly, thinking for a few minutes.

As Rawlings closed the MachStar’s rear deck lid, a staccato of loud popping sounds echoed throughout the chamber. Several spots on the carpeted floor in front of Beth and Koga exploded with dust and several more projectiles punched nickel-sized holes in the MachStar’s rear quarter.

In an instant, Koga was on the ground, rolling toward the far side of the MachStar and pulling Beth with him. They propped themselves against the car’s rear bumper with their weapons drawn. Meanwhile, Rawlings crouched behind the Jeep Wrangler with his gun pointed toward the rear wall punctuated with several dark doorways, including restrooms.

Koga didn’t have to pull back the slide on his pistol; this weapon already had a round in the chamber. Nevertheless, he pulled the slide back far enough to confirm. “Well, I guess we can safely assume that someone doesn’t want us here.”

“You think?” Beth said. “I don’t know about that ‘safely’ part, though.”

Chapter 28

"The shots came from the back. Near the BMW booth, I think," Don Rawlings said from his hiding spot behind the Wrangler. "I'll swing around to the left, you come around the other side, and we'll converge. There could be more than one, so be careful."

"Copy that," Koga responded.

The number of booths and cars in the exhibition hall provided plenty of places to take cover. Koga likened it to urban warfare, only the structures were made of steel, plastic, and rubber.

"How did they know we were here?" asked Beth Hu.

"That's a good question," Koga said. "My guess is they were here to keep an eye on their bomb to make sure it wasn't discovered."

"What's the plan now?"

Koga got to his feet. "Stay here and provide cover. If you see anything on my blind side, shoot it. And try to stay hidden."

Beth nodded.

The dimmed lighting of the West Hall made it possible to move in relative stealth as Koga ran in a crouched position to the far edge of the Song Motors booth. The gunfire had stopped, giving him a chance to breathe and assess their situation. Koga popped a Xanax pill into his mouth to help keep his vision clear and nerves calm. The last thing he wanted to do was lose control and put Beth and Donnie in danger. He took a deep breath and, satisfied with his state of mind, silently counted to three and dove forward, rolling across the aisle to the adjacent Volkswagen stand.

The move was greeted with a barrage of bullets that kicked up pieces of the carpet. One round bounced off the roof of a maroon Volkswagen Golf just as Koga jumped behind it. With every shot, bright orange flashes lit up the BMW stand. Rawlings was right—the shooter was somewhere inside that booth.

And then, a series of *pop-pop-pops* rang out from the opposite direction, directly behind him. It was Beth, who had repositioned herself at the front quarter panel of the MachStar with her firearm pointed at the Nissan booth. Then Koga saw a second shooter—a short, stubby figure dressed in black, hiding behind a Nissan Pathfinder offroading concept vehicle.

Koga shifted his position behind a gray Passat that offered him a view of the neighboring Nissan stand. "We have a second shooter," he said loud enough to be heard.

The second gunman fired a barrage from a Heckler & Koch HK416 automatic rifle, forcing Beth to take cover.

"Not much more I can do here," Beth said as she reloaded her pistol. "I'm pinned down and seriously outgunned."

"Hold your position," Koga instructed, sprinting for the Nissan booth. His move was met with gunfire from two directions as both hidden gunmen tried to trap him in their crossfire. Thankfully for Max, none of them got close as he jumped behind a Nissan Z convertible.

The bad news was the shooters were working as a team. That much was clear. The good news is they weren't very good shooters, at least so far. But neither of them took a single shot in Rawlings' direction. If they weren't yet aware of his presence, it was advantage good guys.

❖

Donald Rawlings had spent his entire eight-year tenure in the military with Naval Special Warfare Command. As a member of SEAL Team Five, he'd been involved in a high number of hostile conflicts, credited with thirty-seven kills in more than a hundred missions.

As he did in previous situations when faced with hostiles, he moved with controlled breaths, quickly and silently advancing toward the first shooter at the back of the hall. He kept his body low and stopped when he reached the Jaguar booth, positioned about fifty yards from the BMW stand. Crouching behind an XJ sedan bathed in pearlescent white paint, Rawlings peeked into the car's leather-lined cabin, where he noticed a chrome, car-shaped object in the cupholder of the center console.

It can't be, can it? Did someone really leave the key fob inside the car?

Rawlings opened the driver-side door as quietly as he could and slipped into the cabin. While keeping his head low, he sat in the driver's seat and picked up the key fob in the cupholder. Sure enough, it was an electric key.

He studied the cockpit. A large round dial on the center console shifted the electronically controlled transmission, and a large display monitor dominated the center dashboard. Putting one hand on the leather-wrapped steering wheel, he pressed the start button with the other, anticipating the roar of a V-8 engine. However, aside from the lights of the instrument cluster blinking on, nothing seemed to happen. It took Rawlings all of two seconds to realize that he was inside an electric vehicle.

Even better, he thought, for there was no engine sound to give away his presence. He pulled down the seat belt and secured it, then touched the brake pedal and twisted the transmission dial to D and pressed the throttle.

The car shot forward with a violent lunge, the XJ's four wide tires shredding the loose carpet. Rawlings switched on the headlights to high beams and kept the throttle pedal floored, navigating the full-size luxury sedan around a Jaguar F-Type sports car, a Ford F-150, and a Tesla Model 4. In seconds, he reached the BMW booth.

The XJ's LED headlights bathed the entire stand in brilliant white light, revealing the confused face of the first shooter. He was a bearded man with frameless spectacles hiding behind a reception counter. The man swung his rifle at the Jag and sprayed the car's front end with a dozen rounds, cracking the windshield and leaving holes and spider-web patterns across the width of the tempered glass. It wasn't enough to slow Rawlings down. He ducked low enough that only his eyes were above the level of the dashboard and kept his foot planted on the accelerator pedal. The Jag side-swiped the a BMW X1 and dove hard into the reception counter, obliterating it and the shooter in an explosion of wood, fiberglass, and blood.

The car stalled right after the driver's airbag deployed, so Rawlings rolled out of the car with his gun in hand. The shooter, who had distinct Middle Eastern features, lay on the carpet with his right leg bent forward at the knee and blood flowing freely from his upper thigh, where a jagged piece of plastic countertop had penetrated the flesh and the femoral artery.

He still stretched his right arm toward his weapon on the floor, only a few feet away from him.

"Don't do it," Rawlings shouted, his pistol pointed at the man's head.

The Arab man flashed him a crooked grin.

"You are Americans," the man said in glee. "You must arrest us, not shoot us. This is why you will always die!"

He turned over and dragged himself toward his rifle, cackling. When his hand reached the shoulder strap, Rawlings fired a single round that entered the right side of the man's forehead, blowing it open in a burst of brain matter and blood as it exited the skull.

No arrest was made.

Chapter 29

The scene was surreal. Despite bullets flying in his direction, Max Koga took a moment to watch a Jaguar XJ sedan seemingly drive itself across the auto show floor, pinballing off another vehicle before colliding into the reception counter inside the BMW booth.

Leave it to Donnie to do things with flair, he thought.

Confident that his friend would take care of the first shooter, Koga returned his attention to the man hiding behind the Nissan Pathfinder SUV.

The short, heavy-set assassin hadn't moved from his spot, but Koga suspected he wouldn't be sticking around for long once he realized his associate was no longer providing him with cover. The short shooter raised his rifle above his hiding place every few minutes to make suppressing fire, but he was only spraying and praying, not aiming.

Koga needed to initiate a response to end this incident now. He moved his position from the rear bumper to the side of the Z Convertible. The top was lowered, giving Koga a full view inside the two-seat cabin. Unfortunately, he didn't see a key, but he did notice that Nissan had equipped the sports car with a conventional six-speed manual gearbox, a rarity these days in the age of the electric vehicle. An idea quickly formed.

When the gunman paused, Koga opened the passenger-side door and pulled down on the steering wheel. It was locked in place. He then glanced at the front tires and noticed they were pointing in the general direction of the Nissan Pathfinder. If he could push the Z forward, it would pass about ten feet in front of the Pathfinder, giving Koga a direct line of sight to the shooter.

Reaching for the shift lever, he yanked it out of first gear and down into Neutral. Then, after releasing the hand brake, he closed the door, staying outside of the vehicle, and pushed with all his might on the base of the front windowsill. Despite being on the carpet, the new Z car was extremely light, so it took little effort to get it rolling. In a crouched position, Koga moved forward with the Z.

The shooter noticed the roadster slowly approaching, provoking him to respond by unloading a few rounds at its front fenders and driver-side door. Despite creating a crooked line of holes in the bodywork, the car kept rolling. While most of the bullets ripped through the Z's bodywork, Max was positioned behind the front wheel, using the car's engine as a solid shield. A few more feet and he would have a clear shot at the shooter.

The gunman reloaded and gave the Z another generous tattoo of lead.

While Koga remained crouched with his gun at the ready, the car rolled right up to the front of the Pathfinder. He stood up from behind the hood of the Z and sent three evenly timed rounds into the gunman's face and chest, knocking him backward to the ground.

As the Z kept rolling, ultimately crashing into the side of a Kia sedan in the next booth, Koga walked toward the downed figure who lay on his back in a spread-eagle position with half his face blown off. There was just enough left for Koga to recognize the dark round, bearded face of a man seated at Badawi's table at the Song Motors dinner.

"Donnie, you okay?" Koga asked.

"Yeah," responded Rawlings from the far side of the hall. "Shooter One is down."

"Shooter Two is down," Koga called back.

"Thataboy. Let's meet at the Song Motors booth and keep your guard up in case there's more," Rawlings said.

Koga picked up the dead man's HK416 and carried the automatic rifle back to where Beth Hu and Rawlings waited.

Rawlings had the same model hanging from his shoulder.

"Yo, man, sweet piece," Rawlings commented, pointing at the rifle

Koga had recovered. Rawlings spoke louder than usual to compensate for everyone's ears still ringing from the gunshots.

Koga asked, "Any of you hurt?"

Rawlings looked over at Beth. "Are you all right?" he asked.

"I'm a little rattled, but no injuries," she answered.

Koga gently put a hand on her shoulder. "Thanks for saving my ass. I owe you one."

She nodded and smiled. "Anytime. I'll make sure you pay up."

"The fact that these guys were here and watching over the place means that there's something here they were protecting," Rawlings said.

"There's definitely something here they don't want us to find," agreed Beth. "And it's probably something that goes boom."

"Knowing al-Ahmed's flair for the dramatic, it's going to be a pretty big explosive device," Koga added. "Which means your hunches were spot on. It's probably hidden in a vehicle, but we don't have the time to go through every one of them now. Do any of you know of any other carmakers from China, Southeast Asia, or the Middle East who might have a booth here?"

"You're the car guy," Rawlings said.

"Well, there's Vantas, Geeley, BYD, Fisker, and Volvo," Koga recalled. "I can't imagine any of them would be in cahoots with Song, but I suppose you never know."

"Aren't Fisker and Volvo from Europe?" Rawlings asked.

"They are, but they were bought by Chinese companies," Koga explained. "And fortunately for us, all the Chinese car companies are in this hall. I'll go take a look at Vantas and BYD. Beth, can you check out Fisker? Donnie, Geeley and Volvo share a booth, so see what you can find there."

The three agents separated. Because the hour was past midnight, no floor workers were present, so it took only fifteen minutes to conduct a quick sweep of the four booths. They regrouped at the Song Motors booth with nothing positive to report.

Koga rubbed his chin. "I'm drawing a complete blank. It must be here."

Beth unfolded the floor map that she had stuffed in her back pocket.

Studying it, her eyes lit up. "It says here that they have turned the entire Concourse Exhibit Hall into a special gallery of future zero-emission vehicles. They're calling it 'Our Green World.' It also says that the press conference with the four company presidents will happen there."

"It makes sense since the theme of the press conference is EV public transportation," Koga said. "The Concourse Exhibit Hall is between the South and West Halls, so it's right in the middle of the Convention Center, ensuring maximum carnage."

"Well, what the hell are we waiting for?" Rawlings said.

Beth took out her cellphone. "Should I call in for help now?"

"Yes, but not with that. Find a landline or a pay phone if you can, because random cellphone signals can set a bomb off. And tell the LAPD to bring a portable cellphone jammer, an OBD2 connector cable, and whatever interface adapters they have, but I need one for an Apple lightning cable," Koga instructed. "If these guys miss their check-in calls, and Nasim al-Ahmed finds out we just took out his goons, he might panic and set the bomb off early."

Chapter 30

Max and Beth followed Rawlings out of the main doorway of the West Exhibit Hall, leaving the place looking like a miniature war zone. It still amazed Koga that the shooting and car crashing hadn't attracted a squad of show security. Descending on the escalator, Rawlings held up a fist to signal the others to stop. The lobby was empty and deathly still.

All three brought up their weapons.

"Who's there?" Koga called out. His voice echoed around the still room.

A man slowly raised his body from behind the Galaxy Court cafeteria counter, next to the base of the escalator. He held a revolver in steady hands. It was the gray-haired security guard, Sergeant Langdon, who had unlocked the door for them earlier in the evening.

"Don't move," Langdon said.

Koga slung his rifle and placed his hands over his head.

"Don't be afraid," Beth said. "Federal agents. You remember us, right? Are you hurt?"

The security man relaxed his grip on the gun. "They hit one of my colleagues. Someone came through the front door and shot her. I radioed for help, but no one came."

"Where is she?" Koga asked, stepping forward from the escalator.

"Next to me. I pulled her in here after the shooter ran up the stairs."

Koga nodded. "That was brave of you—well done. Can I take a look?"

Langdon motioned for Koga to come down to his position.

When Koga stepped behind the lobby counter, he saw a uniformed twenty-something Latino woman lying on her side. Her face was twisted in pain and she clutched her right thigh.

"Bastard got my leg," she gasped.

"What's your name, officer?" Koga asked. She was a rent-a-cop, but such professional respect carried a lot of weight with most of them and reinforced teamwork.

"Mandalito Habenez, sir," she said. "I've only been on the job a week."

"Okay, Mandy, you earned your pay today. Let me have a look at you." Koga handed his rifle to Rawlings and knelt next to her. He gently lifted her hands from the area.

"It burns so bad," Mandy slurred.

Koga ripped open her uniform pants leg from the bullet hole and examined the wound.

"It's through-and-through. This is good. It's gonna hurt like a bastard for a minute, but you'll live. Missed your femur and femoral artery. You'll be doing wind sprints again in no time."

Koga pulled off his belt and wrapped the leg in auto show press releases from behind the lobby counter, tightening his belt around the paper to form a tight seal and stop the blood loss.

"There's the power of the press for ya," he said with fake humor. "Keep the pressure constant on both sides of the leg and don't move around."

"Thank you," Mandy said.

Koga then looked up at Langdon. "LAPD should be here soon. When they arrive, tell 'em we're in the Concourse Hall. Don't forget to mention that we're the good guys. And tell them no cellphones. There might be a bomb threat."

"I'll stay here and wait for the police in case any federal validation is needed," Beth said, stepping through the swinging door. "You guys go on ahead."

Koga nodded. "Sounds good."

Rawlings, who had kept watch, handed Max his rifle.

"Let's do this," he said.

Koga followed Rawlings through the Concourse Walkway to the Concourse Hall. The room was significantly smaller than the South and West Exhibit Halls. In the center was a large dais where the big announcement was most likely going to take place. Rows of seats faced the stage, presumably for the press to occupy.

Around the center section were a half dozen vehicles rarely seen by the public, all of them electric or fuel cell. The largest of these was a sporty-looking full-size SUV with chrome wheels and a CruiseStar badge on its bodywork.

With a swooping silhouette and wide muscular stance, the CruiseStar was indeed an attractive vehicle. Its front end was highlighted by a thin, one-piece headlight that ran across the width of the body. The rear was slightly elevated, giving the entire vehicle the look that it was constantly in motion. Per Stockton Clay, rumors were that the Song CruiseStar, along with the MachStar, were penned by a famous Italian *carrozzeria* whose identity had yet to be disclosed.

"That has to be it," Rawlings said. "You see, bro, I told you chrome rims were making a comeback."

He shook his head. "Still looks pretty tacky to me. Why don't you add gold-stripe tires, too?"

Their conversation was cut short by the sound of the service doors on the far side of the hall rising automatically. The doors led to the outdoor loading dock, which, for the auto show, had been converted into the staging area of a mini test-drive course where guests were given the opportunity to drive electric and fuel cell vehicles with a minder.

Before either could say any more, five randomly spaced gunshots rang out from the loading dock, prompting them to drop to the floor. Koga took shelter behind a prototype Toyota hydrogen engine vehicle, while Rawlings rolled sideways toward the back of the CruiseStar, splattered with blood on its side.

"You hit?" Max shouted. There was no answer. "Donnie, you good?"

Cautiously raising his head to sneak a peek toward the shooters, Koga spotted a lone figure outside leaning across the hood of a Chevrolet Equinox EV with a pistol in his hand. The man briefly moved under some overhead lights, revealing his face and what looked to be a vertical scar through his lips. Koga recognized him as the man in the black hat who had tailed him from the hotel to the art gallery earlier that day.

Pointing his rifle in the man's direction, Koga discharged a dozen rounds of automatic fire into the side of the car, motivating the man to duck behind it. After a few seconds, Koga sprang to his feet and made a mad dash for the CruiseStar where he hovered over Rawlings, who was lying clutching his midsection.

Koga carefully peeled off Rawlings' brown suede jacket, revealing three red stains the size of regulation softballs on his white T-shirt. One was near the shoulder, another in his ribs. The third one, on Rawlings' lower back, caused him the most concern.

Turning Rawlings' body over slowly, Koga checked for exit wounds. He found none. The bullets were still inside him, and it was probably a miracle he was still alive. The first thing to do was to slow the bleeding, so Koga took the suede jacket and tied it around his friend's chest, ensuring there was extra pressure placed over the bleeding rib cage. It wasn't perfect, but it would do for now.

"Yo," Rawlings mumbled, his eyes half open. "You get the shooter?"

"Not yet," Koga answered. "We will. You need to shut up and concentrate on staying awake, Donnie."

Rawlings failed to heed Koga's instructions and slipped back into unconsciousness.

"Don't you die on me, damn it!" Koga yelled. Then the sound of footsteps near the entrance of the hall drew his attention.

He turned to see up-armored LAPD SWAT officers in tactical gear standing in the doorway with their rifles pointed in his direction.

"Put down your weapon and drop to the floor!" one of them shouted.

"Relax, he's with us," Beth said, stepping past the armed men.

"I got a man down," Koga said with urgency. "Active shooter on site."

A half-dozen members of the SWAT unit converged around the Argon men with their rifles at the ready.

"We got this," one said to Max. "The EMTs are right behind us."

As promised, two emergency medical technicians arrived on scene a minute later, placing proper bandages on Rawlings' wounds and putting him onto a motorized gurney. After they carted him away, Koga hurried outside to the test-drive course, where he inspected the vehicles parked there—the shot-up Chevy Equinox EV, a Nissan LEAF, a Tesla Model 1, and a BMW i1. The main gate, the only way to access the loading dock from the outside, was closed and locked.

With his own rifle at the ready, Koga carefully stepped out into the open, looking for any other hiding places. There were none, and yet there was no sign of the man with the scarred lip.

He had vanished into thin air.

Chapter 31

Returning to the Concourse Exhibit Hall, Max Koga was informed by the LAPD that the tactical unit had already started its search for explosive devices inside the South and West Halls of the Convention Center with more than a dozen bomb-sniffing dogs checking each vehicle one by one.

The leader of the SWAT team, a sergeant named Ben Ryder, walked toward the CruiseStar.

"Don't touch that vehicle," Koga cautioned.

Ryder froze in his tracks. "You think a bomb is in there?" he asked.

Koga nodded. "Where is your bomb disposal unit?"

"They're on the way."

"How long until they get here?"

"Twelve minutes."

"We can't wait that long. You all might want to take a couple of steps back," Koga said, peering into the blacked-out windows. Although he could scarcely make out the interior through the front windows, the ones toward the rear were completely painted black from the inside. "There's something definitely in the rear compartment, but I can't make out what it is."

He moved to the back of the CruiseStar and examined the rear hatch. Locked. After trying the other doors, which were all locked, Koga inspected the driver-side door seal, looking for wires or any kind of suspicious rigging. Satisfied that there were none, he raised his rifle and slammed the butt into the window, shattering the glass.

"Are you sure you know what you're doing?" Beth Hu asked nervously.

"I've worked with bomb disposal units in the Navy, and the windows are usually never rigged," Koga said, reaching through the broken glass into the vehicle's cabin and pressing a switch. In a chorus of clicks, all the CruiseStar's doors unlocked simultaneously.

Ryder walked to the back of the vehicle and swung the hatch open. "Well, what do we have here?"

Taking up the entire rear compartment was a large box covered in a black felt tarp. Koga carefully undid the fasteners and pulled it free, exposing a metal box that looked like an extra fuel tank, only this one had a variety of colored wires running into and out of it. The yellow and green ones were connected to a flip phone duct-taped to the side of the unit.

"Now that's what I call a boom box," Ryder said.

"One call activates the detonator, and bang, we all get vaporized. Did you bring the cellphone jammer?" Koga asked.

Ryder handed him a black case with a series of plastic antennas attached to it.

"We have those at the FBI, but I never really knew how they worked," Beth said.

"It intercepts and blocks signals from surrounding cellphone towers before it can reach the phone," Koga explained. "The drawback to these things is that it indiscriminately blocks all cell signals—5G, WiFi, and even nine-one-one emergency calls. That means none of you will be able to make or take a call within a one-mile radius of this thing, so I suggest you guys get far away from here."

"And what are you going to do?" Beth asked.

"I'm gonna go for a drive."

Beth looked at him with a quizzical face. "What on earth for? Now that we have this thing temporarily deactivated, shouldn't we leave the rest to the bomb squad?"

Koga shook his head. "It's not deactivated. And I've had experiences with electronic jammers like this one while I was in the Navy. They're not one hundred percent effective, especially if whoever programmed this thing can switch frequencies. If he gets past the jammer, this bomb can still explode, so I need to get this thing out of here and to a secluded place while we still have time."

"Where on earth would you go?" Beth asked. "We're in the middle of downtown Los Angeles. And how are you going to start the vehicle? There's no key."

Koga smiled. "I made a call to my IT guy beforehand to let him know he may need to assist me, so he installed this handy app. All these cars run on computers these days, meaning we can hack them."

Taking out his sat phone, he fitted the lightning cable adapter to it and connected it to an OBD2 cable. He then plugged the other end of the cable to the CruiseStar's diagnostic port, located under the dashboard. It took exactly two minutes before the instrument panel came to life, and the headlights turned on, eliciting a whoa from Ryder.

"How on earth?" Beth asked. "I thought our cellphone signals were jammed?"

"Mine uses a satellite frequency, so the jammer is pretty much useless against it," Koga explained. "Count us lucky that the terrorists went with a normal flip phone for their bomb and not one of these."

"How did you know you would have the right cable and program?" Ryder asked.

"I noticed that when I first saw the MachStar while it was still on the ship, it still used the standard OBD2 port to run diagnostics, so I figured the case would be the same for the CruiseStar. And I was right. Just so you know, we can also start and kill the engine of most gasoline-powered Chevrolets and Fords remotely, without a key or cable."

"Your little app borders on being illegal," Beth pointed out.

"Everything we do borders on being illegal," Koga replied. Without wasting another moment, he climbed into the CruiseStar's driver's seat.

Once the door gently closed, Beth leaned on the CruiseStar's windowless sill and asked, "Where do you plan on taking this thing?"

"As you said, downtown is too dense. I need to find a place that's wide open. Any suggestions?"

"How about the roof of the parking structure next door?" she said.

"Not secluded enough. Knowing these guys, they put plenty of nails and other sharp things inside the box to ensure maximum casualties, making the bomb dangerous far beyond the blast zone. And I'm sure there's a flammable liquid in here, too, which will set fire to anything nearby. Ideally, I'd like to drive it into the ocean, but I'll never make it to the coast from here without endangering other lives."

"I may be able to help," Ryder broke in. "The closest ocean from here is in Santa Monica. I can get you a police escort all the way to the pier. After we manage the fastest and most effective route, I'll have my officers clear traffic and get you through all the red lights. At this hour, we can be there in maybe fifteen minutes, tops. And the jammer will create an electric bubble around you that should keep the bomb from going off as you travel."

"Now, that sounds like a plan. I can see why they call you L.A.'s finest," Koga said. "Can you set up the escort now, and make sure your people clear the sidewalks, too, before I come through? Keep the caravan at least three hundred feet away in all directions."

"You got it," answered Ryder, relaying the plan to his men by walkie-talkie.

"So, you're really going to do this?" asked Beth.

Koga gave her an unconvincing smile.

"Ever since I was little, I've always wanted to fly a car into the ocean."

Chapter 32

The Song CruiseStar cruised silently on Interstate 10 at an even seventy miles per hour. Max Koga relished in having the entire freeway to himself—something unimaginable on a normal day on one of the most heavily congested stretches of road in the country. As he followed the taillights of four police cruisers three hundred yards ahead, another four brought up his rear at approximately the same distance, all of them with their light bars flashing.

As the digital display on the CruiseStar's clock showed 0300, Koga noticed every exit had already been closed off to keep the public from entering the freeway in front of him.

Sergeant Ben Ryder, who took the role of lead driver of the police escort, kept everyone in the caravan informed of the status of the roads through his police radio.

The convoy reached the Santa Monica city limits in fourteen minutes, which Koga imagined was a record. The same trip usually took him more than an hour during rush hour. The nine-vehicle caravan exited the freeway at Fourth Street, then jumped onto Colorado Avenue, taking it all the way to the Santa Monica Pier, where Koga waved the caravan to stop and disperse as he parked the CruiseStar under the Pier Arch.

"Thanks for the company. I could use you guys on my daily commute to work," he said. "I'll go solo from here. Once I get past the Ferris wheel, I'm bailing, so don't follow too closely, or you might run over me."

"Roger that," Ryder said. "How are you going to get the vehicle past the buildings at the edge of the pier?"

"I'll stay inside until the last possible moment and make sure it's aimed for at gap between them. I'll probably need to carry about thirty miles per hour to break through the guard railing on the other side, so can you make sure the path ahead is clear?"

"It's already wide open. Good luck," Ryder said.

Koga positioned the electric SUV in the middle of the road that extended the length of the pier. He then unbuckled his seat belt and unlatched the driver-side door to ensure a quick exit. The pier stretched a little more than a quarter mile, so there was plenty of runway to get the vehicle to thirty miles per hour, even something as heavy as the CruiseStar carrying a two-thousand-pound bomb in the back.

After placing the shifter into "D" once again, he stomped his right foot onto the throttle pedal. The tires of the CruiseStar momentarily struggled to grab a firm bite on the dusty pavement, but once they did, they shot the three-ton vehicle forward like a cannon.

The SUV reached thirty miles per hour just as the driving surface turned from concrete to wood, marking the point where the pier went over the shoreline. As it passed Pacific Park—the famous playground with the giant solar-powered Ferris wheel—Koga set the cruise control to forty.

With the windows lowered, the cold oncoming air slapped Koga's face while his ears filled with the dinging of the vehicle's fasten-seatbelt alarm. As the CruiseStar neared the far end of the pier, he adjusted the steering wheel so the nose was pointed at the narrow opening between a restaurant and the Harbor Office building. It was going to be tight, but there looked to be just enough space for the extra-wide SUV to get through. While forty miles per hour seemed slower than a turtle's pace on the freeway, it felt like warp speed on the narrow runway of the pier. The buildings came up on him fast.

Now.

Koga flung the driver's door wide open and hurled his body into the cool night air. He hit the wooden-plank deck hard, momentum causing him to roll three times before slamming into the pier's side rail. The impact against the steel bars knocked the wind out of him, but as far as he could tell, nothing inside of him broke. As he pulled himself up, he saw the CruiseStar still accelerating through the opening, breaking off both side mirrors and shooting straight for the pier's edge.

The CruiseStar smashed the guardrail with a loud crunch, breaking the steel bars at their foundation. The large white SUV seemed to hover in space for a moment before its taillights disappeared over the edge, followed by a big splash into the ocean.

Moby Dick lives.

Koga covered his ears, anticipating a colossal explosion, but all he heard was the sound of approaching patrol cars with their sirens on full blast. He stood and dusted off his clothes and jogged over to the pier's edge, looking down at the black of the night sea.

He could barely make out the taillights now, the CruiseStar and its deadly cargo sinking to the bottom of the ocean floor, where it was sin no position to cause harm to anyone.

Chapter 33

Less than an hour after the CruiseStar's dive into the Pacific, the Santa Monica Pier had become a center of operations for the FBI and LAPD. They cordoned off the immediate area around the Harbor Office and the fishing deck off with yellow tape and it was crawling with police officers and federal agents. More than a dozen law-enforcement vehicles lined the length of the pier, their flashing lights reflecting off the gentle waves of the ocean.

A couple of tents had been set up, while divers were already in the water tending to the explosive device. A salvage team stood by to raise the sunken vehicle once police EOD divers deactivated the bomb.

Meanwhile, Koga was escorted to a tent where a female medic tended to a large cut on his elbow. Just as she finished taping him up, Beth Hu walked in.

"Hey, Speed Racer. How are you feeling?" she asked.

"I'm fine, but they insisted I get looked over. Any word on Donnie?"

"Still in surgery. One of the bullets is lodged in his kidney."

Koga cursed under his breath. "If there's a one percent chance of him pulling through, he will. Donnie is the toughest man I've ever known."

Beth took a seat next to him on a portable plastic bench and placed her hand on his shoulder. "Well, it looks like you can check stunt driving off your bucket list. Was it everything you imagined it would be?"

Koga forced a laugh. "Yeah, I felt like a real Joie Chitwood."

"Who?" Beth asked.

"Never mind. But I wasn't in the vehicle when it went into the water, so

I don't know if it counts. I guess the good news is that we have more than enough to implicate Xavier Qiu. Have you guys snatched him up yet?"

Beth didn't answer.

Koga eyed her. "You are bringing Qiu in, aren't you?"

Beth broke eye contact, shifting her gaze outside of the tent.

"Yeah, about that. I'm afraid that's not going to happen."

"*Why not?*"

"I got word on the way down here that he's flown the coop. His entire contingent and their private plane have already left LAX."

"Ugh," said Koga in a tone filled with disappointment.

"It's obvious they knew something about the bomb or they wouldn't have left in such a hurry, right?" Beth said.

"Maybe they had prom dates. Who knows? But it's like they're admitting their own guilt, so why can't we go after them?"

"If they're headed back to Beijing, they're untouchable. We don't have an extradition agreement with China. And even if we did, they would just lawyer up and seek shelter behind their government. Besides, there's nothing to prove they had anything to do with the bomb."

"So that's it? We do nothing?"

"Look on the bright side. They can never come back to America."

Koga said, "Somehow, that doesn't make me feel any better."

Beth nodded.

After sliding off the bench, Koga walked out of the tent, looking for a secluded place, which he found near the Ferris wheel. He had already filled in General Verdy with the details of what occurred at the Convention Center. Verdy took the news about Donald Rawlings hard, but the former general's mind never seemed to waver from the task at hand. He agreed with Koga that the next step was to find out what else Yousef Badawi knew. The jihadist would wake up from his drugged state again soon.

Koga called the main line to The Warehouse, which rang without an answer. He hung up and dialed again. Still, no one answered. He then tried Brian Panackia's personal cellphone, but the call went straight to voicemail.

Something's not right. All lines there are supposed to be manned twenty-four hours a day.

Shoving his phone back into his pocket, Koga hurried to where Beth was briefing two of her FBI colleagues. One of them saw him walk up.

"Well, if it isn't the man of the hour," the shorter, dark Asian man said with a grin.

"Max, let me introduce you to my two superiors," Beth interjected. "This is Special Agent Marty Ragat and Special Agent Eli Erikson."

Koga nodded to them curtly. "Yeah, pleasure," he said, then grabbed Beth by the elbow and pulled her away.

"I need you."

"Hey, I'm busy," she retorted, pulling her arm back.

"Did you drive your car here?" Koga asked.

"It's over there. Why?" she said, pointing to the beige Explorer near the pier entrance.

"Can I borrow it? It's an emergency."

"No, you may not."

"Then I need you to take me somewhere right now."

"What is going on?" Beth asked.

"I'll tell you on the way. And it would be better if I drove."

They hurried to the parked Explorer and bucked themselves in, taking off in the freeway's direction. It wasn't a good idea to reveal the location of Argon's safe house to Beth, but Koga had no other choice. He needed to find out why no one was answering at The Warehouse. It could be nothing, he thought. Maybe there had been a blackout in the Downey area, or the phone lines had temporarily gone down.

But deep in his gut, he couldn't fight the feeling that something terrible had happened.

Chapter 34

Xavier Qiu glanced at the wall clock in his lavish penthouse office atop the Bank of Yidong building in Beijing's Central Business District. He nervously paced the length of the floor, agitated at the prospect of his next appointment. A full day had passed since he returned from Los Angeles, hastily departing after one of the Aqarib men went missing during their media dinner.

His superior had ordered him to leave the country immediately, so he gathered his team and hurried to the airport, where they boarded a private jet headed for Beijing. Not long after takeoff, Qiu had watched a CNN report of a bomb planted in one of Song Motors' display vehicles at the Los Angeles Auto Show. That was too close, he thought then.

They had left damage control and an explanation of their abrupt departure to the hired American public-relations firm that maintained on air that the company had nothing to do with the incident, but the negative effect on their corporate image would be profound. Dreams of ever doing business in America would remain just that, dreams.

Those damned Islamic terrorists had ruined everything.

Qiu pressed a button on his famously uncluttered desk. "Ask Ms. Blackwood to come in, please?" he asked in Mandarin. He stared out of his large office window that overlooked downtown Beijing and reflected on his unlikely ascent as a child from the slums of Daxing to his current position as president of a global car company.

At ten years old, he had run away from home and was picked up off the street by a man who belonged to a small, organized gang syndicate called the Tangs. Qiu's first job was to relay messages and deliver packages in the Beijing area. But as he matured, so did his role. By his fifteenth birthday, he had become a neighborhood boss.

A man affectionately called sifu, or teacher, who rarely showed himself to his members much less to the public, ran the Tangs. It wasn't until Qiu's twentieth birthday that he learned that the Tang sifu was Colonel Chol-Min Seo of the Korean People's Army, and that the Tangs were an organization that serviced the interests of the Democratic People's Republic of Korea.

After losing his own teenage son to cancer, Colonel Seo had taken an immediate liking to young Qiu, and the more he got to know the kid, the more he saw his potential. Qiu was far smarter than anyone else in the gang, so Seo enrolled him in the finest secondary school in Beijing, followed by a four-year stint at Peking University's Guanghua School of Management, where the boy wonder graduated with honors.

They groomed him to be an accountant for the Bank of Yidong in Beijing, a financial institution used by the North Korean government to launder money overseas, but he ended up ascending to vice president after only seven years. Qiu helped Seo, who had since become the DPRK's ambassador to China, to establish Song Motors as a Chinese company with the objective of smuggling drugs and laundering money around the world.

In its first three years, Song Motors made sixty-three million dollars without selling a single vehicle, dealing mostly with Third World countries whose militant despots constantly needed drugs and arms. And they had money, lots of it.

Qiu knew a car company that didn't build cars would attract the attention of the Chinese trade commission before long, so he convinced Seo that Song should develop an actual vehicle to make the company seem like a legitimate business. Seo agreed, and they produced a premium SUV concept vehicle called the CruiseStar—which, to their surprise, made a hundred and fifty million dollars in pre-market orders. The company then drew the interest of a venture capital group from Saudi Arabia, one that secretly sponsored the Aqarib.

Qiu followed up the CruiseStar's success with a prototype super sports car that he predicted could bring in an additional sixty to one hundred million dollars. This would be a gigantic swindle. Like the CruiseStar, the plan was to take orders, but never deliver a single vehicle. If things got too hot, they would simply declare bankruptcy and disappear with the money and take it back to Pyongyang.

Following the U.S.-imposed sanctions on North Korea, the country's Supreme Leader directed his closest circle of advisers to come up with ideas to retaliate against the evil Western regime. It was Qiu who had devised the plan to recruit the Aqarib and help them attack the U.S. While the Tangs had already been supplying fentanyl to the cartels, it was he who concocted the idea to manipulate the jihadists to gradually take out the Mexican gangs and take over the entire drug trade in Mexico. In his mind, it was a brilliant plan to generate a steady flow of income—cash has always been in short supply in North Korea—while being in an ideal position to hurt America without any suspicions falling on them. The Supreme Leader had approved.

Despite his native Chinese nationality, Qiu remained loyal to Pyongyang—and Seo—making him the ideal person to run Song Motors. In return, they compensated him with a seven-figure salary and a penthouse apartment with a chef, a Bentley GT in the garage, and a ceremonial rank of major in the North Korean army.

A loud knock on the door broke Qiu out of his reverie. "Come in," he said in English.

Elena Natase, who went by a dozen different names that included Cynthia Blackwood, stepped through the doorway. She stood a statuesque five-ten, which made her taller than most of the men she encountered in China. Her generous curves, high cheekbones, catlike green eyes, and full ruby lips had compromised many powerful men in her past.

"What do you want?" she asked.

"I'm glad you could make it out of Los Angeles. We couldn't wait for you. Please sit down," Qiu said, gesturing toward one of his ornate and hideously expensive custom-made Power Play Club chairs.

Natase sat and crossed her long legs, exposing a fair amount of skin.

Qiu pretended not to notice. "What does the colonel have planned for me? Am I to be punished? You know that none of what happened in Los Angeles is my fault."

"Is that why you called me here? Why don't you ask him yourself when he gets here?" she responded in Mandarin.

Qiu shifted uneasily in his chair. He wasn't accustomed to being talked to in such a disrespectful manner, especially by a woman, but he knew she held his fate in the palm of her slender hands. And he also knew that she was not one to be crossed.

Her true identity was a closely guarded secret, with only a handful of people even knowing about her existence. She went by many names, and not even Qiu knew which was her real one. Colonel Seo had confided in him that Natase was one of the Supreme Leader's favorite concubines, who also doubled as his most lethal assassin.

According to Seo, the president of Belarus gave her to him as a gift during an official state visit. Natase, who hailed from Klichaw, just west of Minsk, was a member of the Belarusian KGB, and her expertise in killing, disguise and seduction made her a valuable asset for the Supreme Leader.

The phone on Qiu's desk buzzed. He pressed the speaker button and leaned toward the microphone. "Yes?"

"Ambassador Seo is on his way up," his secretary said.

Qiu turned to Natase. "The colonel is here. Please, support me."

Natase laughed. "You're on your own."

The office door swung open. But instead of Colonel Seo, Major Jong-Su Kang entered. He wore a black suit over his stocky, muscular frame, and when taken in together with his dark aviator sunglasses and buzzed haircut, he looked every bit the part of an Asian gangster. But his most distinguishing feature was the long vertical scar that crossed his lips.

"Ah, Major Kang, I see you made it back from Los Angeles safe and sound," Qiu said in Kang's native Korean.

"Yes. I was able to board the same flight as Ms. Elena late last night," Kang said as he performed a quick visual survey of the room, then stepped aside for his boss to enter.

Dressed in baggy pants and a white button-down shirt, Ambassador Chol-Min Seo, who preferred being addressed by his military title, entered the room. He was on the thin side and, at five-foot-eight-inches, stood significantly taller than the average North Korean. While his facial complexion and slick black hair made him appear younger than his fifty-eight years, his body showed signs of age. A critical case of gout in his knees made him bend slightly at the waist when he walked. But when he spoke, he did so forcefully, whether the language was his native Korean or several other tongues that he spoke proficiently.

Seo looked at Natase and addressed her in English. "The Supreme Leader sends his regards. He says he is looking forward to seeing you again very soon."

Natase smiled, and it seemed sincere. "I look forward to seeing him, too. Please tell him I miss him very much."

After taking a seat in another Power Play Club chair, Seo eyed Qiu. "You are lucky to still be alive, Xavier. Your incompetence deserves a thousand painful deaths. The Supreme Leader is very unhappy, as am I."

Qiu wanted to drop to his knees and plead forgiveness, but he held firm, deciding that showing strength now would serve him better.

"Colonel Seo, I did everything you instructed. It is not my fault. The Muslims bungled this mission. It was they who revealed the bomb to the Americans. If everything had gone according to plan, the West would be in a panicked state right now."

The ambassador wagged his finger. "You should watch your words. It was your idea to work with them, so the responsibility ultimately lies with you. You promised a magnificent explosion in the middle of a densely populated American city, with thousands of casualties and the deaths of the leaders of the world's largest car companies, and you did not deliver."

Qiu took a deep breath to calm his nerves. "You are right, of course. What do you ask of me now, colonel?"

"The Supreme Leader has instructed me to shut down Song Motors, at least for the time being. We can't have anyone investigating the company and tying it to the DPRK. To avoid any more scrutiny, we need to offer the world a fall guy, and the Supreme Leader wishes you to fulfill that role."

Seo's words sent Qiu into a quiet panic. "This is inconceivable. I am a global personality, and my absence will be noted. Is there no other way?"

The old man sighed. "There is no other way, regrettably, but don't worry. We'll push the story that your health has taken a nose-dive and that you're resigning immediately to have long-term care. You will be forgotten in due time once Song Motors has disappeared from the scene."

Qiu could have sworn that he heard Natase giggle.

"You will hide in North Korea until this auto show bungle blows over. Once the Muslims carry out their backup attack on America—if the Supreme Leaders so designates—our people here will establish your innocence so that you can return to Beijing within a half year."

Six months. It seemed like a long time to spend in Pyongyang, but in the grand scheme of things, it was something he could endure. "Will I be allowed to keep my title and possessions?"

"I don't see why not. We still have significant influence over many Chinese politicians. You will return a hero," Seo reassured him.

A smile crept onto Qiu's face. "Thank you, *sifu*. And thank you, Supreme Leader," he said, looking upward.

"We have already prepared your statement. We're tying the bomb in Los Angeles to the Aqarib, who have agreed to take responsibility. We're saying that it was just a terrible coincidence that the bomb was placed in a Song Motors vehicle, and the company regrets the damage and loss of life."

Major Kang leaned in and whispered into Seo's ear. After a nod, Seo said to Qiu, "Jong-Su tells me that a journalist named Mack Katana played a part in foiling the Aqarib's plot. Have you heard of him?"

"Yes. He harassed me at the dinner," Qiu answered. "A very unpleasant fellow."

"We've been told by our assets in America that his real name is Maximilian Koga, and he is employed by a secret private military contractor working for the CIA."

" I ... I did not know, of course," Qiu stammered.

"Of course you didn't," Seo snapped. "We know this, and many other urgent things. Which reminds me, Elena, there is a job that I will need your help with," Seo said, turning to Natase.

"How may I be of service?" she asked.

"One of our assets in Beijing has betrayed us, and I would like for you to be present when I invite him to lunch."

Chapter 35

State Council member Wang Wéi stood outside the Great Hall of the People, the center of the Chinese government on the western edge of Tiananmen Square. Dressed in a baggy navy suit, blue tie, and a light overcoat draped across the shoulders, he casually puffed on a Zhonghua cigarette, his fifth of the young day. The smoking and daily consumption of Irish whiskey for the past thirty years had taken their toll on his appearance, and they marked his face with deep wrinkles and pockmarks. The hair on his head was nearly gone.

A white Rolls-Royce Phantom turned onto his street, prompting Wang to flick his cigarette butt into the air and pat down his comb-over with both hands. The car pulled to a stop, and the driver, a young man in his twenties dressed in a black suit, white gloves, and a cap, bolted from the driver's seat and hustled to open the curbside rear door for him.

Wang peered into the empty rear cabin of the car. "Is the ambassador not here? We were supposed to be having lunch together."

The driver bowed. "I truly beg your pardon, sir, but Ambassador Seo was running late, so he asked me to take you directly to his villa. You will dine with him there."

Wang nodded, then bent and stepped into the plush confines of the Rolls, appreciating the soft beige aniline leather and glossy wood.

The driver closed the rear door and returned to his seat. Without as much as a look at his passenger in the mirror, he drove the Phantom away from the curb and into Beijing's congested streets. Wang felt the smooth power delivery of the vehicle and wondered if such a car would ever be in his future.

After a commute of less than fifteen minutes, the Rolls pulled into a gated entrance in the Chaoyang District, near the Third Ring Road.

Seven Ring Roads encircle Beijing. The First Ring Road, built in the 1950s to ease traffic in the inner city, was a small highway that circumscribed the city center. A second, larger ring followed, then a third, and so on. The Ring Roads serve as handy reference points for locals and visitors—the higher the designation of the Ring, the further you were from the city center.

The Rolls-Royce Phantom stopped in front of a large, Victorian-style, three-story mansion with a small carport. It was the first time Wang had visited Chol-Min Seo's home, and he wondered how many more secret villas the North Koreans possessed in China.

The driver killed the engine and jumped out of the car to open the door for the ambassador's guest. As Wang lifted himself from the seat, he noticed three more Rolls-Royces parked along the driveway, each a different model and color.

As millions die of starvation in his country, he and the ruling party live like kings, Wang thought. *Disgusting.*

As he stepped out of the car, Wang was met by Elena Natase, special assistant to the ambassador. What her actual function was remained a mystery to Wang, but she was pleasant to the eyes, so he suspected what some of her jobs entailed. He never objected to her presence.

"Welcome, Councilman Wang," she said in English. "Allow me to take your jacket. Colonel Seo is waiting for you inside."

"It's nice to see you again, Ms. Natase," Wang said, wriggling out of his Prada overcoat. "You know you're welcome to join my office if you ever get bored with the good ambassador."

"I'll keep that in mind, Councilman," she said as they entered the seven-bedroom, ten-bath residence. They walked down a spiral staircase that led to a private meeting room below ground, where she motioned Wang to enter.

Ambassador Seo greeted him inside dressed in his formal Korean People's Army uniform, complete with several rows of obscure, jangling medals and awards he didn't earn. He sat at a round meeting table with Chien Ning, the Minister of Finance for the People's Republic of China.

"Welcome, Mister Wang," Seo greeted. "Please come in and have a seat."

"I didn't expect China's finance minister to be joining us. This is a power lunch if I've ever seen one," Wang said.

Seo laughed out loud. "Well put. I thought it was important for us to discuss the atrocities that occurred in America yesterday, but let us save the shop talk and first eat."

He clapped his hands loudly and two female servers, both dressed in revealing black-and-white outfits, appeared from an adjoining room to place the food in front of the men.

When the food was devoured and plates cleared, Seo turned to the finance minister. "Mr. Chien, our Supreme Leader is very much interested in keeping your government and the Americans from investigating Song Motors. He hoped you can help with that."

Chien crossed his arms. "The simplest and most effective solution would be to shut down the company immediately. Desist, deny, and disappear. In Wuhan several years back, my government did the first two, but couldn't shut the virus lab down in time, which proved costly indeed."

Wanting to take part in the conversation, Wang offered his two cents. "Yes, the Wuhan lab was under so much scrutiny already that shutting it down then would have been taken as an admission of guilt."

"Without a doubt," Chien remarked. "Let's not make that mistake again. Before any dogs come sniffing, shut down the company, colonel, and your Supreme Leader should have nothing to worry about. It's early enough that I can publicly say we dealt with the problem in-house, and our politicians won't need to be involved."

Seo rubbed his chin. "That's a shame. We worked so hard for this, but we can't have your colleagues getting wind of our activities, much less the world, so we will follow your recommendations. We have also prepared someone to take the blame—the president of the company, no less. The Supreme Leader will be very grateful, as your bank account will soon show."

"*Gamsahamnida*," both men said. Thank you.

Putting his wine glass down, Seo leaned forward in his chair. "I have more worrisome news to report. Someone from our organization, or yours, is supplying information to the Americans, specifically to the FBI. This was what led to our problems in Los Angeles. Do any of you know anything about this?"

"Are you implying that there is an American spy in the Chinese government?" Chien asked.

"Not directly, minister. It could easily be someone inside our organization," Seo said.

"What sort of information was passed along?" Wang asked.

"Nothing too sensitive," Seo said. "But enough to have them piece together the connection between the Tangs and Song Motors."

Wang glanced at his Audemars Piguet chronograph. "If I may beg your pardon, colonel, I just remembered I have another appointment that I am late for. Can you please excuse me?"

Seo smiled. "Of course. Thank you for joining us. The Supreme Leader has been appreciative of your cooperation over the years."

"The pleasure has been mine." Wang stood up from his chair and bowed to both men. After taking the stairs up to the ground floor, he grabbed his coat and stepped outside, looking for his ride back to his office.

A bead of sweat ran down the side of his face.

Wang had thought he had taken every precaution, but now he was in danger of being exposed. The only thought in his mind was getting back home and destroying any evidence that linked him to the American FBI agent Beth Hu.

Chapter 36

Waiting for Wang Wéi in the driveway outside Seo's residence was Elena Natase, her black leather boots accentuating her long, perfect legs. "Councilman, our driver is still on his break, so I'll be driving you," she said.

"Fine," he responded. "Can you please take me to my office? I'm late for an important meeting."

She led him to a different Rolls-Royce Phantom, this one red in color, and opened the rear door for him. Wang stepped inside as Natase slid into the driver's seat.

"Please fasten your seatbelt," she said into the rearview mirror.

Natase skillfully guided the large sedan through Beijing's crisscrossing streets, driving with remarkable precision, slicing her way between other cars, scooters, and pedestrians. As they approached the Great Hall of the People, Natase failed to slow down, overshooting the road that led to the entrance of the grand building.

"You were supposed to turn over there," Wang said.

Without responding, Natase instead pushed a button on the dashboard. Wang's seatbelt shoulder strap snapped tightly around his chest, enough to squeeze most of the air out of his lungs.

"*Shénme gu?*" he asked, struggling to free his arm. "What is the meaning of this?"

He reached for the seatbelt buckle with his free hand to undo the latch, but it was stuck in place. When he reached for the door handle, he found that it had been disconnected inside the door.

He was trapped.

In a calm voice, Natase said, "We have at least a two-hour drive ahead of us, councilman, and I would prefer to spend it quietly. You have the option of keeping your mouth shut, or I can help you be silent. Your choice, sir."

Wang struggled to free himself. "I don't know what you're up to, but you're committing a grave crime. You'll go to prison for this."

Natase sighed and pulled the car to the side of the road. She reached over into the glove box and pulled out a large syringe. Propping herself on her knees atop the driver's seat, she faced Wang and stabbed the needle into his thigh.

"What are you doing?" Wang cried, fear clouding his eyes. "If it's money you want, I can arrange it." He started feeling the effects of the drug before the needle was pulled from his leg.

Natase laughed out loud. "Oh, councilman, you couldn't hope to afford me in a thousand lifetimes."

As Wang felt the anesthesia take control, his desperate cry turned into a long, low moan. His body numbed, and he sank into a dreamless slumber.

"If you have a moment, I'd love to show you the Supreme Leader's car collection," Chol-Min Seo said to Minister Chien Ning after Wang had left the room.

Chien removed the cloth napkin from his lap. "I would be honored."

"Splendid. Then follow me." Seo stood up and made his way up the staircase one step at a time. The gout in his knees made the task difficult, but he was determined to get to the top without stopping.

"You should put an elevator in here, ambassador," Chien said.

"Nonsense," Seo said, ignoring the man's obvious discomfort. "It's good to get the exercise."

They stepped into the backyard, featuring a fountain with a statue of Ts'ai Shen, the Chinese god of wealth, in the middle of a small garden. Seo headed toward a large detached garage at the rear of the property, where he punched in an eight-digit code on the wall-mounted control panel. The garage door rose, revealing a dozen classic cars resting inside. "These are the Supreme Leader's latest toys. What do you think, minister?"

There, on the polished concrete floor, were four pre-war era Rolls-Royces, a 1972 Lamborghini Miura, and a gull-winged 1955 Mercedes-Benz 300SL. A coveted 1967 Ferrari P4 sat in the back under a fine layer of dust.

"They are truly magnificent," Chien said. "I myself have a Lamborghini, but it's a Gallardo that I keep in Hong Kong. My true baby is a Nio EP9, but the rest are junk."

He walked among Seo's collection with reverence, not daring to even touch the paint, but bending at the waist to peer into the cabins.

Seo beamed. "Yes, he is quite proud of them. I picked these out for him myself. I think the Miura might be his favorite now."

Chien walked up to a 1931 Rolls-Royce Phantom II, admiring its classic bodywork. "These cars were truly mechanical pieces of art. Nothing like my crappy old Russian Ladas. You have exquisite taste, ambassador—as does the Supreme Leader, of course."

Seo looked at his watch. "I'm afraid I must leave you here, for I too must get to an appointment. The Supreme Leader would like to show his appreciation for your help, so please choose one of the Rolls-Royces as his gift."

Chien turned to Seo, genuinely surprised at the offer. "You must be joking. He has been so generous already. It's really unnecessary."

"Please, minister," he insists. "And we are relying on your continued support, especially regarding your government's new financial-aid package," Seo said.

"Then, if you don't mind, I will take this Phantom II. But how will I get this home? I dare not drive it on public roads."

"Do not worry, minister. We will have it transported to anywhere you like," Seo responded, patting Chien on the back.

"I am humbled by your generosity," the Chinese councilman replied, bowing slightly.

Seo nodded and gestured for his assistant, Major Jong-Su Kang, who drove up in a late-model Rolls-Royce Ghost. "We are needed at the farmhouse," Seo said, slipping into the rear seat of the car. "But no need to hurry. Let's take the scenic route."

The large sedan rode the city's uneven roads like a luxury cruise ship on choppy waters; its ride quality was as smooth as the finest Chinese silk. Before long, they had made it outside Beijing's Seventh Ring, where rolling hills and vast farmlands replaced the sea of concrete buildings. As the peaceful pastoral setting blurred past his window, the soft classical music emanating from the car's Bespoke audio system lulled him to sleep.

Nearly three hours later, the sound of crunching gravel roused Seo from his slumber, signaling that they had arrived at their destination. Kang guided the car onto a private road that led to a small farm, its entrance manned by a trio of men hiding pistols under their belts.

They took one look at Kang and waved him to drive the Rolls-Royce onto the property.

The car pulled to a stop in front of the main house, next to the red Phantom that had been driven by Natase. When Seo stepped out of his car, Elena was there to greet him.

"Have a pleasant trip?" she asked.

"Was the councilman any trouble?"

"Not at all. He's ready for you."

"Excellent. General Kim should be here any moment now," Seo said.

As if on cue, a gray Mercedes-Maybach sedan appeared on the driveway and stopped a few feet away from where Seo and Natase stood. The young driver, dressed in a black suit, rushed to the rear of the car to open the car door for a man in his late sixties with a thin frame and thick graying hair, wearing a loose V-neck sweater and baggy khakis. His short, flat nose supported gold-framed spectacles that made his eyes appear unnaturally large.

"Welcome, general," Seo said. "I hope you had a comfortable trip."

Army General Kim Yon-Ja, the third uncle of the Supreme Leader and the current chief interrogator for the DPRK government, stepped into the bright midday sun and stretched out his arms.

"A wonderful day for a death, is it not, colonel?" he said with a smile that showed off his gold-capped teeth.

Chapter 37

Ambassador Chol-Min Seo showed General Kim Yon-Ja the utmost respect, as did everyone else in the North Korean hierarchy. One bad word from him to the Supreme Leader would mean a one-way ticket to a labor camp. If you were lucky, you would be killed on the spot.

"You look very well," Seo said.

"I see you gained some weight, colonel," Kim responded in Korean. "You need to lay off the cognacs." The old man then looked at Elena Natase. "You, on the other hand, look as vibrant as ever, my dear. When will you be visiting the Supreme Leader again?"

"When this incident is cleared up, I shall fly into his arms at the first opportunity," she said in slightly accented Korean.

Kim clapped his hands together. "So, shall we proceed to our subject? The Supreme Leader is insistent that our traitor suffers greatly."

"He's all prepped and ready for you in the barn," Seo said.

"Excellent. Take me to him."

Seo guided Kim, who walked with a cane, to a large wooden shack at the rear of the property. Inside, Councilman Wang Wéi sat tied to a chair, wearing only his white underpants. Jong-Su Kang stood by his side.

Wang's face went pale when he saw Kim enter the barn. "Please have mercy," he cried.

Kim scoffed as he approached the prisoner. "Do you think you can play double agent with us and get away with it? You are a fool. You shall die slowly and painfully. I'm sure you're familiar with the process known as 'death by a thousand cuts?'"

Being a student of history, Seo indeed was familiar with the torture technique, although he had never seen it carried out. Officially known as Lingchi, it was a form of execution practiced in ancient China that was reserved for the nastiest of criminals. In some Chinese dynasties, it was deemed too cruel and was banned. Lingchi consisted of inflicting cuts to the arms, legs, and chest of the victim with a sharp knife over three to four days, followed by shaving off the nose and ears and then amputating all four limbs. If the person sentenced to this torture still survived, they lopped the head off as a grand finale.

Wang struggled to break himself free, his breaths coming in short spurts. Liquid feces soiled his white underwear and dripped from the chair to the floor.

Kim walked over to a table where a quartet of different-sized knives had been laid in a neat line. "I don't get to practice this one much, so it'll serve as a nice refresher," he said.

To keep Wang from screaming, Kang stuffed a rolled-up handkerchief into his mouth. "This should keep you quiet."

Holding up a hot soldering iron, Kim said to Wang, "I will be merciful and start with your eyes so you won't have to see your body being carved up."

In a warped display of showmanship, Kim dipped the tip of the soldering iron into a small bowl of water, which sizzled upon contact with the hot metal. Kim then held the soldering iron to Wang's face. He hesitated only a moment for Wang to feel the heat and stoke fear, and with one quick thrust, he stabbed the tip into the councilman's right eye. Kim stopped short of pushing it all the way in, instead only inserting the first inch. Wang screamed and his head jerked violently against the leather straps.

"I won't pull it out just yet. I want you to feel the metal inside your skull," Kim said with a smile.

Seo looked away in disgust and noticed that Natase too was averting her eyes from the demonstration.

"Please pay attention," Kim commanded his audience. "It's important to me that you watch." He yanked the iron out. "And learn."

Wang had passed out from the pain.

It was obvious from the gleeful look on Kim's face that he was enjoying himself.

The air reeked of burned flesh, causing Seo to become slightly nauseous. "Shall we wait until he regains consciousness before we continue, general?"

"Yes, there's no sense to this if the subject isn't awake to know what's happening to him," Kim said.

Natase stepped boldly forward. "Why don't we just shoot him in the head and get it over with? Do we really need all of this drama? And if you insist on torturing him, why not waterboard him or bury him alive? It's much less messy and a lot quieter."

Kim's face turned red with anger, his eyes bulging halfway out of their sockets. He took his walking stick and sent it crashing down onto Natase's shoulder, causing her to fall to the ground.

"How *dare* you," he shouted.

Seo jumped in and grabbed the stick from the old man. "Please, general—the Supreme Leader will be furious if you mark up his most prized possession."

"Are you betraying me too, colonel?" Kim asked with a hard look.

"Of course not, but she does not fully understand our ways."

After taking a deep breath, Kim collected himself. "You're right, of course. I get very emotional with my work. She should not be here if she lacks the stomach for it."

"I totally agree," Seo said, handing the old man his cane back.

"I'm so sorry," Natase said. "I just wanted to do what was right for the Supreme Leader."

The sight of the beautiful woman pleading for forgiveness seemed to soften the old man's heart. Kim bent down and stroked her cheek with the back of his wrinkled hand. "I apologize for striking you, but never pass judgment on my work again."

"You are merciful. I'll never disappoint you again, general," she answered.

Kim turned to Seo. "Let me know when the traitor is awake so that I can continue my work. In the meantime, I will rest in the main house." He gestured to Seo. "Show me to my room."

"Of course," Seo answered, hurrying over to the side of the general.

As they walked to the house, Kim spoke to him in a low voice. "I sense something false in that girl. Something about her isn't right. If I were you, I'd keep a watchful eye on that one."

Chapter 38

The Ford Explorer sped down the San Diego Freeway at ninety miles per hour. With both hands on the wheel and his gaze on the road ahead, Koga said to Beth Hu, "I'm taking you to a sensitive location, so I need to trust you to keep quiet about it. I need your word."

Beth said nothing.

"Your word," Koga repeated.

"I'm thinking," she answered. Then, "Okay. I promise."

Just to be safe, though, Koga took a few extra side streets after exiting the freeway to make it difficult for Beth to retrace his route later, should it come to that. When they arrived at the abandoned office complex dubbed The Warehouse, the hour was nearing 0500. Koga braked the Explorer to a stop when he noticed that the chain-link gate that led to the facility was open slightly, with no guard in sight.

"We have trouble," he said, pulling out his handgun.

"What's wrong?" Beth asked.

"The facility has been compromised," Koga said. "Let me check things out first. You stay here and call for help if I don't return in six minutes."

"Like hell I am. I'm coming with you," she responded, unbuckling her seatbelt and drawing her Glock.

Knowing that Beth was more than capable of taking care of herself—and that she was as stubborn as a mule—Koga gave in without resistance. "Okay. Keep behind me and cover my six."

They stepped out of the vehicle, careful to leave their doors open. Koga took the lead, hurrying to the front gate with his firearm in the high ready position, while Beth flanked his rear. Taking shelter behind the corner of a wall, Koga peeked inside and saw Argon's unmarked white delivery truck and three employee cars parked in the lot, one of which was Brian Panackia's GMC Denali.

"I'm going to check out the vehicles. Cover me," he said.

Koga scurried to the truck, placing his hand on its hood. It was cold, indicating that the vehicle had been sitting there for at least thirty minutes. He then moved to the rear of the truck and unlatched its rear roll-up door, throwing it open while pointing his pistol forward. There, inside the cargo space, was the front gate guard lying face up with several red spots on his uniform. Next to him were two other security men who patrolled the perimeter of the grounds, both shot in the same manner.

With his senses heightened, Koga moved quickly to the entrance of The Warehouse, where he immediately noticed the security video cameras lying in pieces on the ground. Using hand gestures to silently instruct Beth to watch the entrance, Koga made his way down the short flight of steps that led to the main door of the building. As he'd anticipated, the keypad on the wall was destroyed.

Slowly pushing on the unlocked door, Koga paused before stepping inside. He allowed his eyes to adjust to the dark interior, then entered. A quarter of the way down the hallway, he saw Brian Panackia lying face down on the carpeted floor. His head rested in a small pool of blood, his eyes wide open, staring blankly at nothing, a single gunshot wound at the base of the skull. There was no need to check for a pulse.

Shot from behind, perhaps execution style. He didn't deserve this.

He recalled Panackia mentioning a wife and a teenage kid. Although Koga knew he would feel sorrow later, his mind and body wouldn't let him dwell on that now. He remained alert while doing his best to suppress the growing anger building within, at least for now.

The first room on the right was the security room, which was empty. A quick sweep of the kitchen and a peek inside Panackia's office showed both undisturbed. Koga proceeded to the interrogation room dubbed the Karaoke Box at the end of the hallway. The door to the room was slightly ajar, casting a sliver of white light across the hallway floor.

In a fluid motion, Koga flung the door open and jumped inside, landing on one knee, his gun held out in front of him, ready to put down anything that moved. Nothing did.

Two men occupied the room, both dead. Abdul Hassan and Yousef Badawi sat in plastic chairs in the middle of the square chamber with their arms bound behind their backs and their heads thrown back. Lurid gashes stretched across the width of their throats, and red pools of blood had spread across the floor around them.

Koga took in the scene. Damn it.

"I'm sorry, Abdul," he said aloud as he walked up to Hassan and closed the dead man's eyes, genuinely remorseful that his life did not end happily. "I'm so sorry."

Koga inspected the rest of the facility, including the other holding chambers, but nothing else had been disturbed. Whoever had infiltrated The Warehouse did so for the sole reason to eliminate these two men. He returned to the entrance, where Beth had kept watch.

"Well, what did you find?" she asked when seeing him approach.

"Our assets are dead. I'm going to call this in. Oh, and thanks for the lift. I'll be in touch," Koga said, discreetly suggesting Beth take her leave.

Ignoring him, Beth took a couple of steps into the hallway.

"Where do you think you're going?" Koga asked, blocking her path.

"I'd like to have a look, too," she said. "Maybe I can help. Give and take, that's how a partnership works, you know."

"Since when are we partners?"

"I distinctly recall you saying earlier that you owed me one for saving your hide."

Koga sighed. "Okay, follow me," he said, leading her in.

With a smile, Beth followed him through the open doorway and into the building.

"Please watch your step," Koga cautioned, pointing to Panackia. "He was a good man."

When they entered the interrogation room, Beth gasped at the grisly sight of the two men seated in their chairs with their throats slit.

"How long ago do you think this happened?" she asked.

"I'm no coroner, but at least two hours. Rigor has already set in."

"Which means, around the time we were at the Convention Center."

"Whoever did this ..." Koga growled, but stopped short when his eye caught an object inside the breast pocket of Badawi's blood-stained shirt. Using the ends of his index and middle finger to keep from putting his prints on it, he pulled out a crumpled piece of thick paper.

"What is it?" Beth asked.

Carefully placing it on the table, Koga used the butt of his gun handle to flatten out the paper, risking DNA contamination, but at least it was minimized.

"It's a loyalty coupon card," he said. "There's no blood on it, so odds are that it was placed there after he died."

Beth walked up to the table. "A loyalty card for what?"

"A restaurant called Carlos D's Mexican Cuisine. There's a stamp of a small taco in one of six boxes, so I guess if you eat there six times, your next meal is free."

"I wonder if it's some kind of trap or a sick joke," Beth remarked.

The wheels in Koga's mind began churning. "Have you ever heard of this place?" he asked.

"Carlos D's? No."

"That makes two of us. Let's move," Koga said, heading for the door.

As they returned to the Explorer, Koga took out his cellphone and reported his findings to Paul Verdy.

"Panackia ... what a tragic loss," Verdy said somberly afterward. "I'm going to send Etienne over there to clean up the place and lock it down. Wait for his team to get there before you go. As of this moment, The Warehouse is officially closed."

"Any word on Donnie?" asked Max.

"The good news is that he's out of surgery. The bad news is he's still unconscious. Doctors are giving him a fifty-fifty chance of pulling through."

"I see. Thanks," Koga said.

Verdy continued. "Ed Womack and Andrew Roberts requested a meeting tomorrow morning. You remember them, right? They want to hear firsthand what happened at the auto show. I'll need you there, and I need you to be sharp, so go get some rest."

"I'd love to, boss, but I'm afraid that will not happen tonight. I think we found a clue, and it'd be bad manners if we didn't check it out."

Chapter 39

An unmarked black Mercedes-Benz van pulled into The Warehouse parking lot thirty minutes after Max Koga's call with Paul Verdy. In the driver's seat was Etienne Bablot, a veteran of France's Special Operations Command. Seated next to him was Al Marks, an ex-CSI officer who'd had a short stint with the FBI. It was the first time Koga had met either of them.

"I wish the circumstances were different, but I'm glad to meet you," Koga said to Bablot through the open driver-side window, shaking hands.

"Likewise," responded Bablot in a slight French accent. "Leave the rest to us. Pity about Brian. He was *bonhomme*, a good-natured man indeed."

"Yeah."

After the van parked in an open space, Koga closed the gate and walked over to the Explorer where Beth Hu waited in the driver's seat.

"Can I offer you a lift?" she asked.

"No, I'm good, thanks." He pointed to his Lexus. "My car is here."

"Did you want to grab breakfast?"

Koga thought about that for a moment, then answered, "Actually, I do. There's a Mexican restaurant in Long Beach I'm thinking of trying out."

Beth smiled. "Well, what a coincidence. I was thinking of exactly the same place. I'll follow you there."

Carlos D's Mexican Cuisine was on Second Street in Belmont Shore, the fashionable part of Long Beach filled with trendy eateries and bars. Beth stopped the Explorer behind Koga's Lexus RC F in front of the storefront where a neon *OPEN* sign flashed in the window.

"Head on a swivel," Koga said as they walked toward the restaurant together.

"Not my first rodeo," Beth responded.

A bell attached to the top of the door tinkled as they walked into the restaurant. A chalkboard sign had the morning breakfast specials and invited them to seat themselves.

The dining area was larger than it appeared from the outside, with seating for about fifty customers. The place was clean, and the air smelled of freshly baked tortillas and bread. On the far wall was a large Mexican flag. The near wall had a dozen framed photographs of the store's celebrity clientele. They were mostly autographed headshots of TV stars and athletes, friends of the owners, but one image in particular caught Koga's eye.

They stepped up to the counter to order from a young woman with a big smile and an old-school restaurant order pad.

"What would you like, sweetie?" she asked Beth.

Beth turned to Koga, who was studying the menu behind the counter. "What are you going to have?"

Koga scanned the specials list. "Let's see. I guess I'll have the chorizo burrito."

"Going with the gut bomb, I see. You're meaner'n me. I'll do the egg-white *rancheros*," she said, putting a hand in her pants pocket. The counter girl made a few fast marks on the order pad, ripped the page off in one pull and stuck it to a carousel of other orders in the window looking into the kitchen.

Beth took out her wallet, but Koga motioned at her. "Please, I got it. Chivalry is not dead."

"Why, thank you, squire," she said, smiling. "I'll find us a place to sit."

Koga grabbed two cups of hot coffee and a table number stand, taking them on a fiberglass tray to the corner booth where Beth sat facing the entry door.

"Looks like a normal restaurant," she said as Koga slid into the seat across from her. "I asked our office to check out this place, but so far, nothing."

Scanning the room, Koga saw a few patrons sipping coffee and an elderly woman warming tortillas on a large, round flattop behind the counter. "I'll be right back," he said, getting up and walking toward the kitchen.

After smiling and saying "good morning" to the tortilla maker, Koga stepped into the open kitchen, where three cooks were busy preparing food orders. He peeked through an open doorway that looked like the stock room, seeing a large refrigerator with glass doors. Like Beth said, there was nothing out of the ordinary here.

"Maybe you were right," he said to Beth upon returning to his seat. "That loyalty card could've been just some sick joke."

They sipped coffee until Juanita emerged with their breakfast orders, placing the larger of the two plates in front of Max.

"They're hot, so be careful. Chili sauce and extra napkins are here. I'll bring refills on your coffee," she said.

The smell of chorizo, eggs, and melted cheese stuffed inside a freshly baked tortilla made Koga's stomach growl, reminding him he hadn't had a proper meal for two days. Without waiting for Beth, he grabbed his fork and went to work. "Now that's what I call comfort food," he said between mouthfuls.

"But you're Japanese-American. Isn't comfort food more like rice and *miso* soup?"

"That, too," Koga said without pausing. "And Spam *musubis*." He had cleared his entire plate before Beth had finished half of hers.

"My God, you inhaled that," she said.

"Do you still visit your mother in Boston?" Koga asked.

Beth paused. "You've been researching me, I see. That means you probably know about my father."

Koga nodded.

"If you're wondering if I ever found out what happened to him, the answer is no," she said.

Before Koga could say anything more, Juanita reappeared to top off their coffee cups. He turned toward her and asked. "Is the owner here? I'd like to give him my regards for the wonderful meal."

"Oh, that is so nice, thanks. Carlos won't be in until about noon, but I'll let him know," she said with a smile.

"How long has this place been open? I saw on Yelp that it has a perfect rating."

"About four years. Yes, we are grateful for the support of happy customers here."

Koga pointed to the wall with the photos. "There are so many celebrities. By the way, who is the man in that one at the top, third from the right? He looks vaguely familiar."

Juanita looked over and counted the images with her hands. "Oh, that's Carlos's father. He's some big shot in Mexico."

"You don't say? Thanks again. You can bet we'll be coming again."

"*Muchas gracias.*" Juanita smiled and returned to the kitchen.

Beth stared at Koga through a wisp of steam rising from her coffee. She wore an amused look on her face. "You should have asked her out. I think she likes you."

"Don't be silly. She was just doing her job."

"Well, this place turned out to be a dead end," Beth said, wiping her mouth with a napkin. "At least the food was good."

He felt he should tell Beth what he had just discovered, but it was important that he proceed alone from here on. Four Argon personnel and two high-value assets were dead because of a leak from within the FBI, CIA, or Argon. Although he trusted her for the most part, he kept to himself that their impromptu breakfast stop had produced the biggest clue yet in tracking down Nasim al-Ahmed.

Chapter 40

Max Koga arrived thirty minutes early for his meeting with FBI Director Ed Womack and CIA Chief Operating Officer Andrew Roberts, the second in as many days. The sit-down was scheduled for nine a.m. inside the CIA's secret Los Angeles office on the west side of town, not far from where Koga lived. After driving the Lexus back to his townhouse, he had time for a quick shower and shave before heading to the unlisted location inside the Wells Tower.

It was Koga's first time at the facility. He was instructed to go to the tenth floor, where he was escorted through a metal detector, given a red-rimmed Visitor badge, and led to a small conference room with a dozen chairs placed around a long rectangular wooden table. There were no windows, and the gray walls were completely bare.

Relieved that he was the first to arrive, Koga took a seat at the far end of the table. A few minutes later, Paul Verdy walked in, followed by Womack and Roberts.

"Thank you all for coming on such short notice," Womack said, sitting down at the head of the table. "Let's not waste any time. First, Max, let me commend your quick-thinking actions of last night. Special Agent Hu reported you single-handedly foiled the terrorist plot at the auto show that would have killed hundreds, at least."

Womack reached forward and offered his hand to Koga, who shook it.

"Thank you," Koga responded. "Beth Hu and Don Rawlings deserve more credit than I do. Without them, we'd have a different conversation right now."

"We're all praying for Donald's recovery—and it's abundantly clear now that Argon's continued contribution is vital to national security," Roberts said.

"About that," the FBI director commented. "I do agree that General Verdy and his team did an outstanding job last night, but let me also remind you, two vital assets were eliminated under their protection. As much as I appreciate what they have done, the FBI needs to play the lead role in the Aqarib and Song Motors operation."

"Wait a minute," Verdy said. "We were the ones who found those men in the first place. We're the ones who uncovered the relationship between Song Motors and the Aqarib. How can you take us off the operation? We've been doing all the legwork."

"I never said you were being completely removed from it, Paul, and you aren't. But we can't have a private company taking the lead on a national security matter of this magnitude. It's bad optics. President Pugh agrees that the government needs to take direct control of this now," said Womack.

"Andy, help me out here," Verdy pleaded.

"I'm sorry, Paul, but the President and Ed have a point. The FBI and CIA should be the ones carrying the heavy load from here on, especially after what our sources discovered in Mexico three days ago."

Koga's ears perked. "What happened in Mexico?"

"You weren't supposed to mention that," Womack grunted, shaking his head. "But now that you did, I suppose I should fill you in. There was a large explosion in Durango last night. By the size of it, we believe it could have been the same type of bomb that was in the vehicle Mr. Koga drove into the ocean. Really high-grade stuff."

"It must have been Nasim al-Ahmed, I'm sure of it. What was the target?" Koga asked.

"A drug-processing factory for the Navarro Cartel," Roberts answered. "The cartel boss, Demetrio Navarro, lost his three-year-old son in the blast. Just hours ago, the family swore revenge on the attackers and is ready to start an all-out war on anyone connected with the incident."

"Maybe we should give them a heads up as to who it was," Koga said.

Womack stood and shook his head. "I'm afraid you guys won't be taking point on this after today. We have already made the decision. We'll update you on a need-to-know basis, of course."

"I'm sorry, Paul, it's out of my hands," Roberts said. He stood and shook Verdy's hand. "We know we wouldn't be here without you guys. We, and the nation, are in your debt." Womack and Roberts exited the room.

"Take note, Max, that's what they usually say when they fire you," Verdy said.

A moment later, two CIA agents appeared in the room to escort the Argon men from the building.

Once in the parking lot, Koga said, "So, is that it? We just go home with our units in our hands?"

Verdy ignored the comment, instead reading a text that had just arrived on his cellphone. "It's from Andy Roberts. He says he has our back, and he wants us to know he said those things because it was what Womack wanted to hear. We'll still be involved."

"That's a relief," Koga responded.

"Yeah, well. If he can bullshit Womack, he can bullshit us. Let's see how things shake out."

Verdy's phone chimed again. He looked down and read the incoming message. "We're wanted at the office. Denise and Raj have something to share with us," he said.

An hour later, the two were seated inside Argon's meeting room in the basement of *Automobile Digest*'s photo studio. Denise Johnson was the first to speak.

"When Max told us about the Chinese criminal organization called the Tangs, we started digging up all we could find, but there wasn't much," she said. "But thanks to Raj, he pieced together enough information from blogs, social media posts, and black sites to find that Xavier Qiu was, and probably still is, a high-ranking member of the Tang organization."

"That hardly comes as a surprise," Koga responded. "The FBI already established that Song Motors and the Tangs were connected."

Denise smiled wryly. "But there's more. Raj?"

Raja Singh stood up and switched on one of the video monitors. On the screen appeared an organizational chart of the Tangs. At the very top was the silhouette of a head designating an unknown subject.

"I've pieced together the leadership profile of the Tangs. By all accounts and purposes, Xavier Qiu is not at the top of the food chain," Raja said. "After researching some very hard-to-access Chinese- and Korean-language sites, it was clear that the chain of command for the Tangs ultimately led to not someone in Beijing—but Pyongyang."

Koga sat up in his chair. "You mean to tell me the North Koreans are in bed with the Aqarib too?"

"That's exactly what I'm telling you," Raja said.

"Talk about your marriage made in hell," Verdy said. "A tyrannical dictator and radical Islamic terrorists, both with no regard for international law, who would love nothing more than see the U.S. burn to the ground."

"In a way, it's brilliant," Koga observed. "Buying into an organization like al-Aqarib and dropping them into Mexico within spitting distance of the U.S. border, while they keep their hands clean. Fairly elegant."

Denise said, "This could make Al-Qaeda and ISIS look like minor-league teams. The DPRK has been using Song Motors as their front, raising capital by dealing drugs and running weapons for the past few years, primarily to third-world countries. With the sanctions, they can't raise hard cash any other way. The citizens starve, but at least the money buys more missiles."

"It makes sense. They've been using shell companies for decades to get around sanctions. They're pros at it," Koga said. "What's our move, boss?"

Verdy crossed his arms and looked frustrated. "Sit tight. All we can do right now is wait on Andy Roberts to get us back in the game."

Koga cleared his throat. "Well then, may I ask for a little time off to take care of some personal things?"

Verdy shot him a suspicious look. "Going somewhere?"

Koga shrugged and a half smile creased his face.

"I hear Mexico is quite nice this time of year."

Chapter 41

Nasim al-Ahmed didn't hide his anger when Ramin Madani, his second in command, informed him that their carefully planned bombing of the Los Angeles Auto Show was unsuccessful. The Aqarib leader raged and sprayed a half-dozen rounds from his AR-15 into the garage wall. If there was anything he was thankful for, it was that the traitors, Abdul Hassan, and Yousef Badawi, had been rightly punished.

"Colonel Seo has asked me to announce that we were the ones responsible for the failed bombing attempt in Los Angeles," al-Ahmed said, folding his prayer mat.

He had spent the past hour on the second-story balcony of Mauricio Duarte's summer retreat to cool his head and pray, despite being told to always remain indoors and hidden from the gaze of American spy satellites that could read *The New York Times* in Red Square. The evening was breezy with a crisp bite to the air, and the sky had just turned dark after a brilliant orange-and-purple sunset.

"We have little choice. Two of our men were killed inside the auto show, and who knows what Abdul and Yousef spilled to the Americans? It makes us look quite incompetent," Madani said.

"Yes, you're right. We spent a lot of time and effort on this plan. To see it all come apart like that is disheartening. But all is not lost, my friend. Yes, we shall indeed claim responsibility. Although the attack was unsuccessful, it was bold in design and ingenious in its potential execution, so it sends a powerful message to the Americans and the rest of the world that we're still here."

"You are wise, my leader," Madani said, bowing his head. "*Allahu Akbar!*"

"*Allahu Akbar!*" Al-Ahmed responded, clenching his fists. "But to think that my own cousin betrayed me ..."

"Abdul always did have a weakness for the material things in life."

A knock on the sliding glass door interrupted them. A young man in his late teens and dressed in a military uniform stood at attention.

"Dinner is ready," he said in Arabic.

Al-Ahmed patted his number two on the back. "Let us eat, my friend."

They entered the house and descended the stairs to the dining room on the ground floor at the rear of the mansion. On a large table were plates of grilled chicken and tortillas. When they sat in their seats, Jayson Spence walked into the room, holding a can of Tecate beer and taking a seat at the far end of the table.

"Has Colonel Seo told you how long I need to be here?" Spence asked.

Al-Ahmed adjusted the patch over his blind eye and cast his remaining gaze at the former assistant chief of security at Argon's safehouse. "He did not, but not long, I hope. And how much has the colonel paid you for betraying your colleagues?" he asked in English.

Spence placed his feet on the table. "I wouldn't know. I don't take orders or payouts from the North Koreans. Mine come from someone else."

Al-Ahmed tore off a piece of tortilla and shoved it into his mouth. "I would very much appreciate it if you can take your feet off the table," he said without looking up.

Spence didn't move.

"Whoever you're working for is also being compensated by Colonel Seo, so it matters little how the hierarchy is arranged. And my men told me it was you who executed the two traitors for us. For that, I thank you," Al-Ahmed said.

"Save it. I didn't do it for you. I get paid to follow orders, man, and that was all I was doing. Following orders."

"Won't the American government suspect you, now that you've suddenly disappeared?" Madani asked.

"I asked for a four-day vacation beforehand. By the time I'm supposed to show up for work again, I'll be sipping a beer on a beach in Seychelles, or maybe relaxing somewhere in Fiji."

"Perhaps you needn't travel far. You're a man who doesn't hesitate to kill. We can use a few like you in our organization," al-Ahmed said.

Spence laughed out loud. "As far as I'm concerned, you radical jihadists are the scum of the earth. I'd rather rot in hell than work for you."

Madani sprang from his chair and reached for his pistol. He stopped short when he saw Spence had already drawn his own Glock and had it pointed at his head.

"Please, put away your weapon," al-Ahmed asked Spence, then turned to Madani. "Ramin, sit and calm down," he ordered in Arabic.

Staring hard into Spence's eyes, Madani lifted his hand off the gun and lowered his body into his seat. Spence returned his pistol back to its holster.

"Good," al-Ahmed said. "Mr. Spence, whatever your thoughts are about us, we really don't care. What's important right now is that we help each other out in obtaining our goals."

"If your goal is to defeat the U.S., you'll never do it, and neither will the North Koreans. You guys might hurt us here or there, but there's absolutely no way in the world you can win. Look at what happened to Al-Qaeda and ISIS."

"We're better organized and far more strategic than they ever were. That's why we will prevail."

"Yeah, we'll see. Good luck with that," Spence said, grabbing his can of beer and holding his middle finger up as he stood and left the room.

Madani clenched his teeth. "I dislike sharing a roof with that infidel, and the gall of him to put his feet on the table like that. When can we rid ourselves of him?"

"Be patient," al-Ahmed urged. "Colonel Seo has told me he's arranging for Spence's passage out of Mexico in the next few days. After that, we'll never have to see him again."

"That's welcome news."

"What concerns me more is the woman, Elena Natase. I'm informed she's on her way here to deliver a message from Colonel Seo. Then, supposedly, she's going to America to kill the man who disrupted our attack."

Madani stroked his beard. "I've never met her, but I hear she's quite deadly. And beautiful."

"I've been to the Supreme Leader's palace in North Korea. It's ten times the size of this house, and he had more than twenty women there, all of them with the faces and figures of angels. He's got black women, white, yellow—all types. We'll have our share of them soon as our reward."

"Maybe instead of telling our martyrs that they'll have seventy virgins in heaven, we should tell them they might be reincarnated as the leader of North Korea," Madani said with a chuckle.

"Yes, our recruitment may triple!"

As both men laughed out loud, Mohammed interrupted them again. "Elena Natase has arrived. She requests to meet with you."

"Understood," Madani said, before sending him away with a wave of his hand. "Speak of the devil."

"Interesting choice of words. Let's go see what she has to say and perhaps we can find out a few things from her," al-Ahmed said, rising from his chair.

Chapter 42

Most every major news network looped the feed of the Song SUV being fished out of the Pacific Ocean by a large crane. On his home TV, Max Koga watched reporters describe a foiled terrorist attack on the Santa Monica Pier, where law-enforcement agents killed the perpetrators and heroically forced the bomb into the ocean.

There was only brief mention of the Los Angeles Auto Show. The FBI had put its own spin on the story. As a result, the L.A. show was reopened after a short postponement to pick up machine-gun brass and repair damages, but the press conference of the four car-company presidents was canceled.

When the newscast changed to politics, Koga switched off the television and prepared for his trip to Culiacán, the capital of Sinaloa, Mexico. He experienced a wave of emotion as he recalled the scene back at The Warehouse—the death of Brian Panackia and Abdul Hassan—followed by the memory of his fallen colleagues. Being constantly active the past couple of days had kept his mind engaged on Song Motors and the Aqarib, but the deafening sound of silence brought back the smell of smoke and the images of that grisly day in Topolobampo in a distinctly blue hue.

He headed for the kitchen to pour himself a large glass of whiskey to wash down a Xanax pill to keep his demons at bay when three loud raps sounded on his front door.

In an instant, Koga turned off the living room lights and fetched a Sig Sauer P224 from the nightstand drawer in his bedroom.

Another three knocks.

Taking a position next to the doorway, he asked, "Who is it?"

"It's Beth, Max," said a familiar voice. "Did I come at a bad time?"

Koga relaxed his shoulders and unlocked the deadbolt. "Come in," he said.

The door opened slowly, revealing Beth Hu holding a leather shoulder bag. Her eyes flicked down to the weapon in Koga's hand. "Is that a gun in your hand, or are you just glad to see me?"

"It's only for the pretty ones who show up at my home unannounced."

"I saw the video camera over the door. It's not hooked up?"

"I'm having a new one put in, so no. What are you doing here?"

"I just wanted to talk about the events of last night," she said.

"Don't know if you heard, but we're no longer part of the operation. Your boss saw to that." Koga was still angry about being left on the beach just as the investigation got hotter.

"I heard. That's what I wanted to talk to you about. Nice digs," she said, walking to a bookshelf on the wall.

"Let me get you something to drink," Koga said, walking into the kitchen. He put the pistol in a drawer.

Beth picked up a frame from a shelf and looked at a photo of an Asian man in a racing suit holding up a large trophy.

"Is this your dad?" she asked.

Koga stepped into the room with a couple of Amstel Lites in his hand and smiled. "Yes. That was the last race he won."

"And this must be your grandfather," she said, picking up a framed black-and-white photo of a young soldier surrounded by other Asian men in uniform.

"Yep. Do me a favor, willya? Take a break from the snooping and sit down?" Koga handed her one of the bottles.

She sat on the sofa and Koga took a seat next to her, raising his drink. "Cheers."

They clinked bottles.

"Looks like you're taking a trip," Beth said, pointing to a packed suitcase in the corner of the room.

"I'm taking some personal time off."

Beth laughed. "Okay, sure you are."

She took a swig of her beer and slid her body closer to his, close enough for Koga to smell the sweet aroma of her perfume. She rested her head on his shoulder. He put his arm around her as he took a swig from his beer bottle. She took his hand and pulled it in, pressing it hard to her chest. Instinctively, Koga leaned in and kissed her on the lips. She responded by pressing her lips more forcefully into his. The entire episode took less than ten seconds, but it surprised him at how naturally it happened.

"I'm still not going to tell you where I'm going," he said.

"I think I can take an educated guess," Beth responded, draping her free arm around his neck and placing her legs over his lap without losing control of her beer.

"You know, I'm not that good with relationships," Koga said.

Beth rolled her eyes. "Give me a break." She kissed him again.

Thrusting his arm under her legs, he scooped her up and carried her into the bedroom.

STAGE THREE
South of the Border

Chapter 43

Mauricio Duarte pulled a 1955 Porsche 550 Spyder into his reserved parking spot in front of the Sinaloa government building, a bland three-story concrete structure in downtown Culiacán Rosales, Mexico. His security detail—four heavily armed men in two black armored Mercedes-Benz E-Class sedans—had escorted him from his home three miles away.

Unlike governors before him, Duarte enjoyed driving himself to work every day. He liked to sample the cars in his collection rather than have them collect dust in his garage. "No hangar queens here. Cars are meant to be driven," he often said.

His stable included Porsches old and new, a Lexus LFA, and a Nissan GT-R, but his favorites were the cars from Stuttgart. No one ever questioned where he acquired the money to buy his toys. The official story was that he had cashed in on several offshore real estate investments, but it was common knowledge that his fortune came from playing ball with drug cartels.

After stepping out of the classic German convertible, he walked a few paces and admired the two-seat silver sports car under the morning sun. The light gleamed across its streamlined body, highlighting the sultry curves of the front and rear fenders. He turned to the bodyguards who waited in the sedans next to him.

"Make sure no one gets near this car. One small mark, even a fingerprint, and I'll have you all lined up and shot, understand?" he said in Spanish.

The lead bodyguard nodded lazily from the driver's seat. He had heard the same threat a hundred times before, but replied with his customary enthusiasm.

"*Si, Gobernador—nosotros entendemos.*" We understand.

His executive assistant met Duarte at the entrance door. Bypassing the security line, they took the express elevator reserved for his use alone to the top floor, where a young intern in her early twenties greeted him with her customary smile. She consistently showed up to work in a skin-tight, low-cut dress that showcased her considerable assets. The executive assistant peeled off toward her office and the intern stayed.

"Good morning, Governor," the woman said with a brilliant white smile framed by ruby lips. She smoothed the wrinkles in her dress. "Are we still on for dinner this evening?"

"Ah, Liliana. I had forgotten. I'll clear my schedule. Book our usual room for afterward?" he asked with a wink.

He walked into his office and settled himself behind his desk, tapping the computer's Return key to awaken the device. As he took a sip from his pre-positioned morning espresso, a soft knock sounded at the door.

"*Ingresar,*" he said. Enter.

Liliana's full figure emerged from behind the door, looking as if she had just stepped off the set of a *telenovela* production.

"Sir, there's a reporter from the United States downstairs," she said. "He isn't on the schedule, but he says that it's very important that he interview you for a story. Something about rare Porsches."

Duarte waved his hand. "I have no time for that. Tell him to make an appointment."

"I did, sir, but he was quite insistent. He asked me to hand this to you." Liliana held up an eight-by-ten-inch envelope sealed with Scotch tape.

"Bring it here," he said.

Duarte tore open the envelope and shook out its contents on his pine-wood desk. Out poured a small bound stack of hundred-dollar bills, a set of car keys, and a color photo of an extremely rare 1986 Porsche 959.

He shoved the stack of cash into the top drawer of his desk. "Did you check his credentials?"

Liliana nodded. "I went to his company website, and he appears to be who he says he is."

Duarte crossed his arms. "I suppose it can't be helped. Show him in. What was his name?"

Liliana read the business card. "Mack Katana, editor-at-large for *Automobile Digest*."

The highly collectible Porsche 959, of which only 249 examples were produced, was high on Duarte's wish list. A recent example had fetched two million dollars at an auction in Pebble Beach.

Liliana returned with the guest and left the room. The man appeared to be a Latino at first, but from his last name, Duarte knew him to be Asian. He wore a wrinkled T-shirt and jeans and shouldered a beat-up duffel bag.

"Señor Katana?" Duarte asked.

Katana stuck out his hand. "Yes. Please call me Mack. I'm with *Automobile Digest*. It's nice to meet you, *Señor Gobernador*," he said in accented Spanish.

Duarte stood up and shook the outstretched hand. "Welcome to the capital of Sinaloa," he said.

"Thank you for taking time out of your busy schedule to meet with me," Katana replied. "Do you mind if we continue this discussion in English? It is my stronger language."

Duarte sat down in his chair and crossed his legs. "Of course, of course. Have a seat. What did you want to talk about today?" he asked, switching effortlessly to English. "That I am impressed by your resolve?"

The man named Katana smiled and walked to the door. "Do you mind if I close this? Some of my questions may be a bit personal in nature."

Duarte shrugged. "*Por qué no?*" Why not?

After shutting the door, Mack Katana turned the lock in the handle.

"There is no need for that," Duarte said. "I assure you that no one will come in without my permission."

Without responding, Mack reached into his bag and pulled out a manila folder, and tossed it on Duarte's desk.

"That is for you. Please take a look," Mack said.

Duarte flashed an uneasy glance at his visitor and opened the folder. Inside were five stacks of paper, each one stapled together at the corner. His face grew hard when he saw the contents on the pages.

"Where did you get this?" he asked.

Mack took a seat in the chair in front of the desk. "That's a dumb question. You know exactly where I got those, governor. From the Caribbean World Bank in the British Virgin Islands. It's where you hide your money."

"I don't know what you're talking about. I do not know what this is."

"Well, let me explain it to you then," Mack said with a laugh. "Those pieces of paper you have in your hands show every deposit made into your account for the past ten years, and we've found some interesting characters who have wired money to you. People we'd like to know more about."

"You are no automotive journalist. Who the hell are you?"

"I'm a concerned American citizen hoping to do something about the illegal drugs coming into my country."

Duarte scoffed. "You need to go talk to the cartels, *mi amigo*. Not me."

"In any case, I'm here to make a deal. You help me and I help you."

Duarte shook his head. "I don't make deals, especially with Americans." He reached for his desk phone but stopped short of the handset when he noticed Katana pointing a small handgun at his chest.

"How did you get that through security?" Duarte asked.

Mack smiled. "Call it tools of the trade. Oh, and I must ask for that money back, too, which I'm sure you already stuffed into your desk or briefcase. You're more than welcome to keep the photo, though."

"You are with the DEA?" Duarte asked.

"That's not important. But now that we've gotten the formalities out of the way, let's get to know each other better, shall we?"

Chapter 44

Aimed at Mauricio Duarte's head was a 5.7mm FN Five-seven handgun purchased from a black-market vendor in downtown Culiacán. Koga reached over the governor's desk and opened the top drawer, where he found the same type of handgun buried underneath the five thousand dollars in cash that had been in the envelope. Koga took the cash and pistol and dropped them inside his bag.

"I'm not here to hurt you, governor. Like I said before, I would like to ask for your help," Koga said.

"What do you want?" Duarte asked.

"We believe you are harboring a known Islamic terrorist in your state. I want to know where he is."

Beads of sweat formed on Duarte's forehead. "I do not know what you're talking about. Please, you are wasting my time and yours. I cannot help you."

Koga leaned forward and picked up the manila folder on the desk and flipped through the pages of bank statements, stopping at the last one. "This shows that large monthly deposits were made into your account for the past two years from a company called Emerald Holdings. We know this company to be associated with North Korea and the Aqarib terror organization."

Duarte stared blankly at his guest. "You are crazy. The account is not mine. The name means nothing to me."

Koga sighed. "You know what, though? You're right. I think I am wasting my time. I will email the copies of these statements to every news outlet in Mexico and the United States. I hope you have a talented lawyer."

"*Si, señor.* I have the best," Duarte responded with a smile.

The governor had balls of steel, that much was sure. It was time to use the ace hidden up his sleeve. "What's your favorite restaurant in Los Angeles, sir?" Koga asked.

"I beg your pardon?" asked Duarte.

"I was just wondering if you had a favorite restaurant in Los Angeles because mine is this quaint little place in Long Beach. I think you've been to it because I could have sworn that I saw your photo on the wall there."

The smile from Duarte's face disappeared.

"Carlos is your only son, correct?" Koga asked. "You've kept him well hidden." Duarte didn't answer. "You even had him change his last name to Delgado. Well, governor, after the U.S. government extradites you to stand trial in America, the FBI will no doubt arrest Carlos and shut down his restaurant. I feel strongly that a connection must exist between him and your millions. Ill-gotten gains, and so on."

"He has done nothing wrong," Duarte protested.

"Oh, I'm sure they'll come up with something. With his daddy's reputation for being one of the most corrupt officials in Mexico, not to mention an agent of the North Korean government *and* a stooge for drug cartels? Finding a reason to lock him up won't be a problem."

Rising from his chair, Koga threw the strap of his duffel bag over his shoulder and walked toward the door. "I'll see myself out."

"Wait," Duarte demanded. "Can you assure me that the contents of that file will not be shared and that you will leave my son alone?"

Koga turned around. "That all depends on you, governor."

Duarte pulled down on the front of his collar, visibly distressed. He said in a soft voice, "The leader of Al-Aqarib is currently at my summer retreat in Mazatlán. Al-Ahmed."

Koga produced a photo of Nasim al-Ahmed and held it in front of Duarte's face. "This man? This man is at your house in Mazatlán?"

The governor nodded. "Yes. He's there."

Eureka.

"You need to tell me everything you know about everyone who's at the house. How many people are there?" Koga asked.

Duarte looked up at the ceiling. "I think four or five inside the house, and they all have weapons. Many, many weapons."

"How many outside?"

"That's difficult to say because the number changes every day. He has pieces of his army arriving every week, and he's also actively recruiting local residents to join his group. At this point, I would say maybe fifteen."

That was considerably more than Koga had expected.

"I need an aerial map of the area around your home. Call it up on your computer. Google Earth will do," Koga instructed.

After punching a few keys on his keyboard, Duarte waited for the image to load as he swiveled the monitor around.

"Where are his men located?" Koga asked.

Duarte pointed to several residences at the base of the hill. "I know he has offered money to the families in these homes to take in some of his men. There are probably a few dozen others spread out here." He pointed to houses in a neighboring block. "And I think some are staying in nearby hotels, probably the cheaper ones, away from the beaches and the tourist spots."

Koga zoomed in and out on different spots of the image. Duarte's retreat was on Isla de Creston, away from the major resorts and tucked away at the end of a small, one-lane road. At the rear of the property was a cliff that dropped into the ocean, making access possible only from the front. Al-Ahmed would have lookouts posted along the road and at the entrance of the property, which meant that Koga would have no chance of getting inside of it unnoticed.

"How high is the bluff? Can we climb it?" he asked.

Duarte shook his head. "I wouldn't have built this house at that location if someone could sneak into my backyard so easily. It drops straight into the ocean, and the base is very jagged and slippery. There's no way to climb it, not even with proper climbing equipment."

"Any other way in or out?"

Duarte pointed to a narrow walkway that twisted away from the side of the property and bled out to a dirt trail. "That's supposed to be a servant's entrance, but we have not used it in ages. The terrorists, I'm sure, don't know about it. It's almost all covered up with shrubbery."

"Can I get through it into the house?"

"There's a gate."

"Do you have the keys to the gate?"

Duarte nodded.

Koga studied the overhead image of the property. Even if he could get onto the property grounds undetected, he still had to deal with armed lookouts and late-arriving reinforcements, not to mention random servants and groundskeepers. The chances of his getting into the compound, killing al-Ahmed, and escaping were not ideal. He needed help.

Turning to Duarte, Koga asked, "How would you feel about being a hero to your people and getting decorated by the United States government?"

"*Pardón?*"

After swiftly grabbing the handset of Duarte's desk phone, Koga held it in front of the governor's face. "I need you to call in your special police force and have them raid your house tomorrow night. Tell them that terrorists have taken over your home. If they're successful in getting al-Ahmed, you will be hailed a hero."

"Our police force doesn't have enough firepower to do anything like that. Besides, most of them are on the Eldorado Cartel's payroll. The only ones who can pull off an operation of this magnitude would be the *federales*, and the only one who can order such a strike is the president of Mexico," Duarte said.

"Then make the call. I'm sure you have his number."

"How am I going to explain Islamic terrorists in my house without incriminating myself?"

"Tell him you've been secretly working with the CIA to lure them in.

I'll make sure the boys and girls at Langley will back your story. That is, if we get al-Ahmed," Koga answered, feeling absolutely no guilt for promising something that he may not be able to deliver.

Duarte crossed his arms, his face set in deep thought. "I don't know. Can you guarantee my safety? The people I am about to betray are very dangerous."

"Of course, you have my word." Koga answered, fairly sure he could keep this promise.

Duarte hesitated. "You place me in a troublesome situation."

"Governor, I'm offering you a clean way out. The DEA has dozens of files like this one on you, just sitting there for the right time to use them. We can make them all disappear, but ultimately, it's your choice whether that happens. You can work with me or against me. Decide carefully, amigo, but decide now."

Duarte swiped the handset from Koga's hand with a glare and punched a button on the phone base.

The executive assistant picked up. "*Si, señor?*"

He barked in his best command voice.

"*Llama al presidente, de inmediato!*" Call the president, immediately!

Chapter 45

It took all of ten minutes to convince Arturo González, the president of Mexico, to mobilize the country's deadly *Policia Federal.* If they could pull it off, it would be a brilliant coup for Duarte, providing a much-needed public relations boost after an affair with his housekeeper had been revealed in the tabloids. Also on the call was Max Koga, who explained that he was there on behalf of the U.S., which wasn't entirely true, but necessary to mention if he was to take part in the operation. In the end, Gonzales permitted Koga's help, but solely as an adviser.

A secure text soon buzzed on Duarte's phone from the Chief Inspector of the *Cuerpo de Fuerzas Especiales*, Hector Arias. It instructed both Duarte and Koga to travel discreetly to the Mayan Beach Hotel the following morning. He would wait for them in Room 216.

After bidding the governor a good morning, Koga left the government building and headed to Culiacán's Botanic Gardens to reset his chi in a quiet environment. After an hour of meditation, he skipped dinner and headed straight to his hotel. Leaving the room dimly lit, he nodded off on the sofa, only to be stirred awake by the sound of automatic gunfire. When he came to, he saw the slain members of his DEA team. They were all there, all seven of them, with Jimmy Slack front and center. They stared at him with somber expressions, their transparent bodies engulfed in a haze of red.

"I'm close, guys. Really close. Just hold on a little longer," Koga said.

Deep down, he knew these apparitions were nothing more than hallucinations, figments of his imagination created by stress and guilt—but they were becoming increasingly real, and he began questioning his sanity. He hoped they would stop visiting once he put an end to Nasim al-Ahmed. That his death would trigger something in his brain that would make them disappear forever. Koga reached for his pill case on the nightstand and popped a Xanax, washing it down with a bottle of water. The ghosts always faded, and when they were gone, he wondered how soon they'd return.

"I'm sure I'll see you guys again. Good night," he said to no one, and went back to sleep.

At daybreak the following morning, Koga stepped through the front doors of his hotel to a waiting black Mercedes-Benz with dark tinted windows.

"Good morning, governor," he said as he dropped himself into the rear seat next to Mauricio Duarte.

Duarte said nothing. Once Max closed the door, the driver pulled the car away from the curb. It was immediately joined by two other black Mercedes sedans, one in front and the other tucking itself behind the governor's car.

"They're my security team," Duarte said.

Koga nodded. "Never leave home without 'em."

During the two-hour drive from Culiacán to Mazatlán, Koga grilled Duarte on the relationship between North Korea and the Aqarib, but the governor professed not to know much.

"They asked me to provide support for the terrorists and help them establish a base here in Sinaloa. That, and arranging for them to take over the Eldorado Cartel," he said.

"How did you accomplish that?" Koga asked. "I can't see the Eldorado's leader giving up his position so easily."

"The Eldorado Cartel was on the verge of collapse, so I suggested to the Aqarib to make a deal with them. So, Nasim al-Ahmed offered the organization ten million dollars in cash and promised to wipe out the local competition. In return, they would hand the leadership role to al-Ahmed on the condition that the main family continued to receive twenty percent of the drug profits."

"Who is your contact in the North Korean government?"

Duarte shifted in his seat.

"Answer the question, governor," Koga demanded.

"It's a colonel in the Korean People's Army. His name is Seo, but I have never met him personally. That is the extent of my knowledge of the North Koreans," Duarte answered uneasily.

The morning rush was still a few hours away when the trio of black sedans pulled into the deserted parking lot of the Mayan Beach Hotel, on the southern tip of Mazatlán. The front door was open, but the lobby of the three-star motel was empty, with not one staffer in sight. Koga and Duarte exited the car as the governor's bodyguards led the way. The four men made their way to Room 216 on the second floor, where Koga pressed the chime button on the wall.

After several seconds, the door cracked open.

"You were not followed?" a man with a thin mustache asked in English from inside the room.

"No, I'm certain we were not," Koga answered.

The Mexican officer then studied Duarte's face and swung the door open all the way.

"Please come in, governor, but your men must stay in the lobby," the mustached man said to the governor in Spanish.

Duarte nodded and waved his hand, sending his detail back down the stairs, before entering the room, followed by Max. The luxury suite offered a pleasant living room area with a small bar. The governor immediately poured himself a glass of cognac.

"I don't understand why I need to be here," he said to the officer. "I have much work to do at the office."

"You're the only one with a detailed knowledge of the property," Koga commented in English.

Duarte let out a disapproving grunt and sat down on the sofa.

The Mexican policeman, wearing a long-sleeve navy blue uniform with a flag of Mexico on his left shoulder, stood in front of the governor. "My name is Hector Arias. I am the chief inspector of the Special Operations Group. I am in charge of this operation, governor."

The Special Operations Group, or GOPES, was the tactical arm of the Mexican Federal Police. Along with the Army's special forces corps, they were the most feared law-enforcement organization in Mexico. The U.S. military trained many of the men working for GOPES, and a few by American PMCs, and not one of them were fans of Governor Duarte because of his known ties to the cartels.

"I'm Max Koga with Argon Securities. We work for the U.S. government," he said.

"It's nice to meet you," Arias greeted him in English. "My associate José is in the adjoining room setting up our surveillance equipment. Would you like to have a look?"

Arias gestured to Koga to join him in the master bedroom, leaving Duarte alone with his cognac. The man named José, dressed like Arias, sat behind a desk with his face buried inside a Panasonic Toughbook computer. Four small television monitors propped up around the room displayed various feeds from cameras placed around Duarte's complex, while several walkie-talkies and cellphones occupied a nearby table.

"We already have teams quietly rounding up Aqarib supporters in the neighborhood," Arias said.

"When are you planning on going in?" Koga asked.

"As soon as we get confirmation that your man is there. A group of ten operatives, including myself, will approach the front gate in an armored vehicle. We'll have a helicopter providing support from the air. There's also a team watching for activity in the surrounding neighborhoods, just in case others decide to join in."

Koga nodded. "Sounds thorough enough. I must ask that I join you when you go in, Chief Inspector Arias. Al-Ahmed uses many body doubles, and I am the only person here who can provide positive ID."

Arias shook his head. "I cannot allow that. You and the governor will stay here and follow us on the monitors. We'll be in constant radio communication."

Koga frowned. "It's your show. Your orders are to kill al-Ahmed, am I correct?"

"Negative. We have been ordered to capture him alive, if possible."

"I strongly suggest that you reconsider. If he's taken alive, jihadists from every corner of the world will rally. Your country, as well as mine, will be victims of many attacks. Keeping him alive will only encourage them and promote kidnappings for trade material. I strongly recommend you put him down like the dog that he is and dispose of the body right away."

"Sorry, but it's not my call. I have my orders from my president. If Nasim al-Ahmed surrenders, we must bring him in alive."

Koga sighed. "Well, then let's hope he's as brave as his followers claim him to be, and he fights to his death. How will you confirm al-Ahmed is inside the house?"

"We're hoping one of our men watching the house will spot him."

"That could take hours or even days."

Arias held out his hands. "I'm open to recommendations."

"Let's send in the governor. He can see if he's in there or not," Koga suggested.

"Are you mad? Why on earth would you want to provide them a valuable hostage?" Arias countered.

"Governor Duarte has al-Ahmed's trust. His presence shouldn't cause any suspicion."

Upon hearing his name mentioned, Duarte wandered into the room. "What's going on?"

"Why on earth would al-Ahmed trust the governor?" Arias asked Koga. "And he is still a governor. We can't use someone of his stature as bait."

Duarte turned around and left the room.

"Come back here," Koga called out, but his request fell on deaf ears. "Trust me, Chief Inspector. This will work."

Arias rubbed his forehead in frustration. "I must clear this with the president," he said, taking out his cellphone. "But does he really need to go in there? Can't he accomplish this task with a phone call?"

"That would arouse suspicion. Besides, al-Ahmed would never get on the line. We must send the governor in. Please call the president," Koga insisted, then stepped out of the master bedroom.

When Koga walked into the living room, the governor looked up at him in panic.

"You mentioned nothing about me going in there," Duarte complained. "It's bad enough that my home will probably suffer heavy damage in the assault. What if he takes me hostage—or kills me?"

Koga grinned. "Think of how the people of Mexico would react to such a brave act. You just might be able to run for president. Well, not if he kills you, of course. But cheer up, those odds are very low."

Duarte's face was so red Koga thought a stroke was possible. "You're a real bastard, you know that?"

Before he could respond, Arias entered the living room. "My boss says he leaves it to my discretion. So, Governor Duarte, I will allow this if you're willing."

Koga smiled. "He's willing. Let's get the good governor prepped for his heroic act."

Chapter 46

Governor Mauricio Duarte's armored Mercedes-Benz E-Class made its way up the long driveway to his summer home. With the governor riding in the back next to his bodyguard, the driver pulled to a stop in front of the metal gate that guarded the property. From seemingly out of nowhere, a thin, bearded man clutching a rifle and dressed in military fatigues appeared.

The governor lowered his window and addressed him in Spanish. "Are you a new recruit?"

The man nodded.

"Where are you from?" Duarte asked.

"Mexico City," the guard said.

"Then you know who I am, right? Please let me in."

"Why are you here?" asked the young guard. "My superiors would like to know."

"I came to fetch my laptop."

The guard unclipped a walkie-talkie from his belt and repeated what he had just heard. A few seconds later, the heavy metal gates swung slowly open, allowing the Mercedes-Benz to enter the large roundabout driveway.

All seemed quiet on the grounds. The carports next to the house were empty, and the blinds on the windows of the main building were shut tight. The driver parked the car in front of the entrance as he normally would and stayed in his seat with the engine running.

Not waiting for him to open his door, the governor stepped out and entered his house with his bodyguard in tow. No sooner had he taken a step inside than a burly Caucasian man with a shaved head whom he had never seen before confronted him.

"Who are you?" Duarte asked in Spanish.

The man responded in English. "What are you doing here? And he stays outside," he said, pointing to the bodyguard.

Duarte held firm and spoke in a commanding tone that was all show and no substance. "This is my house. How dare you tell me what to do?"

The big gringo made a move toward Duarte, provoking the bodyguard to reach under his jacket and produce his pistol. The gringo instantly drew out his own handgun and pointed it at the bodyguard.

"I wouldn't do that if I were you, *amigo*," the man said.

"I am a personal friend of Señor Nasim," Duarte insisted. "And this is my home. Where is he?"

The large man kept his pistol trained on the bodyguard. "I don't know, and I really don't give a shit. Tell your lapdog to stow his weapon."

Duarte scanned the room, hoping to catch a glimpse of al-Ahmed, but he was nowhere to be seen. "I entrusted my home to Señor Nasim, and I demand to see him now."

A moment later, Nasim al-Ahmed emerged from the rear of the house. "What is going on, Mister Spence?" he asked.

Duarte exhaled in relief. "Ah, Señor Nasim. Who is this offensive animal that dares to pull a gun on me in my own house?"

"Perhaps you can tell me why you're here first?" al-Ahmed asked. "The agreement was that you would clear your visits with me beforehand, was it not?"

"I came for my laptop," Duarte said.

After a brief pause, al-Ahmed smiled. "Of course, please come in. But I must insist that you leave your security man outside."

Although he was far from comfortable being left alone, Duarte saw no other alternative than to enter the house without his security man. He ordered the bodyguard to remain outside, and al-Ahmed ordered Spence, his bald gringo, to go upstairs and retrieve Duarte's laptop.

Nervously, Duarte entered the living room under the watchful gaze of al-Ahmed. The governor had noticed several men in camouflage uniforms scattered about the floor when his eyes caught another unfamiliar Caucasian face. This one was infinitely more tempting than the oaf who had greeted him at the front door. She had dark brown hair, an angelic face, and a lean figure.

"Hello, who might you be?" he asked.

The woman sat with her legs crossed and an iPad Pro on her lap. She turned toward the governor. "You're Mauricio Duarte."

He nodded. "At your service, *señorita*."

"The Supreme Leader sends his regards," she said, returning her attention to her tablet.

"You're with the North Koreans? What's going on here, Nasim? You said nothing about having Americans or North Koreans here. That was not part of our agreement."

"You must take that up with Colonel Seo. Having Mister Spence here was not my call," al-Ahmed maintained.

Spence returned to the living room with a small MacBook under his arm. "Is this it?"

"Yes, thank you," Duarte said.

Before handing the laptop over, Spence asked, "What's in there that's so important that you drove all the way here from Culiacán at the crack of dawn?"

"That is none of your business," Duarte snapped. He then turned to al-Ahmed. "Can you please get this animal out of my face?"

"Mister Spence has a point. I would also like to know what made you drive all the way here so early and show up unannounced?" al-Ahmed said.

This wasn't part of the plan. Mack Katana or Max Koga, or whatever his name is, had assured me it would be a cakewalk, Duarte thought—just grab the laptop, confirm Nasim al-Ahmed's presence, and leave. And who is this white gorilla named Spence?

An idea came to the governor. "A news outlet wants to interview me about my family, and they asked for some old personal photos. This request came at the last minute, and I have not backed them up to the cloud yet."

"Then copy what you need here now. In front of us," Spence instructed. "You can't take that out of the house."

"If you insist," Duarte said. He walked over to a desk at the far end of the room, where he fetched a thumb drive from the top drawer. He then sat down on the sofa with the MacBook on his lap.

"I will leave as soon as I copy the files," Duarte said, while Spence positioned himself immediately behind him, looking down at the MacBook's monitor. "A little privacy, por favor?"

Spence smirked. "You have no privacy here."

Elena Natase sighed. "Why don't you guys give him some space? It's his house, after all."

Duarte nodded in appreciation. "Muchas gracias, señorita."

"Do what you must do and leave immediately," al-Ahmed said, exiting the living room. But Spence didn't budge from his position.

When three folders of photo files had completed their transfer, Duarte ejected the drive from the laptop and shoved it into his pocket.

"All done."

Spence grabbed the laptop off the governor's lap and carried it back upstairs.

Natase glanced up from her iPad at Duarte. "Did you get what you needed?" she asked.

"Yes, *señorita*. Thank you for your assistance."

Natase spoke in a hushed tone. "I'm looking forward to seeing your friends soon. Stay safe, governor."

Without trying to decipher what she meant, Duarte wished her a good day and left the house as quickly as he could, walking directly to the waiting Mercedes-Benz outside. As soon as he and his bodyguard were seated in the car, he instructed the driver to leave, his trembling hands struggling to fasten his seatbelt.

Twenty minutes and several detours later, the car returned to the parking lot of the Mayan Beach Hotel, where Max Koga awaited Duarte in the lobby.

"Everything go okay?" Koga asked.

"It did *not* go okay," Duarte sputtered, taking deep breaths to calm his nerves.

"What happened?"

"Nasim al-Ahmed was there. I saw him myself. And a couple of new faces were there, too. A beautiful woman and a nasty gringo named Spence."

"Jay Spence?"

"I am not sure, but he is big, bald, and very unpleasant."

Koga cursed out loud. *Unbelievable*, he thought. The leak hadn't been coming from the CIA or the FBI.

It came from within Argon.

Chapter 47

Hector Arias had dubbed the operation on the governor's summer retreat *La Tormenta*, or "The Squall." After Mauricio Duarte returned and confirmed the presence of Nasim al-Ahmed in his summer home, Arias and his team of twenty special operators huddled around a large table, studying a dozen maps and aerial photographs of all sizes. Duarte was there, too, answering questions about the home's alarm systems, surveillance cameras, and secret rooms.

From the information they had gathered from the governor, the *federales* concocted a simple yet effective plan to infiltrate the property and secure al-Ahmed. The *La Tormenta* surprise attack was to commence at 0300.

As the fateful hour approached, Max Koga wandered into the converted surveillance center in the bedroom of Room 216 of the Mayan Beach Hotel. Three people were manning laptops that showed a half dozen video images. All hell was about to break loose and Koga didn't intend to miss the action.

"As far as you know, José, there's only one team, and they're going through the front, *correcto?*" Koga asked the man behind the largest laptop.

Keeping his eyes on the monitors, José said, "We will have a second vehicle that will follow the first one in as backup; the driveway is too narrow to go in side by side. So we will have two vehicles going through the front gate, nose to tail. We also have a quick-reaction force standing by."

"Sounds good. I'm going to make a fast trip to the lobby and buy some cigarettes from the kiosk. Can I get you anything?" Koga asked.

"No, *gracias*." José shook his head, not taking his eyes off the monitors.

Koga walked past Mauricio Duarte, fast asleep on the sofa. Despite the assurances from the Mexican president that all damage to his property would be paid for, the governor said he couldn't bear to watch his beloved summer retreat being turned into a war zone. So, he drowned his grief in a bottle of cognac, which had effectively anesthetized him.

Once outside, Koga jogged past the governor's security men snoozing comfortably inside their cars and headed straight to a taco shop across the street. The restaurant had long since closed, but Koga was more interested in the late-model GMC Sierra pickup truck that was parked in front. When he reached the vehicle, he quickly inputted the VIN number into the special cellphone app that Raja Singh had created and pushed the activate button.

Click. The doors unlocked, and the engine came to life. "Bless you, Raj," he said aloud as he climbed into the driver's seat.

Driving with the headlights off, Koga took a dusty road that led to the service entrance of the governor's summer home. Once he felt he had reached the correct spot, he parked the truck behind a thick copse of evergreens and killed the engine. It took nearly a minute for him to locate the secret gate, which was largely hidden behind an assortment of bushy undergrowth. But it was there, just as the governor had described.

Keeping low in the moonlit night, he inserted the key that he'd received from Duarte into the gate and turned it. The lock snapped back and the door creaked open, revealing a winding dirt trail up a small rise. He pushed forward in the gloom, clearing branches and leaves out of his way. About fifty yards in, he spotted the outdoor lights of the main house.

Taking a position behind the cover of an overgrown acalypha shrub, he lay flat on his belly and carefully studied the surrounding topography. The trail ended at a carport on the side of the property. To the side of the carport were two men armed with AK-47s seated on a low brick wall under an outdoor light. As guards, they weren't exactly desirable. Their weapons were slung over their shoulders, and they were engaged in friendly conversation about soccer teams, totally oblivious to what was about to go down.

Oblivious was the preferred state.

Gripping his FN handgun, Koga slowly raised his body from the ground until he was on all fours. He was still at least twenty yards from the carport and thirty yards away from the guards, but he had already visualized in his mind what had to be done. He glanced at his watch. It was two minutes until The Squall commenced. He swallowed a Xanax pill to keep his nerves even for what he expected would be a one hell of a firefight, and waited.

Suddenly, a bright orange flash erupted from the front of the property, accompanied by the resonance of heavy gunfire and crunching metal. The lights inside the house switched on almost simultaneously, as shouts in Spanish and Arabic reverberated from inside.

It was showtime.

Startled, the two guards jumped off the wall with their rifles at the ready, but they hesitated, not knowing exactly what to do. Koga sprang from his hiding spot and took off in a sprint toward the two gunmen who faced away from him.

The idea was to take them out without killing them, if possible, but then one guard turned his way. Koga saw the man's eyes grow wide at the sight of a stranger sprinting out of the darkness with a gun pointed at his face. The guard raised his rifle and fired two poorly aimed snapshots that sailed above Koga's head. With no other choice, Koga unloaded three quick rounds from his suppressed pistol, one of them striking the guard's shoulder and spinning him into the second guard. He followed up with six more shots, putting both men down for good.

After stowing his pistol inside his belt, he took the rifles off the guards. He threw one of them into a plastic trash bin nearby and claimed possession of the other, along with extra magazines of ammunition. He ran to the side door and put his ear to it. There were muffled shouts in Arabic coming from inside, but no sound of gunfire, meaning the *federales* hadn't yet infiltrated the house. Koga considered breaching the lock and entering the house, but thought better of it in case there was a small army waiting for him on the other side. He needed a more discreet way to gain entry.

Flattened against the stucco wall and away from the video cameras, he looked around and then ran to the base of a large palm tree, the large trunk of which extended up the side of the house. Its crown swayed next to a small second-story window, one that Koga felt he could squeeze through.

Unfastening the single-point latch of the AK, he swung the strap around the trunk and reattached it. Using the strap to keep his upper body on the tree like a utility lineman, he pushed up with his feet to climb, repeating the process until he reached the top, using a technique he'd learned from Polynesian tree climbers in his native Hawaii. In less than five minutes, he made it to the top of the tree.

Pushing aside the dead leaves, he lined himself even with the small window and straddled the trunk with his legs. After unlatching the sling to free his upper body from the tree, he pointed the rifle at the window and pushed the flash suppressor into the glass, breaking it and creating a small opening, sweeping the rifle barrel around the hole to clear as much glass as he could.

Max paused for a moment in case someone had heard the tinkling of broken glass, but thanks to the mayhem at the front of the property, no one seemed to notice. He rotated himself around the tree until his back was at the building. He secured the AK to his chest in a one-arm bear hug and pulled his feet up, pressing them into the brittle bark of the tree. On the count of three, he kicked with all his might, releasing his grip on the trunk and going airborne into the night.

As he flew through the window opening, pieces of broken glass remaining in the frame carved through the sleeves of his jacket and legs of his pants, but as far as he could tell, he'd suffered no major lacerations. The important thing was that he was in.

Koga raised himself from the carpeted floor. He was in a bathroom. He checked his rifle and stepped into a darkened hallway.

The time had come to meet Nasim al-Ahmed.

Chapter 48

The ground floor of the mansion had become the primary line of defense for Nasim al-Ahmed and his Aqarib soldiers. They positioned themselves at each window, firing at the armored police van that had crashed through the breached gate and powered up the asphalt driveway, spilling out Mexican Army special forces into a coordinated attack formation.

Because Mauricio Duarte's summer home had no second-story windows that faced the driveway, Koga figured the entire floor would be deserted. The Aqarib forces would be concentrated on the ground floor and shooting down the driveway, and al-Ahmed would probably be hiding in the master bedroom. He stole a glance around the corner in that direction and saw a light shining through the crack between the closed double doors.

With the barrel of his AK-47 leading the way, Koga tip-toed toward the light. He was grateful for the carpeted floor that muffled his footsteps. When he reached the door, he stopped to listen to the voices emanating from inside. He immediately recognized the baritone of Jayson Spence.

"Go get Elena Natase. Do you understand? Tell her to get her ass over here now," Spence said aloud.

Koga ducked into an adjacent room just as a tall Aqarib soldier emerged from the master bedroom and hurried past him down the hall.

Seconds later, the tall man returned, accompanied by a woman who left the sweet scent of jasmine in her wake. He glimpsed Cynthia Blackwood, the assistant to Xavier Qiu, as she strolled past him and into the master bedroom.

So, she also goes by Elena Natase.

The *federales* seemed to make progress as the gunfire at the front of the house intensified. Distressed shouts in Spanish and Arabic emanated from downstairs. He had to find Nasim al-Ahmed quickly.

Koga stepped out of the small bedroom and positioned himself near the master bedroom door, where he heard Natase say, "What do you want, Mr. Spence?"

"You and me, we need to get the hell out of here now," Spence said. Something clearly rattled him. "We're gonna be dead meat if we stick around."

Natase may have even chuckled. "What do you propose we do?" she asked in an amused tone.

"The police helicopter has moved to the front of the house, so now's our chance. We can slide down the foundation posts of the rear balcony and make our way off the property through the bushes."

"Ah, the Cirque du Soleil solution. Love it. And if we're caught?"

"We'll be home free once we make it out onto the street. We're two white people; we don't look like them. We just tell them we're tourists out for a stroll."

"Why are you offering to help me?" she asked.

"If you want to stay, be my guest, but I thought your Supreme Leader would be appreciative if I helped his little whore escape."

"You American piece of ...," Natase growled. Her intent was clear as she reached for a Glock 19 on a side table, but before she could reach it, Koga burst into the room and sent the butt of his rifle into the head of the cartel soldier guarding the door. These people are not professionals, Koga thought. As the soldier crumpled to the floor, Spence dropped behind a sofa and Natase ducked behind the king-size bed.

Koga said, "You two both know very well that a round from this AK will easily penetrate your cover. I advise you to come out with your hands in the air before I test that."

Natase was the first to react. She stood up with her back toward Max.

"Please turn around slowly, Ms. Natase, or whatever your name is these days," Koga said without taking his eyes off Spence's position.

She took a step toward the sliding glass door at the back of the room.

"I said *please* ..." Koga's rifle pointed at her.

She stopped and turned her head. "What do you plan to do with me?"

"I haven't figured that out ye ..."

Before he could finish his sentence, Spence popped up from behind the sofa with a Glock 19 in his hand and Max swung the rifle toward his attacker, firing two rounds without properly aiming. Call it dumb luck, but one bullet hit Spence's gun, knocking it from his hand.

With his peripheral vision, Koga saw Natase make a move for the sliding glass door, giving Spence the split second he needed to charge Max, who countered by sidestepping the attack. Koga followed up with a swift reverse roundhouse kick to the gut, which Spence responded by taking the barrel of Koga's weapon with both hands and pulling hard. Koga took a step forward, closing the distance and kneeing Spence in the groin twice, loosening the bald man's grip on the rifle.

After yanking it free, Koga stepped back and pointed the barrel of the gun at Spence's chest. "You killed good men and two valuable assets," Koga growled. "You will pay for what you did, traitor."

"Idiot. You have no idea how deep this thing goes," Spence countered.

"Why did you leave the loyalty card in Yousef Badawi's pocket?"

Spence flashed a puzzled look. "What the hell are you talking about?"

It wasn't him.

In the blink of an eye, Spence's right hand thrust down to his ankle, going for a compact pistol secured in his boot. Half expecting the move, Koga fired two quick rounds into the man's burly chest, sending the oversize *gringo* against the glass patio door. It was clear from the way the rounds failed to produce blood that Spence was wearing a Kevlar vest, so Koga raised his aim and fired three more shots—one smashed the glass door and the other two found their way into Spence's head and neck. The force of the successive blasts sent him stumbling back across the short length of the patio and over the rail into the crashing waves below.

It was now time to deal with Natase. When Koga turned to face her, she had Spence's gun pointed at his forehead.

"Well, this is an awkward situation," she said. "How shall we proceed?"

"Well, we can just kill each other right here and now, or you can drop your weapon and allow me to tie you up," Koga replied.

Flashing a radiant smile, Natase said, "Sounds kinky, but I like option three."

"And that is?"

"You let me go on my merry way, and we both live to see tomorrow. Or, at least I will."

Koga chuckled. "I don't know if you've noticed, but the place is surrounded by Mexican authorities. If you're not apprehended, you'll be taken out in their crossfire."

With the gun still pointed at Koga, Natase moved toward the balcony. Koga let her, watching in silent curiosity what she was up to as she removed her jacket, revealing a compressed backpack underneath. She then climbed onto the railing.

"You're kidding, right," Koga said.

Natase blew him a kiss and jumped.

As he sprinted to the edge of the platform, he saw her descend gracefully with her chute open into the darkness of the night. He then glanced down the cliff wall. It was just as Duarte had said. The drop was steep, at least two-hundred feet into an angry sea. And although the governor said there was no way up or down the slippery cliff, he failed to consider base jumping. After taking a last look at the crashing waves below, Koga stepped back into the house and immediately froze when he noticed a pair of dark, low objects slowly creeping toward him. The light from the indoor lamp illuminated jagged white teeth that gnashed at the air.

Pit bulls. And they sounded pissed off.

Koga held his breath as the two dogs closed in.

Chapter 49

The dogs kept their distance at first, unsure of their superiority and growling long strings of saliva from their mouths. Behind them, a man with wavy gray hair and a bushy black beard held the dogs' leashes in his hands. Koga pointed his rifle at the animals.

"Are these your dogs? Call them off right now if you want them to live," he said.

The man replied in Arabic, which Koga figured wasn't the command for *sit* or *stay*. Koga fired a couple of bullets into the floor, hoping the sound of the gunshots would frighten the dogs, but all they did was cause the man to drop the leashes and flee.

As for the dogs, they crouched lower and seemed to be even angrier.

With remorse, he aimed the rifle at one of the dogs and pulled the trigger. It was met with a hollow click. *Shit*. The previous owner had failed to fill the magazine to capacity. With no time to reach for his pistol and get a shot off, Koga hurled the rifle at the dogs and ran for the master bathroom. He jumped through the doorway head first.

Once he was completely inside, he attempted to kick the door shut, but one dog managed to clamp down on the heel of his right boot. Koga felt the immense power of the muscular beast as it tried to yank him from the room. He kicked the dog's nose with his free leg, but all that did was encourage the animal to pull harder.

As the other dog approached, the rubber sole of his boot tore off, freeing Koga's foot and allowing him to slam the bathroom door shut. The dogs rammed their bodies into the door, trying to force it open, but Koga had already latched it and locked it.

After wiping the sweat from his face with a nearby hand towel, he glanced at his watch. Over twenty minutes had elapsed since the raid began.

What's taking the GOPES so long? They should be here by now.

All but giving up on the prospect of getting Nasim al-Ahmed himself, he concentrated on getting past the dogs without killing them and out of the house. He searched for something he could use as a weapon or shield to keep their razor-sharp teeth at bay.

The thick towel bar mounted on the wall might do the trick. If that didn't work, he would have no choice but to put them down, he determined.

He grabbed the metal rod and pulled down to pry it loose from the wall. It dropped a few inches and then locked into position with a click, like a lever.

What was that?

Quickly turning on the bathroom lights, Koga closely examined the towel bar. It was indeed some form of switch. He then noticed one end of the bathtub was slightly higher than the other. Kneeling at the base of the tub, he ran his hand along a sizable gap that separated the tub from the tiling, placing his fingers inside and pulling up. The near end of the tub lifted upward, revealing a cylindrical shaft with a narrow spiral staircase descending into a long black hole.

It was a secret escape route.

That son of a bitch.

Koga called Mauricio Duarte's cellphone. The line went straight to voicemail, so he tried the main line of the Mayan Beach Hotel, where José answered on the fourth ring.

"Put the governor on. It's urgent," Koga said in Spanish.

"Who is this?" José asked. His voice was barely audible over the barking dogs and gunfire.

"This is Max Koga. There's no time to waste."

"Where are you, *señor?*" José asked. "You need to come back here now."

"Still looking for the cigarette kiosk. Put Governor Duarte on now," Koga said.

"*Un momento,*" José said.

After what seemed like an eternity, Duarte picked up the phone. "What is it?" he said in a perturbed voice.

"You lying bastard. You didn't tell us you had a secret escape built into your master bathroom. Where does it lead?"

The line remained silent.

"You better tell me now, or so help me God, I will make your life very uncomfortable and then I'll kill you," Koga snarled.

"Okay, okay. I'm sorry I didn't mention it to you, but you must understand, I didn't tell you about this escape for my own safety. I have made some very persistent enemies over the years, and I didn't want anyone to know about it."

"Tell me where the escape goes."

"It drops into an underground tunnel that leads to a sewing machine repair shop a half-mile away."

"Does al-Ahmed know about this getaway?"

There was no answer.

"Tell me, *damn you,*" Koga demanded.

"Yes, I mentioned it to him. He was very impressed by it."

"Whatever you do, don't tell the *federales* about it, understand?"

"Yes, I understand," Duarte answered.

"Are there any weapons at the repair shop?"

"There should be a shotgun in the supply room and a pistol under the counter by the cash register."

"Anything else that you forgot to mention?" Koga asked.

"That's everything. No, wait. I have a car parked outside the shop. The keys are on a hook on the wall next to the front door."

Koga unloaded a slew of expletives at the governor and hung up.

Now that the *Policia Federale* was getting close to taking control of the compound, it was only a matter of time before al-Ahmed would use the hidden passageway to disappear once again. But, this time, Koga found himself one step ahead of the terrorist. He owed it all to a couple of killer dogs clawing at the door.

Chapter 50

"Get these people into their vests," Nasim al-Ahmed announced, pointing to three men and one woman in their late twenties standing in the back of the living room of Mauricio Duarte's summer home. He looked at each one of them carefully with his only good eye.

"It's time for you to become martyrs. Your rewards will be great in the next world," the translator said, relaying al-Ahmed's words in Spanish.

Ifran, al-Aqarib's bomb specialist, fitted each of them with black canvas vests padded with C-4 explosives. Ramin Madani, who had no intention of sacrificing this world for the next, stood a few feet away reciting, verses from the Koran under his breath.

Things were not looking good for al-Ahmed and his men. Although the first armored vehicle had been neutralized with an RPG, it had already disgorged its troopers and the only loss was the driver. The terrorists didn't expect the backup vehicle to be even more heavily armed.

The morning sun was getting ready to break the horizon, and the sky glowed a radiant purple to the east, but it was still dark enough for a last attack, al-Ahmed thought.

Mohammed burst into the room, "They have more reinforcements coming, and there's a helicopter above us with a searchlight. What should we do?"

"Keep fighting! I will take care of those reinforcements soon enough," al-Ahmed said.

He then turned to his suicide bombers, all clad in black to make them difficult to see in the dark. "It is up to you to buy us some time. With your heroic acts, the tides of this battle will turn."

"*Allahu Akbar!*" they screamed as one, eyes wide and pupils dilated from the "energy drink" they'd been fed as they prepped for battle. It was largely crystal meth and orange-flavored *Topo Sabores*, with a few shakes of PCP for mood. The result was electrifying.

As Ifran made the final adjustments to the vests, al-Ahmed handed each man an AK-47 rifle. He then looked at the sole woman martyr, the only true Muslim in the group of intended heroes. She donned a black abaya, a loose-fitting robe-like dress, over her suicide vest. "Are you ready, Haifa?" he asked in Arabic.

"I am," the woman said.

He stroked her cheek. "You've been a gallant warrior, and your sacrifice is the key to the survival of our cause. We will send you out first. Keep your arms raised above your head. They'll hesitate to shoot an unarmed woman. When the time is right, you will punish those who defy us."

"I shall glorify Allah and you."

"You'll be remembered for generations," al-Ahmed said to her softly, before turning his attention to the three men. His words were translated into Spanish: "Once Haifa's task is done, it will be your turn. Get as close as you can to that second vehicle and destroy it."

The three men nodded.

"It's time, Ramin," al-Ahmed said.

Madani closed the Koran, placed it on the table, and took Haifa's arm. He walked her to the front entrance of the house and stood next to where several al-Aqarib soldiers were shooting out the window. "May Allah be with you, my child," he said.

Haifa opened the door and stepped outside.

When the demure woman emerged from the house, the Federal Police agents stopped firing and exchanged shouts in Spanish. Haifa walked into the bright spotlight that lit up the front of the mansion with her hands raised high and her head tilted down.

"*Alto!*" an officer called out from the van in back. "Stop!" he repeated in English.

Ignoring his order, Haifa continued to walk toward the first vehicle, which was still smoking from the earlier RPG assault.

Al-Ahmed and Ifran, who held a remote detonator, watched the spectacle from a small window in the kitchen. One of the federale snipers shot at Haifa's feet, sending up a small puff of powdered concrete into the air.

Unfazed, Haifa raised her hands higher and continued forward, slowly nearing the first line of *federale* officers. In her black abaya only the slit for her eyes was visible, and they telegraphed no danger at a distance in the dark.

Another shot rang out, and a sniper bullet went right through her leg, causing her to scream and fall to the ground.

A spotter with powerful binoculars had been scrutinizing the woman closely since she emerged from the house. He titled his head to his boss and spoke a few words. "Stay away," Arias shouted to his team from behind the backup van. "She's wearing a vest ..."

No one came to the woman's aid as she clutched her bloodied leg. With her other arm, she pulled herself forward, her eyes narrowed now and determined.

The scene brought a smile to al-Ahmed's face. It was exactly what he had hoped for. She was buying him valuable time and sowing confusion among his enemies. He patted Ifran on the shoulder. "I will leave the rest to you, my friend."

Ifran put his hands together. "I will pray to Allah for your safe journey."

"And I pray to Him for yours, as well," al-Ahmed said. He gestured to Madani to join him. Together, they ran up the stairway, leaving the fight behind them.

"How do you think they found us? Do you think the governor betrayed us?" Madani asked as they hurried toward the master bedroom.

"Unlikely, but who knows? Colonel Seo assured me he was being compensated handsomely. A man like that would do anything for money—but a man who will betray his country for money will betray us to save his hide. He would incriminate himself as well, but he could have made a deal. I think it's more likely one of our new recruits was careless in communicating with friends or family. The very air here has ears. In any case, it was wise for us to devise a getaway plan."

A loud blast from the front of the property shook the building's foundation and rattled windows, with all the glass in the house's front now blown inward.

Al-Ahmed said, "Haifa has gone to Paradise. I hope she took out a few of the enemy with her."

When they entered the master bedroom, al-Ahmed and Madani paused at the sight of the dead body on the floor.

"What in the world has happened here?" al-Ahmed asked, more to himself than to his number two. "And where is Spence ... and Natase?"

The two pit bulls sitting near the bathroom door jumped to their feet and ran to the men with their tails wagging. As Madani kneeled to pet the dogs, al-Ahmed aimed his rifle at the head of the first dog and fired.

The gray pit bull's forehead exploded and sprayed brain and bone all over Madani. The other pit bull stopped in confusion long enough for al-Ahmed to put a bullet into the side of its head too.

"Why did you do that?" Madani yelled, appalled. He used a hand towel retrieved from the bathroom to clean his face and hands. "I thought you were fond of them."

"There was no other choice, brother. We can't take them with us, and if we leave them here, they can lead our enemies to us. Don't get so worked up over a couple of animals. Now let's get out of here."

Al-Ahmed stepped into the bathroom and walked to the towel bar, which he grabbed and pulled down with both hands. With a click, the front edge of the bathtub came loose and lifted into the air.

Madani pulled the near edge of the tub upward, exposing the hidden passageway. "After you, leader," he said.

With an approving nod, the al-Aqarib boss squeezed his feet through the narrow opening as three more explosions from outside rocked the house. He paid them no attention as he descended into the dark shaft and clambered down a narrow metal ladder.

Chapter 51

After making their way down the ladder, Nasim al-Ahmed and Ramin Madani reached the base of the shaft, where motion-sensor lights winked on to reveal a long tunnel. It was a perfect expression of cartel-tunnel engineering, with a wooden-plank floor, soft LED lighting, fresh air exchanges, and a thoughtful passage tall enough for the two of them to walk through upright.

"I must admit, these Mexicans are expert tunnel builders," al-Ahmed noted, taking the lead. "We can use their skills in Palestine against the Zionists."

"I wish I could see the looks on the Mexican policemen's faces when they don't find us inside the house. By the time they locate this tunnel, we'll be long gone," Madani said with a satisfied chuckle.

"Colonel Seo assured me that his plane awaits us in the fields of Santa Catarina," al-Ahmed said. "But let's hurry. I'm getting a bit claustrophobic."

Walking thirty feet below the center of town, they reached the other end of the extensive passageway in twenty minutes. If what Mauricio Duarte had told them was true, they were now under an abandoned shop on the north side of the small peninsula, with a getaway car parked nearby. In front of them was a metal ladder that led to the surface, to an empty storage room in the back of a sewing-machine shop.

"We are here, leader," Madani said, stepping forward onto the metal ladder that led up. "Allow me to go first and make ensure the coast is clear."

After repositioning the AK-47 strapped to his body, Madani took the ladder rails in both hands and started climbing. When he reached the top step, he pushed away a thin sheet of plywood that covered the exit and climbed out. Al-Ahmed followed, lifting himself into the pitch-dark room.

As they waited for their vision to adjust, a sudden bright orange flash lit up the room with a mammoth explosion magnified in the small space. Al-Ahmed was temporarily blinded and his hands went too late to his ears. But he heard a high-pitched scream.

It had come from Madani, who had covered his eyes with his forearm.

Another flash-bang detonated and al-Ahmed felt hot searing pain in his left thigh; he knew he'd been shot.

As al-Ahmed dropped to the floor, he almost fell backward into the tunnel opening, just as the room lit up from a three-tube fluorescent ceiling light. Both al-Ahmed and Madani shaded their eyes in the sudden brightness, and when their eyes adjusted, they saw an Asian man standing in front of them behind a 12-gauge Mossberg 940 Pro Tactical shotgun.

Max Koga smiled and said in English, "Nasim al-Ahmed, I presume. You have absolutely no idea how much I've been looking forward to meeting you."

❖

Visiting the FBI Los Angeles field office on Wilshire Avenue was something he had never done before, but Paul Verdy knew FBI Director Edward Womack was in town for a meeting about North Korea's involvement with Song Motors.

The receptionist tapped a few keys on her computer keyboard. "I'm sorry, sir, but he just flew back to Washington."

"Then let me talk to the SAC," Verdy demanded.

"General Paul Verdy?" asked a woman from behind.

"Yes, that's me," Paul answered after turning around.

"I'm Karen Thaler, the field office public affairs specialist. I've seen you on CNN," she said, holding out her hand. "It's a pleasure to meet you."

Verdy shook it lightly and skipped the pleasantries. "I need to get an urgent message to Director Womack. He's not answering his phone."

"Well, you're in luck," she said with a warm, disarming smile. "Tony Miller, the Executive Assistant of Counterintelligence, is here. May I show you to his office?"

Verdy's eyes widened, and he grinned. "Yes, please. That would be very helpful."

After receiving his Escorted Visitor badge, Verdy followed Thaler into an elevator that took them to the tenth floor. After exiting, she led him to a large glass office where sat ASAC Anthony Miller, a former U.S. Army officer who had once served in military intelligence under the general in Afghanistan.

Miller rose and bro-hugged his former boss. "It's good to see you again, sir." He turned to Thaler. "Thanks, Karen. I got this from here."

She nodded and left the glass cube, closing the door behind her.

"I'm glad you're here, Tony," Verdy said. "I'm having issues with your new boss. He's not taking my calls."

"Yes, I know. Womack has been told to steer clear of you—as have I," Miller said. "You might want to go to Andrew Roberts at the CIA directly if you have information to share. You guys essentially work for him anyway, right?"

Verdy placed a manila folder on Miller's desk. "Please read the contents in that file and kick it up the food chain. I already sent our findings to Langley. Beth Hu can back parts of this story. She still works directly for you, right?"

Miller didn't respond, but a dark cloud came over his face.

Verdy asked, "What's wrong, Tony?"

"Please keep this quiet, but Special Agent Hu has kinda gone missing," Miller said.

"What do you mean 'kinda gone missing?'"

"Two days ago, she left for China to check on an informant who'd gone dark. She was instructed to report in every eight hours, but we haven't heard from her for the past twenty."

"Jeezus. What the hell are you guys doing in China? You're way out of your jurisdiction."

"Please, general, spare me the lecture. Beth has been investigating the Tangs, who, by the way, are trafficking humans and drugs into the U.S., which makes it part of our jurisdiction."

"Have you sent someone to look for her?"

"Negative. The director doesn't want to involve any more agents until we know more."

"For Christ's sake," Verdy exclaimed, throwing his hands in the air. "This is exactly why amateurs shouldn't be leading our agencies. What did she say on her last call?"

"Nothing much. Only that she was going to talk to some low-level politician in Beijing to find out what happened to her asset. I shared this information with you because I care for Beth, and ..."

"Say no more. We're on it."

"Thank you, sir," Miller said. "I think it's fate that you came here this morning."

Verdy opened the door. "I don't know what you're talking about, Tony. I was never here, and this conversation never took place. Just see that the contents of that folder get to Womack, will you?"

"Who should I say I got them from?" asked the Miller.

"Tell him it fell off a truck for all I care. Just make sure he gets it as soon as possible."

Chapter 52

Twenty minutes had passed since Max Koga entered the sewing machine repair shop from the secret passage in the floor. The shotgun was exactly where Governor Mauricio Duarte said it would be, in the storage closet, and after retrieving it, Koga had waited patiently for his visitors to arrive.

"You move, you die," he warned them.

Ramin Madani gritted his teeth. "You American *dog*. I should have killed you in Mexico when I had the chance."

"Okay, but listen, you don't have to die here tonight," Koga said calmly.

"Ah, but one of us does," Madani declared, reaching to swing his rifle to the front of his body. "*Allahu Ak—*"

Koga squeezed the shotgun trigger, sending nine .33-inch steel ball bearings into Madani's chest that then exited out the back. The power at this close distance was brutal and incredible, with pellets ricocheting around the room after flying out of Madani's body. The doctor fell hard back into the hatch and dropped nine feet into the depths of the tunnel, hitting the floor with a thud.

"I ... I surrender," Nasim al-Ahmed exclaimed after seeing his associate perish next to him.

"Sorry, Nasim, but your presence has been requested by seven of my colleagues on the other side. You remember them, right? The ones you slaughtered in Topolobampo."

Al-Ahmed raised one hand in a non-threatening manner, and slowly lifted the AR-15 strapped to his body with the other, laying it on the floor.

"I am an unarmed prisoner now. You are American. You are not allowed to shoot a helpless man who has given up." He grinned knowingly, as if he had the upper hand. "You must arrest me now. Once I offer my intelligence, I will be in witness protection before your reports are even written."

A wave of nausea came over Koga, as the edges of his vision began to tint red. This animal, who was more than willing to send his comrades to their deaths, was as smug as he was heartless. The urge to empty the next shotgun shell into al-Ahmed's face was desperately tantalizing.

"Why not die a martyr like your friend down there?" Koga gestured to the hole in the floor with the shotgun barrel. "I'll allow you to take your own life here and now ... if you're man enough."

"As long as I'm alive, our cause will carry on," al-Ahmed said. "Therefore, I decline your offer of premature paradise. I still have work to do here."

Koga shrugged. "Thought so. Then take your sidearm out and slide it toward me. And take out everything in your pockets and place them on the floor in front of you—slowly."

Al-Ahmed pulled his pistol out from a holster with his index finger and thumb, dropped it, and kicked it toward Max. He produced a satellite cellphone, a combat knife, and a wallet from his back pockets. Last, he took out keys and a small walkie-talkie from the pouches in his uniform trousers.

"That's everything," al-Ahmed said.

Koga walked up to the terrorist and butt-stroked him in the face with the Mossberg shotgun.

"You are going to regret not taking me up on the offer."

"*Inshallah*," al-Ahmed said, wiping the blood that seeped from the side of his mouth on his sleeve. If Allah wills it.

Grabbing his prisoner by the shirt and hoisting him to his feet, Koga spun al-Ahmed around and pinned him to the wall with the Mossberg while zip-tying the terrorist's hands behind him with the other. He ran his free hand over al-Ahmed's body for a backup search.

"Where are you taking me?" al-Ahmed asked.

There was no reply. Instead, Koga pulled his prisoner to a late '70s Chevrolet Impala parked outside. He unlocked the trunk and lifted the lid.

"Get in," Koga ordered.

"I will not," al-Ahmed resisted.

Koga struck al-Ahmed in the face again with the butt of the shotgun. "Next time, I use the other end."

"You will pay *dearly* for this," al-Ahmed mumbled through bloodied and loose teeth. He rolled awkwardly into the trunk and pulled in his legs.

"Hope you enjoy a pleasant ride," Koga said with a leer, slamming the trunk lid shut. He jumped into the driver's seat of the Impala and cranked the ignition. The car's small-block V-8 awakened with a hard, carbureted cough. He pulled the shifter down into Drive and sped out of the parking lot.

Using the navigation app on his satellite phone, he input the city center of Jalisco, the capital of the state of Durango. The nav app told him it would be a three-and-a-half-hour drive, putting him at his destination around eight o'clock in the morning. Just in time for breakfast.

The Impala drove onto Highway 40D, a relatively new stretch of road that snaked through the rugged Sierra Madre Occidental Mountains. Before this highway was built, drivers traveling from Mazatlán to Jalisco were required to use Highway 40, a wickedly meandering road nicknamed the Devil's Backbone, spending more than seven hours to make the same trip amid exposure to stretches of bad roadway and known bandit activity.

Koga needed none of those extra distractions now.

As the sun crested the horizon, the surrounding hills took on a florescent yellow glow. Down below was a river snaking through a canyon. Just as Koga crossed the Baluarte Bridge, marking the border between Sinaloa and Durango, his Argon cellphone rang. Caller ID showed it was Paul Verdy.

"I'm glad you called, boss. Do I have some news for—" Koga started to say until he was cut off.

"Max, listen up. Beth has gone missing," Verdy said in a flat tone. "I'll have Raj send you the specifics. The FBI will not go looking for her, so I'm sending you."

"Gone missing? How? Where?" Koga asked.

"She took a trip to Beijing and disappeared."

"Beijing? As in China?"

"You know of any other? My admin will find you a flight. Let her know where you are. By the way, where exactly are you right now?"

"Not really sure, but I can tell you I'm currently in possession of a certain one-eyed terrorist," Koga said.

"You son of a bitch—you got the bastard?"

"Aye-firmative. I'll fill you in on the details later, sir. Koga out."

Koga pressed down on the accelerator, getting the Impala to nearly unstable triple-digit speeds on the straights. He reached the border limits of Jalisco a half-hour quicker than what his nav had forecast.

Koga steered the car to the city's industrial sector, where he wandered through the area's crisscrossing streets until he found what he was looking for. On a deserted road just outside of town was an abandoned church, its adobe walls cracked and worn. It hadn't seen a congregation in years.

He drove onto the property and parked the Impala behind the building. After stepping out of the car without killing the engine, he opened the trunk. Al-Ahmed groaned in discomfort. Koga pulled him out to his feet.

"Walk," Koga commanded, leading his prisoner to the boarded entrance of the church.

As al-Ahmed limped along, complaining loudly about his treatment, Koga produced an injector of Argon's knockout drug and jammed the needle into the terrorist's neck.

"What are you doing? What did you inject me ..." al-Ahmed bleated with his one eye wide open before passing out.

"*Buenas noches, Cíclope*," Koga said.

After propping al-Ahmed's limp body up against the front door of the church, Koga returned to his car and parked it two blocks down the road behind a rotting station wagon, then used his cellphone to call a number gotten from Mauricio Duarte the previous day. The conversation in Spanish was quick. He hung up, sank low in the driver's seat, and waited.

❖

The world slowly came back into focus as Nasim al-Ahmed opened his eye. His body hurt all over, as if men had beaten him while he was asleep. The air was unusually cold, and he realized he was in a meat locker with what looked like large cuts of beef hanging from hooks along the walls. He was completely naked, and his arms and legs were secured to a sturdy metal chair.

"Hello," he called out in English. "Anyone here? Bring me some clothes."

A steel door at the far end of the refrigerated room swung open, and five unfamiliar men walked in, taking up positions behind him. Then a sixth man entered. When al-Ahmed saw his face, his heart stopped. Demetrio Navarro, the leader of the Durango Cartel, walked up with a crooked grin.

He said something in Spanish, which al-Ahmed did not understand.

"Please, have mercy," al-Ahmed said in English.

Navarro said in heavily accented English. "You killed my child. My first born. I asked God every day to exact my vengeance. He has heard my prayer."

The backside of Navarro's hand struck the side of al-Ahmed's face. The blow was so forceful that it nearly knocked him and the chair over. Navarro then walked calmly to a nearby table, where he studied the contents on its surface: an assortment of wire cutters; a jerry-rigged cattle prod with thick-gauge wire running from it; a large DieHard truck battery; and a Lincoln Electric MIG welder. Navarro rotated the table, offering al-Ahmed a good look at the equipment.

Upon seeing them, al-Ahmed's eye teared. He suddenly regretted not taking the Asian-American man's offer to take his own life.

"I beg you, please," al-Ahmed said, trembling more from fright now than from the cold.

Navarro didn't answer. He picked up the wire cutters in his hand and placed the jihadist's pinky between its jaws. Even before Navarro squeezed the handles together, Nasim al-Ahmed screamed louder than he had ever screamed before.

Chapter 53

It was early evening when Koga arrived at Los Angeles International Airport, three hours after leaving Durango and ten after bidding adieu to Nasim al-Ahmed, the leader of the Aqarib terror organization. He would have preferred to fly directly to Beijing, but the only way to China from Durango was through Los Angeles, giving him an opportunity to buy some clothes and make a quick stop at the office.

After deplaning, he jumped into his Uber ride, a white, late-model Toyota Camry. The driver was a Middle Eastern woman in her mid-twenties.

"I am taking you to Target?" she asked.

"Yes, and if you could wait outside for me, I'll pay you for your time. My second stop is in Malibu."

"Of course," she said.

Looking down at the app, he saw her name was Badour. She had long, dark hair and thick eyebrows that highlighted an attractive, round face. She drove in silence to the nearest Target store, just off the interstate.

"Be right back," Koga said, hurrying into the store and returning fifteen minutes later with a bulging plastic bag.

"Wow, you certainly bought a lot," Badour noted.

"I'm taking a big trip," Koga said.

She chuckled and asked, "Where are you from?"

"Here, but I grew up in Hawaii," he said.

"I mean, what country are you from?"

"My ethnicity is Japanese."

"I've always wanted to go to Japan. It seems so clean, and everyone there seems so well-mannered."

"May I ask where you're from?" Koga asked.

"Damascus," she said.

"Wow. You've come a long way. I'm glad you made it out of there. Horrible what your country has gone through."

"You know about Syria? Not many do in the U.S."

"What do you think about al-Aqarib?" Koga asked.

When the Toyota slowed to a stop in heavy traffic, Badour peered into the rearview mirror, looking Koga in the eyes. "At first, I thought it was great that they were trying to unite Muslims. Many in my generation don't really care about factions or caliphates. I'm a Shia and my husband is a Sunni, yet we are happy. But it was clear the people in al-Aqarib weren't true Muslims. Their use of violence isn't our way. It's good that Nasim al-Ahmed is no more."

Koga straightened in his seat. "What do you mean 'Nasim al-Ahmed is no more?'"

"It was on the news this morning. They said the Mexican government is making an announcement to say they killed the leader of al-Aqarib."

"Interesting," Koga remarked.

Leave it to Mauricio Duarte to waste no time jumping on an opportunity.

After a thirty-minute ride, the Camry pulled into the *Automobile Digest* photo studio parking lot. After wishing Badour a good day and paying her extra, Koga went directly to the Argon bullpen and Raja Singh.

"Hey, look who's here. I hear you had quite the vacation, world traveler," Singh said.

"Yeah, kinda. And thanks for digging up Mauricio Duarte's bank transactions so quickly. I don't know how you do it."

Koga gave him a thumbs-up and entered his office. On his desk was a new Apple laptop and a large envelope that contained a stack of Chinese yuan notes and five thousand American dollars. There was also a new passport and other documents in the name of Mick Mifune—the boss certainly had a way of coming up with terrible aliases—and a notebook detailing the political situation and topography of Beijing, which was a travel book of sorts for government agents. Scribbled on the cover of the notebook was the name of the CIA's Beijing station chief with a note. "He will have a vehicle pick you up at the airport. He's on our side. Use him. —Paul."

Koga stuffed the items into his Oakley bag and then called Singh on the interoffice phone. "Raj, you got a minute?"

"Be right there," Singh said, appearing in Koga's doorway a moment later. "What's up?" he asked.

"Have you been following the al-Ahmed situation?" asked Max.

Singh nodded. "I've seen classified reports saying he was found in a public trash bin near Jalisco, missing a few fingers and toes and both his ears. Apparently, his body was covered with many burn marks. Pretty horrible. Was that you?"

"No," Koga answered. "Well, not directly. By the way, I need you to do me a favor. You heard that Jayson Spence was working for the Aqarib, yes?"

Singh nodded. "Paul briefed us after you called it in."

"Well, Spence said that this whole thing went deeper than I knew. And that got me thinking. He didn't have access to a lot of the information that was leaked, including the raid on al-Ahmed's San Diego cell. So, I'm sure there's another suspect, one that's higher in the food chain. I'm regretting not keeping him alive ... "

"What do you need me to do?"

"Dig up whatever you can on everyone who knew about the SEAL raid in Mexico, the one where they saved my hide, as well as the FBI raid on that cell in San Diego. Check emails and personal texts if you can."

"Got it," Singh said, turning to return to his workstation.

"Oh, and Raj?" Koga said, calling him back. "Let's just keep this between ourselves for now."

Chapter 54

Without knowing exactly how long he was going to be out of the country, Max Koga elected not to leave either of his cars to the uncertain security of the airport long-term parking lot. He instead took another Uber back to LAX just as the sun descended under the western horizon. But before heading for the airport, he had one important stop to make. While sitting in the rear seat of yet another Toyota Camry, his cellphone buzzed. It was Verdy.

"Max," his boss greeted somberly. "The hospital just called. Rawlings didn't make it."

The sentence was met with silence. It took Koga several seconds to process the information, and even once he had, there was nothing to say.

"I'm sorry, Max. I know how close the two of you were," Verdy said.

"What happened?" Koga finally asked.

"He went into cardiac arrest during the third operation. The doctors said it happened while they were attempting to take out the last bullet. I'm headed there now."

Koga felt his head go light, and a feeling of nausea set in. "I was on my way to see him just now. Shit, I was so sure he was going to pull through. He was the toughest son of a bitch I ever met."

Taking deep breaths to calm his nerves, Koga ended the call just as the Camry pulled into the parking lot of the Good Samaritan Hospital. After asking the hospital receptionist for Donald Rawlings' room number, he followed the signs to the intensive-care wing to a suite at the end of a short hallway. He hesitated to enter the room, afraid to see what was behind the door. But he stepped in. The first thing to catch his eye wasn't Rawlings lying on the bed but an African American woman seated next to him.

"I'm sorry. I hope I'm not interrupting," Koga said.

The woman spun around. "Who are you?" she asked.

"I'm Max. And you are?"

"Donald spoke about you often," she said through reddened eyes. She then stood from her seat. "My name is Ameri."

Ameri was at least two inches taller than Koga, with long, lean legs under a knee-length skirt. The bronze color of her skin shone under the fluorescent ceiling light, as did her straight brown hair. She wore little makeup but didn't need any; she had just a smidgen applied to her high cheekbones. The exotic nature of her appearance made guessing her age difficult. Koga would have put her in her late twenties or early thirties.

Stepping past her, Koga approached the bed where Rawlings lay. He stood there for a minute, studying his friend's serene face, then touching his arm. Although Koga had seen death plenty of times before, this one was different, even from the time when Jimmy Slack was killed in front of his eyes. The sight of his best friend, who was filled with humor and energy, resting in such a still state, and without expression, seemed more than surreal. He felt his eyes well up, but he refused to let the tears fall.

"You bastard. You damned, stinking bastard," Koga murmured. "We were supposed to retire in a couple of huts in Kauai when we're done saving the world."

Ameri began sobbing loudly, dropping back down into her chair.

Releasing Rawlings' arm, Koga then turned to the young woman. "I don't think we've ever met. You're related to Donnie how?"

She took a tissue from her handbag and blotted her eyes. "Donald and I were dating. We've been together for the last six months or so."

"He never mentioned you to me."

"We had our reasons," she said.

"Would you like to share them?"

Ameri eyed Koga from head to toe. "Donald told me you were the most trustworthy person alive."

Koga seated himself in an empty chair. "I'm all ears."

"Back when I was in San Diego, I was involved in a terrible marriage. My husband was a raging alcoholic, and he liked to beat on me. One day Donald saw him strike me in broad daylight, so he confronted him. My husband didn't appreciate being talked down to and took a swing at him. Donald broke his arm."

Koga chuckled, glancing at Rawlings. "Sounds like Donnie."

"Yes, only my husband was a Navy captain."

Koga raised an eyebrow. "Oh."

"He tried to have Donald arrested, but couldn't because Donald apparently had friends in high places. A deal was made for Donald to be honorably discharged. I filed for divorce, but my husband refused to sign the papers, saying he still wanted to work things out. I wanted no part of him anymore, so I moved out. That's when Donald said it was okay to stay with him. One thing led to another and ..."

"Donnie definitely had a way of making every aspect of his life an adventure. A captain, huh? That explains why he left the Navy."

Ameri nodded.

Rising from his chair, Koga gazed upon his friend's face for the last time. "I'll see you on the other side, bruddah. Rest peacefully." He then headed for the door.

"Where are you going?" Ameri asked.

"To make sure I lose no more people who are close to me," Koga said without turning around.

STAGE FOUR
Into the Red

Chapter 55

Of all the airports Max Koga had visited over the years, Beijing Capital International Airport was among the most modern and clean. Large and artfully designed, the general atmosphere of the facility reminded him of Narita International Airport in Tokyo, with shiny tiled floors and blue signs with both Chinese and English characters.

What set Beijing Capital apart from its Japanese counterpart was its customer service, or lack thereof. At Narita, the airport staff went out of their way to assist and serve their guests, what the Japanese call *omotenashi*. The staff at Beijing Capital didn't seem to care whether you lived or died.

After disembarking from the United Airlines Boeing 777 aircraft, Koga stopped and asked an attendant where to find the best ground transportation. His first attempt was totally ignored. The second prompted a loud response in Mandarin, evidently an annoyed one.

"English, please?" Koga said.

The middle-aged man retorted in his native tongue, then stalked away.

Koga followed the other passengers through immigration and then to the arrivals lounge, where an Asian man in a black suit held up a placard with "M. Mifune" written across it in thin marker letters. With his compact roller suitcase at his side and Oakley bag hanging from his shoulder, Koga approached him.

"I'm Mick," he said.

The man bowed and smiled. "Stan Yu at your service. Please follow me,

Mr. Mifune," the man responded in flawless English.

Koga followed him outside, walking past a row of waiting taxis. They stopped next to a Buick minivan, a China-market-only model, parked by the curb.

"Please get in. We're friends of Mr. Paul," Yu said.

He placed the luggage into the rear compartment as Koga climbed inside. In the driver's seat was an older man with salt-and-pepper hair, wearing a white polo shirt and khakis.

"Welcome to China," he said, pulling the Buick away from its parking spot and leaving the attendant behind at the curb.

"Are you a friend of my Uncle Sam?" Koga asked.

"Yes, he sends his regards. The station chief wishes you to join him for lunch."

With the radio station playing classic American rock music, the minivan made its way into the heart of the city. Traffic on the highway flowed smoothly at first, but once Koga and his driver entered the inner Ring Roads, congestion steadily increased until finally they came to a dead stop.

"And I thought the traffic in Los Angeles was bad," Koga remarked.

"This city has been constantly growing for the past one hundred years," the driver said. "Beijing's first Ring Road—the highway that circumnavigates the city center—was established in the 1970s, although many here say that it was much earlier than that. As people flocked here, the city needed to expand geographically, so they built a second Ring Road, followed by a third, then a fourth. They just opened the Seventh Ring Road, which is located more than a hundred miles from the city center."

"How many more of these until we get to our destination?" Koga asked.

"We're almost there. It's just inside the Third Ring," the driver said.

As promised, the Buick exited the expressway a few minutes later and pulled into an area called *Nanluoguxiang*, an old town characterized by *hutongs*—narrow streets lined with traditional courtyard buildings. It was one of several "old towns" in Beijing in which the principal attractions were its specialty shops and distinctive food offerings. Because no motor vehicles were allowed inside, the Buick stopped near the southern entrance.

"Go down that walkway. Just follow the flow of people," the driver instructed as he opened the automatic side door. "You'll see a teahouse on the right-hand side with yellow lanterns. The chief is in the back room. Take your things with you. You'll not be returning to this vehicle."

After thanking the driver, Koga stepped out of the vehicle and onto the cracked sidewalk. A powerful stench overwhelmed his nostrils. It was no secret that China probably had the worst air quality in the world, and the rank aroma of smoke and chemicals made breathing a chore. He pulled a white handkerchief from his left rear pocket and covered his nose and mouth with his free hand, making his way down the main pathway.

The main *hutong* was lined with many shops that included fabric stores, cafés, and even a boutique hotel. There seemed to be an even mix of Chinese locals and Caucasian tourists strolling through the street. And there were small government-installed video cameras everywhere. Big Brother was always watching in China. About a hundred yards in, he spotted an establishment with yellow lanterns hanging from a low roof. The teahouse resembled an old Chinese residence, with a narrow entranceway set between two large windows.

When he walked through the open door, Koga saw tables positioned randomly in the center of the room, with about half of them occupied by patrons snacking on dumplings or sipping tea.

Further in was a narrow passageway that appeared to lead to a private area. A woman who stood barely five feet tall and wore enough makeup to double as a Chinese opera performer greeted him in Mandarin.

"Huānyíng. Qǐngwèn kèrén yǒu jǐ wèi?"

"English?" Koga requested with a tentative smile.

"Welcome. How many people?" she asked in a thick accent.

"I'm meeting a friend who is already here."

"Ah, yes," she said. "He told me you were coming. Follow me." She led Koga to one of two private rooms in the back.

Inside the room was an Asian man in his mid- to late-forties, dressed in a black button-down shirt and gray slacks. He sat on a cushion atop an elevated wooden floor. In front of him was a low table, with an ornate teapot and two small ceramic teacups. Koga stowed his suitcase and Oakley against the wall and removed his shoes, taking a seat across from his host.

"Thanks for arranging transportation," he said. "You must be Charlie Wong."

"I'm the station chief here. It's good to meet you, Mister Koga. I've heard a lot about you from Paul," Wong said, extending his hand. Koga shook it.

"Please call me Max. What can you tell me about Agent Hu?"

After pouring tea into Koga's cup, Wong took a sip from his own. "Not much, I'm afraid. I do know that she was investigating the Tangs, a criminal organization made up mostly of North Korean expats and funded by Pyongyang. Word on the street is that it's the Tangs that have her."

"Have they asked for a ransom or demand?"

"Not yet, although we were expecting an offer for a prisoner swap. We've been keeping an eye on the North Korean embassy, but we have seen no sign of her or any suspicious movements by the North Koreans."

"Do you think that she's still alive?" Koga asked.

"Again, I don't know, but I suspect so. She makes poor trading material if she's dead."

"There's that." Koga took a sip of his tea. It was warm, unsweetened, and bitter. "Can you tell me more about the Tangs?"

"The DCIA said we were to leave the Tangs alone for now. If he or anyone else at Langley got wind that I was helping you, I'd probably be sent off to Tibet. I'm only doing this because Paul is a good friend of mine."

Wong placed a black sports bag onto the table and slid it toward Koga. "I prepared this myself, but you didn't get it from me. There's information about the gang in there. Hangouts, some photos and names of the leaders, and other stuff. But just to be clear: If you get into trouble, I'll deny any knowledge of you. You're a private citizen here on vacation for all we know."

"I have no problem with that. Plausible deniability. That's the PMC way of life," Koga said as he unzipped the bag. Inside he found a sat phone, a holstered Walther PPK handgun, a suppressor, extra full magazines, thin gloves, and a large sealed envelope.

"I'll want the gun back when you're done," Wong said.

Koga zipped the bag shut. "I'll take care of it as if it were my very own."

"From what I've heard about you, that's not reassuring. There's a number programmed into the satellite phone inside the bag. Call it only in an emergency." He tilted his head over his shoulder. "I've arranged for you to leave through the back door."

Koga's stomach growled. "Do you mind if I order some chow first? The food here smells amazing—and from what you've told me so far, I'm going to have a long day ahead of me."

Chapter 56

The staff at the Royale Hotel Beijing had grasped the concept of customer service better than the folks at the Beijing Capital International Airport. Trained by American and Japanese hoteliers, the workers at the Royale knew that foreign business travelers liked to be pampered, and they often tipped well.

When the valet spotted Koga step out of a taxi in front of the entranceway, the young man ran to him to relieve him of his suitcase and guide him to the check-in counter. A woman there greeted Koga warmly and offered a hot towel and a glass of water with a slice of lime inside to occupy him while she logged him into the hotel computer by his passport number.

The lobby had a quaint, classically Asian feel to it, with dark wood floors, traditional Chinese-style wooden chairs, and tables placed around a giant salt-water aquarium. Paul Verdy's administrative assistant had arranged for the four-star hotel because of its central location in the business district.

"As with many high-end hotels in a communist capital city, there's the likelihood the government bugs the rooms and monitors with hidden cameras, so take extra precautions," she had suggested to him over the phone.

As soon as he entered his room, he swept it for listening devices and cameras with an ingenious device built into his watch. The room was clean. He then sat on his bed and opened the folder provided to him by CIA Station Chief Charlie Wong.

For such an old organization, the Tangs had remained remarkably low profile. While the gang's lower and middle ranks were composed of Chinese street thugs, the upper echelon of leadership consisted of North Korean agents, all of them members of the Korean People's Army. Ranked by the CIA as the fifth-most powerful criminal organization in China, the Tangs had cells in South Korea, Macau, Taiwan, and Japan, and were expanding throughout Southeast Asia.

In fact, the random abduction of Japanese citizens in the early Eighties—grabbed in broad daylight and whisked away to North Korea to teach KPA soldiers the Japanese language and culture—was believed to have been carried out by the Tangs. The organization had its hand in everything from drug dealing to kidnapping and extortion. It also operated an exclusive nightclub called the Red Note in the fashionable Sanlitun district of Beijing, where it often conducted business with Chinese politicians and celebrities. The file mentioned that the North Korean ambassador to China and suspected Tangs leader, Colonel Chol-Min Seo, made frequent visits there.

It's as good a place as any to start.

After unpacking his suitcase, Koga peeled off forty hundred-yuan notes from his bundle of Chinese cash and stuffed them into his pants pocket. He then shoved five American one-hundred-dollar bills into the other pocket and, with the handgun and holster stowed under his belt in the small of his back, he took the elevator to the lobby.

A young man in his mid to late twenties, dressed in a hotel uniform with a nametag that read "Chen Yen-Jung," greeted Koga with a smile as he approached the concierge desk.

"How may I help you?" Yen-Jung asked with a hint of a British accent.

Koga took a seat at the concierge desk. "I would like to hire a driver for a couple of days. One who speaks good English."

Yen-Jung took out a folder from under the table and opened it to the first page, reading down the columns of entries. "There are several reliable services we're contracted with. Do you have a preference?"

Without so much as a glance, Koga closed the folder shut. "I need someone who can also act as a guide. You know, show me some of the 'non-tourist' spots in the city. Someone discreet," he whispered. Yen-Jung didn't immediately respond, but instead studied Koga's face.

He surveyed the lobby and, when satisfied that no one was within earshot, whispered, "I'm sure that can be arranged. I know a person who handles, um, special requests. It will cost more than the normal service, if that's all right."

"That's fine."

"Then I have the perfect person," said Yen-Jung. "Please do not mention this to anyone at the hotel." He pulled out a notepad and scribbled a name and number on the top sheet of paper.

"Thank you," Koga said, taking out some Chinese cash from his pocket.

Yen-Jung barely moved his lips when he spoke. "Not here. Give it to the driver. He's actually my cousin."

Koga nodded and stowed the money back in his pocket.

"Thank you, and please contact the front desk if you have any more questions. Good day," Yen-Jung announced in a loud voice while shaking Koga's hand.

After ripping up and throwing away the piece of paper that the helpful concierge handed him, Koga stepped outside and dialed the number that he had memorized at first glance.

"*Wéi*," a scratchy voice answered on the third ring.

Koga spoke slowly and clearly. "Is this Benjamin Xu?"

"Who is this?" the voice asked in broken English.

"I'm Mick, and I received your number from your cousin at the Royale Hotel. He said I can hire you as a driver for a couple of days."

"Yes. My rate is three hundred U.S. dollars per day," Xu said.

Koga thought he could negotiate that price down to about fifty bucks if he wanted, but he had neither the time nor the inclination to haggle at this point. "I'll pay you five hundred if your service is good," Koga offered.

"Mister, I will be there in fifteen minutes," Xu said before hanging up.

Exactly fourteen minutes later, a light brown, slightly beat-up vintage Toyota Land Cruiser drove up the hotel driveway, stopping short of the valet sign. A lanky man wearing Ray-Ban aviator sunglasses and an untucked blue Aloha shirt stepped out. He walked to the hotel entrance, right past Max.

"Xu?" Koga called out.

The man stopped, turned around, and slid his glasses down his nose to get a better look. "Mr. Mick? I thought you were a white man."

"I'm close enough." Koga liked what he saw. Xu's clothes and attitude showed he was an open-minded individual, one who would do just about anything for the right price. He reminded Koga of a modern-day Han Solo, without the make-believe bravado or the Wookie.

"I'm American, although I may not look it," Koga said.

"Sure, of course. As long as you pay, you can be whatever you want. I don't care," Xu responded, walking back to his SUV and opening the rear door for his client. "And call me Big Ben."

Ignoring him, Koga walked over to the Toyota, opened the front passenger door, and plopped himself into the seat. "I enjoy sitting up front."

"Very good, mister." Xu closed the rear door and took his position behind the steering wheel.

Koga held up two one-hundred-dollar bills. "You get the rest when we're done."

Xu took the money and shoved it into his breast pocket. "Where you want to go? Do you want pretty girls? I know the best massage parlors."

"How about a club called the Red Note?"

Xu shot Koga a hard look. "Red Note? That's a very exclusive place. You need a special pass to get in. Do you have a membership or an invitation?"

"More or less," Koga said.

"Okay, but I can take you to better clubs. I know them all."

Koga shook his head. "Nope. I want to go to the Red Note."

"Lots of dangerous people hang out there," warned Xu.

"I'm counting on it, Big Ben. I'm counting on it. Now drive."

Chapter 57

The Red Note was at the south end of Bar Street in Sunlitun, where Beijing's upwardly mobile went to shop, dine, and drink. If you partied in the city, Bar Street was a good place to start. The area was known for its array of bars, catering especially to foreign tourists and expats.

The sun was just about to set when Max Koga and Ben Xu reached Bar Street. The sidewalks were rather empty, but Big Ben assured him that the place would be hopping with a wide assortment of people as soon as nightfall came. He pointed to a two-story brick building at the corner of the main intersection. "That's the club you want, but it's not open yet. No one there."

The Land Cruiser slowly passed the brick structure on the far side of the street. It had a sign in front that read: "Red Note. A Modern Jazz and Rock Club" along with Chinese characters that probably said the same thing.

"Pull over here and let me out," Koga instructed.

"You sure you don't want a massage first?" Xu asked.

"I'm sure. I'll call you when I need you. Stay within two minutes of here."

"Okay, no problem. I'll wait for you down the street," Xu said, stopping the car to let Koga out. "Text me when you need me."

Koga stepped away from the vehicle and a white-haired woman sitting behind a low wooden table on the sidewalk stared at him with wide eyes. She gasped and pointed at him, shouting something to him in Mandarin.

"I'm sorry, ma'am, I don't speak Chinese," Koga said.

Recklessly parking his Toyota along the sidewalk, Xu rushed over to shout something to the woman in Mandarin. He put his hand on Koga's back and urged him away. "You go, boss. These fortune tellers always looking for business. Pay them no attention."

"What's she saying?"

"She say she see spirits on your back."

"What, like ghosts?"

Xu nodded. "Yes, ghosts. Just ignore her."

Koga paused and turned back to the old woman. "Ask her what she sees."

Xu translated the question and received a quick response. "She say there are spirits of six men and a woman on your back. She has never seen so many attached to one person. They all look very sad."

What the ... It had to be more than just a coincidence.

"This isn't some kind of trick you play on foreigners, is it?" Koga asked.

Xu put up his hands. "I've never seen her in my life. And why would I go to all the trouble?"

"You have a point. Ask her why they're with me."

Xu and the woman swapped several words and then he turned to Koga and said, "She say they worry about you, and they only want to help you."

"Really? Why?"

Xu looked at him with a surprised expression. "You believe her?"

"I don't know. I've heard stranger things that were true. What do you think?"

"In China, we believe unhappy spirits attach to living people randomly, but Westerners think this is a joke."

"Then can you ask her what the hell they want?" Koga asked, taking a seat on the small stool across from the woman. "Tell her I'll pay."

Xu shrugged. "Okay, boss. It's your money."

The woman took Koga's hands and held them on the table countertop. She closed her eyes and muttered. Xu translated her words in real time.

"They seem to be your friends, and they care for you a lot. They will not rest until your job is finished," Xu said.

"But I've already avenged them. They should be satisfied now."

The psychic continued speaking with her eyes still closed.

"No, they are not content. That is why they cling to you."

"Is this why I always feel so tired lately?"

"Yes, they are feeding off your *chi*, your spiritual energy."

"Ask her that if I bring to justice the people responsible for their deaths, will they find peace and leave me alone?"

The psychic's face hardened with intense concentration. She then let out a deep breath and opened her eyes. "Wǒ bù zhīdào."

"She say she doesn't know," Xu translated.

The woman muttered something else in Mandarin.

"And she say that she doesn't think it is vengeance they want."

"How long do they plan on sticking around?" asked Koga.

The psychic answered as if understanding his words, "*Zhīdào nǐ nénggòu zhōngyú zhǎodào xīnzhōng lǐ dì níngjìng.*"

"Until you find peace in your heart," Xu translated.

Koga took six hundred yuan from his wallet and handed it to the woman. "*Xiè xiè,*" he said. Thank you. "I still have many questions, but I feel somewhat less crazy than before, thanks to you." He took her hands in his and grasped them warmly, smiling with appreciation.

Upon seeing the cash, equivalent to nearly one hundred American dollars, Xu clapped his hands and asked, "Hey, how about translation tip for me?"

"All in good time, Big Ben. Now, I have some work to do, so please disappear and wait for my call." Xu scurried back to his parked Land Cruiser.

Great, thought Koga. Not only does my vision tint when I face danger, but I have dead spirits piggybacking me.

Although he couldn't embrace the supernatural without skepticism, the fortune teller's words had provided him with fresh motivation to find Beth Hu and see this business through to the very end.

It was the only way for everyone, living and dead, to find peace.

Chapter 58

Big Ben Xu drove away and Koga headed to a small bar with an outdoor patio and a direct line of sight to the Red Note's front door. After taking a seat at a small table, a server wearing a UCLA T-shirt approached with a hammered silver tray bearing a ceramic teapot and cup.

"What you want to order, please?" he asked in English, placing the cup on the table and pouring the tea.

"Just something to snack on and a beer," Koga said.

"We have sandwich and French fries."

"What is he making?" Koga asked, pointing to a man baking what looked like crepes on a small round stove inside the store.

"Chinese pancake, called *jianbing*. He making it for himself. It's breakfast food," the man said. "He just woke up."

"I'll have what he's having."

"It's not on menu, but I see if he make extra," the waiter said, walking into the building.

Koga watched as the cook cleaned his small portable stove with a wet cloth, the water droplets sizzling on the worn surface and issuing steam into the air. He dropped a dripping ladle of batter on its surface and spread it until it was paper thin. After cracking an egg on top of it, he sprinkled some salt, scallions, and chili sauce over the medley, then folded it twice and placed it inside a paper wrapper. The waiter brought the crepe dish to Koga's table, still steaming from the griddle.

After inspecting the *jianbing*, Koga carefully bit off a corner of it and chewed slowly. The texture of the crepe was soft and exploded with flavor, with just the right amount of saltiness to offset the sweetness of the dough.

He ate and kept an eye on the brick building. A pair of American female college students, a blonde and a brunette, sat at a nearby table, observing him and whispering.

The blonde woman turned toward Max. "Hey sir, is this place open?"

"I think so. I just ordered," Koga said.

She blinked her bloodshot eyes. "You speak really good English."

"Thanks, I've been working on it. By the way, have either of you ever been to that club over there?" he said, pointing to the Red Note.

The blonde shook her head. The brunette, who seemed less affected by whatever they had been drinking or smoking, said, "That place is super exclusive. You can't get in unless they know you and have a lot of money."

As Koga sipped his tea, a blue Subaru WRX STI pulled up to the front of the Red Note, its exhaust note burbling off the building walls of the narrow street. When the passenger door opened, a thin man wearing a black T-shirt and gray slacks jumped out. He unlocked the Red Note's front door and entered the building. The Subaru then drove away. Seeing the powerful road car suddenly reminded Koga of the race car driven by his father in his last World Rally Championship race.

Finishing his early evening meal, Koga left a hundred yuan note on the table, bid the girls adieu, and strolled toward the Red Note. Xu had been right about this district—as soon as the skies darkened, bar street came alive. The shops were all lit up like video games, many with music broadcast into the street from storefront speakers, and the sidewalks had become filled with college students and businessmen. None of them approached the Red Note.

When he reached the bar's front door, Koga pounded on the hard metal surface three times. A pair of brown eyes appeared behind a speakeasy grill, followed by what seemed to be angry words in Mandarin.

Koga shrugged. "I'm American."

"We not open," the man behind the door said in accented English.

"Your camera broken?" Koga asked, pointing at the video camera attached to the wall.

"No, I see better this way. Closed. Go away."

Just before he closed the grill door, Koga held up a wad of American hundred-dollar notes. "Are you sure about that?"

"What you want here?"

"Oh, just some fun. I heard I could meet lots of pretty girls here, especially nice Chinese ones who speak good English."

"No girls here now, but come back at nine. We make sure you have good time," the man said, nodding with a broad fake smile.

Koga pulled another bill from the wad and held it in front of the eyes. "May I have a beer now? I'm very thirsty."

"There are many other bars open. Go there and come back at nine."

"I only drink at classy places, not dumps like those," Koga said, peeling off another hundred.

The eyes locked onto the three hundred dollars. "Okay, one beer, five minutes. I need to set up for opening time."

The sliding cover to the speakeasy grill closed, followed by the click of a deadbolt. Koga took a couple of steps back, and at the precise moment the door unlatched, he launched himself forward, driving his shoulder into the metal door with the ferocity of an angry linebacker. The force of the impact sent the manager flying backward into the restaurant. As he fell onto the wooden floor, Koga stepped into the building and shut the door behind him, his Walther PPK already in his hand.

The manager sat up and raised his arms when he saw Koga's firearm pointed his way. "Hey, mister, take it easy," he said.

With his right thumb, Koga flipped the safety off. "Now, about those nice Chinese girls who speak good English ..."

Chapter 59

Three days had passed since Beth Hu had been abducted, but she felt it was like three weeks. She'd spent most of the first two days with a black bag over her head in a small, nondescript massage room located somewhere within the greater Beijing area. Where exactly, she had no clue.

In front of her was a twin-size bed covered with white towels, and next to it was a medicine cabinet holding plastic containers of what looked to be therapeutic oils. A ceiling fan circulated the scent of ginger and tobacco smoke throughout the room, while a single upright lamp provided the only source of light. The melody of Chinese string music played faintly from a speaker mounted to the wall.

She had entered the country under a pseudonym and spoke with no one of consequence since her plane touched down. After checking into her hotel, she had taken a taxi to the Song Motors office to confirm that it truly had closed. There was nothing there except empty office spaces, with a few tables and chairs left behind. She took another taxi to a shopping mall near Beijing University, where Councilman Wang Wéi, her asset in the Chinese government, dined four nights a week.

Wait there long enough, and he would show eventually, she thought.

When dinner time rolled along, Bistro Chinois was filled to near capacity, but Beth managed to sweet talk the host into seating her at a small table in the back. Once settled, a man in his fifties dressed in a white jacket and a black bowtie brought her a glass of water and asked for her order in Mandarin.

"I'm new here, but my friend, Councilman Wang, recommended this place," Beth replied in the same tongue.

The waiter flashed his large white teeth. "Ah, Councilman Wang. Yes, I have served him many times. Such an interesting man."

"He told me he would come tonight, but I don't see him," Beth said.

The waiter rubbed his chin. "Come to think of it, I haven't seen the councilman for a while, which is quite odd. He has been coming here three to four times a week for the past ten years."

"I see. Then I suppose I'll have whatever the chef recommends tonight," Beth said, scanning the restaurant for a familiar face.

"Right away," the waiter said.

After a hearty three-course meal with no appearance by Wang, Beth left the establishment. She headed in the direction of the train station to return to her hotel when two large men blocked her way on the sidewalk. Before she could react, a dark green minivan screeched to an abrupt stop next to her. Three men wearing black ski masks spilled out of the vehicle and took hold of her, forcing her inside. They secured her wrists and covered her head with a black sack. Only a few minutes later, she found herself in the massage room, where the only human contact she had was with a Chinese kid named Kevin, who brought her a couple of meals.

The Tangs had discovered her identity, but how did they know about her arrival in China so quickly?

The door to the room unlocked. Expecting to see Kevin with her lunch, she stepped back when she instead saw a stocky man with a large scar on his lip.

"Who the hell are you?" she asked in Mandarin.

The man answered in English. "Sit down over there."

"Bugger off," answered Beth.

"Suit yourself," the man said as he stepped to the side to allow a taller man with greased black hair to enter. Beth recognized him from the photos at the FBI offices.

It was Ambassador Chol-Min Seo of the DPRK.

"Hello, Ms. Hu," he addressed her in English.

"You have the wrong person. My name is Katie Chang. You can verify this with my passport. I'm an American citizen, and I demand to be freed."

Seo laughed. "Come now, Ms. Hu—or shall I address you by your title, Special Agent?—please don't think me a fool, and I will accord you the same courtesy. I know exactly who you are. You're an FBI agent investigating the disappearance of our mutual friend, Councilman Wang Wéi."

"I don't know who or what you're talking about."

"I also know that you were at the Los Angeles Auto Show, where you and your friends removed a bomb from the facility. My assistant, Major Kang here, said that he saw you as plain as day."

Beth glanced over at the imposing figure. He didn't look familiar, but he projected an aura of cruelty. In the corner of her vision, she observed that he'd left the door ajar.

Seo continued. "Let me tell you what's going to happen. You'll be glad to hear that we'll treat you quite humanely ..."

Beth cut him off. "Like attacking me in the middle of the street and keeping me here against my will?"

"Let me assure you that, by our standards, that is just short of VIP treatment," Seo said. "So, where was I? Oh, yes. You'll fly to Pyongyang tonight on our private jet. There, you'll be tried as a spy by our highest court."

"But I'm on Chinese soil."

"We'll say that we caught you snooping inside the North Korean embassy," Seo said. "I'm sure I don't have to tell you that embassy property is North Korean soil."

"My people know I'm here."

"No matter. We will broadcast your trial all over the world. Everyone will see how the U.S. actively spies on our country."

Giving no sort of warning, Beth leaped forward with her right fist flying toward Seo's jaw. But before it could reach its intended target, Kang stepped in and slapped it down. He followed with an open-hand strike to Beth's shoulder that sent her flying into the opposite wall. The impact knocked the wind out of her as she fell to the ground.

Kang walked over and lifted her by the arm.

She responded by kicking his legs, but her Nike running shoes bounced off his tree-trunk thighs like paper spitballs.

Seo barked something in Korean and Kang released Beth's arm.

"I admire your fight, Ms. Hu," he said. "The Supreme Leader likes women with grit. Perhaps he will make a deal with you."

"What kind of deal?" Beth asked, trying to catch her breath.

"He may offer you the privilege of becoming one of his concubines."

Beth laughed. "I'd rather rot in hell."

"That can also be arranged," Seo said with a smile. "I will accompany you to Pyongyang, so, as you Americans say, I'll catch you later."

The colonel walked out of the chamber, followed by Kang, who shut and locked the door behind them.

All alone in the room again, Beth lay on the bed and stared up at the ceiling. Tears welled in her eyes, not at the prospect of being executed or spending the rest of her life in a North Korean labor camp, but out of frustration for not being able to do anything about it.

Chapter 60

Max Koga kept the business end of his handgun trained on the manager of the Red Note, who remained seated on the floor with his hands raised in the air.

"You don't know who you are messing with," the man warned.

"Nor do you, brah. Lie face down," Koga ordered.

The thin man let out a sigh, turning his body over and lying spread-eagled on the floor. Koga ran his hands over his captive's body and removed a small-caliber Beretta in the man's pocket. He took the weapon and shoved it into his Nike combat boot. He patted down the man's torso, finding a phone and a wallet that he removed and threw against the far wall.

"And I thought civilians weren't allowed to carry guns here. Now sit up slowly," Koga instructed, stepping back.

The manager lifted himself on all fours, swiveled his body around, and sat with his legs stretched out in front of him.

"Where's the American woman?" Koga asked.

"What American woman?" the manager said.

"You know which one." Koga raised his pistol to the man's face. "I'm sure you realize what's going to happen if you don't answer."

Before the man could respond, Koga heard the loud exhaust of a car from the rear of the jazz club. The engine shut off, followed by the sound of the rear door of the building being opened. Whoever it was had stepped into the kitchen and was headed his way. Quickly and quietly, Koga moved behind a partition while keeping the gun aimed at the manager. He put his index finger to his lips, gesturing for the manager to stay quiet. The service door that led to the kitchen swung open, and a rotund man stepped into the main dining room. He saw his colleague sitting on the floor and barked something to him in Mandarin.

"Don't move," Koga said, stepping out from his hiding spot. "Sit down next to your friend. Sit. *Zuò*."

The fat man looked at Koga with a surprised expression, but there was no fear there. With a confident smile on his face, he reached for the back of his belt.

"Don't do it," Koga reiterated, pointing the pistol at the big man's chest.

Either the fat man ignored him or didn't understand the command, because in the next instant he produced a small chrome revolver and pointed the barrel in Koga's direction.

Instinctively, Koga took dead aim at the center of the man's chest and fired two rounds. The bullets left two spreading red blotches on his white shirt as the fat man fell back, causing the wood floor to shake when he hit home.

The poor bugger must have thought my gun was a fake.

Without even looking the dead man's way, Koga walked over to the manager and lifted him up by his shirt. He forced the muzzle of his pistol into the manager's mouth.

"Do you see what happens when you don't listen to instructions?" Koga bellowed. "You'll meet the same fate if you don't do as I say. What is your name?"

"Ning ... Ning. My name is Ning," the manager slurred around the metal gun barrel.

"Okay, Ning Ning, I'm going to make it very simple for you. I know you're a member of the Tangs. Tell me where the American woman is, or I shoot you right now." Koga pulled the gun out of the manager's mouth long enough to permit him to draw a breath and speak.

"Only one Ning. My name is Ning."

"I don't care, brah. Where's the girl?"

"She's at the massage parlor. They're keeping her there until they move her," he said.

"Move her where?"

"I don't know. Probably out of the country."

"Has she been hurt in any way?"

Ning shook his head. "I don't think so."

"For your sake, she'd better not be. Where's this massage parlor?"

"It's very close, about ten minutes by car."

Koga kicked the dead fat man's revolver away and shoved Ning toward his former comrade. "You're going to take me there. Grab the car keys from your friend."

Ning quickly rose to his feet and did as he was told, pulling out a large keyless remote from his colleague's front pocket.

"Good," Koga said. "Slide it on the floor toward me."

Ning put the key fob on the floor and pushed it toward Max, who stopped it with his foot.

With his gun and eyes trained on Ning, Koga bent and picked up the fob. "Now, turn around and head for the kitchen."

Grabbing the back of Ning's collar, Koga pushed him through the swinging service door and forced him out the rear exit, where the blue Subaru WRX STI he'd seen earlier sat in a reserved parking spot. He pushed twice on the key fob, unlocking all four doors of the car. "Get in, slowly. You're driving."

Without hesitating, Ning did as he was told while Koga slid into the rear seat directly behind the driver's seat. He shoved the gun barrel hard against the base of Ning's skull.

"We're going to the massage parlor," Koga said. "Once there, park fifty meters away where I can see the front entrance. Do you understand?"

Ning nodded and pushed the start button that triggered the Subaru's turbocharged flat-four engine to life. He backed the car out of the alley and onto the main road. With the cold metal barrel of Koga's gun pressed against the back of his neck, Ning drove for ten minutes until he reached the outer border of the Suntilun area, pulling over on a narrow side road. He pointed to a building half a block away.

"She's in there."

The two-story building had a bright neon sign on the second-story wall. It read "Heaven's Gate" in English.

"What floor? What room?" Koga asked.

"Probably second floor. That's where they keep the special guests."

"Drive around the corner and park inside that alley up ahead."

Ning paused. "You're going to kill me?" he asked.

"Only if you don't do precisely as I tell you."

Ning guided the compact sedan into the alley, pulling up next to a large trash container overflowing with bulging white plastic bags, many ripped open by rats the size of house cats and spilling garbage on the street. Evidently, it was the trash man's day off.

"Get out slowly," Koga instructed.

As Ning stepped out of the car, Koga matched his movements, keeping the gun pointed in the gangster's direction the entire time. He then pressed the bottom button on the key fob, which released the trunk lid. After moving to the rear of the car, he took out a small tool kit that he always kept in his pocket and broke off the internal trunk release handle.

"Get in," he ordered Ning.

Ning looked at him, puzzled. "What? Why?"

"Get into the trunk. Do it now, or I shoot you and then I put you in anyway."

The prisoner climbed in, mumbling something incoherent in his native tongue. As he closed the lid, Koga gave Ning a quick wink and headed toward Heaven's Gate.

Chapter 61

From the outside, Heaven's Gate looked like any of the other massage parlors scattered throughout the city. Not knowing what to expect inside, Max Koga pushed on the glass door and stepped into a waiting room that looked eerily similar to the one from his neighborhood walk-in clinic. There were old chairs lined up against the wall near a reception window and stacks of magazines rested on a side table, but the room was devoid of people.

Max walked up to the reception window where a woman appeared behind the plexiglass germ barrier separating him from the countertop.

"Please sign in," she said in English with a strong accent. "You look Japanese. Are you from Tokyo?"

After signing "Mauricio Duarte" on the dotted line, he said, "No, I'm Sinaloan."

She gave him a confused look. "Where? Oh, no matter. What kind of girl you like?"

"One that speaks perfect English," Koga replied.

"Okay, can do. More expensive. Two thousand yuan for one hour." She raised her index finger.

Koga did a quick calculation in his head. "That's like three hundred American dollars," he fake-protested. "She'd better be worth it."

"All worth it here, sailor," the woman said with a sly grin.

Koga slid the cash through a slot cut into the bottom of the plastic screen. The woman scooped up the money and zipped it into a fanny pack worn in front. She disappeared into the back, reappearing a moment later in the adjacent doorway. She was dressed in a traditional Asian *cheongsam* dress right out of *Flower Drum Song*, and she was quite attractive up close. Koga put her age at around forty.

"Please come this way," she said with a smile.

He followed her through a long hallway lined with five closed doors on each side, ending at a spiral staircase.

"Where do those stairs go?" Koga asked.

"That special VIP room. Very expensive. Only members allowed there," she said while opening the nearest door on the right. She then gestured for him to enter. "Please wait in here and take your clothes off. I bring you our best girl speaking English."

It was the first time Koga had been in an Asian massage room. It was nothing like what he had expected. Where he envisioned elaborate Chinese art on the walls with lush carpeting and silk screens, this room had minimal furnishings—a twin-sized bed, a chair, and a nightstand holding neatly folded towels. The room reeked of tobacco smoke and perfume of indeterminate brand. The walls were bare save for a metal hook holding a white linen robe on a plastic hanger.

Instead of stripping off his clothes, Koga quietly opened the door and looked down the dimly lit hallway in both directions. As he had hoped, it was deserted. He stepped out of the room and made his way to the spiral staircase. He was nearly there when one of the doors that lined the hallway swung open and a young woman dressed in a see-through white nightie appeared. She jumped in surprise at the sight of the stranger.

Koga held up his hands. "I'm looking for the bathroom. Please be quiet. *Shhhh*." She responded by shouting something at him in Mandarin.

The thought of striking her and knocking her out cold crossed Koga's mind. Before he could do it, the madam burst out of the reception office.

"Where you going?" she asked, walking in his direction. "I say wait in the room."

The time for role-playing was over. Koga pushed aside the young masseuse and pulled his Walther from under his belt, hoping that the sight of the firearm would scare the women away. Instead, they began talking even louder. Evidently, their clientele had pulled handguns in here before.

Ignoring them, Koga ran up the staircase to the second floor, which was only two rooms. Both doors were shut and locked. Koga kicked in the first door. The room was empty. He went to the second door and kicked that one in. Nobody home.

Either he had arrived too late or that Ning Ning had tricked him. He turned to make his way back down the stairs when a cacophony of men's voices and pounding footsteps from below stopped him cold.

Shit.

Koga stopped and knelt on one knee, waiting to see if anyone climbed the stairs. Then, a single unfamiliar voice called out to him.

"Mr. Koga, we know who you are. I advise you to place your weapon on the floor and come down slowly."

Double shit.

Without knowing how many men were gathered below, Koga weighed his options. He saw no other way out of the building other than through the front door, since neither of the VIP rooms had windows large enough for him to climb through.

The man's voice sounded again. "I have your friend Beth Hu with me. If you don't unload your weapon and toss it down the stairs immediately, I will shoot her."

Koga froze.

"Max. If you really are up there, don't listen to him. I'll be okay."

It was Beth's voice.

Relieved she was still alive, Koga relaxed his shoulders.

"Okay, you win," he shouted. "Let her go and we'll forget all of this ever happened."

The suggestion was met by a hearty laugh.

"An amusing offer, but I'm afraid I must decline. Now, throw your firearm down the stairs and come down with your arms raised. You have three seconds or Agent Hu gets her bullet."

"Don't listen to him. I'll be all ..." The sharp sound of a face slap cut Beth's statement short.

The notion to go Butch and Sundance crossed Koga's mind. Jump down the stairs, shoot everything in sight, and go out in a blaze of glory. But the thought of Beth being hurt left him no real choice but to do as he was told. He reinserted the magazine and jacked in a fresh round, leaving the Walther ready to fire when he flung it down the stairs.

I might get lucky, he thought.

But the weapon bounced down the metal stairs and then fell to the floor without discharging.

"Thank you. Now come down with your hands over your head. Slowly," the voice instructed.

Raising his arms in the air, Koga descended the stairs one step at a time. Upon reaching the ground floor he was confronted by eight men, all brandishing weapons pointed in his direction. Behind them, he saw Beth with her arm being held by a person he recognized immediately. It was the man with the scarred lip who'd shot Donald Rawlings. Next to him was another familiar face, although he had never met the man in person—North Korea's ambassador to China, Chol-Min Seo.

"It's nice to meet you, Ambassador Seo," Koga said.

"Please, call me colonel," Seo responded. "And I think you've already met Major Jong-Su Kang."

A wave of intense anger fumed from within, as Koga wanted nothing more than to rush the North Korean mob and snap Kang's neck. His vision began to tint red, but he fought the overwhelming desire to go into full postal mode. He nodded to Seo as he positioned his body to hide the Beretta in his boot, but Seo hollered something in Mandarin to his men, provoking one of them to pat Koga down. The gangster smiled when he felt the metal object on Koga's ankle, taking the small gun from its hiding spot.

The man confiscated his other possessions too, including his personal cellphone, the sat phone he received from Wong, the wad of cash, and his pill case. Another man stepped forward and bound Koga's wrists behind his back with a pair of plastic zip cuffs.

"I must congratulate you on foiling al-Aqarib's bomb attack in Los Angeles," Seo said as he stepped forward.

"I have no idea what you're talking about," Koga answered, keeping his eyes on Beth.

She returned his gaze with a worried expression.

"And I'm sure you had something to do with Nasim al-Ahmed's regrettable end. Is it safe to assume so?" asked Seo.

"Again, absolutely no idea what you're talking about."

"Well, Mr. Koga, do you know what's going to happen now?"

"We're all going karaoke?"

Seo laughed out loud. "That is funny. But after I explain what we have in store for the two of you, I don't think you'll be in the mood for making jokes. First, we're going to take Ms. Hu to Pyongyang, where she will be tried and found guilty of espionage."

Beth struggled to break free.

"You grabbed me off a public street in the middle of Beijing. You won't get away with this."

Seo wagged a finger in Beth's direction. "We destroyed the cameras on that street beforehand, so there'll be no one to contradict our story. As for you, Mr. Koga, you're going back up to the special VIP room where we will kill one of the girls working here in front of your eyes. And then you shall die by drug overdose. Can you guess what's going to be all over the newscasts tomorrow?"

The cruelty and simplicity of the plan were modestly impressive. "You are one colossal piece of garbage, you know that?"

"Imagine the shame your country will experience when an American agent is found dead in a brothel in China, overdosed on heroin after murdering a young woman."

The words sent Koga into a fit of rage, as he could no longer contain his compulsions. He delivered a head butt to the gangster next to him. Once his right side was free, he sent a reverse roundhouse kick to the man behind him, knocking him backward into several other henchmen who toppled backward like falling bowling pins.

When he turned toward Beth, two men climbed onto Koga's back, with one of them putting a chokehold around his neck. Koga tried to shake them off, but the others joined in and forced him down to a knee. For the finale, Kang slammed his boot into Koga's jaw, opening up a deep gash just inside the mouth. It was the end of a hopeless attack.

"Goodbye, Mr. Maximilian Koga. I wish you a nice, um, trip," Seo said, laughing at his own joke. He turned and walked out of the hallway, forcing Beth out the door ahead of him.

On his knees with nearly a dozen men keeping him down, Koga sneered with blood seeping from his mouth: "You will see me again, you bastard—and when I do, I'm going to kill you."

But his words had no effect. Even Koga knew his threats were hollow.

Chapter 62

Three men lifted Max Koga to his feet while the other five trained their firearms on him from ten feet away. They forced him back up the spiral stairs to one of the VIP rooms where, once inside, they placed him in a chair and secured his legs with zip cuffs.

"Guys, you can still do the right thing here. Let me go and there's a big reward in it for you," Koga said.

The three gangsters locking him down ignored him. When they finished tightening the plastic straps, they left as another hoodlum entered—a large, muscular thug built like Arnold Schwarzenegger in his prime. In his hand was a slender Chinese girl dressed in the same sheer nightie as the other masseuses. He threw her onto the bed just as another man appeared. This one was much older than the others, probably in his mid- to late-sixties, with thick gray hair and thin, gold-framed spectacles. Using a walking stick for support, he limped to the hysterical girl.

Paying no attention to Koga, the older man was transfixed by the young woman, licking his lips as Chinese Mr. Olympia secured her arms and legs to the bed posts. The woman cried and resisted but to no avail.

"Stop. I'll do anything you say," Koga pleaded.

The older man looked Koga's way. He spoke in heavily accented English. "I am General Kim Yon-Ja of the Korean People's Army. In my country, I am sometimes called The Artist because of my special skills. You both will be my canvas today."

General Kim was unfamiliar to Koga, but he wasn't exactly a Communist version of Mister Rogers.

"Do what you want with me, but leave the girl alone. She has nothing to do with any of this," Koga demanded.

"So noble. What you're saying is that you'll do whatever I say if I let this girl go?" Kim asked.

"That's exactly what I'm saying."

"I'm very interested in your offer," Kim said, looking up and down Koga's sweating body. "But I'm afraid I have my orders. This woman was caught stealing money from her customers, so she must be punished."

The young masseuse continued to struggle, her screams muffled by a cloth gag.

"Hold still, my dear," Kim said, producing a syringe from a small medicine bag that he pulled out from under the bed. Inside the brown leather bag was also a rubber tourniquet. He tossed it to Chinese Mr. Olympia, who wrapped it around the young woman's left arm.

It was hard to watch, but Koga locked his eyes on the woman's face. Despite knowing that she didn't understand him, he said in as comforting a tone as possible.

"I'm so sorry. You don't deserve this. I hope you can take some comfort in knowing that you won't be going alone."

Just as Kim stabbed the needle into the woman's arm, the sound of automatic gunfire erupted from the ground floor, followed by shouts and screams.

A thin, bearded Tang gangster in a polo shirt came pounding up the stairs, opened the door and stopped in the doorway. Kim shouted something to him in Korean, but the man stared blankly into space and fell forward with three holes in his back.

Both Kim and Chinese Mr. Olympia retreated to the back of the room as a slender woman with medium-length brown hair, wearing goggles and clad in black body armor, appeared in the doorway. She stepped over the corpse and, standing in a modified Weaver stance—one foot forward and both hands on the weapon—she fired multiple shots from a machine pistol at the two men. In three seconds, she had discharged a half dozen rounds—the first three perforating Kim's frail body, and the other three taking out Chinese Mr. Olympia—and just like that, two gangsters and one North Korean general were dead.

The woman turned to him and removed her goggles.

Koga's eyes nearly popped out of their sockets when he saw her face. "Cynthia Blackwood? Or is it Elena Natase? Whatever the hell your name is—how? Why?"

"I'm here to pay you back for what you did in Mexico," she said, taking out a large knife.

Koga wondered what part of his body she was going to cut off first. But to his grateful surprise, she knelt in front of him and severed the plastic cuffs around his wrists and ankles.

"Thank you," he said. "But as I remember it, I held you at gunpoint and threatened to kill you in Mexico."

Natase smiled. "I knew you wouldn't kill me."

"Yeah?"

She tossed back her thick brown hair. "I'm not into Asian guys, but you caught my eye."

Where did I hear that before?

Koga's jaw dropped. "You were the one on the motorcycle that night in Venice, who bought me the drink and hired those thugs to beat me up."

Natase shrugged her shoulders.

"I can't believe I didn't recognize you," Koga continued. "It's incredible what makeup and a wig can do. And why did you pay those guys to rough me up again?"

"I wanted to see if you could handle yourself. I needed to know if you were someone I could rely on."

"Rely on? Who *are* you?" asked Max.

"Like I'm going to tell you."

Mentally taking a step back to visualize the picture in its entirety, Koga said, "You're an agent spying on North Korea. That much is obvious. But for who? Your methods don't suggest SAS, MI6, or BND—and I'd know if you were CIA. Then are you FSB, Russian intelligence?"

Natase shrugged her shoulders a second time.

Koga kept going. "North Korea and Russia may be loose allies, but they don't really trust each other. You were sent to keep tabs on the North Korean government, notably the Supreme Leader, but your cover must have been in danger of compromise and you needed to get out, and fast. So, you used me to create a distraction to help you."

"And you delivered, especially in Mexico," she said. "Everyone in Pyongyang thinks I'm dead, and I'm free to go back home with nobody the wiser."

Then another piece of the puzzle snapped into place. "It was you who left that restaurant loyalty card in Yusef Badawi's pocket."

Natase smiled. "But just so you know, it wasn't me, nor was it my idea, to kill those people at your safe house. That was all Mr. Spence's doing, and I had no way of stopping him."

"I believe you. But why save me now?"

"My superiors, and yours, would like nothing better than to see Colonel Seo out of the picture. His radical political agenda and eagerness to use nuclear weapons make our government very uneasy. The man is certifiably insane."

"I agree, but ... wait, you've followed me since I arrived in Beijing?"

"We've been tracking you pretty steadily since you left Mexico."

A large Caucasian man appeared in the doorway holding an Izhmash AK-9 assault rifle. He uttered a few words to Natase in what sounded like Russian and then disappeared back down the stairs.

"I must go," she said. "It's been fun. Here's one last present for you." She handed him a folded piece of paper. "On this is the address and coordinates of a private airfield where Colonel Seo secretly keeps a private jet that takes him to and from North Korea. I'm sure he's headed there now, along with your FBI friend."

Koga took the piece of paper from her. "Thank you. And thank you for saving my life."

Natase gave Koga a kiss on the cheek and headed for the exit. "Happy hunting," she said with a wink. "The Kremlin is depending on you."

"Will I ever see you again?" Koga asked, but she was gone before he finished his sentence.

Chapter 63

Koga was torqued about being used by the Russian government. After its debacle in Ukraine, he was genuinely surprised the country would have the resources and energy to keep an eye on North Korea, who have long been an ally. Although they disposed of their disgraced dictator president, the new principals in the Kremlin were still probably a bit on edge and besides, who can blame them for being concerned of a man-child despot living next door with access to a nuclear arsenal?

But Blackwood/Natase had saved his life and for that he was grateful, whomever she worked for in the end.

It was now time to move. Koga hurriedly rose from his chair and rushed to the bed where the bound masseuse lay. The syringe was still stuck in her arm. Thankfully, most of the drug was still in the casing. He pulled the needle out and used a towel to rub away a tiny droplet of blood that leaked from the puncture. She had passed out from sheer terror, but she was still breathing. He shook her by the shoulders.

"Hey, hey, wake up. You're safe now," he said, but there was no response. She'll make it, Koga thought, but Beth won't if I don't get going.

Taking the handgun from the cold, dead grasp of Chinese Mr. Olympia, Koga stepped over the body of General Kim Yon-Ja and made his way down the stairs. The rickety spiral staircase creaked with every careful step. On the ground floor were dead bodies scattered the length of the hallway, with blood splattered on the carpet and walls. He counted two collateral female bodies and six male gangsters—which meant one gangster was unaccounted for.

After inspecting the massage rooms, he walked to the madam's office near the lobby, where he carefully pushed the door open and entered, pistol first. Immediately, he spotted Gangster Number Eight, an Asian man, under a large metal desk with his hands over his head, trembling with fright.

"Hey, you," Koga called out. "Peek-a-boo ..."

The man panted heavily but didn't look up.

"Do you understand English?" Koga asked in a calm tone. "Look at me."

The man slowly raised his head and turned to look at him. The guy appeared to be no more than eighteen years old, just a kid.

"Don't-don't, don't shoo-shoot me," he wheezed in English. "I want not to die."

"I won't shoot you, bruddah. What is your name?" Koga asked.

"Kevin."

"Please come out from under the desk, Kevin."

Kevin did as he was told and raised his hands in the air, prompting Koga to lower his weapon.

"Why are you breathing like that?" Koga asked.

The kid coughed and struggled to catch his breath. "I have asthma."

"You have an inhaler?"

"Yes." The kid patted his pocket where Koga made out the imprint of the familiar short tube.

"Go ahead and take a jolt. Then I need you to do me a favor, after which you can go home, all right?" Koga said.

Kevin inhaled a burst from his medication and nodded.

"Okay, call the police and tell them what happened here, but leave me out of it. Tell them another gang attacked you. Say it was the Triads or something. And have them bring an ambulance. There's an unconscious girl upstairs who's hurt. Make sure she gets help. Go ahead, call now."

Kevin took out his cellphone and spoke for a minute. Then he said to Koga, "They come now."

"Good. Did you see where the people who did this went?"

"No. I was hiding here."

It was fortunate that the kid had stayed out of sight. Koga was pretty sure he would be dead if Blackwood/Natase or her partner had seen him.

Emergency sirens wailed in the distance and were getting louder. "Go back home and never join a gang again," Koga said.

Kevin bowed and bolted up the stairs at a full sprint.

After reentering the hallway, Koga found the man who had searched him lying face down at the base of the stairs. After reclaiming his possessions, he grabbed an AK-47 off another dead gangster and exited Heaven's Gate as casually as he had entered. He rushed to the alley where the Subaru WRX STI was parked and popped open the trunk with the electronic key fob.

"Get out," Koga said to Ning.

Ning lifted his body from the tight compartment.

"What happened in there? Did you find your girl?" he asked.

Koga answered with a swift backhand across the face that sent Ning into a half spin. "You lured me into a trap, you pile of shit. Your Tang friends were there waiting for me—that's what happened in there. But they're all dead now, and you know what? It's time for you to get on that bus too."

"I don't know about any trap. I just manage the club. They're all dead? You killed them all?" Ning asked.

"Go stand against that wall over there," Koga ordered, pointing to a concrete wall next to the car.

"I have a family. Please, don't kill me," Ning pleaded.

"I have family and you were going to kill me, dipshit. Count to one hundred slowly. When you finish, you can go, Ning Ning. But if you turn around before that, my associate, who's watching from a nearby building, will shoot you in the head. Nod if you understand."

Ning nodded. "It's still only one Ning, though." He started counting, Koga dropped the AK on the rear seat of the Subaru and jumped in. After switching the navigation controls to English, he input the address of the private airfield that he received from Blackwood/Natase. A few seconds later, the screen highlighted the quickest route—an eighty-mile journey on a looping highway. The topographical map of the area on his cellphone told him the airfield was within the Lianhuashan Forest.

Max shifted into first gear and floored the throttle, pointing the WRX STI onto the main road like a race car leaving pit lane, knowing full well that the odds of catching up to Beth Hu and her captors were slim.

Chapter 64

Ambassador Chol-Min Seo regarded Beth Hu in the rear seat next to him. His gaze lingered on her toned legs that extended as she stretched. "You are beautiful. You may avoid the labor camps yet if the Supreme Leader takes a liking to you."

They were in Seo's Rolls-Royce Phantom with Major Jong-Su Kang driving at breakneck speed for the airport and a private jet awaiting their arrival. Beth looked out the window and wondered why Max Koga was in Beijing. The only practical explanation, she surmised, was that he had come looking for her. She turned to the ambassador.

"If you spare Max's life, I'll do whatever you ask," she said. "Anything."

Seo smiled a grim leer. "I'm afraid it's too late. There is no doubt he is already dead."

The ambassador was probably right, Beth thought. Surrounded by at least eight armed men, he had no weapon of his own and no backup. She hoped, at the very least, that Max had met his end painlessly.

At first, she thought she had imagined it, but Beth noticed that the plastic cuff around her right wrist had come loose. She pretended to shift in her seat while subtly twisting her right arm behind her back to see how much slack there was.

With a bit of work, she felt she could free her wrist. She worked the cuff up her hand, but she realized she needed to move her arm more to get her hand completely through. She needed a distraction.

"So, what's your story? If you're such a big shot in the North Korean government, why are you still a colonel?" Beth asked.

Seo shot her a stern look. "Why are you Americans always so damned disrespectful?"

"I'm just saying," Beth said.

"My father brought shame to our family, so they executed him. My mother, sister, and I were thrown into labor camps," Seo explained. "After our previous leader's passing, the Supreme Leader pardoned me because of my past service to him and asked me to serve as one of his chief advisers. Because of the crimes of my father, I haven't been allowed to attain a rank higher than my current one, at least not yet."

"What on earth did your father do?"

"I'm afraid I'm not at liberty to discuss that with you, Ms. Hu."

"You and the Supreme Leader, are you guys, like, besties or something?" asked Beth with a grin.

"They chose me to attend college in Switzerland with him. It was my job to safeguard him and ensure his destiny wasn't diverted by the evil ways of the Western world."

"Such a heartfelt story. Are your mom and sister still in the labor camp?"

Seo paused in thought. "My mother died a few years ago. As for my sister, I do not know what has become of her."

"You don't seem to care much about your family."

"My country is my family," Seo answered with conviction.

"How can you be so proud of such an oppressive regime? Look at the people in your country. They're dying of starvation while your leader spends money building up his arsenal and living it up like a rock star. That's a crime against humanity."

"It is you Americans who are forcing us to do this. All of you should die horrible deaths. If you would just stay out of our business and leave this part of the world alone, we wouldn't need to take these measures to protect ourselves," he exclaimed.

"And what gives you the right to kidnap me?"

Seo stared Beth in the eyes. "I hate your country and everything it stands for, and it has been my dream since I was young to strike you down. But I know trying to engage America directly in war would be suicide. I'm not stupid, nor is the Supreme Leader. I told him there are other effective ways to fight you, as al-Qaeda, ISIS, and the Russians have shown us."

As the ambassador kept talking, Beth moved the zip tie steadily up her hand. The perspiration on her skin acted as a lubricant, helping the plastic strap slide onto the base of the thumb. A fake cough timed with one last tug ... and *voila*, her arms were free.

As the Rolls slowed to a stop at a traffic light, Beth surveyed the scene outside. They were just past the Sixth Ring Road and, while traffic was sparse, there were still some signs of life nearby. A few cars drove across the intersection in front of them, while one vehicle was stopped on the other side of the light. It was now or never.

Beth went straight for Seo's face. Although she failed to gouge his eyes with her thumbs as she wanted, she left a deep scratch on his cheek, causing him to retreat to the far side of the cabin.

"Kang!" Seo called out.

Using her left arm to push down his guard, Beth sent an elbow onto Seo's cheekbone, stunning the ambassador. As Kang turned around, she pulled on the door handle, unlocking and opening the door in one swift move, then jumped outside and rolled onto the tarmac.

Seo picked up his gun and pointed it in Beth's direction. "Stop or I'll shoot!" he shouted.

Go ahead—I'll take a swift death any day over a slow one in a labor camp.

Beth ran to the back of the car, hoping to find a taxi or, better yet, a patrol officer in the street. She then noticed a pair of headlights approaching, prompting her to run to the middle of the road and wave her arms in the air. The Nissan Sylphy braked hard, its front bumper stopping inches away from Beth's knees.

Running to the side of the Sylphy, she said to the driver in Mandarin, "Please help me, I've been kidnapped. Those men back there have guns. Call the police."

The driver-side window lowered. "Get in, quickly," the man behind the wheel said.

More than happy to oblige, Beth opened the rear door and jumped in, huddling on the rear floor. When all four of the Nissan's doors locked simultaneously, she looked up to see the driver and passenger turned in their seats, the latter pointing a gun at Beth.

A moment later, Seo walked toward the car holding a bloodied handkerchief to his face. He knocked on the window, prompting the driver to unlock the doors, which he did. The ambassador then slid into the seat next to Beth.

"Do you think we're dumb enough not to travel in groups? We have another two cars ahead of us, too, just for your information," he said.

Seo blotted his face where Beth had left a gouge that bled freely.

"I would smash your face and break your bones one at a time if I didn't think it would displease our Supreme Leader," Seo said. The white handkerchief was almost completely red now, but the wound was bleeding less as coagulation set in. "Then again, I may be able to engineer your return to me once the Supreme Leader is tired of you." His eyes blazed and his face creased with a terrible smile. "I will look forward to that day."

Recognizing that she had bungled her only opportunity for escape, Beth buried her face into her hands. There was now nothing standing between her and Pyongyang. She only hoped that her stay in the Hermit Kingdom wouldn't be a long one, and that a deal could be made between her country and the Supreme Leader before she suffered too greatly.

Otherwise, she would never see home again.

Chapter 65

When Koga reached the outer precincts of Beijing, he slowed the Subaru's pace from ninety miles per hour to just over forty so he could search for the entrance to an unmarked and little used logging trail he'd seen on his cellphone mapping.

With about a half hour to make up, he'd need to average double the speed limit to catch Colonel Chol-Min Seo and Beth Hu if he stayed on the highway, and by doing that, he risked being pulled over for speeding. He needed to look for a shortcut. The navigation app on his phone showed an old unused logging trail that sliced through the forest. It could shorten the total distance to the airfield by about a third.

According to Koga's calculations, if he could average fifty miles per hour through that stretch, he might beat Seo to the airfield with some time to spare. Without knowing the width and the surface condition of the trail, it would be a risky move. But he had no choice.

Koga took out the satellite phone he received from Beijing CIA station chief Charlie Wong and speed-dialed a pre-programmed number.

"This better be good," Wong answered.

"I wouldn't have called if it weren't. I found Beth Hu, but she's being taken to a secret airfield somewhere around the Lianhuashan Forest about a hundred miles from the city."

"She's alive?" Wong asked.

"As of about an hour ago, yes. Colonel Seo plans to take her to Pyongyang and put her on trial as a spy. I'm in pursuit, but I need help. They have at least a dozen heavily armed men."

"I wish I could, Max," Wong said, "but sending in our men is out of the question. However, what I can do is quietly leak the news to some of my contacts in the Chinese government. They all know about the so-called 'private airfield.' It's like the worst-kept secret ever. Rumor has it that even the Supreme Leader has used it to fly secretly into China to party in Beijing and secretly lobby with those in the Chinese government. That is, when he doesn't have time to use that ridiculous green and yellow train. But if Seo is trying to smuggle a U.S. citizen out of the country, that would give the Chinese ample excuse to shut it down. They can put the blame squarely on Seo so the Supreme Leader doesn't lose face."

"If you can convince them to act, how long will it take reinforcements to get there? Colonel Seo is en route as we speak."

"Hard to say. A couple of hours, maybe less."

"That's way too long."

"It's the best I can do. And I can't stress this enough, Koga—do not get arrested by the Ministry of State Security or the People's Armed Police Force. Chances are you'll never be heard from again."

"What if they get Beth?" Koga asked.

"I think I can get her released if I can convince them she's on a diplomatic mission. I have people in the Chinese state department who owe me some favors."

"That's the best thing I've heard all day. Please hurry. Koga out."

Not a minute after ending the call, he spotted the entrance to the closed logging trail. A flimsy yellow chain blocked the entrance. He flicked on the Subaru's high beams and neatly hand-braked onto the dirt path, busting the chain in two. The car was stable and controllable, and it rotated easily into the narrow gap in the tree line.

He selected first gear, side-stepped the clutch, and instantly went to wide-open throttle. The engine screamed in turbocharged glee as the STI's four drive wheels clawed at the dirt road surface, rocketing the sedan forward. The Subaru nav was scrolling the route so that he could anticipate upcoming corners at speed, but the roadway was narrower than Max had hoped with little runoff, and one mistake could wad up the car with him in it.

Reminds me of the SCCA Rallycross events back in Hawaii, Koga reflected.

Eyes flicking at the speedometer, Koga upshifted to fourth gear on a longer straight and flattened the accelerator. The engine responded with an eager howl. The high beams illuminated about five hundred feet in front of the car, but this gave Koga only a split second at these velocities to react to the road ahead because the scrolling nav map was about a second behind his actual position on the road. He would let off the throttle and counter-steer to rotate the all-wheel-drive car sideways through the turns, dragging the rear bumper through thick evergreen tree branches but so far keeping it off their trunks.

Another coat of paint and Koga would have bounced off that last one.

The thing he feared most was a deer or some other animal wandering onto the trail and getting pinned in the bright LED headlights because there was no shoulder here. You went forward, or you went back. The obstruction needn't even be as large as a deer; striking a decent-sized beaver at high speed likely would cripple the cooling system with animal debris shotgunning into the radiators, not to mention a sudden impact with a random tree that might have fallen across the trail.

Koga tried not to think about that, but his right foot involuntarily lifted off the accelerator just a hair then. A quick glance at the trip meter showed he was halfway through the pass. His pace was good, so he let his shoulders and speed relax a bit more.

For a moment, he thought of his father, who had made his living racing through hazardous off-road trails just like this one, constantly balancing the vehicle on the edge of speed and catastrophe. He wished the old man was his navigator on this raid.

Then without warning, the roadway about a hundred feet in front of him disappeared from the headlights, showing only an empty black hole ahead. It was the next thing Koga feared most—a drop-off.

With no hope of even slowing the car, Koga threw the dice. He downshifted to third and floored the throttle, hoping to clear whatever gully lay ahead. The engine screamed with a high turbocharger whine and the Subaru surged forward, pressing him back into the Recaro seat.

He felt the car drive up a small incline before being shot toward the night sky. Not knowing how far he was going to fly—or fall—he braced for impact, expecting the worst. It was then that he wished he was secured by a six-point racing harness instead of the street-standard lap and shoulder belt.

The Subaru glided through the air for what seemed like an eternity, and then all four of its tires hit the ground at the same time. The initial impact jolted every bone in Koga's body. He bit his tongue and chipped a tooth. The car bounced forward a couple of times before finally coming to rest on a flat patch of ground. Koga steered the car left and right to keep it centered on the trail and finally braked to a stop.

He opened his eyes and looked around. As far as he could tell, the car was still in one piece. No smoke rose from under the car's hood, nor were there any ugly sounds of metal clanking. And the engine was still running.

Damn, I'm good, Koga thought with a laugh out loud. Sometimes, it's better to be lucky. He ran his lacerated tongue over the chipped tooth, looking into the rearview mirror to see the chip was much smaller than it seemed to a swollen tongue.

Sweaty celebration over, he shifted into first and pressed on, hoping that no other obstacles stood between him and the airfield.

Chapter 66

Paul Verdy parked his Infiniti QX60 in the reserved spot for his weekly appearance at the Argon Securities corporate headquarters. He took the elevator to the fifth floor and wandered through the main workspace with briefcase in hand, exchanging morning greetings with his staff.

Once in his office, he plopped down behind his large mahogany desk. Almost immediately, his interoffice phone buzzed. It was his administrative assistant, Naomi, a forty-year-old former flight attendant with a spectacular long-term memory and an aptitude for numbers.

"It's Etienne on line one," she said through the speaker.

Verdy punched a lighted button on his desk phone and picked up the receiver. "How did it go? Talk to me."

"How did what go, boss?" asked Etienne Bablot in his customary slight French accent. "The cleanup or the extraction?"

"Both."

"You'll be glad to hear that The Warehouse is now just an old abandoned building. We cleaned it thoroughly and even sprinkled pixie dust everywhere for good measure."

"Good. And what about our favorite former automotive CEO, Mr. Karl Goan?"

"Well, about that. We had a—how do you say—slight hitch. We were able to break him out of jail, but there are cameras everywhere in South Korea, and I think Mr. Goan may have been exposed when his surgical mask fell off while leaving the getaway car."

"Did you get him out or not?" Verdy asked.

There was a pause, followed by a slurping sound. "*Bien sûr.* Of course. The team and I are having a lemonade with him now at his penthouse in Dubai."

Verdy breathed a sigh of relief. "Well done. Now, get back here as soon as you can. And make sure Monsieur Goan wires us the remaining balance before you leave his sight."

Not ten seconds after hanging up, his desk phone buzzed again.

"Andrew Roberts from CIA is holding on line two," Naomi said.

Verdy punched another lighted button. "What can I do for you, Andy?"

"Hello, general. Sorry to bother you. I heard about Donald Rawlings."

"News travels fast," Verdy said.

"And how is Max getting on in China? Has he located Agent Hu yet?"

"I haven't heard from him," Verdy said. "Do you know if Womack has sent any of his agents there to look for her?"

"Not that I know of. I wanted to tell you, Paul, that they put your file describing the link between the Aqarib and the North Koreans on the shelf. I know you hand-delivered it yourself. No one wants to do anything about it. It's a damned travesty."

"Listen, Andy, I need to go now, but I'll be in touch if I hear anything more. Keep fighting the good fight."

"Will do, general. You do the same. Talk soon."

Verdy closed his eyes in thought. Then he rose from his chair, grabbed his briefcase, and walked out of his office.

"Leaving already, boss?" asked Naomi, who sat behind a desk right outside his glass office. "Should I ask where you're going?"

Verdy only shook his head and hurried out of the building. He jumped into his SUV and sped out of the parking lot.

Chapter 67

It took Max Koga about a half hour more to clear the logging trail, several minutes quicker than he'd expected. Once the road descended into a wide valley, it straightened out into a narrow, unmarked access trail, which, according to the Subaru's navigation system, led to the secret airfield. The driving surface turned to dirt once again, but this time, the road was wider and flatter than the logging trail, allowing the Subaru to cruise at a comfortable seventy miles per hour until the roadway ended at a heavy metal gate.

A chain-link fence surrounded the compound, giving it the aura of an abandoned military compound. Switching off the headlights and driving up to the entrance slowly, Koga scanned the area for guards and dogs. All clear. He stopped the car, leaving the engine on, and walked to the gate, which was secured by a thick metal cable and a padlock. Taking out his pocket tool kit, complete with a set of lock picks, he went to work on the padlock, snapping it open in seconds.

Careful not to kick up dust, Koga drove his car slowly into the facility. After closing the gate behind him and refastening the lock, he headed toward the only airplane hangar on the compound. It was then that he noticed several headlights appear behind him on the access road.

They're right on time.

Parking his car out of view, Koga picked the lock on the hangar's main door and switched on the flashlight app on his cellphone. The hangar was a large one, big enough to house at least two good-sized aircraft, but sitting in the middle of the structure was just one, a stark white Cessna Citation XLS Gen2 business jet with no registration markings. The airstair was lowered, which Koga took as an invitation to climb aboard.

The jet's cabin was first-class luxury, with a roomy eight plush leather seats on a thickly carpeted floor. A framed official portrait of the Supreme Leader hung on the forward bulkhead, his dour expression glaring aft into the cabin.

Koga sat down in the back and stuffed his cellphone into his pocket, immersing himself in complete darkness. The only thing visible was a faint red mist creeping into the peripherals of his vision. But instead of going for his pill case, he allowed the red in, letting it provide a gratifying rush of adrenaline to fill his body. His mind and body were now ready for whatever was about to come.

A few minutes later, the lights of the hangar flickered on, signaling the arrival of Colonel Chol-Min Seo and his entourage. The main hangar door rose slowly open, and Koga risked a careful peek out of the window. He counted six vehicles and sixteen men, including Seo and Major Jong-Su Kang. Beth Hu was visible in the rear seat of a compact Nissan sedan stopped on the pad outside the hangar.

The Rolls entered the hangar and stopped about fifty feet from the plane. Kang stepped out of the driver's seat and, with a meaty paw that encircled her slender upper arm, escorted Beth from the Nissan to the rear cabin of the Rolls, seating her next to Seo. He then gestured for two men in pilots' uniforms to board the aircraft.

Perfect, thought Max. If I can take out the pilots first, it would ground the jet and give the Chinese secret police more time to arrive.

Dropping to the floor to keep from being seen through the plane's open windows, Koga crawled to just inside the jet door and waited. The first man up the airstair was presumably the pilot in command, judging by four thin silver stripes on his jacket sleeve. When he stepped onto the flight deck, Koga slammed the butt of his gun onto the base of his skull, instantly knocking him out. Before the pilot hit the floor, Koga caught his falling body and pulled him deeper into the plane, stuffing him in the shadow of the forward bulkhead under a framed photo of the Supreme Leader's unblinking gaze. The co-pilot was nearly all the way in when Koga's grip on the unconscious pilot slipped, sending the limp body onto the cabin floor with a heavy thud.

The sound caused the co-pilot to stop at the top of the stairs, just short of the open doorway.

"*Byung-Ho?*" he called out to the pilot.

"Yes," Koga answered softly, hoping he sounded at least a little like the pilot.

The co-pilot stepped back down the stairs, pointing toward the plane door. "*Bihaeng-gi an-e nugungaga issda,*" he shouted, which Koga guessed was something along the lines of *There's someone inside the plane.*

Cursing under his breath, Koga retreated into the aircraft as a small army of men gathered at the foot of the stairs with their weapons drawn. At the rear was Kang, holding a Makarov pistol and barking orders in Korean. With his best-laid plan having gone quickly into the toilet, Koga stuck his AK-47 out the doorway with the barrel pointed down at the men.

"Sorry I have to do this, boys," he said, squeezing the trigger.

Instead of raising their weapons and firing at Koga, the gaggle of gangsters scattered to evade the AK's automatic fire. But it never came.

The rifle failed to fire. Koga rechecked the safety and it was off. The damned thing had jammed. He needed to clear it fast, but one gangster, armed with what looked like a hunting rifle, was already making his way up the stairs. From the way he held his weapon, the poor sod obviously didn't know the first thing about firearms.

When the man reached the halfway point of the stairway, Koga pulled out his pistol and shot him twice in the chest. With a loud shriek, the man tumbled back down the stairs.

The others took a step back and unloaded their rounds into the plane's open doorway and fuselage. Dozens of bullets ripped through metal as Koga dropped to the floor and took shelter behind the seats. One bullet caught the receiver of his AK-47, rendering the weapon useless and spraying Koga's face with metal fragments.

Koga could hear Seo shouting angrily from outside the hangar, and the gunfire ceased.

With the element of surprise gone and his firepower drastically reduced, Koga found himself trapped inside the aircraft like a rat in a fancy trap, without the faintest idea on what to do next.

Chapter 68

When he heard the gunshot resonate from within the aircraft, Colonel Chol-Min Seo had taken cover behind his Rolls-Royce. His heart nearly stopped when his men began unloading their magazines into the jet's fuselage.

"Stop, you idiots—you're damaging the Supreme Leader's plane!" Seo barked in Korean after stepping out from behind the Phantom.

Major Jong-Su Kang ran to Seo's position behind the car. "We have a problem, sir," he said.

"You don't say. Who on earth is inside our plane?" Seo asked.

Kang swallowed hard before answering. "It is the American—Koga."

Seo looked back at the major, perplexed. "Are you mad? Max Koga is dead."

"It is him, sir. I saw his face."

He dismissed Kang with a wave of the hand and shouted in Mandarin in the aircraft's direction. "I am Colonel Chol-Min Seo of the Korean People's Army. I demand you to identify yourself now."

No response.

After waiting a minute, Seo tried again. "Throw your weapon down and come out with your hands in the air immediately. I promise you will not be harmed."

This time, a familiar voice sounded from inside the plane.

"Didn't we just do this back at the massage parlor? I suggest you employ a different angle, because I have all the time in the world and enough ammunition to take on half of China," the voice responded in English.

The blood flushed from Seo's face.

"I don't believe it," he said to himself. It *was* Max Koga.

A dozen questions rushed through Seo's mind at once, but one was the most important. How is he not dead?

Seo looked at Beth Hu, who remained inside the car's rear cabin with her wrists securely bound behind her back.

"Well, what do you propose I do?" he asked through the open rear door.

"I would do as he says," Beth replied.

"So, you're saying I should let you go?"

"We can all still walk away from this."

Seo smiled. "We shall see." He then lifted his head up above the car's roof. "What is it you propose, Mr. Koga?" he shouted in English.

"Let Ms. Hu drive away alone in one of your cars," Koga replied from his hiding spot. "Once she's off the property, I want all of you to leave the premises. Then, I'll leave quietly myself. The Chinese authorities are already on their way here. If you play your cards right, colonel, everyone goes home free and alive."

"I'm sorry, but that is not going to happen," Seo retorted. "You say you're heavily armed, but if so, why did you shoot only once from a handgun and take out only one of my men? Why didn't you try to kill them all? You had the opportunity. I am inclined to believe that you are not well-armed at all."

"I strongly discourage you from taking that chance," Koga said.

"There's only one of you and nearly fifteen of us, so yes, I will take the chance," Seo answered. He turned to Kang and said to him in Korean, "Mr. Koga is not to leave this hangar alive. Is that understood?"

Kang nodded.

His bluff called, Koga knew the odds were now stacked even more heavily against him than before. He only hoped to stall until the People's Armed Police arrived ... if they arrived at all.

He took out the satellite phone and rang Charlie Wong.

"Good, you're still alive," Wong greeted.

"Not for long unless the PAP gets here like now," Koga said.

"They're on their way. The air units just left their base. They'll be there in no more than an hour."

"I don't *have* an hour," Koga exclaimed, ending the call.

No longer able to rely on the Chinese to rescue him in time, Koga crawled to the plane's entrance and pressed the "door close" button on the wall that automatically brought the airstair up to merge back into the aircraft. Once it was within reach, he pulled it in, locked it in place, and walked over to the downed pilot.

"Get up," he said, lightly kicking him on the thigh. "I need you to fly the plane."

No response.

Koga grabbed him by the shirt and slapped his face. "Wake up."

The pilot's mouth opened wide, but his eyes remained shut. He was breathing, but he wasn't going to wake up any time soon.

So much for Plan A.

Koga headed for the cockpit, staying low to avoid the hangar light coming into the flight deck windows. Although he had no experience piloting a jet, he was licensed to fly single-engine prop planes. The two were vastly different, but all he wanted to do was switch on the engines and taxi the Citation around the runway for as long as he could.

How hard could it be? he thought, until he saw the bewildering panels of controls that surrounded the captain's chair.

On to Plan C.

Returning to where the pilot lay moaning, Koga peeled off the man's uniform jacket and pulled off his own black polo shirt. Now dressed in Koga's gray undershirt, the unconscious man was dragged to one of the window seats near the airstair and seat-belted upright into the seat. After propping him up to look like he was holding a gun, Koga hid behind another chair and waited.

Not a minute had elapsed when, as Koga had anticipated, a gunman tried to penetrate the plane. Koga waited quietly from behind his hiding spot.

Suddenly, the man surged into the cabin with his gun ready. His eyes darted to the figure seated in the shadows, and he squeezed off two quick rounds at shadows.

The dead pilot slumped forward, hit with gangster bullets.

The shooter proudly declared to his colleagues in his native tongue, presumably, that he had eliminated the enemy. They were the last words he would utter.

Koga rose from his crouch behind an adjacent chair and shot the gangster in the belly. He fell face forward just inside the cabin and Koga rushed forward to roll him out of the way when he noticed a second man making his way up the airstair.

Koga let loose a shot at him without taking aim. The bullet missed its mark, but it sent the man running back down for cover. Contemplating his next move, Koga risked a glance out a window to see the rest of the gangsters repositioning themselves in dispersed groups around the hangar.

This is not good. They're getting organized.

Everything around him had become tinted in a deep shade of red. Though his enemies were now employing improved combat tactics, giving him little chance of coming out alive, Koga didn't feel the least bit concerned.

Chapter 69

It was now time for Plan D.

Koga could feel his heart beating when he picked up the damaged AK-47. It was just a piece of metallic junk at this point, so he hurled it out the airplane door, aiming for the far corner of the hangar. As the eyes of the gangsters focused on the weapon sailing through the air, Koga picked up the pistol that belonged to the man he had just shot and leaped through the doorway, clearing the airstair and touching down with both feet on the hangar floor.

The gangsters saw Koga exit the plane and fired their guns his way. He responded by taking off in a full sprint toward the parked Rolls-Royce, shooting at the gunmen around him with a pistol in each hand. His aim was on point as he picked off three men behind a large tool chest with the Makarov while his Walther sent bullets into another two attackers hiding ineffectively behind a stack of wooden boxes.

Seeing Koga approach, Colonel Chol-Min Seo moved inside the Rolls-Royce's rear cabin, taking a seat next to Beth and slamming the door shut. "Your boyfriend is certifiably insane," he said.

Koga maintained his pace despite a bullet grazing his shoulder. Once he was about ten feet from the Rolls, he dropped to the floor and slid sideways as rounds flew over his body from all angles. He kept sliding until his entire body slid underneath the car intending to pop out the other side, but friction stopped him short. Koga planted both feet and pushed, but his feet slipped on a small puddle of water—condensation from the car's air conditioning unit. He tried again, but his boots failed to establish a firm grip on the polished concrete floor. He was stuck.

The gangsters slowly came out of their hiding places and gradually made their way to the front of the Rolls. Koga's last chance at saving himself would have been to shoot their feet and legs as they neared, but he was pointed in the wrong direction—his head under the rear axle. He had no choice but to shoot blindly toward his feet and hope to take a few out while trying to wiggle out the other side.

Either way, it was painfully obvious that this was where his adventure was going to end.

Going out with guns blazing is not a bad way to go, he thought.

Readying himself for his final attack, he paused when he caught wind of a familiar sound. It was the distant thumping of rotor blades breaking the still of the night. He repositioned his head and caught a peek of the unmistakable markings of China's People's Armed Police in a trio of Harbin WZ-19 light attack helicopters approaching the hangar, three abreast.

The PAP had a reputation for being one of the most merciless law-enforcement agencies in all of Asia, with the very mention of its name causing terror among the masses, but on this occasion, Max was absolutely ecstatic to see them.

Chapter 70

The appearance of the three choppers, their chain guns pointed into the hangar, sent the gangsters into a panic. They took off in every direction. The two outboard helos in the phalanx hovered with ominous intent while the center chopper landed on the concrete pad and disgorged a half-dozen heavily armed policemen onto the main runway.

Colonel Chol-Min Seo stepped slowly from the Rolls, raised his hands into the air, and walked toward the oncoming People's Armed Police agents, shouting to them in Mandarin.

Koga scrambled out from under the car and rushed to Beth Hu, who remained in the rear cabin. He produced his pocket tool and freed her wrists of the zip cuffs.

"Are you hurt?" he asked.

Beth embraced him as soon as her arms were free. "I'm so glad you're alive. I thought you were ..."

"You weren't the only one," Koga said. "What was Seo shouting?"

Beth laughed. "He said he's a diplomat, that he was abducted and being held prisoner. Don't know how he's going to sell that one, though. But how on earth did you get away from ..."

Koga took hold of her shoulders. "Time for all that later." He gestured to the front of the hangar where the police were forcing the bad guys to the floor and restraining them.

"That's the People's Armed Police, a nasty paramilitary force I want no part of. Let them take you in, though. The CIA station chief says he can handle your release, so just stick to your story of being on vacation and that these guys kidnapped you off the street."

She kissed him hard on the mouth.

Koga reluctantly pushed her away. "I gotta run. See you back in L.A."

Leaving Beth behind, Koga exited from the door opposite the police and made a dash for the rear door of the hangar. Gunfire had erupted throughout the airfield by the time he reached the hidden Subaru. He stopped short of opening the driver-side door, reconsidering his initial decision to jump into the car. The airfield had only one access point, and it was now being watched by an attack helicopter. There was little chance that he could outrun the chopper, much less avoid the ground reinforcements that were undoubtedly on their way.

Looks like I'm walking.

Staying low to the ground, he jogged to the darkest section of the border fence and climbed. Once over the other side, he stayed inside the forest, keeping the access trail in his sights and letting the trees provide cover from any more choppers.

He took out his personal cellphone.

"*Wéi?*" Big Ben Xu answered.

"It's me. I need to be picked up," Koga said.

"Oh, hey, boss. Are you at the Red Note?"

"Not exactly. I'm going to give you an address to an airfield near the mountains. Call me when you're twenty minutes away and park the car on the side of the road. Don't go near the airfield."

"Airfield?" Xu asked. "What airfield?"

"It's a long and complicated story, but if you can get there within two hours, there's another hundred dollars in it for you."

"I am on the way," Xu said, ending the call.

Koga assessed his location on the cellphone nav, then pushed on. He could hardly believe he'd escaped the mayhem with his hide intact. He was making good progress when he heard a tree branch snap behind him. He froze for a few seconds and then spun around with his Walther PPK raised, expecting to see a deer or a wild boar. Instead, in front of him was a different animal, one that was much more dangerous and sinister. One with a scar on his lips.

"Fancy meeting you here, Major Kang," Koga said.

Major Jong-Su Kang appeared out of the shadows with his Makarov pointed at Koga's chest. "Put down your weapon," he said in good English.

Koga scoffed at the remark. "In America, we call this a standoff. I shoot you, you shoot me, and we both die."

"I will be happy to die for my country."

"Well then, that's your patriotic privilege, I guess," Koga said, keeping the muzzle of his weapon trained on Kang's head and watching for the slightest movement from his adversary's trigger finger.

"Let us settle this like men. No weapons. We fight hand-to-hand. Only one of us goes home."

Koga shot him a puzzled look. "What? No. You are not *samurai*."

"Then what? We kill each other here?" asked Kang.

Koga took a moment before answering. He wanted nothing more than to kill the man who took his best friend's life. But as things stood, then he would have to die too, or at the least, suffer a nasty gunshot wound. Was it worth it?

Yeah, it was.

As Koga put pressure on his trigger, Kang spoke again.

"The colonel will blame *me* for his failure. That's the kind of man he is. I'll be thrown into a labor camp with my family unless I kill you. Only then will there be the possibility of mercy from the colonel and the Supreme Leader."

"Yeah, well, not my problem," Koga said. Then it dawned on him that Kang probably preferred to die here rather than return to his homeland empty-handed—but if so, why hadn't he taken the shot yet?

"I want to defect," Kang said. "Will you take me in?"

And there it is.

"Not a chance," was Koga's answer.

"So, what do we do?" asked Kang.

"Throw away your piece, and I'll dance with you."

With a sneer that bent the scar on his lip, Kang nodded once and tossed his handgun aside.

When Koga followed suit, the burly North Korean bent low and charged forward like a mad bull. He was faster than Koga had anticipated, and in an instant, Kang had his shoulder buried into Koga's abdomen, sending him reeling backward.

With his vision seeping red, Koga covered up as Kang threw an overhand right. The force of the punch broke through his defense and landed on his temple, making Koga's knees slightly buckle—there was no doubt Kang was definitely the stronger of the two. Max decided then that the only chance he had of beating this opponent was taking him to the ground.

Using a low kick as a feint, Koga closed the gap between him and Kang, wrapping an arm around the man's thick waist and then throwing him over his hip, sending him to the ground with a heavy thud. Koga swiftly took hold of Kang's foot and assumed a saddle position, triangulating his legs around one of Kang's legs. Koga then hooked the lower part of that leg with his own foot, known in *jiu-jitsu* as an inside heel hook. Immediately, he applied pressure, lots of it, until he felt Kang's knee tear and ankle snap.

The big North Korean let out a loud bellow.

In one fluid motion, Koga sprang off Kang and fetched his Walther. He briefly searched for the Makarov the North Korean major had cast aside earlier but didn't see it in the immediate vicinity. He walked to his defeated adversary, who sat on the ground in front of him, wincing in pain.

"Do it," Kang said, closing his eyes.

"I don't think so. You don't get an easy out." Koga lowered his weapon. "Have fun back home."

Without looking back, Koga continued to the meeting point with Big Ben Xu, the tint in his vision already returning to normal. When the main road came into view, he heard the forest echo with the sound of a single gunshot.

Chapter 71

The job of chief operating officer for the CIA required one to be an inherently light sleeper, for a call requiring immediate action could come day or night. So, when Andrew Roberts' agency iPhone vibrated on the bedside nightstand, he sat up immediately and took the call.

It was an encrypted message from "Fruitfly." After punching in his six-digit passcode, he pressed the green icon. The message was brief and to the point: *We need to meet asap.*

Rubbing his eyes, Roberts rose out of bed and headed for the bathroom to splash water on his face. The quaint two-story home in West Virginia had become a lonely island that provided refuge from the elements since his wife of twenty-five years had passed two winters ago. The warmth of the place, and his life, had gone with his wife. He threw on his robe and headed toward the stairs, where he saw the kitchen lights were on.

I don't recall even entering the kitchen last night.

He reached into the drawer of a side table in the second-floor hallway and grabbed a Glock 19, one of several firearms placed around the residence. Holding the pistol at the ready, he descended the stairs and approached the kitchen, where he softly pushed the swinging door open. He looked inside. It was empty.

When Roberts turned to clear the living room, he saw the outline of a figure sitting in his favorite reading chair.

"Who the hell are you?" he asked, pointing the handgun at the intruder.

The lamp next to the chair turned on. There sat Maximilian Koga.

"Koga? What the hell are you doing here? How the hell did you get in here?"

"Good evening, Mr. Roberts," Koga said. "That message you got from 'Fruitfly?' That was me."

"I don't know what you're talking about," Roberts replied, contemplating whether to shoot the unwelcome guest. Here was an uninvited intruder spying on a CIA exec. A regrettable mistaken-identity shooting would be justified. The gun in Roberts' hand rose.

Then another voice sounded from the other side of the room.

"Don't be stupid, Andy." It was Ed Womack, the director of the FBI.

Roberts kept his gun trained on Max but his head turned to Womack.

"What's the meaning of this? Breaking into my house in the middle of the night? I'll have you both arrested."

"My agents have the house surrounded. It's you who is under arrest," Womack said.

Koga held up a stack of papers. "We did some background into your finances, and for an intelligence professional, you've been kinda sloppy. It looks like you've been receiving large amounts of money from some very bad people."

"That's absurd," Roberts shot back.

"It says here that Pyongyang's Room 39 has been making regular payments to a company based in Antigua called Wolf Creek Industries, owned by a man named Ivan Krylenko," Koga said. "Ring a bell?"

"Nope."

"Well, that's odd," Koga responded, scratching his head. "Ivan Krylenko is the name of your late brother-in-law, isn't it? Oh, and this phone from which I just sent that text to you? It belongs to Jayson Spence, who you knew quite well. You hired him several years ago, way before he joined Argon, to help you with a hostage extraction a few years back."

"Never heard of him," Roberts maintained.

"No matter. He's dead now. He went down with the Aqarib in Mexico."

"I'm going to call my lawyer," Roberts said.

Koga pretended not to hear. "Only six people knew I was in China: General Verdy, Denise, Raj, Beijing Station Chief Charlie Wong, and two of his men. And I know for a fact that neither Mr. Wong nor his men relayed that information to you or anyone else. But General Verdy said that somehow you knew. How did you know I was in China, Mr. Roberts?"

"Your passport blipped when you left the country."

"Yeah, only I was traveling under a name never used before."

Perspiration accumulated on Roberts' forehead. "I'm not saying anything more without my lawyer present."

"Then allow me to fill in the blanks," Koga said. "The North Koreans told you I was in China. This is how I see it: The Tangs felt that, after abducting Beth, someone might come looking for her, so they took precautions by setting a trap for whoever might show up. And stupid me, I walked right into it. Then, someone from the Tangs told you they had caught me, and you unknowingly incriminated yourself to General Verdy during your phone call with him."

"You can't prove that."

Koga rose from the chair and stabbed his finger in Roberts' direction. "Oh, but I can. It was you who notified Nasim al-Ahmed of the DEA operation in Mexico that got my team slaughtered. It was you who notified him of the FBI's raid on the San Diego cell that turned up empty. You also ordered Spence to take out our assets at the safe house and then informed Seo of Beth's presence in China."

Roberts remained silent, his gaze jumping between Koga and Womack. "I didn't direct Spence to kill anyone. He did that on his own."

"It doesn't matter. You're a scumbag and a traitor," Koga said.

"I'm none of those things," Roberts protested.

Womack asked, "Why, Andy? Why?"

Roberts lowered his weapon and took a seat on the sofa. "I've worked my ass off for this country ever since I joined the army. After I got to Langley, I dedicated my life to protecting it. I saw some terrible things over the years, but I never hesitated to do what was necessary. The only thing that kept me balanced through it all was my wife, Yaryna, who I met when I was stationed in Ukraine. I brought her back here, and we were happy. But six years ago, she was diagnosed with a rare type of Alzheimer's. The doctors could do nothing and gave her months, maybe a year, to live."

"It's unusual for Alzheimer's to take someone so quickly," Koga said.

"Usually, people with the disease live from three to fifteen years, but Yaryna's case was different. Almost as soon as they diagnosed her, her condition went downhill fast. In less than a week, she'd forgotten that we were married. Within a month, she no longer recognized me. There were experimental drug programs going on in the U.S., and I pleaded to the government for her to be granted access to them, but I was refused. It was a living hell."

Koga started to protest, to say Roberts's wife was insufficient cause for treason, but how do you say that to a man desperate to save the woman he loved?

"While I was in Japan a few years ago," Roberts continued, "I led an investigation on a rogue Russian scientist who had nearly perfected methods of curing fatal diseases with nanotechnology. Ask your friend Stockton Clay about it. He was in the middle of the whole thing. Well, that scientist died in a plane crash, and all his work was supposedly destroyed. But a year later, while Yaryna was ill, and I was running an operation in Seoul, I was approached by a stranger claiming that he had some early experimental samples left, and he offered them for my wife."

"And that man was Colonel Chol-Min Seo?" Womack asked.

"Yes, it was. Of course, I refused, and I was going to report the approach to my superiors, but Seo convinced me to take Yaryna to a clinic in a place called Shenyang, where one of his doctors injected her with the nanobots. Her condition improved immediately—I mean, as I watched. It was astounding. Seo said that the nanites were imperfect experimental samples and could become fatal to the host in several years, but they would fully restore her faculties for the short term, allowing her to live out her life normally." Roberts half-smiled. "As my wife."

"So, you made a deal?" Koga said.

"It was a hard decision. In the end, I felt I owed it to my wife. And that extra time we had together was priceless. When Seo came calling to collect on his part of the deal last year, I kept my end of the bargain."

"It's tragic, Andy. I'm sorry for what you went through, but I still need to take you in." Womack said.

"Yeah, I know." Roberts nodded. "It is what it is. I'd do it again."

Koga walked over to Roberts. "I'll need your weapon."

Womack remained in the shadows, taking no chances, his weapon trained on Roberts. If the CIA officer even took a deep breath while holding his gun, Womack was going to shoot, but not to kill. That might be what Roberts would want.

Roberts pondered the Glock for a few more seconds, then offered it to Koga with the grip end first. "It was the Aqarib and the North Koreans that did the killing, not me. I can live with the choices I made."

"A lot of good people died because of you—including my men at the DEA. Their memories haunt me to this day. I hope they now haunt you too," Koga said.

Womack ordered Roberts to stand and be cuffed, then he escorted the CIA exec out of the house just as support teams arrived with flashing blue Kojak lights on unmarked sedans.

Chapter 72

Details of the arrest of CIA Chief Operations Officer Andrew Roberts were kept from the media. A week after he was taken into custody, Paul Verdy called a meeting at Argon headquarters in Marina Del Rey. Max Koga was the first to arrive, followed closely by Denise Johnson.

"Good to see you," Koga said. He hugged her tightly.

"How's Beth?" she asked.

"Don't know. I haven't seen her since China. I think they've buried her in meetings and paperwork. That, or she's been avoiding the epic hero who selflessly rescued her at great personal peril," Koga replied with a laugh.

"Yeah, probably that latter one, huh?" Denise said with a grin.

They seated themselves on either side of the conference table and Raja Singh joined them.

"Hello, Max," Singh said with a two-finger salute. "I just want to say in all seriousness that you are the baddest guy on the face of the earth."

Koga laughed. "I beg to differ, Raj—*you* are the baddest. Without you, we'd still be knocking down doors in San Diego."

"Totally agree," Denise concurred, raising both thumbs. "But it's just not the same without Donald here."

The room fell silent. They cast their gaze in different directions, remembering their fallen friend.

"He's still with us," Koga said. "He's probably looking down at us right now and drinking a celestial beer."

The conversation was cut short by the arrival of Paul Verdy, who took his customary seat at the head of the table.

"Sorry to keep you waiting. How's everyone?" he asked.

"That depends on why we're here, sir," Koga said.

Verdy folded his hands on the table. "Well, first things first. I want to commend you all on your recent work on the Song Motors and Al-Aqarib case."

"Whatever became of our favorite North Korean colonel?" Koga asked.

"Ambassador Chol-Min Seo was arrested by Chinese domestic intelligence police at the remote airfield outside of Beijing and officially charged with homicides, kidnapping, and gun crimes. As a representative of the North Korean government, he was accorded diplomatic immunity and shipped back to Pyongyang the next day. No word on his fate, but the North Koreans assured the Chinese government that he would be reprimanded appropriately."

"The colonel most likely has a date with an anti-aircraft cannon. And what of Andrew Roberts?" Denise asked.

"He's awaiting trial. My friends in the White House say they will keep the proceedings as quiet as possible, but that's not to say word will leak out, and the proverbial shit will hit the proverbial fan. Anyway, I asked that any refs to Argon's involvement be redacted from the record."

"I genuinely feel bad for the guy," Singh said.

"Don't," snapped Koga. "His selfish actions came at the cost of a lot of valuable lives."

Verdy cleared his throat. "But that's not why I called you in today. With respect to our recent performance, the president himself has asked that the role of Argon Securities be expanded. We'll now assist the CIA, FBI, ATF, and DEA, meaning you guys are going to get very busy until we can staff up."

"Bring it on," Singh exclaimed.

"There's still hope for President Pugh yet. I'm glad he's not like the clown we had in the White House a few terms ago," Denise noted. "Although I had my doubts at first."

Verdy continued. "Because of all your hard work, I want all of you to take ten days leave. Enjoy life and come back fresh. You earned it, and you deserve it." He stood and took a moment to look each of his operators in the eyes. "Thank you, people. Thank you very much." He turned and left the room.

"I've got nowhere else to go, so I'll probably be in the office most of the time anyway," Singh said.

Koga smiled. "I just may see you there, Raj. And you?" he asked Denise.

"I think I'll go on a trip with my husband if he can get time off work."

"You're married?" asked Max. "Am I the last one to know this?"

"Ha, maybe. Yeah, five years. See you later," she said, digging into her purse for her car keys as she left.

Singh followed her out, leaving Koga alone at the table. He pulled out his cellphone and began typing a text.

Hey Beth, how are you? Haven't heard from you in a while. I got some time off. Any plans next week?

He read the text back to himself, paused, and deleted it without hitting *Send.*

It was the first time Koga was alone in his townhouse since joining Argon, and it seemed quieter than before. Night had fallen, but he was in no mood to go out. The events of the past week had taken their toll on his psyche and body, and he still had Donald Rawlings' memorial to prepare for. It was not something he was looking forward to. Deep in his heart, he still refused to believe that his friend was truly gone.

With nothing worth watching on the television and being too lazy to pick up a book, he switched off his phone, lay in bed, and stared at the ceiling, allowing the dark veil of sleep to descend over him like a fog.

Koga knew they would come, but this time, he welcomed their visit. Real or not, he wanted to ensure they were satisfied that he had avenged them.

Like always, it began with the sound of gunfire. The shots were faint at first, but they gradually grew in volume. In fact, they had become so loud that it roused him. It took him several seconds to realize that it wasn't imaginary gunfire that had filled his ears, but the sound of someone knocking on his front door. He threw on a T-shirt, walked across the living room, and looked at the security system monitor mounted on the wall.

On his front porch stood Beth Hu.

"Well, hey," he said, opening the door. He leaned in and hugged her. "I'm so glad to see you. Is everything all right?"

She stepped into the living room, holding a bottle of wine and two long-stemmed crystal glasses. "It took forever to get processed out of China," she said. "I just got back a couple of days ago. Besides, you could have called or texted me, you know."

"I figured you'd be up to your ears in paperwork, and I didn't want to be a bother."

"Well, I kinda was up to my ears in paperwork, but did it occur to you I might enjoy being bothered? Anyway, you weren't answering your phone, so I called Denise, and she said you were home. I thought we'd celebrate," she said, holding up the wine bottle and the delicate glasses.

"Celebrate what?" asked Max.

"Oh, I don't know—maybe the fact that we're still alive after what we went through in Beijing?"

"I'd love that, but can I take a rain check? I'm expecting a few friends to show up."

"At this hour?" she asked with a surprised look.

"Sorry," he said, shrugging. He glanced at the clock on the wall. It showed nearly midnight, which meant that he'd been asleep for nearly two hours. It was odd that Slack and Co. hadn't shown up. They usually appeared a few minutes into his slumber when he didn't take a Xanax first ... which reinforced the notion that they were figments of his screwed-up brain.

Beth placed the wine bottle on the counter.

"Well ... okay. I know a brush-off when I see one. Oh, and I wanted to say how sorry I was about Donnie. I miss him."

"Me too," Koga responded somberly.

"This is for you," she said, pointing to the wine bottle. "Call me sometime if you can wedge me into your hectic schedule."

As she turned to leave, Koga saw the gift was a Silver Oak Cabernet from Napa Valley, one of his favorite wines. Then, through the rear sliding glass door, he saw his fallen team members standing in his dimly lit backyard with smiles on their faces, looking as content as he had ever seen them. But in the blink of an eye, they were gone. He kept his vision fixed on the backyard, wondering if they'd return. They didn't.

That's it? Not even a "well done" from you guys?

Koga felt a weight lifted from his shoulders. He knew then that his friends were at peace, at long last.

"On second thought," he called out to Beth before she could leave. "Shall we open this baby up now?"

Beth stopped at the doorway. "What about your guests?"

"Oh, them? They, uh ... " Koga glanced back out the rear glass door and stopped. There, standing alone where the others had been, was Donald Rawlings, with his arms crossed and a faint smile on his face. After a two-fingers scout salute, he too vanished into the night.

"What about your guests?" Beth repeated.

Koga smiled warmly. "You know, I don't think they're coming tonight. In fact, I don't think they'll ever come again."

Epilogue

Gradually getting up to speed with Argon Securities' various projects was time-consuming but not challenging. Maximilian Koga took a sip of hot, black coffee from his mug and kicked his feet onto his desk. The day was still in its infancy—the video feed from an exterior camera showed the summer sun was just showing its face over the Malibu mountains.

He was alone in the old photo lab of *Automobile Digest* that had been converted into the task force office. Looking at empty shelves against the wall, he felt a wave of melancholy at the prospect of having to leave; arrangements were being made for the team to return to Argon's headquarters in Marina Del Rey at the end of the week. It was too bad, Koga thought. He had grown accustomed to the quiet nature of the old magazine building.

Only a month had passed since he joined Argon, although it felt like he'd packed a year into those four weeks.

As if on cue, Koga's cellphone buzzed. Looking down at the screen, he saw it was from Beth.

Where have you gone off to? Free for dinner tomorrow night? the text read.

Koga waited a couple of minutes before writing back. *In the office getting caught up*, he replied. *Dinner sounds great. Call u later?*

She responded with a thumb's-up emoji and a smiley face.

He couldn't remember the last time the simple thought of a woman had made him smile. To think that only two months before, he'd been at the lowest point in his thirty-something-year existence, facing expulsion from the DEA, and having no clue where he was headed. Then came the death of his best friend. But life felt simpler now, and simple was really good.

Pondering where to take Beth out to dinner, he nearly spit his coffee into the air when Paul Verdy's booming voice exploded into the room from over Koga's shoulder.

"I knew I'd find you here," Verdy said, his imposing figure filling up the doorway. "Come with me. We're going on a drive."

Sliding his feet off the desk and putting down his mug, Koga grabbed his old leather Navy jacket that hung from his chair. "Where we goin', boss?"

"We'll talk about it in the car," Verdy answered, turning around and leading the way out of the building.

Verdy guided his Infiniti SUV onto Highway 101 and headed north. The notorious Los Angeles rush-hour traffic had yet to peak, so they could maintain an even sixty miles per hour all the way to the L.A. county line.

"So, where are we headed again?" Koga asked, accustomed to his boss' reluctance to reveal a destination until the second or third ask.

"A CIA safehouse. We're taking possession of a high-level asset," Verdy said. "Director Nigel McKeen wants to hand him over to us because he doesn't know who to trust right now after the Roberts fiasco. It may only be temporary, but he thinks this asset can help us with our next assignment. I'll fill all of you in on that later."

"May I ask who this mystery man is?" Koga asked.

"The simple version is, he was planted here at a young age by China's spy agency, but he got turned by us about ten years back. That's when he began supplying Langley with intel while pretending to spy for the MSS."

Koga nodded. "Okay, a classic double agent."

"That's right. But a while back, he believed his bosses in Beijing were getting suspicious, so to protect his family, he asked the CIA to take him off the grid. And they complied."

"And he's been in hiding ever since?"

"Affirmative. McKeen flew him in last night to one of Langley's safehouses in Santa Maria, which is where we're headed now."

"What about the others? Denise, our new guy, Greg, and Raj?"

"They'll be brought in later. No one outside of only a handful of people knows that he's been in hiding. I wanted you to meet him first and get a feel for what we might get involved in."

"Sounds simple enough. Hey, does this mean we get to stay in our offices at the *Digest*?" Koga asked.

"Trust me, Max. This ain't gonna be simple. You'll see."

After two hours on the highway, Verdy guided the QX60 on a winding road that led to a deserted winery. A gate, with a weathered metal sign that read NO TRESPASSING in bright red, blocked the entrance to a long dirt driveway that cut into an empty dirt field where grapes once grew.

Verdy stopped the SUV at the gate, rolled down the window and faced a small camera mounted on a nearby fence post. A moment later, the gate swung open.

As the vehicle made its way onto the property, Koga noticed a small concrete building about a hundred feet away, behind a large oak tree. So that's where the guards are stationed, he surmised.

Verdy stopped in front of the main building, a rundown house that resembled a Victorian-style home. He killed the engine and stepped out. Koga followed. A tall, well-built Caucasian man with brown hair and an unusually bushy mustache met them at the front door. He wore a light black jacket, gray turtleneck, and khakis.

Verdy said, "Is this house for sale?"

The man responded, "It is not. It needs paint and new plumbing."

"In that case," Verdy said, "we must have the wrong location."

The protocols satisfied, the man smiled and opened the door wide.

"General," the man said, smiling and extending his hand. "I'm Supervisory Agent Mitchell Snowhill."

"Good to meet you." Verdy gestured to Koga. "This is my chief intelligence officer, Max Koga."

Snowhill extended his hand, which Koga shook. He led the two men into the building.

The interior of the building was a commonplace, spacious home, with a grand living room at its center and cedar plank floors. An oversize rock fireplace gave the place a warm, homely ambiance. Sitting in a reading chair in the far corner was a trim Asian man scrolling through a tablet, his legs crossed and his head resting on his hand. Koga guessed he was in his early sixties.

The man looked up from his tablet to the new arrivals, then stood and bowed his head. He was shorter than average, but his straight posture and lean build suggested that he was still physically active, maybe an avid golfer judging by his red Nike polo shirt and white stretch trousers.

Or a military man.

Verdy spoke first. "It's nice to see you again, doctor."

The Asian man smiled and shook Verdy's hand. "Good to see you as well, general." He looked at Koga. "And this is the young man Director McKeen mentioned?"

Verdy nodded.

The man offered his hand to Koga. "It's very nice to meet you, my friend. My name is Qiang Hu. I've been told that you are a friend of my daughter, Beth."

It took a moment for Koga to fully comprehend what the well-mannered Asian doctor had just said. He looked at Verdy.

"Does Beth ... ?"

Verdy shook his head.

Koga's first thought was *You've got to be kidding me* ... followed by the notion that his simple way of life had just come to a sudden end.

Acknowledgments

This work would not have been possible without the support of a clan of wonderfully talented people, who didn't just assist in the production of this novel but motivated me to keep putting words down onto paper until the dang thing was finished.

My heartfelt thanks to *Dan Frio, Jim Hall,* and *David Lovett* for their incredible editing skills and knowledge of all things cars and weapons. Without their expertise, the book would have lacked the realism and detail required to make it a convincing read.

A heartfelt thank you to my good friends James Chen and Giacomo Enzo Chen for their great expertise in Chinese culture and insights into the city of Beijing. My appreciation also goes to Karen Marks for sharing her knowledge of the human brain and psychiatric disorders.

Special accolades to my business manager and close friend, Mike Gin, who's always pushing me to keep writing.

And, of course, nothing could have been possible without my family's support. I dedicate this work to my late mother.

— *Sam Mitani*
Los Angles, California
March 2023

This narrative is a work of fiction. Nothing in this work constitutes an official release of U.S. Government information. Any discussions or depictions of methods, tactics, equipment, fact or opinion are solely the product of the author's imagination.

Nothing in this work reflects nor should be construed as any official position or view of the U.S. Government, nor any of its departments, policies, or personnel.

Nothing in this work of fiction should be construed as asserting or implying a U.S. Government authentication or confirmation of information presented herein, nor any endorsement whatsoever of the author's views, which are and remain his own.

About the author

Sam Mitani was born in Tokyo, Japan, and moved to Southern California with his family at the age of two, where he grew up.

He was the first Asian-American senior staff member of an English-language major automobile publication, and is best known for his work as International Editor for *Road & Track* magazine, where he was a staff editor for 22 years. Among his many automotive firsts, Sam was a member of the first American motorcycle tour of Vietnam since the war. The exploits of this trek were chronicled in *Cycle World* magazine.

In 2010, he set a class land speed record at the Bonneville Salt Flats in a modified four-cylinder Suzuki Kizashi family sedan, clocking 203.73 mph. This run also qualified him to join the exclusive and prestigious Bonneville Salt Flats 200-mph Club.

Sam holds a 6th-degree black belt in judo and has previously placed third at the World Masters Championship International Competition in São Paulo, Brazil.

His debut novel, *The Prototype*, was published in 2018.

For more information on this and other exciting new authors, please see ForcePoseidon.com
contact@ForcePoseidon.com

Printed in the USA
CPSIA information can be obtained
at www.ICGtesting.com
LVHW041035290923
759640LV00013B/25/J

9 781737 520061